DELICIOUS
Surrender

A DOMINANT BILLIONAIRE ROMANCE

LUCE SUTHERLAND

Edited by Kristen Corrects, Inc.
Cover art design by Kari March Designs (www.karimarch.com)
Cover Model: Abram Hodgens (www.abramhodgens.com)
Photographer: Sarah Mireya Photography (www.sarahmireya.us)
Stylist: Natalie Fuller, SisterStyling (www.sisterstyling.com)
Book formatting: Christine Lee

ISBN: 979-8-9916408-1-7   Paperpack
ISBN: 979-8-9916408-0-0   eBook

First edition published 2025

Dedication

To my husband, a.k.a. facilitating man of my dreams, for your love and encouragement from the very beginning to this moment of completion. Until you came along, I wasn't a finisher. You helped fuel my passionate imagination through any means necessary, and I love you for that—and for believing in me when I didn't. And just because there are parts of you in this book doesn't mean you should read it. In fact, maybe you shouldn't.

To my BFF, MP. We should have been sisters, and in many ways we are. We love the same things, sometimes the same men, always the same book boyfriends. The hotter the better. You are my person. Not because you're smart as hell, or an exceptional mentor, but because you are a woman with kickass courage. I am blessed to be on the receiving end of your SUN, MOON, and STAR power. I can say with absolute certainty: This book would not exist without you. You have been there from its conception, through my doubts and fatigue, into the third trimester and delivery. No one has given me more insight, feedback, editorial assistance, and encouragement than you. I love you, babe.

"Mom, did you do your homework last night? How many words did you write this week?" To my beloved son, thank you for believing in me and keeping me on track. You have been incredibly supportive of my writing endeavors, even knowing that I was taking a giant leap into the world of *smutty* erotic romance! Your encouragement means the world to me, and I couldn't have done this without you. With all my love, CPTN–to the moon and back.

Playlist

"Wrecked" – Imagine Dragons
"Uninvited" – Alanis Morissette
"Suddenly I See" – K.T. Tunstall
"The Road Less Traveled" – Lauren Alaina
"Ain't Nobody" – Chaka Khan
"On My Mind" – Ellie Goulding
"Nice to Meet Ya" – Niall Horan
"Baby Did a Bad Bad Thing" – Chris Isaak
"Sinnerman" – Nina Simone
"When the Night Comes" – Joe Cocker
"Never Let Me Go" – Florence + The Machine
"Big Girls Cry" – Sia
"My Silver Lining" – First Aid Kit
"Don't Call Me Up" – Mabel
"Let Her Go" – Passenger
"Symphony" – Clean Bandit
"Surrender" – Natalie Taylor
"What is Life" – George Harrison

1

Good Riddance

Fifteen minutes. That's all it took to close the book on the relationship. Ross and his toothbrush, two T-shirts, and a pair of ratty slippers were gone. A bitter chill hung in the room. It had nothing to do with regret and everything to do with the freezing February wind that blew in when he stormed out of her flat.

The relationship experiment was a failure. So much for being a *normal* girlfriend. Normal meant shedding a few tears when you broke up. Normal meant not hiding your desires for months then swinging a wrecking ball into your carefully constructed house of cards. Brynne was through making excuses for Ross. The only one she was fooling with the charade was herself. She finally told Ross one of her fantasies and he flipped out and called her sick and twisted.

It brought her relief to finally voice her truth. Researching BDSM for her novel had unlocked a Pandora's box of carnal curiosity.

Finishing the book consumed every spare hour for the past six months, which made it easy to ignore what was missing with Ross. Her best friend would congratulate her on the decision to dump him, but her father would wonder why she couldn't hold on to a man.

She planted herself on the one good cushion of her secondhand couch and texted Jared. Never a fan of the starchy accountant, he wasted no time reminding her of Ross's unworthiness. Deep down, she knew it was the truth. The problem was, she always chose the safe option. Safe meant a maximum of three dates with men she could not see herself falling for. Then it was easy to avoid getting tied down. And easy to leave.

Three texts and a phone call later and Jared had coerced her to ditch her sweats and head to their favorite hangout for drinks.

He waved from across the crowded restaurant. She scooted into the booth, yanked off her mittens, and grabbed the gin and tonic he'd ordered for her.

He raised his glass, and she did the same. "Cheers, babe! Congrats on giving that wanker the boot!"

Brynne sighed and clinked her glass to his half-finished Cosmo. "Cheers to that, J. I only wish I figured out what you saw within the first month."

"Don't be so hard on yourself! Most people thought he was a catch. On paper, I guess he was. Good job, no bad habits, decent looking."

Brynne groaned loudly. "You're being kind. He was an uptight vanilla cupcake without icing. I mistook his high-handedness for dominance and his selfishness for confidence. I can't help feeling like a fool."

"Shush now. Do you remember what you told me when I broke up with Harry? You said it was good practice because it showed me what I don't want in my life." He pursed his lips and winked.

"You were right."

"Okay. You've got a point. But I've had enough. It was better when I kept to the three-date rule. I'm not built for a real relationship, and I don't have time for one. Without distraction, I can concentrate on polishing the book. Do I even need a man if I have a drawer full of batteries?"

"Hold on. You don't have to give up on the species, Bree. I am sure there is a man out there who can tame the dirty, bad girl inside of you!"

She snorted. "I'm not so sure, J. I don't know if I can give up control. If we're talking fantasies, I want a man strong enough to toss me over his shoulder, wicked enough to tie me to the bed, and skilled enough to tease me to the brink."

Jared grinned at her. "Christ, isn't that what we all want?"

She laughed without humor. "In a book boyfriend, yes, but that's impossible in real life. The thought police have created men who tiptoe around us, like they tiptoe around the clitoris. It would be nice to find a guy who knows how to operate my console and maybe even write some new code."

He slapped the table and laughed. "Hon, if I knew where to find them, I'd be rich! But since you're free now, you can embrace your dark side. Speaking of your saucy alter ego, how's the writing going?"

The deadline for her manuscript was fast approaching. She had put her heart and soul into it for the last eighteen months, and failure was not an option.

"Editing is torture. I need to stop over-analyzing it." She blew out her breath. "I will deliver it by the first of March or die trying."

"You've got this. I have no doubt!"

"I hope so. My aunt Josie's longtime agent agreed to review the full manuscript, as a favor to her. She may represent me or tell me to go back to the drawing board."

"Okay, so stop obsessing and trust that you did your best. It will go through more revisions before they send it to publishers, right?"

"Yeah, that's how it's supposed to work. Honestly, I don't know how my aunt did this twenty-six times."

"She did it one book at a time, and so will you." Jared raised his glass. "Here's to using your newfound freedom and finishing that hot and juicy romance."

Encouragement from Jared and Aunt Josie kept her toiling at her computer every night after work, but it took every ounce of discipline for Brynne to finish on schedule. After pressing send on her manuscript, she and Jared celebrated by getting drunk and doing karaoke at their favorite bar.

Two years earlier, they started at the *London Mirror* on the same day. God only knew where she would be if he hadn't taken her under his wing. Probably murdered and left in an alley in Croydon. She arrived in London with two suitcases and a reservation for four nights in a shitty hotel twenty miles from downtown. When she showed him where she was looking for an apartment, he ripped up the list and helped her find a great flat in Brixton.

Jared was an amazing press photographer, but his passion was black-and-white erotic photography. He couldn't make a living from it, so he took a job that paid the rent. The night his boyfriend dumped him, they went to a bar after work and got hammered. She confessed she was writing a BDSM-themed romance, and he admitted to moonlighting at an exclusive gentleman's club that held fabulous fetish parties. That night, they shared many secrets, and a special friendship was born.

After two months with no news from the agent, Brynne was inconsolable. Jared was a saint, but she knew he was getting tired of her negative self-talk.

She checked her email incessantly and considered sending a follow-up, but Josie assured her it could take several months. Seven weeks and three days later, she woke up to an email from the Wade & Stewart Literary Agency. Her thoughts began flitting like a bee in a pollination frenzy. One flower of doubt, one bloom of hope. Doubt had plagued her for weeks, but the waiting was over. She piled up her pillows and opened the email.

Dear Brynne,

You've done a good job with your characters and have created a compelling story that kept me engaged most of the way, but you missed the mark on delivering the type of erotically charged scenes that readers want in this genre. Dig deeper into the true dynamics of a dominant and submissive relationship and make sure the characters have an attraction that sizzles.

One of my preferred publishing houses is planning to launch a new line of more erotic stories. They are looking for darker romances with kinky themes and more explicit sex.

This genre is not in my wheelhouse, but when you have completed a rewrite, I'll have my team take another look at it. You've done well, so don't give up.

Josie and I haven't been able to connect. Please be sure to pass along my good wishes when you see her.

Best regards,
Linda

Guilt nagged her. It had been months since she'd visited Aunt Josie. With her singular focus on revising the book, she'd put off making a trip to Skye. Josie was her biggest cheerleader and had consistently encouraged Brynne to fulfill her dreams of being an author. Her racy Regency-era novels about strong, adventurous women and dashing, dominant men allowed Brynne to find her own author voice.

The writing was on the wall. Studying other erotic writers and watching kinky videos wasn't enough. At thirty-two, she was no shy wallflower, but her quest to understand the dynamics of BDSM had missed the mark.

It was time to explore the world of dominance and submission— and it was going to require *hands-on* experience.

She punched out a text to Jared:

Brynne: *Jared. I want you to get me an interview at Dominus. I'm done trying to figure out the scene on my own.*

Jared: *Oy vey! OK I'll try to get you an interview but only as a server. They may not hire you - you have no experience as a sub.*

Brynne: *I want to see the real stuff and maybe I'll meet a real Dom there who can teach me the ropes. I can pretend to be submissive. How hard can that be?*

Jared: *Christ, you don't have a submissive bone in your body. Or if you do, it's hidden by that big chip on your shoulder.*

2

Club Dominus

Spring was being held for ransom by a cold, damp fog that blanketed the city. Brynne walked up the steps of the majestic four-story Georgian and took a deep breath. Without Google Maps, she would have walked right past the entrance.

An engraved foundation stone proved the building had been around at the turn of the century, and the imposing black gate made her wonder if it was meant to keep people out or lock them in. Shaking off her nerves, she pressed the buzzer.

She was applying to one of the last private, men-only establishments in London. Club Dominus was a rich man's fetish club. Exorbitant fees ensured that only the very wealthy or very connected could enjoy the fine cuisine and other more deviant pursuits that membership offered.

Jared tried to talk her out of it, but Brynne ultimately convinced him it was the safest way to get firsthand exposure to the scene, even if she'd only be observing the guests as a server. He helped her fill out the outrageous questionnaire, and three days later, they called her for an interview.

Ringing the call button one more time, Brynne steeled herself for the next step in her erotic education.

"You may enter."

The gravelly voice made her hair stand up. An audible click released the latch on the gate. The tall oak door swung open, and she admired the grand two-story foyer with its gleaming black-and-white marble floors and miles of polished wood. Ornately framed oil paintings filled the walls of the impressive staircase and reminded Brynne of a museum. It smelled like lemon polish, old books, and leather.

Her gaze landed on the withered butler who was looking at her like an exterminator would a wayward cockroach.

She pasted on a phony beautiful smile and said, "I'm here for an interview. My name is—"

He cut her off with a wave of his white-gloved hand. "I'm quite aware of who you are, Miss Larimore. Now, if you would please follow me."

"Sure, of course," she said, then hastily added, "sir."

She followed closely as he tottered down the stairs to the lower level.

They entered a long, wide hallway with dark paneled walls and many closed doors that begged to be investigated. He opened one such unmarked door to a small windowless room and stepped aside so she could enter. "Your meeting is not for another fifteen minutes, so you will wait here until I fetch you. No wandering off, do you understand?"

"Yes." She gave his back a mock salute.

Were all English butlers so starched? She wouldn't know. This was her first encounter. Perhaps only when they were dealing with the riffraff, which she surely was.

Taking advantage of the chance to check her appearance, she kicked off her uncomfortable heels and padded over to the large ornate mirror on the opposite wall. Strands of auburn hair had come out of her messy bun, so she did her best to pin the stray bits back and carefully reapplied her lipstick. When the old man returned, he huffed his impatience as she scrambled to put her shoes on.

He led the way to another closed door and knocked. Brynne noticed a Scottish crest on the opposite wall and was about to ask him about it when the door opened, and all thoughts fled.

A giant of a man filled the opening. Her breath stalled as she took in the massive chest and thick arms bulging beneath a snug navy sweater. Her eyes traveled up in slow motion until she met the man's amused gaze and blushed. He was the most beautiful Black man she had ever seen. Eyes the color of cognac were framed by lashes most women would kill for. She stood five-foot-six in heels, but he was easily a foot taller than her.

"You must be Brynne," he said in a deep baritone. "I'm Garrick Hunt, manager of Club Dominus." His hand dwarfed hers, but his grip was gentle. She couldn't help but smile back, reddening when his eyes twinkled in amusement at her wide-eyed appraisal.

He gestured to the sitting area. "Have a seat. I'll be right back."

"Mount Garrick" disappeared into the hallway, and she sat in the middle of the oversized leather chesterfield. Anxiety made her fidgety. She had to get this right. Jared had been hesitant to give her any details about the club, insisting he was under a strict NDA.

Garrick returned with a sheaf of papers. "I'm a little old-fashioned. I like printouts, so I can jot notes as we go." He sat in one of the two club chairs bookending the coffee table. "You can sit here. I don't bite." He pointed to the seat nearest to him.

Brynne slid across the leather cushions. Her face heated as she struggled to straighten her skirt, which had twisted and ridden up her thighs.

Garrick cleared his throat and leaned back casually, giving the impression it was an informal conversation between friends.

"I quite liked your answers to our interview questions." He smiled. "You took a rather original approach, particularly with how you would manage a challenging guest."

"Thank you. I believe it's about being charming and disarming and never offending a customer."

"True, however, you haven't worked in an environment where the customer is not only right, but they might enjoy meting out punishment for a perceived insult or minor mistake." His eyes never left hers, and it was disquieting.

"No, I haven't, but I have experience defusing situations when a customer is inebriated or looking to pick a fight." She added, "I worked in some pretty rowdy places during college in Toronto."

"Ah, Canada! Of course, I was trying to place your accent and the funny way you say *aboot*." He chuckled as he flipped a page over and continued. "What made you relocate to London?"

"I was born in the UK—in Inverness actually—but we moved to Canada when I was eight. Every summer, I used to visit my aunt in the Highlands. By my late twenties, I wanted a change of scene, and London was always at the top of my list." He didn't need to know why she abruptly left her promising position at a well-known magazine to grovel for an entry-level copyeditor job at the *London Mirror*.

"So, Brynne, tell me, when did you first know you were submissive?" His dark eyes met hers and held.

Thank god Jared told her to expect this question. She just prayed he didn't think her answer was ridiculous.

She cleared her throat. "I've known since I was about eleven. I used to tie up my dolls. Harley Davidson Ken would kidnap Barbie and take her away to his lair. He would have his wicked way with her until Malibu Ken came to her rescue. But not before she had been, um, mistreated."

Garrick was chuckling, and she let out the breath she had been holding.

"How many men, or women, have mastered you, Brynne?"

"Two," she lied. "I was in a relationship until recently. We broke up a few months ago." At least that part was true.

"That's too bad. If you don't mind me asking, why did you part ways?"

She met his gaze and stretched the truth some more. "He was cheating on me and going to clubs with other women."

Garrick shook his head. "Unfortunate. You are better off without him."

"Thanks, I agree. He was a total douche."

Garrick smiled and flipped to the next page. "There will be plenty of situations, especially during our fetish nights, where you might find yourself lavished with attention. I assure you we take every precaution to ensure the safety of our staff. Our members represent London's elite and are generally a civilized bunch. You can expect them to flirt and proposition you—harmlessly, of course."

Brynne nodded and smiled. "I think it's a pity nobody flirts anymore. Men can't even give a compliment because it's politically incorrect and often considered harassment."

Garrick leaned forward, piercing her with his dark eyes. "Believe me, they will flirt. You must be prepared to dodge, deflect, and flirt back so there are no bruised egos."

"I can handle that," she said confidently. There were plenty of times she had to evade wayward hands and unwanted attention while slinging cocktails and chicken wings.

Garrick went on, "During our fetish parties, members will expect absolute obedience, and they may push your buttons to test it."

Brynne's eyes widened, and she wondered what would happen if she lost her temper or really fucked something up. "What if I accidentally spill a drink?"

Garrick steepled his fingers and touched his lips as he mulled over the question.

"Master Gage or I would decide on the punishment. If you spilled a drink without breaking glass, you would get on your hands and knees to wipe it up. We might make you pull your skirt up, so your arse is on display as you do it."

Brynne inhaled sharply and bit her tongue.

"If you broke the glass, someone else would need to clean it up, and you might receive a spanking for being clumsy."

"Um, I would do my best not to let that happen," she whispered.

"Does that mean spanking doesn't turn you on?" Garrick studied her, measuring and assessing. It seemed like an innocent question, but it did not fool her.

"I—I do like being spanked, but being punished in front of your guests would be…" She shivered just thinking about it. "Mortifying."

Garrick rose and retrieved a folder from his desk. "Our members' privacy is more important than anything else, as you saw from the comprehensive NDA we emailed." He placed the three-page document on the coffee table. "Here is a printed copy you can sign for me now."

Brynne took the fancy pen he offered and signed the last page. She had read it from top to bottom and knew she couldn't tell anyone what went on in this place.

"Now, all we need is the reference from a Dom or someone known in the scene who will vouch for you."

Brynne nodded absently, but then realization dawned. Her hands twisted in her lap. Could she have misheard him? "I have—I mean Jared Blackwood has vouched for me. Is that what you mean?"

"No, sweetheart, I mean a legitimate letter of reference that lets us know someone properly trained to behave with grace and obedience in all circumstances you may experience here at the club."

Her eyes widened as she struggled to gather her thoughts. "I, um, I will get that for you."

"Good. Bring it when you come back for the second interview with Master Gage. He owns Dominus, and all candidates must meet his approval before we offer employment."

Garrick rose and pressed a buzzer by the door. She stood and tugged her wrinkled skirt down, wiping the perspiration off her palms.

He turned and gave Brynne his business card. "Call the main number when you have your reference letter, and they will set up your next appointment."

"Thank you, will do. It was a pleasure to meet you, Mr. Hunt. I really appreciate your time."

"Same. Take good care, Brynne. Wait right out here for Miles. He will escort you out."

Brynne was itching to call Jared, but it would have to wait. As she waited for the butler, she overheard raised voices behind the door across the hall.

"I don't give a fuck about your finances, Sierra. You should have thought of that before you lied to me."

Brynne held her breath and stood there, curious to hear more.

"If you need money, perhaps you should sell some of your designer handbags—or pawn the ring you decided to keep. I'm sure you could raise a hundred thousand pounds." The accent was distinctly Scottish, and his voice dripped with contempt.

A woman's voice pierced the silence. "You are such a bastard! After everything we've shared, how can you be so callous?"

"You don't really want me to answer that, do you? I have work to do. See yourself out."

Brynne moved quickly down the hall when the conversation ended. The door swung open, and a tall, stunning blonde started toward her.

Her icy scowl pinned Brynne to the spot. "What the hell are you looking at?"

Brynne backed up until she felt the wall at her back. This was one of those times she wished for three more inches of height.

The woman curled her over-injected lips in contempt. "Are you one of those doormat subs who needs to be told what to do every hour of the day?"

"Excuse me?" Brynne recognized that haughty face from somewhere. When a wave of cloying perfume reached her nose, recognition dawned. She was the spokesmodel for a horrid fragrance that was featured all over Harrods last year. That scent always gave her a headache.

Before she could respond, a man appeared in the doorway. "Do yourself a favor, Sierra, and leave now."

Brynne lost the ability to speak, but her brain catalogued his features one by one and transmitted unadulterated hunger through her bloodstream, straight to her core. He was her darkest fantasies brought to life. His jaw was rigid, his fists clenched at his sides. He looked positively lethal. She had the urge to run but was rooted to the spot.

The woman's screechy voice interrupted her perusal. "You're a sick fuck, and I'm going to make sure everyone in our social circle knows it."

"Go ahead. We'll see how your pristine reputation weathers the gossip that ensues."

"I hate you."

He shook his head, clearly at the end of his patience. "Go."

She turned on her heel and strode toward the staircase, then turned back, catching Brynne's eye for a second before she spat, "You will be sorry."

"I already am." His barely audible response raised the hair on her neck.

Once the blonde viper was out of sight, he stalked toward her. Brynne didn't realize she was inching away until she bumped into a table and almost toppled it.

The man reached past her to steady the wobbling lamp. "Why are you loitering in this hall?"

He stood close enough to singe her skin with his heat. His eyes raked over her like shards of green ice with the power to wound. She stammered, "Uh, Garrick told me to wait here for the butler after my interview."

He made a strange sound in his throat. "Submissive or server?"

"Server."

"Have you signed the NDA?"

She nodded.

"Good. You'll do well to forget everything you saw and heard today." He looked her up and down. "I trust you are bright enough to find your way to the front door?"

Her chin jutted, and she met his disdain with her own. "I was just following Mr. Hunt's explicit instructions."

"Good for you. We like that in our employees." His mouth

turned up slightly at the corners, causing her to stare at it. "What we don't like…is impertinence."

Her face was hot, and she hated how her body cowered under his stare. The old man reappeared and cleared his throat, saving her from saying something stupid. He wrung his hands and bowed. "My apologies, sir. Multiple deliveries came to the front entrance and delayed me. I will see the lady out."

"It was no trouble at all, Miles."

She watched him gently pat the man on the shoulder, the harsh tone gone from his voice.

"Don't hurry on the steps. You've got to take it easy until that hip is back in fighting form."

"Yes, sir, thank you, sir."

He turned with a curt nod to Brynne and disappeared down the hall. Miles led her back to the entrance. She had barely stepped onto the portico when the door slammed shut at her back and freezing rain stung her cheeks.

What the actual fuck? Who was that guy? Why was her heart pounding in her ears? And what was the deal with that woman?

No doubt the tall, obnoxious Scotsman was the owner and Master of Dominus.

Nice work, Brynne. You made a lousy first impression.

The encounter almost made her forget the other disaster. The small matter of a reference letter from someone in the scene!

Brynne dug her cell phone out of her bag and started down the street. Jared picked up after half a ring. "How did it go? Did you get the job?"

"No, not even close! I'm trying not to get hysterical here in the middle of Covent fucking Garden." She stopped and put her hand over her mouth so no one passing by would hear her. "Apparently, I need a reference from a real Dom!"

"What? You can't be serious?"

"Oh, I'm deadly serious," she growled into the phone.

"Wait, did you do what I told you? Did you act reserved and *submissive*?"

Jared had warned her not to get prickly, but how dare he assume she failed?

"Dammit, I acted the right way!" Her voice was drawing attention from passersby. "Garrick put me at ease. He was very nice, but that's not enough. He needs this letter. Without it, I'm screwed." Sighing heavily, she added, "I also had a run-in with a gorgeous but horrible man."

"Geez, girl. What did he look like?"

"Tall, dark hair, chiseled jaw, chilling green eyes… And he probably has pointy teeth."

"That would be Master Gage."

"Yeah, I figured. He made me weak at the knees—until he opened his mouth. I'm disgusted to say I probably would have stripped naked if he'd told me to."

"Too bad he didn't. Then you might have gotten the job without going to a local dungeon for a reference."

She heard him chuckling into the phone and wanted to throttle him. "Jared, this is not funny. What the hell am I going to do?"

"I know someone. She is wonderful, and if I tell her you're a novice, I am sure she will go easy on you."

Brynne felt herself go pale. "Are you joking? Who is she? Wait, are you suggesting I go see your dominatrix friend?" Her mouth went dry at the idea of experiencing a real-life scene, after thinking about it for so long.

"Yes. It's better than paying a stranger."

"Bloody hell. Can't I pay for the service and get a letter, without, you know?" she couldn't bring herself to finish.

"Oh sweetie, that's not how it works. A proper Domme won't fake this kind of thing. Mistress Patricia is well known across Europe—a reference from her will guarantee you the job. The only thing is, she won't say she instructed you unless she did."

"Fuck. Me."

"No, not unless she's attracted to you, and it's not one of your hard limits."

"Christ, Jared, that's not what I meant, and you know it!" Brynne groaned loudly. "Look, I've got to go. I'm drenched and heading underground. We'll talk tomorrow at work, okay?"

"Don't worry, Bree, it will be fine. You'll see. Bye."

She punched the end call icon and stomped down the steps. She could not believe her luck. It wasn't like she expected success without hard work, but without Club Dominus, she would have to venture into the creepier fetish nightclubs. The thought of going to an actual dominatrix made her stomach flutter…and something else she refused to acknowledge.

Her thoughts returned to Gage. The man was annoyingly gorgeous and so bloody rude. When he was towering over her, she felt like a rabbit in the sights of a hawk. What did it say about her, that she wondered what it would be like to be caught?

3

A Special Letter of Reference

It was ten past nine when Brynne slid into her cube, hoping to go unnoticed.

No such luck. The city editor's assistant, the prim and pointy-nosed Margaret Smythe, peered over the wall of her cubicle. "Late again, Brynne?" she said in her condescending tone.

"There was a delay on the underground. It was beyond my control." Brynne was past caring if this owlish woman reported all her transgressions to her boss. Early on, she'd played the game to make a good impression. Today, she was in no mood to explain herself.

"One would think you don't want this job."

"Then one would be quite mistaken, Margaret." Brynne turned away to pull her PC out of her backpack, ending the exchange. The woman huffed and walked away.

Brynne spent the better part of the morning proofreading a tedious article for the Life & Culture section. It was almost noon when her phone buzzed. Jared was back from photographing the gallery opening and wanted to meet.

Jared: *Bree, I'm at the café. Got us a table if you can take lunch.*

Brynne: *On my way.*

The noon rush was in full swing, but he had a table in the back with her favorite tuna on rye waiting. She maneuvered through the tables and saw he was grinning mischievously. Before she sat down, he blurted, "I have news!"

"Don't tell me, the Nash Gallery wants to exhibit your stuff?" she asked.

"I wish. No, I have news from Mistress Patricia!"

Her head snapped up. "God, keep your voice down. There could be people from work nearby!"

"Right! Sorry. I just never thought I would hear from her so quickly." He looked around to ensure no one was within earshot. "She has agreed to meet you."

Brynne's hands went to her forehead, then she covered her eyes. "Oh. My. God." She couldn't believe Jared got her an appointment so quickly. This was all moving so fast.

"I know, right!" Jared was gleeful. "She is in very high demand, but she will do this favor for me. She can fit you in next Saturday."

Brynne's fingers pressed hard against her temples. She had never been with a woman—but it wasn't about that. It was anxiety and uncertainty at the thought of finally doing something she had never experienced before. "Jared, I don't know about this."

"You've got to go. I accepted for you." He got all serious, his mouth a stern line. "There is no turning back now. My reputation is on the line."

"J, you know I love you, but you shouldn't have made this commitment without talking to me first! If she's as good as you say, she will know I'm not submissive." Brynne looked down at her sandwich and shook her head. "I would rather just interview her, and she can explain all the power dynamics to me."

"Hon, you have already done lots of research. You've *talked* to enough people about the how and the why, and you've watched enough videos to understand the mechanics." He sighed and put his hand on hers. "But all that will not help you get inside your characters' heads and make them real."

Brynne knew he was right, and it was annoying as hell. Shaking off his hand, she glowered at him and bit into her sandwich. Twenty minutes later, they walked back to the office in silence. Thankfully, Jared knew better than to press her.

She had no time to think with Ms. Smarmy Smythe watching her every move. After staring at the same page for an hour, she went to make a hot chocolate. Her boss, Nigel, was in the staff kitchen pouring himself a coffee.

"Hey Brynne, I meant to tell you how impressed I was with your work on that last piece you fixed up for Edwards. It's a good thing you checked her facts and caught those errors before we went to print. It could have been a disaster."

"Thanks, Nigel. Glad I could help." Brynne smiled brightly, thrilled at finally being noticed for her editing skills. She often wondered if his PA had poisoned his opinion of her. Maybe her fears were unfounded.

"I've seen what you are capable of and will send you more. Keep it up." She stood there for a few minutes, basking in the compliments about her work.

The week flew by. Brynne worked late three nights in a row. Nigel, true to his word, kept calling on her to edit more of the higher-profile articles. She welcomed the added responsibilities.

By Thursday, she was exhausted from obsessing about the upcoming *session*. Begging Jared for more insights on Patricia proved fruitless. He told her that anticipation was like foreplay and that the mystery would add to the experience. *Thanks for nothing, J.* She called him every name in the book and stopped answering his texts.

Madame Patricia's assistant sent a confirmation email that was comprehensive and explicit. She expected punctuality, immediate compliance with instructions, and proper use of safe words. Upon arrival, Brynne would complete the hard and soft limits questionnaire. Lingerie was optional for modesty; however, it might get damaged during the scene. The fee of £275 cash was required upfront for this custom "test your limits" session and a reference letter would be provided shortly after.

Brynne splurged on a taxi to cover the distance to the industrial area of East London. It reminded her of Toronto's waterfront and her first full-time job. *Toronto Life & Style* magazine was her first big break out of university. It provided an abundant education— particularly in how men could be duplicitous bastards.

She forced herself back to the present as the taxi pulled up in front of the old yellow brick building. The structure was two city blocks long, and the barred windows reminded her of a prison, not an office building.

Pulling her collar up against the wind, Brynne hunted for the entrance to the Valentine Agency. Anxiety churned in her stomach as she pressed the buzzer. Had she lost her mind letting Jared talk her into this? Working at the club was one thing, but submitting to a professional Domme was quite another.

A cheerful, melodic voice came over the intercom. "Come on up, luv. Take the stairs to the second floor. We're at the end."

Brynne entered a well-appointed reception room and was greeted by a striking woman in a tailored gray suit, white silk blouse, and sexy suede slingbacks. Taking Brynne's extended hand, she said, "It's lovely to meet you, Brynne. I'm Patricia."

Her welcoming manner put Brynne at ease. "It's great to meet you, too. Thank you so much for agreeing to meet me on such short notice."

She tilted her head and smiled playfully. "That Jared is a special young man. You must be close friends for him to call in such a favor."

"He is. We've been best friends ever since I moved to London two years ago."

"Please take a seat in my office. I'm going to lock the door, as I've sent my assistant home for the evening."

Mistress Patricia was not at all what she expected. No black leather outfit, short spiky hair, or blood-red lipstick. Honey-blonde hair framed her delicate features, and her twinkling blue eyes projected warmth, acceptance, and something else Brynne couldn't put her finger on.

The office smelled like orange blossoms and vanilla. It was feminine and elegant, against the backdrop of exposed brick and wide plank floors. She sat in front of the antique writing desk and pulled out her notebook. When Patricia returned, she asked if it would be okay to take notes.

"Yes, of course," she replied as she sat down and donned a pair of purple reading glasses. "I'd like to get to know you before we begin."

Brynne's tension and dread released like steam from a boiling pot.

Thank god they weren't immediately heading to the dungeon. "That would be great!" she blurted, adding, "I guess you know I am not very experienced?"

"We were all inexperienced at one time, Brynne. It takes nerve to explore something new."

Brynne let out her breath. "Thank you for that." She absently pressed her hands to her thighs and continued. "The truth is, I've wanted to explore this part of myself for a long time." She swallowed, shocked at how truthful she was being—not just to Mistress Patricia, but also to herself. "I haven't found the best way or the right person."

"Tell me about the first inkling you had that you were submissive."

She flushed a little and let out her breath. "The thing is, I don't know if I am. There are things I fantasize about, but I've never been with anyone who likes the same things."

Each time she bared her soul, it got easier. Brynne described her failed attempts to find a strong, confident partner—someone who wouldn't crumble the way her father had when her mother left. His fragility frightened her and made her determined never to be that vulnerable. Her three-date rule in college kept her from sharing her secret fantasies with anyone. Patricia listened and nodded, never making her feel silly.

"You aren't what I expected at all," Brynne admitted.

She smiled and winked. "Believe me, I hear that all the time."

"Do I pay you now?" Brynne waited for direction.

"All in good time. First things first," she said as she tapped her computer mouse and opened a file. "Who has requested the reference letter?"

"It's for Club Dominus. I've interviewed for a job there and—"

"Oh, how wonderful!" she exclaimed. "So, this will be for Master Gage?"

"Yes. Garrick, the manager, requested it before I have the final interview with Gage. I met him briefly. He was very intimidating." Brynne couldn't help herself and asked, "Is he always so scary?"

Patricia took off her glasses and looked wistful. Her eyes were the color of sapphires, and Brynne fell deeper under her spell.

"Gage MacLeod is quite a stunning specimen, and unlike any man I've ever met. He can be deeply passionate one moment and cold as ice the next. That dark magnetism draws you into his orbit—but beware, he is emotionally unavailable."

Brynne swallowed and mouthed the word, "Oh."

"The sad thing is he doesn't play in clubs anymore, even in Berlin, where we originally met. He was always aloof, but he's become cynical and reclusive since—well, it doesn't matter. You just stay out of trouble, and he won't bother you."

Brynne's curiosity was piqued even though she knew it was in her best interests to stay under the radar.

Patricia's nails clicked on the keyboard, pulling her back to the present. "During our session, we will discover what you like, what you don't like, and what turns you on whether you like it or not." She continued like a professor laying out a class lesson. "Often there are things, or specific restraints, for example, which will trigger a reaction you didn't expect. Like if I deprived you of sight—or the ability to speak."

Brynne's pen stopped midair and her cheeks burned at the implication. More disconcerting was her body's reaction as sensations whirred to life between her legs.

"Ultimately, you will have to trust me, Brynne. When we go into my studio, you become my submissive, and you do exactly as I say." She peered over the top of her glasses. "Do you understand the rules of engagement?"

"Yes." Brynne nodded. "May I ask a question?"

"Of course. Now is the time to ask."

"What if I don't... I mean, what if someone you are instructing misbehaves?"

Patricia stopped typing and paused before answering. "In my experience, when that happens, there are two probable reasons. One, the sub doesn't have respect for the Dom and is withholding the gift of their obedience. The other possibility is that he or she wants to push their buttons to instigate harsher punishment or more *attention*." Patricia waited for her to finish writing and asked what she thought.

She nibbled on the end of her pen. "I am not sure why, but my personality has always been a bit, um, oppositional. As a kid, I got attention by being bad. In this situation it's hard to judge whether to test the boundaries when I don't know how harsh the punishment will be."

"You will likely know right away. Pain is not always a deterrent; for some, it's highly enjoyable."

"To be honest, I have fantasies like lots of women," Brynne said, "but they're more about being forced to comply, not submitting willingly."

"I appreciate your openness, dear. But you should know most Doms demand obedience. For some, it is the most essential element, because it shows a commitment and devotion to pleasing them. It is also irrefutable proof that everything is by choice and not done under threat."

Brynne wrote everything down, then looked up to see Patricia was waiting for her full attention.

"The number-one rule is that your submission is voluntary. It must never be forced, or even coerced." Her expression softened. It was almost nostalgic. "Personally, I view it as a gift."

"I see. A Dominant cannot have what they need unless the sub is willing to give it."

"Exactly. It is a delicate balance of power that requires full trust. One could argue the submissive wields more power because they can always stop a scene. The skilled Dom can push the boundaries when they know exactly how far their sub likes to go. It's up to you to make them aware of what you will and won't do. For example, if you decide a hard limit is no ass play, your Dom must respect that."

Brynne swallowed. Patricia peered over her glasses and said, "Sweetie, you are wound so tight, one tap with a crop, and I think you could come undone."

"Is it that obvious?"

She winked. "Only to the discerning eye."

Patricia rose from her desk and suggested they sit on the couch to talk through the next set of questions. She glided over to the wall unit and accessed a well-stocked bar. Brynne admired the way her pencil skirt showed off her hourglass shape and toned legs. She poured two glasses of a deep plum-colored liquid and handed one to Brynne.

"This is my favorite sweet sherry. It will help calm your nerves." She took a seat on the sofa. "It's highly unusual for me to take on someone I know nothing about. Since this is for Dominus, I need to be *thorough*."

Brynne sank onto the sofa and took a tentative sip. The rich sweet wine warmed her, and for the first time in a week, she relaxed.

Patricia raised her glass. "To discovering the submissive in you, Brynne."

They clinked glasses, and Brynne smiled tentatively. "May I ask, how did you get into this line of work?"

"When I was twenty-eight, I started my own headhunting business with a bank loan and a dream. A lot of psychology is involved in coaching candidates to change companies. I had a knack for reading personalities and could spot the ones who needed to be pushed harder to reach their potential. Some needed to be strong-armed, while others needed coddling."

Patricia's eyes lit with excitement. "As I built my business, I found that I really enjoyed using those skills to help people take risks. One day, a gorgeous software executive of about thirty asked me if I would punish him if he didn't take the lucrative job I'd sourced for him." She laughed. "I told him I would beat him black and blue. He came to my office the next day and begged me to do it."

"Wow." Brynne couldn't hide her admiration.

Patricia returned to peeling the onion. "Tell me a little about your childhood, parents, and where you grew up?"

Brynne wrestled with where to begin. "I was born in Scotland, but when I was eight, we moved to Canada. Not long after, my mother left. She packed up, told my dad she didn't want to be a wife or mother anymore, and left to find a more exciting life."

Brynne kept her face devoid of emotion. "I should have been devastated, but I wasn't. She rarely took notice of me, dressed me in ugly clothes, and chopped my hair like a boy. It took me a few years to realize that she wanted to minimize the attention people gave me. She wasn't happy unless the spotlight was on her."

"Is she still alive?" Patricia asked.

Brynne tensed. "I have no idea and couldn't care less."

"How did your father cope with her leaving?"

Jesus, she is dredging up some old memories. "He was a mess. Depressed, drank too much…so I took care of him. I became the lady of the house." Taking another sip of liquid courage, she continued, "I really didn't mind. He eventually pulled himself together."

Patricia continued with the questions and Brynne let it all tumble out of her. It was cathartic. They drank and nibbled on crackers, grapes, and a rich creamy brie that Patricia pulled out of her mini fridge. She asked about her high school experiences and Brynne explained she was "a late bloomer" who only had one so-called boyfriend.

"In grade thirteen a boy I had a crush on asked me out for an actual date. Ryan Woodberry was his name. He picked me up in his dad's posh Mercedes and I was overjoyed. Halfway through the drive-in movie and a bottle of wine, he begged me for a blow job." Brynne giggled. "I eventually caved. That night I learned I had a talent, and that power was far more intoxicating than the wine."

"What happened?" Patricia leaned forward, eagerly.

"I guess I had something to prove. Maybe I wanted all the boys to know they missed out on a gem, so I went down on him like a champion. When he came, I swallowed because I thought only a wimp would spit!"

Patricia clapped her hands and laughed. "That is fabulous! Did he worship the ground you walked on after that?"

Brynne's smile faltered. "No, actually. We dated for a few weeks, until I found out he was seeing another girl."

"That little shit!" Patricia exclaimed.

"Yeah." The memories came flooding back. That was the first of many disappointing experiences with boys.

She looked at her quizzically. "So, you were still a virgin by the end of high school?"

Smiling playfully, Brynne replied, "Absolutely! My dad always told me to keep my legs closed. So instead, I opened my mouth!" Laughing, she added, "I'm sure that's not what he intended."

"I bet not! Your experiences were pretty limited up to that point. Did you go crazy at university?"

"No, not really. In year two, my dad was diagnosed with cancer, so I switched to part-time. I was helping at home, so I dated very little. My only boyfriend was cautious and dependable. Basically, I called all the shots. I popped my cherry with him but got bored a month later and broke up with him. My girlfriends called me the man eater because after that I never dated a guy more than three times. When they wanted more, I ditched them. By graduation, I'd found erotica and a five-speed vibrator, but had no clue what I wanted in a man."

Patricia poured them each more sherry and asked without preamble, "Tell me what you think about when you masturbate."

OMG. She'd only shared that once, and it turned out badly. Those secrets remained in a mythical lockbox under her bed.

When she remained mute, Patricia reassured her, "There's nothing I haven't heard, Brynne. If you haven't read the book *My Secret Garden* by Nancy Friday, I will lend you my copy." She retrieved a worn paperback from her bookshelf and handed it to Brynne. "Fantasies can be an accelerant to help ignite your desires. We all have them—and you'll see they run the gamut."

"I've never heard of this book." She handled it gently as the binding was coming apart and pages were loose.

"That's because they published it before you were born, dear." Patricia grinned. "It did for a generation what *Fifty Shades* did for this one. It proved women think about sex as much as men. Our fantasies are vivid, integral parts of our sexuality."

Brynne carefully considered what she said next. "I have a recurring fantasy of being helpless and unable to stop what is happening because I'm tied down. Sometimes I'm kidnapped or overpowered by a man who is bent on having his way with me...not by force, but by arousing me against my will."

She saw no shock or judgment on Patricia's face but wasn't willing to divulge any of her other deviant thoughts. Those would remain unacknowledged for now.

"I am glad you feel comfortable sharing your experiences with me, Brynne. I think I know what you need. You had a lot of responsibility as a young girl—the man who was supposed to take care of you couldn't, and no one has made you feel safe and cared for."

Patricia's eyes were dark and hypnotic, and she couldn't look away. "Mmm. It would be wonderful to stop worrying and let go."

Her expression changed, and Brynne felt the imperceptible shift. "We have both been drinking, so I cannot take you into the playroom now."

She couldn't hide her disappointment. She wanted it so badly she could taste it.

"That doesn't mean we can't see if you can surrender some of that ironclad control."

Brynne waited, holding her breath.

"Get on your knees and come here." She pointed to the floor at her feet.

Her breathing stalled; her eyes wide.

"As a rule, I don't ask twice. I expect immediate obedience, or you will be punished."

Brynne scrambled to the floor and kept her eyes down. Patricia had morphed into a Domme before her eyes.

She reached across and undid Brynne's hair. "What a beautiful shade of red." She moved closer and took her time running her fingers through it. "Is it natural, or will I find another color down below?"

Brynne whispered, her mouth suddenly dry, "It's mine. My natural color, I mean. Mistress."

Patricia smiled. "Have you ever been with a woman, Brynne?"

She shook her head and bit her lip.

She cupped the back of Brynne's head and took a fistful of her hair. "You are very beautiful, more so because I don't think you realize it."

The grip on her hair tightened. Patricia pulled her head back until their gazes met. Brynne's heart pounded in her chest. She was mesmerized.

"I would like to kiss you." Patricia moved closer. "With your permission."

Brynne flushed with arousal. "Yes, please, Mistress."

She lingered, her hand tightening in Brynne's hair. She leaned in and ran a thumb over her bottom lip. "Put your hands behind your back and keep them there."

Brynne did as she was told and licked her lips, anticipating the kiss.

"I may want to do more than kiss you, pet. Do you consent to my touching you?"

Brynne's body was on fire, her clothes felt too tight, and she craved the kiss and whatever else this gorgeous woman wanted from her. Her voice was breathless and hungry. "Yes, please! I want this. What are you waiting for?"

"There's the rebellious little girl coming out to play." She tsked, let go of her hair, and sat back.

"What's wrong?" Brynne's voice sounded shrill to her own ears.

"Sweetheart, you have just learned your first lesson of submission."

"I'm sorry," she pleaded. "Please give me another chance."

"In order to get what you want, you must learn to be obedient and patient. Your Domme decides what, when, how fast or slow. Not you."

"I didn't mean to. I'm so sorry." Brynne could cry. She wanted to reverse time and go back.

"Brynne." She placed a finger on her lips. "I will see you for your proper session on Monday evening." She left Brynne kneeling on the carpet and went to her desk. "I will give you the limits questionnaire to take with you. Be here at five thirty. Make sure you eat something beforehand, but no alcohol."

Brynne rose and could not meet her eyes. She took the paper and tucked it into her purse with the book.

"I'm glad we went a little off course tonight and got to know each other. It will make your session that much more…" Her indigo eyes twinkled. "Rewarding."

4

Submitting to Mistress Patricia

What a rookie mistake! Brynne was ashamed, and it stung. During the ride home, she stewed on what might have happened if she had shut up and waited. That confident, elegant woman wanted to kiss her! And she'd wanted it just as badly.

When she got home, she was in a fine state of pique and horny as hell. She cursed herself for not replacing her broken vibrator so she would have to resort to an old-fashioned hand job. Brynne stripped and flung herself down on her bed. She closed her eyes and imagined Patricia's mouth on hers. On her breasts. Between her legs. Then she imagined being made to reciprocate.

Her fingers found their purpose, dipping into her wetness and circling her clit until she was writhing in need. She rolled onto her stomach and slid two fingers up inside herself. Grinding down hard on the palm of her hand, she came, her body shuddering as she groaned into her bedspread. It barely took the edge off. Brynne used her other hand to push her fingers deeper inside and began plunging them in and out. With images of Patricia looming over her, a crop in her hand, she tapped her g-spot and screamed out a second delicious orgasm.

She woke several hours later, with her hands still between her legs. Her stomach growled as she stumbled to the kitchen to make some tea and toast. She sat at her kitchen table and pulled out the limits questionnaire. She had never seen a list like this before. No wonder her book was not hitting the mark. It was sorely lacking in some of the kinkier activities in the D/s scene.

Instructions at the top of the form indicated she was supposed to record a letter next to each item: [N] No way; [Y] Yes interested; [M] Maybe / Might try; [D] Don't Know.

It seemed simple enough. Except the list was anything but.

Bondage and Suspension	
Blindfolds	Bondage (light)
Bondage (heavy)	Immobilization
Leather restraints	Chains
Ropes	Intricate (Japanese) rope bondage
Rope body harness	Arm & leg sleeves (armbinders)
Harnesses (leather)	Harnesses (rope)
Cuffs (leather)	Cuffs (metal)
Manacles & irons	Gags (cloth)
Gags (ball)	Gags (tape)
Gags (phallic)	Gags (ring)
Gags (inflatable)	Mouth bits
Full head hoods	Mummification/plastic wrapping
Straitjackets	Suspension (upright)
Suspension (horizontal)	Suspension (inverted)

Voyeurism / Exhibitionism

Forced nudity (private)		Exhibitionism	
Modeling for erotic photos		Video (watching others)	
Voyeurism (watching others)			

Impact / Percussion

Spanking		Flogging	
Single-tail whips		Canes	
Belts / strapping		Leather straps	
Riding crops		Hairbrushes	
Wooden paddles		Slapping (ass, breasts, genitals)	
Face slapping		Hair pulling	

Sexual Activity

Fellatio / cunnilingus		Swallowing cum	
Cumming on partner		Hand jobs	
Anal sex		Anal plugs (small)	
Anal plugs (large)		Anal beads	
Vibrator on genitals		Masturbation	
Fisting		Forced masturbation	
Double penetration (mouth+)		Orgasm control	
Double penetration (anal+)		Triple penetration using toys	

Sensation Play

Abrasion		Scratching	
Biting		Tickling	
Kissing		Zapping (electricity)	
Ice cubes		Wax play	
Clothespins		Nipple weights	
Nipple clamps		Nipple suction	

Humiliation		
Teasing	Humiliation (private)	
Verbal humiliation	Humiliation (public)	
Spitting		

Roleplaying		
Fear play	Fantasy abandonment	
Fantasy kidnapping	Interrogation	
Sleep deprivation	Pretend rape	
Multiple partners at once	Initiation rites	
Religious scenes	Medical scenes	
Prison scenes	Schoolroom scenes	

Service and Restrictive Behavior		
Following orders	Forced servitude	
Restrictive rules on behavior	Eye contact restrictions	
Speech restrictions	Kneeling	
Begging	Standing in a corner	
Massage		

She got halfway through the first page and stopped at *forced masturbation*, unable to process anymore. At two a.m., she crawled under the covers and tried to erase the deviant images floating around in her head.

Sunday dawned dark and gray. The smell of rain had wafted through her bedroom window, bringing a damp chill with it. She woke up tangled in her sheets after tossing and turning all night. After a hot shower, she decided it was a perfect day to stay home in her flannel pajamas and do some editing. But first she needed to take a closer look at the limits list. It was hard to admit how many items she ticked with a D for *Don't have a clue!*

Plastic wrap never came up in her book research and she had no interest in breath play, electricity, or spitting. WTF? On a second read through, she changed some *No way*s to *Maybe*s, so she didn't come across as a total novice. They couldn't cover a fraction of the list in one hour, anyway.

Jared phoned and wanted all the details. She omitted what had almost happened between them and shared only that they drank sherry and hung out in her office talking for two hours.

"Wow! She must really like you, Bree."

"She is very easy to talk to. I bared my bloody soul. But you didn't tell me how beautiful she is."

He chuckled. "You were already intimidated. I didn't want to tell you she was a goddess. You would have freaked out more."

"That was a good call." Brynne smirked. "I was enough of a basket case."

Even though she was curious, she didn't ask about the questionnaire or his feelings about those activities. Some things were best left a mystery between them. They ended the call when Aunt Josie rang, saving her from further awkwardness.

Brynne groaned in agony when her alarm sounded on Monday morning. It was crucial to arrive an hour early to work. She couldn't afford any hassles today from Margaret. Jared asked her out for coffee, but she made excuses about a tight deadline. In truth, she didn't want to discuss what might happen later that night. Thankfully, Nigel and Margaret were not around when she ducked out at four o'clock. She raced home and took a bath, ensuring every nook and cranny was silky smooth.

She donned the sheer stockings and sexy garter belt she'd purchased to entice Ross. Although it had been a wasted effort on him, she was glad she treated herself to the sexy ensemble with a matching bra and panty set in pale purple.

By the time she arrived, her body was buzzing with arousal and anxiety about all the things that might happen. Brynne was loath to admit some of the shocking items on the list made her pulse race.

Patricia's assistant was tidying up her desk when she arrived. "Hi, you must be Brynne." The forty-something woman beckoned her forward. "Do you have your list with you?"

Brynne pulled it out of her bag, hesitant to hand it over.

"I'm just going to run it through the copier; I'll give Patricia the original, and you can keep a copy for yourself."

"Okay, th-thank you," she mumbled.

When the assistant put it face down into the machine without looking at it, Brynne let air back into her lungs. She handed the copy to Brynne and placed the other in an envelope and sealed it.

"Through that door, you will find the changing room. When you're ready, head on into the studio. Patricia will meet you there in fifteen minutes sharp. I'm heading out and will lock the door behind me." She made quick work of putting her trench coat on and smiled mischievously. "Have fun, my dear!"

Brynne went into the small changing room and hung her coat up. She saw an envelope with her name on the front, in bold script. Quickly tearing it open, she sat on the red leather chaise to read it.

> *Brynne,*
>
> *When you pass through the door to my playroom, you are giving yourself willingly into my care for a safe, sane, and consensual scene. While in this room, I expect you to obey me without hesitation. Failing to do so will result in swift punishment.*
>
> *I will respect the limits you have set down. You have the*

right and responsibility to use your safe words appropriately. Red will stop the scene. Yellow will pause the scene to allow you to communicate any issues to me. Green is your consent to continue.

If you are gagged, I will give you a bell to hold. If you drop the bell, the scene stops. Shake the bell and I will pause. But only one time. Ringing it a second time will stop the scene.

Per our earlier email exchange, you have acknowledged receipt of the rules and safety precautions I take while you are under my care, and you confirm your consent again by entering the room.

When you enter, you will kneel on the mat beside the St Andrew's cross. Clasp your hands behind your back and keep your eyes on the floor. You will address me as Mistress—and speak only when given permission. Leave your shoes off.

M.

She found a well-appointed bathroom, and a bare steel door that screamed secret dungeon. Brynne used the facilities and ran cold water on her wrists. She stared at her reflection in the mirror and gave herself a pep talk. *Do as you're told and don't fuck this up, Brynne. This is an opportunity to open the door to this new world—to experience this lifestyle.* Almost as an afterthought, she thought about her book and Linda's advice. *What better way to understand a dominant-submissive scene than to try it?*

With trembling hands, she removed her dress and jewelry and locked them in the small locker with her purse. *Am I doing this for the novel, or to satisfy my carnal curiosity?*

Fear seized her chest—she'd forgotten to check the time. Without delay, she hurried into the next room, positioned herself as directed, and waited, heart thumping in her ears. She didn't dare to look around in case she was being watched.

A door clicked shut, and Brynne shivered. She heard heels clicking on the hardwood, and then stunning knee-high leather boots with lethal stiletto heels and ornate pewter buckles came into view.

A gentle hand was on her chin, raising her bowed head. Brynne's gaze traveled up a pair of shapely legs clad in fishnet stockings, past a black satin all-in-one corset that accentuated Patricia's hourglass figure. She wore her hair pulled back in a high braid. Two arctic blue eyes stared back at her. Her ruby red mouth was a contradiction. It begged to be kissed while warning off anyone who dared to try.

She used a black riding crop that hung from one wrist to hold Brynne's chin up. "You have much to learn of patience, Brynne."

Brynne was not sure if she should speak and silently pleaded for guidance.

"Good girl. You may answer me when I ask a question. If I make a statement, I don't expect a response. Whether I bestow a gift or a punishment upon you, I expect you to say, 'Thank you, Mistress.'" She reached behind Brynne to pull something off the wall. "Do you understand?"

"Yes, Mistress," she murmured.

"Put your arms above your head."

Brynne complied at once.

Patricia buckled leather cuffs tightly onto each of her wrists, then pulled a chain down from the ceiling and hooked it through rings on the cuffs. She stepped away from Brynne to press a button on the wall, and the chain above her head pulled Brynne's handcuffs upward with a soft whirring sound. The machine slowly dragged Brynne up until she was perched on her tiptoes. She exhaled in relief when it lowered slightly so her heels were back on the floor.

Mistress Patricia took her time and explored her captive body, dragging the wide leather tongue of the crop down the sensitive skin of her upper arm. Brynne shook as it tickled her under the arm. Next, Patricia scraped it across the tops of her breasts and then slowly back and forth over her sensitive nipples, causing them to strain against the satin of her bra. Brynne unconsciously tried to maneuver it into contact again and received a sharp, stinging smack on her tender skin.

"Ow!" That shocked her out of her dream state.

"Oh sweetie, that was nothing," Patricia scolded. She pulled the cups of her bra down and tucked the material underneath, making Brynne's breasts jut out.

A moment later, she felt the blindfold being tied snugly behind her head. The air left her lungs, and she whimpered in helpless arousal.

She felt Patricia standing close. Warm breath was on her cheek, then she felt her tongue trail along her lower lip. "Such a pretty little mouth you have, Brynne. It doesn't look big enough to take a cock, but we both know it can."

Brynne gasped and closed her mouth, feeling self-conscious.

"Perhaps I should have you demonstrate your skills on my strap-on?"

A hand tightened in her hair, pulling Brynne's head back. Patricia nibbled on her bottom lip, then she kissed her—tentatively at first and then more hungrily. It was a sensual assault, and Brynne's body swayed toward her. Their tongues entwined, and Brynne couldn't get enough. It was soft, so different from kissing a man. When Patricia stepped back, she moaned her dismay.

"I've looked carefully at your limits list, and I'm pleased to see you are willing to push the envelope a little. It will be my pleasure to oblige."

Brynne heard her moving around behind her. The sound of a little bell made her pussy react with a gush of wet heat. Patricia placed the bell in her left hand. "Hold on tight to it, pet. If you want me to stop, all you need to do is drop it."

She gripped the little bell hard. "Yes, Mistress."

Brynne felt cuffs being fastened to her ankles, then her legs were nudged apart. She heard the cuffs being attached to rings embedded in the floor. Patricia was behind her again, and Brynne shivered in anticipation. She played with her breasts, squeezing and pinching her overly sensitive nipples until Brynne gasped.

"I believe the instructions you received from my assistant were clear on what to wear. Any lingerie was at risk of being damaged."

Brynne bit her lip to stop herself from answering. Patricia sounded annoyed, causing anxiety to roil in the pit of her stomach.

"I can tell this is expensive, so rather than cutting it off, I will punish you instead." She unfastened her bra and pulled it roughly over her head and out of the way.

"Thank you, Mistress. I'm very sorry. I wanted to look sexy for you."

"I'll tell you what I find sexy, pet. You getting wet for me. Whether it's your tears, your puss, or maybe just saliva dripping out of your gagged mouth."

Brynne was stunned when Patricia forced her mouth open and pushed a hard ball past her lips. It was swiftly buckled behind her head, tight enough that she couldn't dislodge it. She fought to keep from freaking out and wrapped her fingers tightly around the bell. She was trembling in reaction until Patricia twisted her nipples hard enough to make her whine loudly into the gag.

"Now, I'm going to make you a pretty rope harness. I want to see these voluptuous breasts bound, so they stand out for punishment. I'm so glad you ticked that box."

Patricia wound several cords around her back and chest, above and below her breasts, compressing the flesh between. The rough strands tightened around Brynne's sensitive skin, and she worked to calm her breathing. *I'm not going to drop the bell*, she told herself, but it sounded more like a command of desperation.

She tied the two bands together, so Brynne's breasts swelled and stood out. Brynne was stunned at how sensitive and full they felt, and it sent a surge of sensation to her core. Her desire was outweighing her anxiety. She felt rope being wound around her hips several times, and then Patricia explained she was using a few well-placed knots to increase her pleasure. The sensual timbre of her voice increased Brynne's excitement. Strangely, she also realized that she felt safe.

When Patricia pulled the ropes taut between her legs, she positioned them directly over her pulsing clit. The diabolical knots pressed her soaked panties tightly against both her openings. She moaned into the gag; secretly glad she couldn't plead for release. Adding to her turmoil was the realization that saliva was dripping down her chin and onto her bound breasts.

"What a delicious sight you are." Patricia's soft hands glided like a whisper over her, caressing her breasts, her stomach, and the curve of her ass.

Brynne pushed her ass out in a blatant offering. She was aware of the consequences of what she was doing, and Mistress Patricia didn't disappoint.

"Somebody is trying to top from below," she said as she pulled her panties up, roughly tucking the material under the rope, baring her ass completely. "Seems I've been too soft with you and need to take corrective measures. You were impatient on Saturday, you wore lingerie that I had to make allowances for, and you have tried to *direct* my attention, instead of being attuned to what your Mistress wants from you."

Brynne heard clinking behind her where various implements hung. She tried to say "I'm sorry" but it was inaudible. Heels clicked ominously closer and stopped behind her.

"I'm going to give you four strikes for each one of those misdemeanors. Twelve in total."

Brynne whimpered.

"This wide leather strap won't sting like the crop or bruise as much, so you should be grateful for small mercies."

"Mmm," she mumbled, and braced for impact.

It was unexpected when instead Patricia pushed a padded bench up against the front of her thighs and said, "I'd rather have you bent over for this."

The whirring started lowering her arms. Her relief was short-lived when Patricia pushed her down over the cool leather platform. She refastened her wrists to the sides of the bench, trapping her there. Then she unhooked the ankle cuffs and brought her legs together, locking them to a new hook on the floor.

"Don't move, my pet, or I may miss my target. And that will get you extra."

Thwack! The first blow shocked Brynne, and she yowled into the gag. Radiating heat followed the harsh sting. The blows rained down on her backside, with no time in between. Patricia aimed her strap all over her butt and thighs until Brynne was squirming against her bonds and squealing for mercy. Her mind played a back-and-forth dialogue, one side urging her to drop the bell—and the other, more defiant side refusing to do it. Each time she jerked and bent her knees, the rope between her legs tantalized her clit. The pain began to blend into a fiery heat, and she realized that by pressing against the bench and squirming, her release was imminent. When the strap hit its target one last time, the symphony of sensations brought on a violent, earth-shattering orgasm.

Tears had been threatening, but with that cataclysmic release, the floodgates opened. Patricia dropped the whip and stood up against

Brynne's flaming ass, her hands quickly releasing the gag and the blindfold. Brynne was sobbing, not because it hurt, but because it was a cathartic release. As a rule, Brynne didn't do *vulnerable*. With Patricia, she let herself go, safe in the knowledge she would take care of her.

Patricia held her tightly until her tears were spent. When she released the cuffs, Brynne was grateful not to be standing, fearing she could crumble to the floor. Patricia helped her up and led her to the satin-covered bed at the other end of the room.

She gave her some tissues to wipe her nose and smiled. "You are positively radiant, Brynne."

As Brynne came down off her high, she became self-conscious. The rope harness was still wreaking havoc on her body, and she felt raw and exposed. Patricia, as if reading her mind, lay down beside her and pulled a soft fleece blanket over them both.

"You responded in a way that I've only seen a few times before. It was pure and beautiful."

"Th-thank you. That was beyond anything in my imagination." Brynne smiled shyly. "I've never come so hard in my life."

"What did you like the best?"

"Being helpless and unable to see or speak. And the ropes feel like an extension of you holding me, squeezing me so intimately. It's hard to explain how safe they made me feel."

"I know how it feels, sweetie. I was a bottom before I discovered how much I liked to top."

"Oh, wow." Brynne smiled. "I guess that's what makes you so good at knowing just how much and how hard. I thought the strap would hurt more, but after the initial shock, it was…" She paused, searching for the word. "Sublime."

Patricia chuckled and tucked a strand of Brynne's hair behind her ear. "Let's get you untied."

The sleek black Mercedes pulled away with Brynne cocooned in the back. She had the letter in her purse and soaked panties in the pocket of her coat. Patricia made her eat an apple with peanut butter and then insisted that her chauffeur would take Brynne home.

When they walked down to meet the car, Brynne was struggling to convey the magnitude of what she felt. "I don't know how to thank you. I…"

"No need to thank me, sweetie. I had as much fun as you did, and I hope we meet again."

Before Brynne could reply, Patricia handed her a bottle of water and kissed her on both cheeks.

"Drink this—it has electrolytes. And when you get home, have some carbs, then a hot shower and go to bed. Mistress's orders."

She shut the car door and waved them off. Brynne sank into the heated seat and closed her eyes. She couldn't help but replay every moment of the night in her head.

The experience caused an irrevocable shift inside. Could those desires continue to be ignored? Should she lock them back up? Could she?

The sensations were unlike anything she had experienced in her life. Sure, she had looked at scenes like that on the internet, but they paled compared to the real thing. Christ, if she didn't rein in her thoughts, her growing arousal was going to wet the expensive leather seat.

One thing is for certain. It's no longer a question of what do I want, but how do I get what I need?

5

Interview with the Devil

Three sleepless nights later, the big day was here. She had the hard-fought reference letter and a few tender bruises to prove she was a tough cookie. Brynne never expected to enjoy being bound, blindfolded, and spanked. She wasn't naturally submissive. This was probably caused by her recent overload on porn and erotic literature. Right? She would get over it soon enough. It was crucial research for the book, that's all. At least that's what she kept telling herself.

She knew the drill this time. After ringing the bell, the front gate clicked open. Miles deposited her in the same small waiting room, and she saluted his retreating form. She started pacing back and forth, talking to herself. "Don't let this dude intimidate you with his snarky attitude. You didn't come this far to be turned down for a waitressing job! Forget how hot he is and imagine him in his underwear... No, never mind, scratch that. He gets off on being a mean motherfucker, so don't let him get to you!"

She stared at herself in the mirror, legs apart, hands planted on her hips. "You've got this!"

After power posing, she sat down and picked up a glossy entertainment magazine from the coffee table. Her eyes lit on the bondage magazine underneath.

Gazing at the erotic photos felt as forbidden as sneaking into her aunt's liquor cabinet when she was fifteen. The centerfold showed a demonstration of Shibari, a type of erotic rope bondage. The intricate pattern of symmetrical knots reminded her of the way Patricia had tied her. The look of rapture in the woman's eyes felt all too familiar.

A sudden noise at the door caused Brynne to screech and drop the magazine. She leaped up as Miles opened the door. Would he ever look at her without frowning?

She smoothed her skirt and tucked a wayward tendril of hair behind her ear, feigning a confidence she no longer felt. Silently, she followed him down the hall, chanting a mantra in her head. *Don't lose your cool, don't lose your cool!*

Miles knocked and stepped aside. She looked to him for guidance, but his face was blank. A voice as sweet and dark as molasses replied from behind the door. "Aye, come in. I'll be right there."

Brynne entered and looked around. Seeing no one behind the large mahogany desk, she took in the beautifully appointed office. A massive leather couch dominated the room. Dark charcoal gray walls, antique gold sconces, stunning herringbone wood floors, and a thick Persian carpet created the feeling of a sumptuous cave. There was a distinctive scent in the air, a hint of sandalwood and citrus. The lightly woodsy smell reminded her of her favorite incense, calming her nerves a little.

A door opened behind the massive desk, and he walked in. It took every ounce of self-control she possessed not to gasp.

Her heart thrummed loudly in her ears and her fingers clenched the portfolio in her hands.

"Have a seat." He pointed to the chair facing the desk. His Scottish accent was less pronounced than the other day, but the deep pitch of his voice still thrummed along her nerve endings.

She could feel his eyes on her, following her every step. Relieved to make it to the chair without incident, she sat down quickly and winced when her sore bottom hit the wood. If he noticed, he didn't let on.

She went to pull a notebook and pen from her handbag and realized it wasn't on the floor or behind her chair.

He interrupted her restless fidgeting. "What seems to be the problem, Miss Larimore?"

"I think I left my purse in the other room. I—" she stammered.

"You can get it when our meeting is over. It will be perfectly safe."

"Of course. Thank you, sir." For a split second she saw something flare in his eyes, but it was swiftly replaced by a stern interrogator's face.

"As you know, I make the final decision about whether to hire you. Or not."

To keep from smiling like a nervous schoolgirl, she bit down on her lip and nodded.

While he looked over her application, Brynne drank in the sight of him. His angular jawline was sharply cut, shadowed with just the right amount of designer stubble which added to his formidable aura. There was an edge to his handsomeness, refined, and yet dangerous. This man would own any room he walked into, without needing to say a word.

She was taking notice of his long-tapered fingers and smooth, trimmed nails when he noisily cleared his throat. Her breath stuttered to a halt as she came back to reality and noticed his piercing eyes trained on her. Was he trying to unlock her secrets? Uncover her lies? She tried and failed to hold his gaze. It was like looking at an eclipse without proper eye protection.

"I've read Garrick's notes and your responses to our interview questions, but I'm curious why you're interested in working at Dominus. Many of our members are older, some even twice your age. Are you looking for a new master—or perhaps a sugar daddy?"

Brynne's mouth dropped open before she could stop it. "No, I'm not interested in finding either! I'm here because your club puts safety above all. You carefully vet your clientele, and that makes it better than the other fetish clubs in London." She clasped her hands together to keep from fidgeting. "I have another day job, so discretion is important to me."

"What is this other job?"

He'd obviously never read her resume, and that irritated her. "I'm a copy editor at the *London Mirror*. I don't want anyone to know I, this…" She paused, at a loss for words.

"This deviant side of your personality?" He smiled…if you could call that weird contortion of his mouth a smile.

Her lips compressed, and she reminded herself this was a test. "I don't think of it as *deviant*. But yes, I keep my private life private." She looked down at her lap and mentally scolded herself for getting agitated.

"I'm sure I don't need to remind you discretion and privacy are the two most important facets of this job. You signed an NDA, so if you dared to write a story about this club, you would kiss your career goodbye." His eyes burned through another layer of her armor.

Brynne licked her lips, her mouth parched. "I am not a reporter. I'm here for personal reasons and because I need the extra money. I've no interest in participating, I just want to watch." Her eyes widened and her gaze flew to his. "I didn't mean that the way it sounded."

One perfect eyebrow lifted. "So, you just want to serve drinks and play the voyeur rather than take part as one of our submissives?" His fingers grazed the coarse shadow along his jawline. "You said you have no interest in finding a master. Why is that?"

"I recently broke up with my boyfriend. He wasn't—it wasn't what I hoped. So, I just want to take my time and figure things out."

Gage smirked and cleared his throat. "When did you last tend bar?"

"Throughout college. I worked the bar on weeknights and waitressed on weekends." She felt like a specimen under a microscope. *Just breathe, Brynne.*

"You think you can create a cocktail especially for my club?"

That was unexpected. "Sure." Brynne scanned the bottles on the shelves behind him, noting his expensive taste in scotch. "I'd use an old-fashioned glass with a ball of ice, add three ounces of Macallan twelve-year, one ounce of amaretto, and a splash of orange bitters. And I would garnish it with an orange peel."

"Sounds interesting. And what would you call it?"

"Well, Smooth Operator is already taken." She racked her brain, then an idea hit her. "How about The Devil's Lash?"

"Cute," he said, without a trace of humor. "Can you name the four whisky regions of Scotland?"

Was that a trick question? "I think you mean the five regions. Campbeltown, Highland, Islay, Lowland, and Speyside." She looked to his sideboard and added, "Judging by your collection, you're partial to Macallan single malts."

His eyes narrowed. "You like scotch?"

"I like Glenmorangie Original, but to be honest, I'm more of a Hendricks and tonic girl." She grinned. "Does that disqualify me?"

"No, but your cheekiness might."

Her heart fluttered. "I'm sorry," she said, then quickly added, "sir."

A muscle twitched in his jaw. "Did Garrick explain what impertinence might get you?"

Later, she would ask herself why she goaded him. With an impish smile, she said, "A sound spanking?"

He leaned back in his big leather chair and studied her. The silence was unnerving. Her little joke fell flatter than flat. Jared had drilled it into her head—she was supposed to be meek and mild. So far, she was batting zero.

"I'll wager you will receive your fair share of spankings here. Are you a masochist?"

"What? No!" she said, suppressing the urge to giggle.

Gage made a notation on the page, and Brynne gripped the folder in her lap.

"There will be occasions when you'll enter the private rooms to refresh ice and drinks while a scene is going on. You think you can handle that?"

"Yes, of course. But I thought there was no drinking when you do a scene?"

"That is true. Those taking part in the scene won't be drinking, but the people watching can enjoy alcoholic beverages."

She mouthed a soundless "Oh" as realization dawned. Club members could play or watch the spectacle, and if she was lucky, she would get to see all of it. She sat forward and spoke with conviction. "I promise to do my job well and give you no reason to find fault with me."

"Hmm. That would be a pity," he said, with a ghost of a smile.

Brynne's eyes widened, and she shifted in her seat.

"Do you have the reference letter?"

She started at his abrupt tone and pulled the linen envelope out of the wrinkled portfolio. It bore a distinctive seal, with an ornate P in the middle of the blood-red wax. It was addressed to Master Gage, Club Dominus.

He took it and looked back at her, his eyebrows raised in surprise. "Mistress Patricia vouched for you?"

"Yes." Brynne worried her bottom lip. "Is there a problem?"

"Not a problem, just a surprise." He sliced the envelope open and took the letter out. "Why don't you fetch your handbag while I read this?"

Brynne jumped at the chance to leave the room and compose herself. She hurried down the hall, berating herself. She needed to get a grip. While grabbing her purse, she saw the magazine on the floor and quickly set it back where she found it. After a few calming breaths, she walked back into the lion's den.

Gage had poured himself a drink and was reading the reference letter with an amused smile.

The tip of her shoe caught the carpet, and she tumbled to her knees. "Fuck," she hissed through gritted teeth.

He leaped up and was beside her before she could gather herself and the contents of her purse off the floor. "I'm sorry. I caught the edge of the rug." She looked up, and he was looming over her, eyes glittering. She dragged her gaze away and retrieved a lipstick and a pen that had rolled toward his desk. This close, she felt the heat of his body, and his distinctive scent surrounded her. It was a divine blend of cedar, orange, and something else she couldn't put her finger on. Shaking herself out of a trance, she tucked her belongings into her handbag, and he helped her to her feet.

"I hope you are not this clumsy when carrying a tray of drinks?"

Her hackles rose at his derisive tone, and so did her chin. "No, I assure you I am not."

He dropped her arm abruptly and sat down behind his desk. "So, tell me, how did you come to know one of the most prominent Dommes in Europe?"

She squared her shoulders and took a deep breath. "My friend Jared, who works here part time, he introduced me. He did all the black-and-white erotic photos for her studio." She wondered if Gage remembered who he was. "He's an amazing photographer."

"Is that so?" He took a mouthful of the scotch, and her mouth watered watching him swallow it. "Patricia speaks highly of you. Although it states quite plainly"—he tapped the paper with a long, tanned finger—"that you need a firm hand."

Brynne squared her shoulders. "That's only because she was testing my limits."

"Well…" He carefully put the letter back in the envelope as he spoke. "I can say with certainty, we will *test* your limits, too."

"Does that mean I've got the job?" she asked, ignoring the other remark.

"Against my better judgment, I will give you a chance." Gage used the phone on his desk and punched three numbers. "Garrick, I'm going to give your little Tinkerbell a job." He paused. "Aye, we'll see." In response to whatever Garrick said, he replied, "Mistress Patricia." He looked up at Brynne, his eyes searing hers with their intensity. "Please email her Sonya's info and get her to rush the uniforms. Aye. Tiaraidh an dràsda."

Brynne recognized the Gaelic sign off, "Bye for now," and then registered what he'd said. "Tinkerbell?"

"Everyone here gets a nickname that Garrick chooses, based on appearance and personality. The members will not know your real name."

She wanted to argue against the childish name but thought better of it. "Okay. I understand. You mentioned something about uniforms?" Until this moment, she hadn't considered what sort of outfit she might have to wear. Her hands fidgeted in her lap.

Gage's smile looked positively wicked. "Oh, didn't Garrick tell you what you will wear?"

Brynne felt a shiver of unease. "No, he didn't cover that."

"Dinna fash. It's nothing to worry about." She could tell he was enjoying her discomfort. "Servers in the lounge wear a sexy French maid's outfit for regular nights, and our next fetish night will have an Arabian nights theme, so Sonya will also measure you for a harem girl costume."

Brynne swallowed hard. "I see."

"Make sure you get to the seamstress this week to be measured."

She nodded. Well, that was that. Her fate was sealed. When he stood, she followed and took his outstretched hand. His heat engulfed her palm, and she felt a frisson run up her arm.

"Your hand is freezing!" He clasped her hand in both of his and warmed it. Little did he know he was heating another part of her body.

She shrugged and tried to sound casual. "Cold hands, warm heart."

He dropped her hand quickly, then ushered her out into the hall. "Take a seat in the waiting room. Garrick will bring you the paperwork to get you on the payroll."

"Thank you for giving me this opportunity. You won't be sorry… Mister, uh, Gage. Sir."

With a nod, he said, "Aye, let's hope not," and shut the door.

Gage sat down and took another sip of the 1824 Limited Release. It calmed him like nothing else could. He had enjoyed provoking the lass. She wasn't very tall, but her body was curvy and lush. Garrick knew he had a thing for natural redheads, and he chose a fitting nickname. His friend was probably hoping to arouse his interest, since it had been over three months since he'd been out with anyone. He coaxed him to give her a chance if she had the balls to come back with a reference letter. Well, she had done better than that. Securing one from Patricia Valentine was quite a coup.

She was a distraction that he didn't need, but it had been so long since anyone had amused him. He imagined all the ways he could make her blush or, better yet, lose her cool. Her hourglass shape would be stunning in the uniform. There were more than a few clues she had a fiery temper to go with that hair. If he was lucky, she might find herself tossed over his knee.

She'd looked so bloody tempting kneeling on the floor, staring up at him with those doe eyes. He caught himself thinking about training that impertinence out of her. Her eyes went from light amber to the color of dark chocolate when she became flustered.

Shaking those ridiculous thoughts away, he pondered the letter from Mistress Patricia. It had been a long time since they'd crossed paths. She had come for the grand opening and to their first fetish night, but she preferred the younger clientele of Club Verboten. While he knew she wouldn't write a letter for just anyone, his instincts told him there was something more to Brynne. She didn't behave like a submissive—there was too much rebellion in her. There had to be another agenda at play. His bet was that she was looking for a rich husband, and what better place than a club that catered to London's elite? Membership was a half a million pounds. Within these walls, discretion was assured, and powerful men could be unencumbered by the usual social mores.

He would need to keep a close eye on her—not just because of the way her heart-shaped ass filled out a skirt, but because he couldn't afford any mishaps at the club. Even if his prick found the little pixie captivating, he would not break his own policy regarding dalliances with staff. He had created it for good reason.

Although several months had passed since he broke his engagement with Sierra, the wounds were still raw. She proved how mercenary a woman could be. He should have known, since his mother was the queen of the mercenaries, but it was still a shock when he learned of the lengths his fiancée would go to get him to the altar. She could have earned a BAFTA for her performances in the bedroom. He was grateful that he overheard her speaking to her best friend about how she was *suffering* until the day when she could stop pretending to enjoy giving him head and doing his bidding in the bedroom. She also planned to demand that he sell the club and become *respectable*.

He was well rid of her. Plenty of women wanted to date him, though he had no interest in vanilla sex. For now, he remained unattached and would not try to find a submissive to play with. His mother had political aspirations and implored him to keep his "dirty dalliances," as she called them, under wraps. Maybe it was time to consider a trip to New York or Houston where he could play in complete anonymity?

To get his mind off his self-imposed celibacy, he pulled up the latest investment pitches sent from his office in Edinburgh. He needed to make some decisions soon about the proposals now that they had Ministry approval. The local planning councils had finally approved the zoning and construction plans. There were a few more parcels of land to acquire to bring the plan together. A substantial investment of his own capital was at stake. It wasn't a profit-driven venture, it was a passion project.

Garrick knocked and poked his head in. "I was just seeing Tink off."

"Come on in. Will you have a wee dram?"

Garrick chuckled. "If it's the 1824 you're offering, I'm in."

Gage poured his friend a drink and asked him point-blank, "You think she's got what it takes?"

Garrick savored the scotch before answering. "Oh, I think she's one tough cookie. Perhaps not as mild-mannered as the rest of the crew, but that will make it more interesting."

Gage rubbed his jaw. "Aye, interesting until she slaps someone for taking liberties, like pinching her behind." He smiled wickedly. "Hell, those curvy thighs are just begging for the palm of someone's hand."

Garrick's eyes widened at his admission. "I made sure she knows what to expect. Our paperwork leaves nothing to chance, either. The members will proposition her. They might get a little touchy, but the floor monitors will keep a close watch, as always."

Gage hoped he was right. He blew out a breath. "I suppose if she loses her cool, the consequences will give everyone an entertaining spectacle—and a look at her bare arse."

"I hope the little pixie blows a head gasket and we get a front-row seat." Garrick took another sip and chuckled.

Gage laughed, but something had been on his mind since Brynne left. "Maybe we should tell Sonya to make her outfits less revealing. It might save some trouble in the long run."

Garrick looked at him skeptically. "Mate, are you going soft in your old age? We are in the business of liquor, sex, and entertainment. If she sells more drinks because her tits are on display, then that's a good thing."

He groaned. "Maybe, but we are not here to feed innocent lambs to slaughter." Frankly, Gage didn't want to be distracted by her breasts spilling out of her uniform, nor did he want the guests to lose their heads over her. He tossed back the rest of his drink and stood. "I'm going to head out. I've got meetings in Edinburgh tomorrow—but I'll see you on Friday. Keep the machine running."

"Will do, man. Safe travels."

6

A Rough Start and
A Rude Russian

Brynne lay in bed and replayed the interview in her head. Against all odds, she got the job. Aunt Josie taught her to never give up when pursuing her dreams. She cleared one major hurdle, but many more would follow! Mr. Big Dick Energy, was one of them. Too much testosterone and arrogance in one hell of a hot package. One minute Gage was cold and suspicious, and the next she swore there was something else radiating from his eyes.

From the top of his wavy dark hair to the soles of his handmade Italian shoes, he was sinfully delicious. Too bad, when he opened his mouth, he ruined her fantasy. His don't-fuck-with-me attitude should not appeal. Except it did. Is this what a dog feels like in heat? At the mercy of nature? According to Darwin's theory of natural selection, her body had just chosen her alpha.

She punched her pillow. "Sorry Mr. Darwin, I'm not falling for a man who wants to control my every move. It doesn't matter because he is a million miles out of my league. Even if he is the man to deliver on my wicked fantasies, it's best to forget him."

The next day, Nigel gave her two more stories to edit on a tight deadline. She was glad of the diversion. She and Jared got takeout for lunch and found a patio table that gave them some measure of privacy. He pried all the juicy details out of her about the interview.

"I survived my meeting with his royal highness, Lord and Master of Club D." She rolled her eyes and bowed her head mockingly. "So what if he is the hottest thing on two legs? Guys like that are usually selfish in bed. Women fall all over themselves for the looks or the money. I learned a long time ago to avoid hunks because they don't have to work at relationships, and more often than not, they are self-absorbed."

Jared spoke in a low voice. "A security monitor told me he was engaged until a few months ago. He found out his fiancée was lying to him, so he broke it off. He hasn't been seen with anyone since."

Her eyebrows shot up. "I bet it was that Sierra chick who I saw after my interview with Garrick. Are you telling me this so I feel sorry for him?"

"No babe, but sometimes good-looking men can be misunderstood. Women are calculating in their pursuit of looks and money without a thought to the guy's feelings."

Brynne saw Jared looking pensive as he chewed the last bite of his cheeseburger. "I know that's happened to you, J." She grinned, trying to lighten his mood. "It must be hard when boys come after you because of your tight butt and muscly biceps, and they never bother to ask you about your hopes and dreams."

"It's a cross I have to bear." He smiled, but it did not reach his pale blue eyes.

Jared was model handsome. His dark blond hair was long on top, and he kept his undercut fade perfect by going to his stylist every four weeks. The man always dressed impeccably, no matter the occasion. A scout discovered him at seventeen, and he modeled for three years. She remembered some of his stories. It was soul-crushing work, and he got hooked on amphetamines to keep his energy up and his weight down. The pressure to look perfect took its toll.

It must be hard to be treated like a sex object. *Not that I would know how that feels.*

"Listen, I intend to keep out of his way. Which means I do my job; I watch and learn." She leaned in and lowered her voice. "I think he's just waiting for me to fuck up, so I get my ass whooped."

Jared laughed so loudly that a couple walking by turned and stared at them. He gave them a withering look, and they quickly turned away. "Hon, you better be ready. There is a very good chance you'll get your you-know-what *whooped*." He laughed again, this time putting his hand over his mouth.

"Stop! I'm trying not to think about that. But really, it felt like he grudgingly gave me the job and doesn't trust me at all. He was so surprised by the letter from Patricia, I swear he thought I'd forged it."

"That is Master Gage. He's suspicious as fuck. He has to be, to keep the club and its members secure. They pay him a ton of money to have a safe place to play."

"That's another thing." Brynne wrinkled her nose. "Do I have to call him that?"

"I sure would. All the staff who do scenes show him that respect. Didn't he tell you how to address him?"

"Nope. He never properly introduced himself and I avoided it by calling him 'sir.'" Brynne filled him in on the klutzy fall she took in his office. Jared laughed and asked if she saw the kinky magazines in the waiting room.

"Yes! How did you know? Did you see them when you interviewed?"

"Yup. The room has a two-way mirror, and they video all the candidates while they wait."

"What?! You're joking?" Her mind played back that day and her hand went to her mouth.

"Bill, the head bartender, told me. He saw it on the computer screen in Garrick's office." He stared at her ashen face. "What did you do in there, Bree?"

"Oh, nothing really," she said, dropping her head in her hands. "Just talked smack about the boss while trying to calm my nerves. Then I power posed in front of the mirror. Christ, I may get fired before I even start!"

He patted her hand. "Don't worry. If he wasn't watching it live, it's not likely he will go back to find it."

That information did not quell her nerves.

"Shit, I have to get back, and we don't want you to be late either. Mustn't give Margaret a reason to spank your bum!"

"You're hilarious," she said, rolling her eyes. "She would probably jump at the chance."

On the walk back, Brynne asked if he would come to the seamstress with her after work, but he had a date, so she went on her own.

Sonya was very pleasant, and she put Brynne at ease. After measuring the usual body parts, she took down the circumference of her neck, wrists, thighs, and ankles.

"What do they need those for?"

"We take those to make you a set of cuffs and a collar, dear. We have many different outfits depending on the type of party Master Gage is hosting."

"Of course, how silly of me." She gritted her teeth at the thought of calling him that. It was bad enough she was on videotape calling him a mean motherfucker. It would not be good to tell Sonya what she thought of the king of douche-dom.

"I will have your weeknight uniforms ready by Thursday. That's your first shift, right?"

Brynne chewed her bottom lip. "Yes. I don't know how I'll make it on time if I have to stop here first."

"Don't worry, I'll have them delivered to the club."

Sonya handed her a list of instructions about the outfits, which were never to be worn outside the club. They would be dry cleaned and replaced in her locker for the next shift. From what she could see, the French maid's outfit seemed reasonable. What worried her were the *special* outfits they created for the fetish parties. She thanked Sonya and cursed Gage as she made her way to the train.

Thursday sucked. Margaret gave her an article to fact-check at four thirty p.m. so she was late leaving the paper. She claimed Nigel asked for her specifically, but Brynne wondered. She got it done and delivered the thumb drive back to the dragon lady's empty desk. It took ten minutes to get a taxi because it was pouring, and her umbrella was lying on the floor under her desk.

At 5:55 p.m., she rang the buzzer. The imperious voice of her favorite butler came through the intercom. "Staff must use the rear entrance."

"Miles, I will be late because I don't know where that is. Please, can you let me in? I won't use this door ever again."

"Not possible, miss. Walk to the corner, two buildings west, make a right at Bedford, and follow the lane to the black awning.

Take the steps down to the employee entrance and ring the bell."

She swore and stomped down the steps. Rain pelted her as she jogged two city blocks, found the lane, and ran some more, cursing the old fart the whole way. In the time it took, she could have been inside getting changed. *Fucking hell.*

By the time she reached the entrance and rang the bell, she was out of breath and in a rage. The clock was ticking in her head like a time bomb. She punched the bell twice more just as the door opened. She looked up to see a pair of cold green eyes and shook her head in despair. Brynne rarely cried, but the censure in his face was almost her undoing. She looked at him, her voice barely audible. "No one told me about the staff entrance. I'm sorry, I went to the front door. I didn't know." She took a breath and added, "It, it won't happen again."

While she was suffering from verbal diarrhea, he stepped forward and pulled her into the small vestibule by the lapels of her soaked trench coat.

Gage's eyes looked her up and down. "No, I'm sure it won't. Garrick will give you an access badge for this door next week. If you make it through the weekend."

Brynne felt her temper rising. Her chin lifted in challenge. "I'm no quitter. Now, if you'll excuse me, I have to get ready."

She ducked out of the enclosed space and hurried to the locker room, mumbling under her breath. That bastard tweaked her temper again. If she was going to survive, she'd better work on her poker face. He enjoyed twisting her in knots and was betting on her to give up. Well, she had no intention of letting him win. She never backed down, sometimes to her utter detriment.

Thank god there was a hairdryer and various other toiletries and hair products in the ladies' changing room. She quickly repaired her hair and reapplied her makeup. The uniform was hanging in her locker. When she got it on and looked in the full-length mirror, she bit her lip and shook her head. "You've got to be kidding."

The frilly white blouse with cap sleeves covered the essentials, but the black corset-style dress cinched her waist and undercut her breasts, blatantly pushing them up. The black skirt only reached mid-thigh, and it too had ruffles around the bottom. A white lace apron completed the ridiculous French maid ensemble. It was over the top, and Brynne guessed that was the point. She carefully put on her seamed stockings and black high heels and touched up her lipstick. Facing her reflection, she took a deep breath and said, "Don't let these bastards get to you!"

She went up to the main floor in search of Garrick. As she entered the lounge, all eyes turned to look at her and conversations stalled. Brynne concentrated on ignoring them and walked toward the man behind the bar. She reached for the polished brass rail and held on to it for support. The gray-haired barkeep had a kind smile and a bushy mustache. "You must be the new girl. I'm Bill, head bartender."

Relieved, she said, "Hi Bill, I'm Br—"

He stopped her with a hand on her wrist and a shake of his head. "Tinkerbell is the name you'll go by, missy. I've got your name tag right here." He winked and whispered, "No one needs to know your real name."

"Got it. Thanks, Bill." She took the tag from him and attached it to her blouse.

"Go into the back and ask for Melinda—you'll train with her tonight." He gestured to the two doors between the bar and a glass-enclosed wine room. "She's the tall platinum blonde. You can't miss her."

In the back of the house, she saw Garrick first. He was speaking to a busser, reprimanding him for something, so she hung back and looked for Melinda. Bill was right. She was about five feet ten in her heels and very slim—everywhere, except for her boobs! Brynne wondered how she kept from toppling over. Melinda hurried over and surprised Brynne by hugging her. "You must be Tinkerbell! I'm Melinda the Good Witch. I'm so happy to meet you!" Her voice was sweet, like a Southern belle.

"Nice to meet you too, Melinda. Can I ask, do you think I can get my name changed? I would rather not have Tinkerbell. It's ridiculous."

Melinda giggled but didn't reply. Garrick's deep baritone behind her made her jump. "I choose the names, Tink. So, I'm afraid you are stuck with it."

"Um, right." She flushed. "Sorry, Garrick. Understood."

"You will shadow Mel tonight and help her with the drinks and food service. We serve light fare in the lounge until ten o'clock." He handed her a leather-bound book. "Familiarize yourself with the menu. If people want a broader menu, they can go to the dining room—but that kitchen closes at nine thirty."

Brynne nodded and took the menu. Melinda grabbed her arm and linked it with her own. "Come on, the natives must be restless. I ducked out to the powder room. And Bettie went home early, so they're running me off my feet."

The night passed quickly. She received a few leering looks, one stray hand on her bottom, and two proposals of marriage. It was easy to smile and divert their attentions and she giggled at the outrageous request for a kiss. By nine, her feet were killing her. She would have to get a pair of shoes with a lower heel. Melinda was sweet and kept a running commentary on how everything needed to be done, so one doesn't *get into hot water*, as she called it. With the members, she had perfected a flirtatious yet chaste demeanor. She blushed easily and deflected any would-be suitors by pretending to be offended. Brynne watched and learned.

It was near closing time, and there was one table left with two burly dudes who could be mafia enforcers or bouncers for an exclusive nightclub. They'd ordered a full bottle of Stolichnaya Elit and had finished three quarters of it. Brynne thought she heard them speaking Russian, but they always stopped when she came near. She was putting away mixes behind the bar when a third man joined them. His aura was a disturbing combination of power and menace. He was easily six feet tall, dressed in a dark-blue bespoke suit that accentuated his massive shoulders. From her vantage point, she watched the other two men stand and show deference to him. They offered him the vodka, but he waved them off and turned to look toward the bar.

His eyes met hers, and her first instinct was to flee. Her stomach dropped with a feeling of inevitability—this predator had just spotted prey. Melinda was not back, so she couldn't ignore the demand in his gaze. She smoothed down her skirt and hurried over. "Yes sir, may I get you something to drink?"

Hazel eyes raked her over from head to toe. Then he smiled. His perfect white teeth had her thinking of Little Red Riding Hood and the Big Bad Wolf. He shifted closer and looked down at the name tag on her chest. "Tinkerbell?"

She dug her fingernails into her palm and looked at his bristly jaw to avoid his eyes. "Yes."

He tilted her chin up, forcing her to meet his gaze. "Such fire in those dark eyes, devushka." His voice was deep and raspy, like he'd just smoked a pack of unfiltered cigarettes. It made the hair rise on the back of her neck. He let go of her chin, but his eyes never left hers. "Fizzy Aqua Panna with a lime."

She nodded. "Rocks?"

"Da," he said. She froze as he tucked a stay hair behind her ear, then spun away and went to the bar. She was shaking and fumbling with the bottle when Melinda came back.

"Where did we put the limes?"

Mel retrieved them from the fridge and dressed the glass. "You look spooked, doll. I can take his drink over."

Brynne nodded, relief relaxing her shoulders. "That guy unnerved me a bit."

"He does that to everyone. That's Dimitri Ivanov. He's the biggest manufacturer of steel in Russia. Scary mother." She took the glass and a cocktail napkin. "I've got this. Take a breather in the back."

She felt like a chickenshit, but Brynne was glad to escape.

From the kitchen, she heard raised voices and panicked. Somebody wasn't happy. Brynne made a snap decision to duck down the back stairs.

She could hear Melinda's raised voice. She didn't want to leave her alone any longer and walked back up to see her standing there in the doorway, telling the giant man he wasn't allowed in the back. When he saw Brynne, he stalked toward her. "Why didn't *you* bring my drink, Kiska?"

Brynne stammered out, "I had to use the ladies' room."

He nodded, appeased for the moment. "I want you to serve me when I am here. Only you. Understand?"

"Yes, sure."

"Horosho. Spasibo." He cleared his throat, but it still sounded raspy. "I mean, good, thank you."

They both sighed when he went back to his table.

"My goodness, Tink," Melinda said. "He's got a thing for you."

"Where the hell is Bill? I felt very vulnerable out there."

"Good question." Melinda looked at her watch. "Will you

be okay? I'll pop downstairs and see if I can find him. The security monitor is back."

"Sure. I'll be fine," she said, concealing her agitation.

Brynne kept herself busy tidying the area behind the bar, turning all the bottles so the labels were facing front. When she turned back, Dimitri was leaning over the counter, watching her. She squealed in shock and jumped back, dropping a plastic jug of orange juice. How did he move within a few feet without her noticing? He toyed with an ornate gold ring on his baby finger, drawing her eyes to the tattoos on his enormous hands. This close, she could see more ink on the thick cords of his neck beneath his collar. Finally, she met his eyes; they made her feel like she was an item on the menu. She broke out of her daze to retrieve the bottle of juice and said, "Thank god that wasn't a priceless bottle of scotch."

He shrugged. "Da. I would pay for any bottle you dropped because of me."

She focused on putting the mixes in the fridge and feigned a casual tone. "That wouldn't be necessary, but thank you."

He took advantage of her proximity and clasped her forearm. She pulled away, but his grip lessened enough to slide to her wrist. He looked at his large hand, dwarfing her wrist. "So delicate, my little Kiska."

She tried to tug free, but he held fast. "What does that mean?"

His mouth curved in a smile. "*Pure* is the literal translation. Where I come from, it means *kitten*." He turned her clenched fist over and pried her fingers open. "You are a little cat, prepared to fight. I like that in my women."

"Let me go, please." She hated how weak her voice sounded.

His thick, calloused fingers held fast. "Do I frighten you?" he said with a gleam in his eye.

Brynne's mouth dried, and she couldn't push any words out.

Don't let him see how he unnerves you. She watched as he entwined his fingers in hers and spread her hand open, then with his forefinger he lightly traced the lines on her palm, one by one. His touch was so at odds with his size, it left a trail of sensation in its wake. She tugged again, and he let her hand go. She realized why when Garrick came up and greeted him.

"Mr. Ivanov, it's good to see you. It's been a while. Can we get you anything for last call? We are closing shortly." His tone was friendly, with an undertone of steel.

Dimitri looked at him, and his lips curled in an insincere smile. "I will have a blueberry tea served by Miss Tinkerbell."

"Certainly. She'll bring it over as soon as it's ready."

The expectation was clear. Ivanov nodded and strode back to the table.

Garrick looked at her, his eyes narrowed. "What are you waiting for? Go brew some orange pekoe, and I'll prep the liqueurs."

Brynne hurried to the back. She prepped the teapot and made a tray with a couple of shortbread biscuits and a cloth napkin to wrap the snifter.

Garrick gave her the Grand Marnier and amaretto mixture. She walked carefully over to the table, concentrating on each step. Dimitri had removed his jacket and was sitting back, his crisp white shirt revealing a hard, muscular chest and flat stomach. His legs were blatantly spread, as if waiting for someone to kneel between them. The silky material of his pants clung to his massive thighs. Brynne refused to meet his eyes and laid the tray carefully on the table in front of him. She was turning away when he grabbed her wrist.

"Kiska, pour the tea for me? Pozhaluysta. *Please.*"

Her feet were aching, and she was tired. She wanted to jam her heel into his shiny brown shoes and tell him to fuck off. Instead, she looked at him with a phony smile and said, "Of course, your *excellency*."

She was pouring the tea when he burst out laughing. If she didn't have a good grip on the pot, it might have landed on his legs. Brynne couldn't help noticing his friends were scowling at her.

Dimitri patted the shoulder of the man closest to him. "Ya lyublyu zhenshchin s ogon'kom—I like a little fire in my women." One smirked, and the other forced a laugh. She guessed women didn't speak to him like that very often.

She made her escape straight into the back and found Garrick there. "That guy is one scary bastard!" Her voice was high pitched, giving away her anxiety. "Security wasn't here when he came in. I was on my own."

Garrick took her gently by the shoulders. "Hey Tink, take a deep breath. Nothing happened. You are safe. I will investigate, as that should not have happened."

She hugged herself. Her eyes were bright with unshed tears.

His voice lowered. "If you can't handle a guy like him, maybe you should reconsider this job."

Brynne shook her head. That was all she needed to hear. "I'm no quitter." She stated it for the second time tonight. But did she believe it?

He pulled a paper out of his jacket. "Here, it's a taxi chit. Cars are on standby at the back entrance for you when it gets late. You can get going now. I'll close up."

She nodded and started for the stairs.

"And Tink, you best get another pair of shoes. I'm all for high heels, but you'll be crippled unless you get something with a lower heel. Find something sexy but functional."

She stared at him and nodded her head absently.

Brynne quickly changed and hung her uniform on the rack under her name tag. She was glad that her sneakers had dried over the course of the evening. When she exited out the back, a black cab flashed his headlights and pulled up.

The trip home was fast, the rain having let up hours ago. She entered her apartment and leaned up against her front door and sighed. What a night! But she survived it.

Brynne dropped her stuff and kicked off her shoes, making a beeline for the fridge. She uncorked the open bottle of chianti and poured it into the only clean mug in her entire apartment. She made a plate of cheddar cheese and crackers to fill the void in her stomach. In the future, she would have to scarf down some food before her shift. All she'd managed was to nibble on some nuts during her trips to the kitchen. At least she would lose weight with all the running back and forth.

She sank into her old couch and took a swig of the chilled wine, unable to stop thinking about the big Russian and the unnerving way he looked at her, like he wanted to own her. He was polite and surprisingly gentle when he took her hand, but she sensed a barely contained aggression emanating from his linebacker-size frame.

When she crawled into bed a short time later, it was another tall, overbearing bastard that she cursed. Why didn't Gage come up to the lounge during her shift? After their run-in at the back door, he didn't appear again. She should have been glad, but in truth, she was disappointed.

7

Temptation & Trouble

Gage arrived at his London penthouse at nine thirty p.m., frustrated and hungry. He had planned to review his VC team's assessment of a small software startup, but his concentration was shot. He'd made excuses and canceled dinner with his mother to get back to London a day early. When Garrick questioned him, he denied it had anything to do with seeing the new girl in her uniform.

She looked as *tempting* as he'd imagined. It took all his resolve not to go up to the bar. Instead, he'd watched her for an hour from his office video feed, like a perverted voyeur.

Disgusted with himself, he left the club and went home to burn off this pent-up energy in the gym. He couldn't get the vision of Brynne out of his head. When he pulled her in from the rain, smudges of mascara had marred her fair skin, and wet strands of auburn hair were stuck to her rosy cheeks. She'd been breathless and infuriated, hammering the doorbell, but when she saw it was him, all the fire went out of her eyes and her shoulders sank. She was on the verge of tears. Thankfully, his callous remark remedied that, and she looked like she wanted to punch him instead.

No matter how amusing it was, he did not need this distraction. He had not yet forgotten being made a fool of. Sierra had him believing she loved him *and* his dominant nature, and he'd been attracted to her classic, flawless style. She never had a hair out of place, and she was not prone to messes—emotional or otherwise. She was just like him. Oh so carefully *contained*.

There was further damning proof that he'd lost his edge. By failing to do his usual background checks, he had never uncovered the dire state of Sierra's finances. She came from old money; however, the family coffers were dwindling fast through a series of poor investments and her father's gambling. Gage viciously pummeled the speed bag as another realization dawned on him. Sierra didn't mind being tied to his bed because it meant she didn't have to participate! She could lie there, taking one for king and country. He'd been blind and stupid, seeing willing submission, in what was, in fact, indifference. That his mother loved her should have been his first clue. Sierra needed a rich husband, and it was clear she would do just about anything to get one, including selling herself to the devil.

He was done and had zero interest in doing dinners or making small talk. For now, he was content to look down the barrel of celibacy. While his mother was seeking a judicial appointment, he would remain under the radar. That meant no visits to UK clubs— even the underground ones.

His mother had almost lost her mind when he told her he was opening a fetish club. It didn't matter that he used another name in London. She was certain they would somehow link it back to her. In three years, no one had made the connection.

Although he never fully unleashed his dominance with Sierra, it was there, locked away, waiting to be freed. His fists were aching, but his mind was clear when he finished his boxing routine.

After a hot shower, he found a serving of spaghetti Bolognese in the fridge, compliments of his housekeeper. He poured a glass of Brunello di Montalcino and opened the rooftop patio doors to let the sounds of the city drift in. His phone pinged.

Garrick: *All is quiet. We're closed for the night.*

Gage: *Thanks, man.*

Garrick: *We might have a problem. Dimitri is back in London. He has set his sights on Tink.*

Gage leaned back and sighed, pinching the bridge of his nose. *Not Dimitri.* He was one of the first members to invest, before they had a following. While Gage appreciated the referrals of several foreign billionaires, he didn't like the man. Once he learned of Dimitri's failed bid to buy the building Dominus was housed in, he became even more guarded.

Gage: *Fuck. Call me.*

Gage picked up the call the moment it rang. "What happened?"

"His comrades spent a few hours polishing off a bottle of Stoli. Tink was the only one in the bar when he came in."

"Where the fuck were Bill and the security guard?"

"Bill had gone to the cellar, and the guard was called upstairs."

"Unacceptable."

"I agree. Anyway, he got under her skin. Mel came back and brought him the drink he ordered."

"I'm sure that didn't go over well." Gage knew the man and what kind of service he demanded.

"No, it didn't, but I smoothed things over. Brynne brought him a tea before I sent her home."

"And she didn't dump it in his lap?" Gage secretly hoped she did so he could mete out a punishment.

"No. She maintained her cool. I'm not sure what she said to him before she left the table, but he laughed like I've never heard before."

Gage rubbed his chin. "We'll need to keep a close eye on him. And, G, I want to know why security left the floor. His ass should be out the door."

Garrick was apologetic. "I'll handle it, Gage. Don't worry. I'll see you tomorrow."

"Thanks, man. Have a good night."

By the time Gage went to bed, he knew what he had to do. If it was in her best interests, maybe he could reconcile how much of a prick he was going to be. The only consolation would be the amusement it would bring, however short-lived.

Gage arrived at the club by three o'clock on Friday afternoon. He'd worked from his penthouse most of the day, digging deeper into the financials of the company he was considering investing in. The club was still quiet when he found Garrick alone in his office.

"Hey." He strolled in and took a seat. "Did you speak with Bill?"

"Yeah, I made it crystal clear that someone must always be on the floor. I told him Dimitri showed an avid interest in Tink and that under no circumstances was she to be left alone with him."

"Good. And the AWOL security guy?"

"Tore a strip off him—and told him the safety of our staff was the most important element of his job, and if he failed at that ever again, I would fire him."

Gage decided to share his plan with Garrick. "I am going to compel Tink to quit. We both know that Dimitri hates to lose—and he's recently discovered that it was my political connections that won me the real estate deal, even though he outbid me by a million pounds. And now with this infatuation with Brynne? I don't like it."

Garrick paused and studied Gage. "He has always skated the line, but never crossed it. He doesn't want to lose his membership. We'll keep a close eye on him."

"Listen, she's a novice and cannot handle a Dom like him. That's why I need to get her to quit. It will just be easier."

He could read the doubt in his friend's eyes. "How do you plan to do that? She strikes me as a determined little thing."

"Aye, you are right. But for her own good and my peace of mind, she needs to go."

Garrick shook his head. "It's a pity. I've taken a liking to the little spitfire. Why don't you just sack her?"

Gage looked at his friend, wondering if he was entertaining similar carnal thoughts. That didn't sit well with him. "No, I intend to teach her a lesson. She came here playing at being submissive, and I don't believe she is. I'll put it to the test. By the time I'm done, she will give up and quit."

Garrick's mouth crooked. "I hope you're right, boss."

Brynne was at the paper early on Friday so that she could finish by four thirty and be at the club on time. Jared was in Liverpool on assignment, so they didn't catch up. She had everything with her and was at the back entrance with plenty of time to spare. She ate a homemade ham and cheese sandwich and had a quick shower before changing into her uniform. As she put the outfit on, she mumbled under her breath, "Chauvinists still rule the world, Brynne. Get used to it."

Melinda arrived as she was finishing her makeup. She wanted to know how everything turned out last night. Brynne shared the incident at the bar and Garrick coming to her rescue.

She put her hand reassuringly on Brynne's shoulder. "I wouldn't worry, Ivanov has several girlfriends—all stunning and all submissive masochists. He will bring one or more of them to the Arabian fetish night. Hopefully, he was just having a bit of fun with you."

If that was his type of woman, did that mean he was a Dominant sadist? Brynne shuddered. "I sure as hell hope so, Mel. I'll see you upstairs."

The guests kept her and Melinda running until Bettie arrived around seven o'clock to provide cover. Many of the guests were in for dinner and drinks before going upstairs later. Several of them flirted and told her how *lovely* she looked in her uniform. It was easy to blush and laugh off the teasing.

Garrick came into the bar and summoned Brynne over. "I need you to collect Gage's dinner from the chef and take it down to his office. He has already placed the order, and it will be up shortly."

"Sure. On it."

Brynne found the main kitchen and asked someone to point out the head chef. He was the man barking orders and checking the plated entrées. Waiters scurried around collecting orders.

"I'm here for Gage's dinner," she said when he looked up impatiently over the prep table.

"Okay, miss, it will be a few minutes. Wait over there, you're a distraction to my cooks. They are liable to burn something if you stand there in your little tart's outfit."

His dismissive wave set her teeth on edge. Brynne felt conspicuous and moved out of the way. Mel told her that only men served in the main dining room. Members could bring their wives and girlfriends on the weekends for dinner. They relegated *tarts* to the lounge.

Her mouth watered when she saw the grilled pork chop, mashed potatoes, and green beans. As she was prepping the tray, the chef snapped at her not to forget the soup.

She whispered her thanks, grateful she didn't leave without it. After grabbing the cutlery and a napkin, she headed downstairs. Two flights down in high heels, while balancing a tray, winded her. Why couldn't the arrogant prick get his own dinner?

It was difficult to knock, so she kicked the door twice with the toe of her shoe.

The beast growled a reply, beckoning her to come into his lair.

She tried to twist the doorknob and almost toppled the tray. "It's locked!"

Seconds later, the door swung open, and he glowered down at her. She scowled back, but he had turned away, pointing imperiously to his desk. His phone was to his ear while he paced to the other end of his office. Brynne didn't see an empty space to put down the tray, so she waited to ask him to move his papers. She saw a very erotic scene on his computer screen and wondered if that was happening somewhere in the club.

She pulled her eyes away from the monitor when she heard him finishing his call.

"Thanks, Cole. That sounds great. See you then." Gage hung up the phone and scowled at her. "What took you so long? And why didn't you cover the dishes? My food is probably cold now."

This is a test. Just a test. Don't throw the soup on him. "I didn't see any covers. I'm sorry. It won't happen again."

"It better not." He crossed his arms and looked expectantly. "What are you standing there for? Put the tray down."

"The food is getting even colder while I'm standing here waiting for you to move your papers. Unless you don't care if I plop this right down on top of them?"

He glared at her. "How considerate of you."

She rolled her eyes while he gathered the documents. He was baiting her, but she would not fall into his trap.

"Are you sure you wouldn't like me to get you a fresh entrée?" Her voice dripped with saccharine sweetness.

He looked sideways at her, and she couldn't conceal an impish smile.

"I'm sure," he snapped. "But you can replenish my ice. And you forgot the bottle of sparkling water I ordered."

"Oh, certainly. I'll get right on that. *Sir.*" She hurried to the door.

"Aren't you forgetting something, Red?"

She turned around, her face blank.

He pointed to the ice bucket on the credenza.

"Oh, how silly of me!" she trilled, putting her hand to her open mouth. With an exaggerated sway in her hips, she swept up the container and sauntered out.

As soon as the door was shut, expletives spewed out of her mouth. "Pompous son of a bitch!" She stomped up the stairs to the bar kitchen and threw the watery ice in the sink. As she refilled the bucket, she eyed the box of salt on a shelf nearby. The prick deserved it—but it could get her fired, or worse.

Brynne was leaving when Mel flew through the door into the kitchen. "Where have you been, Tink? We could use your help."

"Sorry Mel, I had to get his royal *highness* dinner from upstairs.

I'll be right back after I take his water and fresh ice down."

"Seriously? It's for Gage?"

"Yes, why?

"Because he usually eats in the dining room when he's here. And he has a fridge in his office stocked with water."

Brynne looked at Mel, and her hands balled into fists. "I knew he was yanking my chain. That bastard. He has his own fridge?"

"Uh-huh, in the cupboard behind his desk." Looking worried, she added, "Wait, what are you going to do?"

Brynne's eyes narrowed. "Nothing he doesn't deserve."

The office door was closed, so she had to put the bottles down to knock and open the door. As she bent to pick up the Perrier, ice spilled out and flew across the hardwood.

"Oh shite!" She scurried to the sideboard to put everything down. "Do you have a garbage bin?"

Gage rolled his chair back and handed her the small wastebasket. He watched her with a smirk on his too-handsome face.

Brynne bent down to pick up the melting cubes. She heard him inhale and realized she was giving him an eyeful. Pleased to get a reaction, she deliberately bent at the waist to collect the rest.

"You missed some under the coffee table." His voice sounded strangled.

"Oh! Thank you, sir," she said sweetly, and got on her hands and knees to find the rest. She heard his chair creak. "Do you have a spare napkin so I can wipe up the water? I wouldn't want anyone to slip."

"It's fine," he ground out. "Take the tray and get back to work."

"Of course, let me get that." She went to the side of his desk, and he handed her the tray. She glimpsed another naked woman on his screen. That one was tied spread-eagled on a four-poster bed, blindfolded. The dishes almost tipped off the tray, but she righted them just in time.

"See something you like, Red?"

Brynne stared at the picture and kept up the game. "Mmm, looks interesting. Are you looking to improve your technique?"

He cleared his throat. "I have had no complaints about my technique."

She looked at him, feigning innocence. "Oh, you let your submissive speak?"

His brows rose, and he smiled wickedly. "Of course. Eventually, I remove her gag so she can thank me *properly.*"

Brynne blushed deeply and backed away. "Ha, ha, funny. Well, I'd better go, and let you get back to your important porn."

She hurried back to the lounge, which was packed. Sparring with him was exhilarating…and dangerous. If she had any second thoughts about the salt, it was too late now!

By eleven o'clock Brynne was counting the minutes until her shift was over. Thank god Dimitri the Terrible did not make an appearance. She and Bettie were clearing empty tables when Gage walked into the lounge. He stopped to chat with a few of the remaining guests. She grabbed a tray and headed to the kitchen before he got to the bar. Regretting her rash actions, she prayed he didn't use any of the tainted ice.

Luck was on her side. Gage was gone when she returned to say goodnight to Bettie and Bill.

He gave her a taxi chit and said, "Tink, stop by Master Gage's office before you leave."

Uh oh. "Okay, sure. Did he say what he wanted?"

He looked at her like she had two heads. "He doesn't have to tell anyone what he wants." His gaze hardened. "I would hate to think you've forgotten that already."

"Um, no, of course not. Sorry Bill."

"Get going, Tink, and have a good night."

"Thanks, same to you." Dread plagued Brynne as she went down the back steps. What on earth had she been thinking? She was a rookie playing with a professional.

She knocked and waited, ringing her hands. The door swung open, and he stood there, looking her over. She instantly regretted not changing out of her uniform before coming to see him. Her hair had come undone, she had no lipstick left, and food stains marred her skirt.

"Please come in, Miss Larimore. I'd like a word with you." He stepped aside, and she went toward the chair opposite his desk. "Not there. Take a seat on the chesterfield."

She perched on the edge of the cushion and waited for the inevitable.

Gage was leaning on the edge of his desk with his arms crossed. "Tell me, do you like working here?"

"Yes, I do. I like it very much, sir."

"I presume you read all the employment documents thoroughly and you understand what we expect of you?"

She stammered, "Yes, I understand. I want to apologize for being impertinent before. I—"

He interrupted. "Do you know what I hate, Miss Larimore?"

Her eyes widened. "Disrespectful behavior and dis-disobedience?"

"No. Guess again."

"Um, cold food?" She didn't think that was it, but her mind was blank.

"No, but that is on the list. I hate insincere apologies, especially when I know the person isn't truly sorry. It's like a lie, and I hate lies as much as meaningless excuses." He went over to his bar and took down a bottle of scotch and a glass. He was lifting the lid on the ice bucket when Brynne croaked. "Wait. Please."

He turned. "Excuse me?"

She wrung her hands in her lap. "I had a moment of insanity earlier and I—I put salt in your ice bucket."

He looked awestruck and stared at her. "Salt?"

"Yes, I truly am sorry. I was angry, it was stupid." She looked down, unable to meet his eyes. "And I guess you'll want to fire me."

"That's one thing I want to do," he said under his breath. He poured himself a straight scotch and perched on the edge of his desk. After a healthy swig, he shook his head, his mouth a hard line.

Brynne waited for the ax to fall, her teeth worrying her bottom lip.

"Let's try this again. I'm going to ask you some questions. Your answers, and your honesty—or lack thereof—will determine if you have a job when you leave here."

She gazed at his rigid jaw and shivered. "Okay."

"Were you sorry that my food was cold?"

She swallowed hard. "No, but I didn't miss the lids on purpose. I missed them because I was in a hurry."

He nodded. "What possessed you to put salt in my ice?"

She exhaled, knowing she was damned if she told him the truth and damned if she didn't. "When I went to get the water, Mel asked why I wasn't helping, and I explained I was getting you dinner and then water and ice. She said you always have a supply in your office, so I felt like you were punishing me by making me run up and down the stairs for things you already had in here."

His eyes narrowed. "Maybe I wanted to test whether you would behave properly when exasperated."

"And I failed the test," she murmured.

"Indeed, you did. But you must have known that your behavior would have consequences?"

"Well, yes, but…" She faltered, unable to look at him.

"And yet you did it, anyway. So either you crave punishment, or you need more motivation to follow the rules."

Her face flushed as he went on.

"In my club, we have these specific rules for a reason."

She nodded.

He stood and paced back and forth, taking sips of his room temperature scotch. "Our members pay handsomely for helpful, pliant, beautiful young women to serve them. They pay for the privilege of flirting, teasing, and even spanking them when necessary."

Seizing the moment, she blurted, "Could you maybe just spank me instead of firing me?"

He stopped mid-stride, his eyes glittering down on her. "You haven't seemed to grasp that it is your job to follow orders eagerly, however tiring or humiliating they might be."

She waited, not sure what he would do next.

"If you still want this job, you will have to be punished properly. Tomorrow evening, we will let our guests know that you've been naughty, and they'll get the chance to paddle your behind in the Pareo playroom upstairs."

Brynne's eyes widened.

"You'll wear a leather collar that has the name tag *Bad Girl*, and since you cannot seem to control your errant mouth, I may decide to make you wear a gag."

Brynne sucked in a breath, shocked at his words. Her clothes felt unbearably tight, and she shifted uncomfortably.

Gage went and sat behind his desk and ran a hand roughly through his hair. He looked as out of sorts as she had ever seen him.

She wrestled with acute embarrassment. "Thank you for the second chance, sir."

"This is your *only* chance, Brynne. I don't waste my time with novices. Now get your ass out of my sight before I change my mind."

She scrambled for the door as fast as her legs would carry her. She was almost through when he said, "By the way, have someone show you where the service lift is. I don't expect you to run up and down the stairs with my food."

She nodded and shut the door.

"Well, shit. It would have been nice to know about the elevator two days ago."

Changing quickly, Brynne packed up and was out the back door in ten minutes. Once in the taxi, she checked her messages. Three were from Jared, and one from her dad, who was traveling around the Maritimes with his new wife. Every few weeks, he would send an update on their adventures. Brynne was glad he had found companionship after all those years alone.

Jared asked if she was working Saturday night because he was called in for a shift. She rubbed her forehead at the thought of him being there and possibly seeing her get punished.

Brynne:	Hey J. I've missed you. Lots to tell you. I fucked things up today.
Jared:	What happened?!
Brynne:	Long story :-(
Jared:	Uh-huh, did Master G take you over his knee?
Brynne:	OMG. No, but I wish he had. He's going to let others spank me tomorrow instead.
Jared:	Oh shit.
Brynne:	FML. I'm such an idiot.
Jared:	Did you lose your temper??
Brynne:	No, well yes. I hate he can rile me so easily. He is so calm, it's maddening.
Jared:	Lolz

Brynne: *He lectured me like my high school principal. I wanted to punch him. BTW my uniform is redick. Seriously mortifying.*

Jared: *I am sure you look sexy as hell in it ;-)*

Brynne: *Pfft. I'm exhausted, my feet r killing me. I need a new pair of work shoes.*

Jared: *Why don't we go shopping tomorrow?*

Brynne: *That would be great.*

Jared: *Cool. Call me at 10 to wake me up.
Night Bree <3*

Brynne: *Night J xo.*

Gage poured himself another scotch and sat on the warm cushion Brynne had just vacated. Christ, the way she pushed his buttons was ballsy. He hated to admit it, but it impressed him. Just a little.

She deserved to be tossed over his knee. God knows he wanted to, but she wanted it, too. No matter what, he had to maintain the upper hand. When she bent over and flashed her ass and then crawled around after the ice, his cock came alive. Thankfully, he had been sitting behind his desk. He rubbed his chin and thought about the punishment planned for tomorrow. It should teach her a humiliating lesson.

The extra embarrassment of an audience should deter further cheeky behavior. He doubted it and secretly hoped she didn't give in and quit yet. The game was just getting interesting.

8

Baby Did a Bad, Bad Thing

Brynne woke after a fitful night, out of sorts. She hit the snooze button a second time and the snippets of a dream floated somewhere between sleep and wakefulness. She was lying over Gage's lap, her panties pulled down to her knees. He was caressing her bare cheeks, and she knew he was about to spank her. One hand pressed the small of her back and the other lifted… She braced for it, her body tingling in anticipation.

And then the alarm jarred her awake.

Damn! Banishing the arousal that lingered, she called Jared and jumped into the shower.

They met at noon to wander through the Selfridges shoe emporium downtown. After trying on ten styles, she found the perfect pair of lace-up booties with a comfortable two-inch heel.

When they stopped for a cappuccino, Jared demanded that she spill the juicy details of her run-in with Gage.

"I will, I promise. But I have to ask you something first. Have you ever met the scary, giant Russian guy Dimitri?"

The coffee cup froze halfway to his mouth. "Bree, he is richer than God, and the scariest dude I've ever laid eyes on. He was in Russia for the last four months."

"Well, he's back, and I had to serve him! He made me so on edge. You know I can handle overzealous admirers, but this was different. It was like he marked me or something. Have you seen him upstairs, you know, in action?"

"No, but I wish I had; he is so frickin' hot!"

Brynne chided him, "You're crazy, J. He's hot like a nuclear meltdown—and probably fatal if you get too close!" She shook her head and added, "Melinda told me he sometimes brings two subs with him to fetish night. That's pretty crazy."

"I've heard that but haven't seen it. One of my friends witnessed a scene at another club where the rules are less strict."

"And?"

"Apparently, he prefers to use a crop because he likes to leave marks. The guy said he tied the two girls together and made them pleasure each other while everyone watched."

Brynne shivered and sipped her coffee. "Jesus. I hope he goes back to Russia soon."

"You are safe at Dominus, Bree. Garrick and Gage have the best security, plus there are high-ranking members of Scotland Yard in the club regularly."

Brynne took a deep breath. "I know he can't hurt me, but he's messing with my head. You know?"

Jared waved his hands. "Okay, we haven't got much time. Tell me what the hell you did to piss off the boss?"

He listened to her tale of ice and woe and warned her for the second time she was playing with fire.

"Babe, Gage doesn't joke around. I've never seen him even crack a smile. He expects everyone to follow his rules and won't hesitate to fire anyone who doesn't."

"Well, maybe I'm winning him over and thawing his frozen sense of humor?"

"I wouldn't count on it."

Jared told her what he had heard from the other staff at the club. Gage used to frequent the underground scene in London and Berlin but hadn't been seen anywhere in ages.

"Apparently, back in the day, he had a different sub on his arm every few weeks."

Brynne listened and said absently, "I wonder what it would be like to do a scene with him?"

Jared's eyebrows shot up. "Have you lost your mind? He's the kind of Dom that expects total submission and proper behavior. Don't take this the wrong way, but you aren't a natural submissive. Your defiance simmers below the surface, ready to do battle. I know Ross made you feel like shit when you shared your fantasies, but he was not worthy. Not even close." He took her hand and squeezed. "I saw it with my own eyes. The more confident you became, the more he tried to tamp down your sparkle."

"You're right. I was blind. He was slowly isolating me and undermining my belief in myself. Why couldn't I see his possessiveness for what it was?" Brynne blew out a deep breath. "All I wanted was for him to take charge in the bedroom, but he was so not the guy for that!"

"Bree, just be patient. You will find someone who gets you when you least expect it. But Gage is a Ph.D. level in D/s, and you are in kindergarten. So please, please, put him out of your mind."

She smiled, knowing he was just trying to protect her. "I might find him attractive, but you have nothing to worry about. He's an asshole, and he doesn't even like me." She chuckled. "You are worrying for nothing."

Jared rolled his eyes. "Yeah, well, you just behave yourself. Remember to follow the damn rules, and everything will be fine."

Brynne smiled and kissed him on the cheek. "You're a worrywart, Jared and I love you for it. I'm off. Hope I will see you tonight."

Jared gave her a squeeze and waved as he took the steps to the other subway platform. As her train pulled away from the station, she noodled on their conversation. Sure, she was curious about what made her bad-tempered boss tick, but her mission was not to get involved with a man, it was to understand the whole dominant/submissive dynamic. The book would not rewrite itself, and she hadn't touched it in days. This fascination with bondage and discipline was just a passing fancy and nothing to do with being dominated. Taking orders and submitting herself to a man like Gage MacLeod? *Of course not…*

She had one more stop to make before Brixton station. When she left the Naughty & Nice store, she had a smile on her face and a spring in her step.

A few hours later, she was at Dominus and a nervous energy had taken hold of her. She felt like a hummingbird in a sustained hover, her wings and heart fluttering madly. She stopped pacing long enough to rifle through her backpack and found a crumpled chocolate-covered granola bar. Chocolate always helped settle her nerves. She devoured it and got back to finishing her hair and makeup. After changing into her uniform, she added one last item to her outfit. It wouldn't save her from the humiliation of being spanked, but it was a little protective armor.

Brynne was on her way to the stairs when Garrick stopped her.

"I wasn't sure you were going to be back, Tink. I understand you have earned yourself some punishment tonight?"

Brynne looked at his twinkling dark eyes and then at the floor. "Yes, sir."

Although he was a large man, Brynne never felt intimidated by his size or demeanor. He was like a protective teddy bear, unlike his boss, who reminded her of a feral jungle cat.

"Gage is waiting for you in his office." His mouth twitched.

She nodded and smoothed the nonexistent wrinkles in her skirt. *Here goes nothing.* Taking a deep breath, she knocked on the door.

"Aye, who is it?" He sounded more curt than usual.

"Tinkerbell."

"Come in." The chill in his voice hit her like a Scottish wind in November. The hope that he might have softened his stance overnight went up in smoke.

She walked in and stopped a few feet inside the door. Unsure of what to say or do, she stared at the carpet and clasped her fidgety hands together.

"On your knees," he said, his voice gruff as he stood.

Her wide eyes flew to his. She wanted to pretend she didn't hear him, but he was pointing to the floor where she stood. She lowered herself to the carpet and focused on his immaculate wing tips when they came into view.

He picked something up from the coffee table, the slight jingling of metal increasing her anxiety. In the back of her mind, she made a mental note to remember how she felt. *This would be a good feeling to incorporate into the book.*

Gage gently tipped her face up so she could see what he held in his hand. Brynne swallowed hard, but the lump remained lodged in her throat. His face gave nothing of his feelings away as he fastened the white leather collar around her slender neck. He tucked two fingers against her skin as he fastened the buckle snugly. She wondered if he could feel the hammering of her pulse. Her palms were damp, her hands now fisted at her sides. The collar felt heavy and humiliating, as it was meant to. She refused to meet his eyes, staring instead at his belt buckle.

"Hold up your wrists." His accent was more pronounced, and it raised the hair on her arms. Was he affected by this exercise? She raised her arms up and watched him buckle matching white leather cuffs to each wrist.

He showed her a silver oval tag engraved with the words *Bad Girl* before he attached it to the front D-ring on the collar. "This will let everyone know why you are collared tonight."

Brynne looked right through him and refused to let him see her fear.

"I have one additional item, but I'm undecided on whether you need it."

She looked at what he had in his hand and balked. Her eyes implored him to show mercy. Pleading would give him the justification to use the gag in his hand.

His mouth twisted into a wicked grin as he toyed with her. Time dragged, and neither spoke, until he dropped the ball gag on the table and picked up a small-link chain, about eighteen inches long. Without a word, he clipped her wrist cuffs together and returned to his desk.

She stared after him incredulously. *How am I supposed to do my job with my hands chained together?*

"You may go now, Red. But if I hear you've been at all sassy"—he looked pointedly at the table—"I will reconsider that."

She exhaled and rose, her cheeks and neck flushed. "Yes sir. Thank you, sir."

The jingling chain mocked her as she hurried to the locker

room. She sat in a toilet cubicle for ten minutes, talking herself out of running home. What the hell just happened? When he put the collar and cuffs on, she had the strangest sensation that her blood was thickening and causing certain parts of her body to heat and swell.

It was clear this was a game for him, one he fully expected to win. Brynne had to pretend that the restraints didn't affect her. Right? Or was she supposed to be acting contrite? What would the heroine in her story be feeling in this situation? Remorse? A true submissive wouldn't pretend she was cool as a cucumber; she would try to get back in his good graces. Sucking up was not her strong suit. God help her, this would be harder than pretending indifference.

When she got back up to the kitchen, Melinda was there getting an order.

"Hey Tink! Glad you're here! Could you help me? The order for table four is up and I've got my hands full. Things are hopping tonight."

"Sure, happy to help." She was grateful Mel didn't comment on her appearance.

Brynne awkwardly picked up the serving tray, spreading her chained hands as far apart as possible, hoping she wouldn't lose its precarious balance. *Imagine if I accidentally spilled this tray on someone—then I'd really be in trouble.* She navigated through the tables, aware that the noise in the room was gradually diminishing. As she reached the table with two elderly gentlemen, conversation had given way to the clink of glasses and the sound of cutlery on plates.

"Which one of you ordered the medium rare burger with cheddar?" she asked quietly.

"That would be me, Miss Tinkerbell." The balding man in the pinstriped suit grinned at her. "And I'm looking forward to hearing what you did to piss off Master Gage."

Brynne was about to say something flippant but stopped herself.

"If I told you, I'm sure I would get in even more trouble, sir. You wouldn't want that, would you?" She maneuvered the tray carefully and put the plates down, taking care not to catch the annoying chain on their glasses.

The other man chuckled. "I wouldn't mind seeing that, Tink. I have signed up to give you a spanking later."

She cringed at the reminder, but her pride would not let it show. She cleared her throat and asked, "May I get you anything else?"

The first man patted her hand. "I'll have another Dalwhinnie fifteen straight up, and my friend will have a pint of Guinness."

He turned to the man and said, "Don't torment the girl, Douglas. You'll have your chance later."

Brynne escaped to the bar and punched in the drink order. Bill snickered at the collar and cuffs. "Not sure what you did, lass, but you've caused quite a stir tonight."

Brynne shook her head and sighed. "After I deliver these drinks, I would really like to know what I'm in for."

Bill smiled and handed her the scotch and the beer. "Sure thing. Stop over at table nineteen first. Those fellas just sat down, then I'll fill you in on tonight's festivities."

She delivered the beverages without incident and was about to take the orders of the new table when one of the men grasped the dangling tag and pulled her slowly down to his level. Before he could finish asking her how *bad* she was, a tall, hulking security monitor was beside them, deftly prying the man's fingers off the tag and getting in between them.

He casually addressed the man and his friends. "Sirs, we do not allow our waitstaff to be manhandled. Should you wish to enjoy the company of a skilled submissive, you may investigate the upper floors later."

The man sneered. "I know the rules man, I was just going to say something to her. You didn't need to go all sphincter police on me."

"Yes, well, she can hear quite fine standing right beside you." Turning to Brynne, he said, "Do you have all the drink orders, Miss?"

"Just two so far. I was just going to ask what you would like, sir?" Brynne pasted on a smile for the jerkoff with the dirty blonde hair. He stared at her, then huffed out his order of a Rusty Nail. The guard escorted her back to the bar and alerted Bill to keep an eye on those guys while she entered the order.

Brynne waited for the drinks, feeling certain she was being watched. Damn the collar and cuffs. There was an air of predatory anticipation in the bar, and she felt like a fox before the hunt.

As she returned to the table, she heard one man say to his friend, "We should get to punish the bad girls every night, don't you think, Roger?"

The blonde dude looked up at her as she placed the drinks down, licking his lips suggestively. "Definitely agree, mate, especially the ones with attitude."

Brynne held her tongue. The last glass was almost on the table when his hand found its way to the back of her thigh, just below the hem of her skirt. She jerked back and spilled his drink onto the table, splashing his pants. He jumped up angrily. Brynne was apologizing when, out of the corner of her eye, she saw a large man striding toward them, his face a mask of fury. Brynne shook and almost dropped the glass. Dimitri arrived at the table at the same moment as Bill. The three men stood staring at each other, and she knew she needed to defuse the situation.

She grabbed the bar towel Bill had in his hand and mopped up the drink. "Bill, I was terribly clumsy and spilled the Rusty Nail. Would you be a dear and make another one, please?"

Bill looked pointedly at her, and she was relieved when he

retreated. There was enough testosterone at the table without him trying to referee.

Dimitri was staring at her; she saw his eyes narrow a fraction when he read the tag on the collar. He looked at the man who had touched her like he was an insect, rage still blazing from his eyes. She put her hand on his forearm and squeezed. "Mr. Ivanov, thank you for coming to my rescue, but as you can see, everything is fine."

His gaze softened slightly, but his words were sharp and ragged like a serrated knife. "This man put his hand on you, and if he knows what's good for him, he will apologize."

The blond guy withered under his stare. It was obvious he was no match for the Russian, and one fist could easily crush him. He backed away, his hands up in surrender. "No harm, no foul, Ivanov. I'm sorry, I was out of line."

Dimitri shook his head in disgust. "Nyet. You need to say sorry to her, not me."

The man was beet red, his head bobbing up and down. "I'm very sorry, Tinkerbell. I meant you no harm and hope you can forgive me."

Brynne nodded quickly, wanting to escape the situation. Dimitri was being a strange combination of lethal and protective. She definitely didn't like all this attention.

"Thank you, sir. I'm sorry for spilling your drink and causing a commotion." She stepped out of the way when Bill brought the new cocktail and made to leave with him. Dimitri followed them over to the bar. He leaned in and rested his elbows on the polished wood. She could feel the tension coming off him in waves.

"You have been bad?" he asked, rubbing the stubble on his jaw.

"I, uh, got into a little trouble, yes," Brynne said, looking down at her feet.

"I would like to punish you, but I must know the crime. Then I will know how hard to be."

Brynne's mouth fell open, and she looked to Bill for help. Before he could respond, Gage came up beside her and placed a hand on her lower back.

"Dimitri, welcome back to Dominus. Garrick told me you were in London. I trust business has been treating you well." Gage greeted him politely, but Brynne saw how rigid his body was when he shook Dimitri's hand.

Turning to her, his face a mask of indifference, he said, "Tink, take your break now."

Dimitri watched her go, and he didn't look happy about it. "Da, Gage. Business is excellent. I'm here for a month and supervising the final touches on my yacht. You must come out for a cruise when I take delivery in a few weeks. She is a beauty."

Gage nodded. "Sounds brilliant. I'd love to." *When hell freezes over.* He wouldn't be caught dead on this man's yacht. "Let us know if you need anything, and enjoy your evening."

Dimitri popped some peanuts into his mouth, then said casually, "I want Tinkerbell to serve my table when she comes back."

There were no outward signs of his feelings on this subject. But when Gage spoke, his voice had dropped several octaves. "She is serving a private event tonight, so I'm afraid that's not possible."

Dimitri studied him, probably deciding if he believed the excuse or not. "Pity. Well then, I expect her to serve my table when I come tomorrow night." He put his hand on Gage's shoulder, the way a friend might, but it was a blatant act of dominance. "You can make that happen for me, can't you, old friend?"

Gage watched Dimitri walk away. He gritted his teeth and turned to Bill.

"Let me see who has signed up to punish our little troublemaker?" Bill passed him the sheet, and he went in the back to find Brynne.

She was in the kitchen, pacing back and forth, when Gage found her.

"Change of plans for this evening, Red. There is a private party on the third floor that Bettie was going to serve, but I'm putting you up there instead of her."

"Okay," she said, her brow crinkling.

Gage glanced at the paper in his hand, his mouth a hard line. "There are five members who signed up to punish you, so unless I want a riot on my hands, we honor that plan."

"Five?" She gulped.

He looked pointedly at her. "You are lucky. Bill pulled the sheet down early so it wouldn't exceed a manageable number for your first time."

"Th-thank you for that."

Gage watched her chewing on her bottom lip. "Don't thank me yet. Each one gets five strokes." He ran a hand through his hair and continued, "Bill will discreetly let them know to be in the Pareo play area at nine thirty p.m. If the dinner party isn't finished, Bettie will cover."

She was fidgeting with the chain, looking pensive.

"If you want to back out and quit, now is your chance."

"No, sir. I earned this punishment. And someone will supervise, right?"

He got the feeling that her stubborn pride regularly got her into trouble, and he wondered what she had to prove. "I'll be overseeing your punishment. And if you use your safe word, it stops."

"I understand."

"The dinner party has already gathered in the Veni Vidi Vici room, so check in upstairs and get your bearings. Garrick will let Bettie know of the switch. You will owe her one and should share your tips with her. The parties usually net a tidy bonus."

"Absolutely I will. What kind of party is it?"

He watched her face transform. Uncertainty gave way to curiosity, lighting her darkened pupils with excitement. Without a doubt, she would be lousy at poker.

"A small dinner celebration for one of our most esteemed members from Scotland Yard. That's all you need to know. They have hired a couple of subs to entertain, and the dining room staff will bring dinner in. You will just need to run the bar, keep the wine flowing throughout dinner, and clear a few dishes."

"Okay, got it. I'll head up."

"One more thing, Red."

Brynne looked expectantly at him. He drew her wrists forward and unbuckled the cuffs and then the collar.

"You won't be needing these until later."

Her irises had turned to the color of espresso and that pouting bottom lip was begging to be nibbled.

"Go," he growled. "And for god's sake, try to stay out of trouble."

It took every ounce of self-restraint he had not to watch her go up the steps. He headed to his office cursing Garrick, his mother, his ex-fiancée and his libido, which chose this moment to come out of hibernation.

9

Private Party.
Public Performance

Her pulse was racing, and her body was hot all over when she reached the third floor—and it wasn't from sprinting up the stairs. When Gage closed the distance between them and took the cuffs off, his scent hit her like a psychedelic drug. She knew nothing about LSD, but guessed it was similarly mind altering.

Aunt Josie's voice kept replaying in her head: "Be careful what you wish for, sweetie." She was getting what she had long fantasized about, and it scared her shitless. There was no turning back now—her education was getting a jumpstart, thanks to Dimitri. Access to a private party so soon! It would be a boon if she got to witness an actual scene.

She wandered down the wide corridor, noticing the Latin names in decorative brass script above each entrance. Each door was upholstered in dark green leather, accented with lacquered strips of wood and black iron rails. They looked just like the old steamer trunk she had discovered as a young girl in Aunt Josie's house.

Brynne remembered that first summer she spent with her aunt on Skye. Josephine Lamond was a trailblazer in her time. She never married, but she had countless male friends and admirers. She was Brynne's idol. Josie wrote racy historical romances. The covers featured beautiful heroines held possessively in the arms of a larger-than-life hero in tight white breeches. She was an overly curious twelve-year-old and almost fell off a ladder attempting to get to the top shelf of the bookcase. However, her grandest discovery came a few years later when she found the trunk in the closet under the stairs.

She tried the lock multiple times, knowing there had to be something interesting inside. When her aunt went to town on Saturday afternoons, she searched every corner of the little cottage. It took weeks to unearth the skeleton key taped to the back of a picture frame. Brynne would never forget the strange feelings that came over her when she found the magazines. The black-and-white photographs from the 1950s featured the famous pinup queen, Bettie Page...in vintage lingerie and bondage. They were her first exposure to that world, and they left an indelible mark.

Garrick came up from behind, startling her. "So, Dimitri is at it again?"

"I'm afraid so. Did Gage fill you in?"

"I didn't get any details. He just said we needed to move you from the lounge and reduce the chances of a brawl breaking out."

"It got tense, but I calmed him down. At least he didn't hit the guy who overstepped, so it wasn't too bad."

Garrick's eyes narrowed. "It's our job to prevent things from escalating. If Gage thought there was the chance of an issue, I trust his instincts. They are never wrong." His voice was low and harsh. "It was the right call to take you out of the room."

She regretted making light of it. "Sorry, Garrick." Jesus. Was the Russian that dangerous? "I appreciate it, I do. And I hope Bettie isn't upset that I'm taking the private party."

Garrick's tone was short. "She'll understand. Now, let me explain what you will and won't do while in that room."

Ten minutes later, Brynne's stomach was doing flips. She didn't want to ruin this opportunity by forgetting the rules. If she did well, there could be other chances to work up here and watch people doing scenes.

When she entered the room, she fought to keep her eyes on the floor and recited Garrick's last instructions in her head. "Don't stare at anyone; practice being invisible. Your job is to be demure, discreet, and don't speak unless spoken to."

She smiled at the security dude stationed inside. He gave her a curt nod and shut the door without making a sound. Brynne scanned the large dining table to check whose glasses needed refilling when her gaze landed on the centerpiece and froze.

Positioned in the middle of the table was a naked human sculpture. Brynne forgot everything as she drank in the sight of the naked woman secured to a raised leather platform. Her arms were fastened over her head with black leather wrist cuffs attached to rings embedded in the table.

Brynne's palms dampened when she saw how they'd restrained her. Each leg was bent at the knee and held by a wide leather strap binding ankle to thigh. The woman's skin glistened with oil. A black satin blindfold covered her eyes, and she held a small apple in her mouth, cradled by her ruby red lips.

Brynne realized she was being anything but invisible and tore her gaze away from the mesmerizing sight. She hurried to the portable bar cart in the corner. Bettie had stocked up the liquors and mixes and there was a long table against the back wall with a selection of red and white wines.

The man at the head of the table was obviously their host. All but two guests listened raptly as he told them a story about a stakeout. His mustache was neatly trimmed, and he kept his salt-and-pepper hair shaved close to his scalp. Brynne noticed the way he commanded the room. She took her time studying the guests and wondered how the eclectic group became friends.

They ranged in age from late thirties to late fifties. She recalled Gage mentioning Scotland Yard, but most of these guys did not look like they worked in law enforcement. One was clad in black leather and two others were dressed like models for *GQ*.

She kept stealing glances at the woman on the table. Guests nibbled from an array of fruit decorating her body. Someone had placed plump raspberries on each nipple and the juices from strawberries and watermelon left traces on her polished skin.

A tall, striking man came over to the bar. He wore his jet-black hair tied back, accentuating his high cheekbones and dark-brown eyes.

"What happened to Bettie?" His accent was distinctly Italian. He eyeballed her name tag and added, "Tinkerbell?"

Brynne smiled. "She was called away, and they asked me to cover." It wasn't a total lie; she just hoped the switch didn't disappoint them.

His eyes probed, causing her pulse to flutter. "Are you a submissive, Bella?"

"No. I mean yes, but not the way you mean." She lowered her voice. "I'm here to tend bar, not perform any other duties for the party." She felt her face heating as he studied her.

"I see. That is a shame." He chuckled and said, "Let's see how well you make a Manhattan."

"Certainly, sir. Straight up or on the rocks?"

"Rocks."

She prepared the cocktail, having learned how to perfect it for her father, who preferred it with Canadian rye. After placing it on the bar, she grinned playfully. "Please tell me you are a purist and prefer cherries over a lemon peel?"

"Si, cherries. Grazie," he said, his eyes glinting.

She added two sour marasca cherries on a stir stick and presented the drink. "I hope you like it."

He took a sip and hummed in delight. "You're an excellent mixologist, Tinker-bella." He winked and returned to his seat near the end of the table.

It was then that she noticed the other submissive on display at the other end of the room. Her hand flew to her mouth in shock. How had she missed seeing the man with a stunning body mounted on a St. Andrew's Cross? His position meant the guest of honor could admire his beautiful form throughout dinner. A leather hood hid most of his face but left his mouth visible. His body was perfection, well-muscled without an ounce of excess, made more tempting by his spread-eagled position. His skin was glistening with oil too, accentuating every curve of muscle. The cuffs held him taut, and his erection was bulging, trying to escape the leather pouch covering it.

Brynne's mouth dried, and she felt suddenly warm. The guest of honor rose to speak to his guests and jolted her out of her trance. "Thank you all for coming tonight to celebrate with me. Our first course will appear soon, but I want to play a little game before it arrives."

Murmurs sounded around the room as they waited for him to continue. He pulled a purple velvet pouch off the table and passed it to the first person to his left. "Pull one card out and pass the bag along."

Their excitement was palpable as each person took a playing card out of the bag.

"Each card represents either a punishment or a reward for our two slaves: Achilles and Helen of Troy. Depending on which card you draw, you get to mete out one or the other. If you have a spade, you'll punish our handsome stallion on the wall. A diamond means he gets a reward. And if you draw a heart, you will give Helen pleasure, but a club means distress or teasing *without* release."

The woman on the table shivered, and her wrist cuffs rattled the rings on the table. Brynne's pulsed picked up its pace, and she squeezed her legs together in sympathy. Or was it envy?

The gentleman who ordered the Manhattan waved his card in the air. "John, if we want to trade, is that possible?"

John nodded. "That would be acceptable, Massimo—if someone wants to swap with you."

"Molto bene." He stood and addressed the group. "I have a spade but would like to trade for a heart. Who is interested in switching?"

The man opposite him rose and said, "Deal!" The man in black leather had been stealing glances at Achilles every few minutes. He looked pleased with the switch. Everyone else seemed satisfied with their cards.

John walked to a tall cabinet in the corner near the cross and opened the doors to reveal a wide selection of implements. Brynne sucked in a breath when she saw the floggers, clamps, restraints, and sex toys of various colors and sizes. He turned to the group. "Who has the highest spade?"

A tall, slim man with glasses rose, flashed the Queen of Spades, and walked to the open cabinet.

"Choose your instrument of pain, Oscar. You have the honor of going first."

Oscar took his time perusing the shelves and chose a flogger in blood-red leather. He turned to the table and waved his choice for everyone to see.

Massimo clapped his hands. "Great choice Oscar, the deerskin is perfect to warm him up."

The man restrained on the cross clenched his fists when he heard what the item was. She watched the rise and fall of his chest, feeling acute anticipation. Oscar stood beside him and trailed a hand over his chest, grazing his nipples.

"Now, now, Oscar, yours is a punishment card. You must refrain from caressing Achilles; the one holding a diamond gets to do that."

Oscar bristled at being reprimanded, judging by the shift in his stance. He turned back to Achilles and mumbled something. With shocking quickness, the flogger landed across the spread-eagled man's muscled thighs. He jumped in reaction and bit his lip, but no sound escaped. The flogger landed again, inches below his groin. Oscar increased the pace and intensity by landing several blows on his stomach and upper body, and the man jerked against the cross. A rosy blush spread across his chest and sleek flat abs. The captive held his composure without so much as a murmur.

"Thank you, Oscar. Nice work," John said.

Oscar hung the flogger back on the hook and walked up to the bar. His eyes were black, his expression lit with excitement.

"What can I get you, sir?" Brynne kept her voice low.

"I'll have a double bourbon on the rocks. Maker's Mark, if you have it."

"Yes, of course," Brynne said, and poured the drink without delay. He nodded and turned without a word, returning to his seat.

"Who has the high diamond?" John asked. A handsome, sandy-haired man showed his card to the group and stood.

"Ben gets to raise the stakes, but remember, don't let him come."

Ben took off his beautifully cut suit jacket and hung it on the back of his chair. He nodded at John as he straightened his cufflinks. With a wink, he said, "Never fear. I know how to *edge* a slave." Bypassing the cabinet, he went straight up to the cross and leaned in close. He whispered something to Achilles that was inaudible. Ben took his time, hands roaming over his glistening chest, circling, and then pinching his nipples to hardness. He ran a finger along the young man's jaw, then tugged at his bottom lip. His fingers dipped inside his mouth.

"Wet them," he said, in a deep Irish accent. The deep pitch of his voice skittered along Brynne's nerves as she watched the sub do as he was told.

With newly damp fingers, he played with his nipples. His other hand grasped the pouch and squeezed, causing a groan to escape.

"Permission to bare Achilles's *sword*?"

John chuckled. "Permission granted."

Ben wasted no time in undoing the snaps and pulling the leather away. He stepped to the side so everyone could see the beautiful erection jutting from his body. The head was dark with need. Cock tears had gathered at the seam. Brynne unconsciously licked her lips and could not look away. When John cleared his throat, she jumped up in surprise. Being so absorbed in the scene, she hadn't noticed him standing next to the bar.

"I'm sorry," she blurted, blushing to the roots of her hair.

He grinned at her, his eyes twinkling in amusement. "Perhaps I should punish you for your inattention." He winked and added, "I'll have a Hendrick's and tonic."

She swallowed, her eyes wide. "Excellent choice."

"So, you're the new girl everyone's been talking about?"

Brynne winced. "Bad news travels fast."

He chuckled. "You're fresh meat, love. Don't worry, the novelty will wear off soon enough."

"I hope so," she said, handing him the drink.

John raised his glass in her direction and sat back down. The scene unfolding at the other end of the room re-captured her attention. Ben was dragging a feather along the underside of the prisoner's arms and down his torso, all the while massaging oil up and down the length of his prick. Brynne overheard Achilles's sharp intake of breath and watched his taut body shudder as the Irishman continued to torment him.

John took control again. "Thank you, Ben. Now we'll call upon the holder of the other spade to bring our gladiator back down to earth."

"That's me." A man with ebony skin and mischief in his eyes rose from the table. He was well over six feet of lean muscle and sculpted cheekbones.

While he stood at the cabinet perusing the items, Brynne salivated over his perfect butt. What would he do to poor Achilles? It didn't matter. She was already impatient for what might happen next.

She couldn't see what he chose because he stood in front of the cross, his large frame blocking everyone's view. When Achilles moaned low, her body shuddered in reaction to the obvious discomfort in his tone. The sounds in the room were subdued. Everyone was holding their breath, listening for signs of his resistance or surrender. Another distressed groan followed by the tinkle of a bell. Achilles sucked in his breath, and it was obvious his tormentor was fastening something between his legs. When he stepped aside, a collective sigh passed around the room. Brynne would give anything for a gin and tonic to wet her parched throat. She swallowed a gasp, seeing the clamps fastened to his nipples with small bells to signal his duress. The Black man had also wrapped several leather straps tightly around the base of his penis and balls. If Brynne thought his cock looked hungry before, it was positively ravenous now. She swallowed hard and reached for a bottle of water.

A buzz sounded, and the security guard moved to the door. He peered through the small window first and then allowed the three servers to enter. They made quick work of clearing empty dishes and then set down the salad course. Brynne circled the table with the wine and topped everyone up. Once she retreated, John raised his glass.

"A toast to Master Gage, who gave us this delicious 2001 Barolo."

"Hear, hear!"

"Cheers," the guests chimed in.

Everyone except John clinked glasses and dug into their salads. He dropped his napkin on his chair and walked in front of the captive, strung up for his amusement. He leaned in to Achilles, his mouth close to his ear as he unfastened the hooks holding the cuffs to the corners of the cross. Achilles nodded and dropped to his knees, the bells from his nipple clamps echoing off the paneled walls. John took a dining chair and placed it in the corner facing the room. From her vantage point at the other end, Brynne could see everything. Part of her wondered if John did that on purpose, and her pulse quickened. She reluctantly pried her gaze away and focused on wiping the bar, but couldn't ignore the sounds coming from that corner. The unbuckling of a belt, the sound of a zipper, and the swish of trousers being drawn down. When Brynne looked back up, Achilles was kneeling between John's legs with his cock cradled in his grasp.

"Tut, tut," he said, his tone gruff. "No hands." He drew the young man's arms behind his back and clipped the cuffs together.

"These bells are a distraction." He swiftly tossed the clamps to the floor. Achilles moaned as the blood rushed back to the tortured tips and he whispered his thanks.

"I'm sure you are glad to be rid of them. Now you can show me just how much."

Achilles nodded, raised himself to a kneeling position, and opened his mouth. The hood covered his eyes, so he waited to be directed. John's jaw clenched; his steely blue eyes glittered as he pulled the open mouth toward him. Achilles took the smooth round head into his mouth, tentatively at first, running his tongue over the crown, then down the sides, letting his saliva coat the stem. He took him into his mouth and descended slowly, propelling himself forward a little further each time. John closed his eyes and let his head fall back. Achilles coated the entire length of it with swirling strokes, sucking on the way up, licking on the way down. He increased the intensity, forcing himself down farther each time, and Brynne swore she heard the sound of it thudding against the back of his throat. John clenched his fists and began thrusting himself forward to meet every stroke. They were both oblivious to the onlookers.

Everyone had ceased eating. They stared, mesmerized by the erotic sounds of a cock being worshiped. John gripped the arms of the chair; he was getting close, swelling, and growing under Achilles's proficient tongue. The next time he pushed himself down, the entire length disappeared into his throat. He remained there, and Brynne could see the tendons in his neck working, swallowing the head over and over.

John let out a keening cry of ecstasy, his legs twitching as every drop was wrung from his body. Only then did Achilles pull himself off to rest his forehead on the older man's thigh. His chest rose and fell as he drew in deep breaths. To Brynne's surprise, John started undoing the laces at the back of the hood. Once they were loosened, he stood and pulled Achilles to his feet in front of him. Yanking off the leather covering, he took his face in his hands and kissed him deeply. John's large right hand concealed much of his face from Brynne, but a strange feeling of recognition dawned. They turned slightly from the table, so they were both shielded from prying eyes.

She watched John take hold of the young man's rock-hard prick. It wasn't long before his manipulations brought Achilles to completion. Another all-encompassing kiss muffled his groans.

Then Brynne saw his profile properly, and she nearly fainted.

10

Tink's Punishment

Holy fucking fuckazoids!

She had no way out of the room, so she scooted down and pretended to fix her shoelace. There was a crack between the bar and the wall where she watched John pull his pants up and put a robe around her best friend. He led Jared to the door and kissed him lightly on the mouth.

"Thank you for a wonderful gift, Achilles. I hope I'll see you next weekend at Fetish night."

"You will," Jared murmured, and left.

Thank god he didn't see her. Brynne was stunned and hot all over. Her mind was racing. Had he done that before? Did they know each other well? Could she ever tell him she'd witnessed that? She had to digest the whole thing and try to act normal. If she ever got the nerve, she would ask him how he did that thing with this throat.

They released Helen, the lovely centerpiece, from the table for a break, but planned to bring her back for the dessert course and more card games. Brynne looked forward to seeing more. She served more wine and cocktails after the entrée was served. She had completely lost track of the time, so when Bettie arrived a short time later to take over, her stomach dropped. There was still time to bolt for the nearest exit.

Gage was talking to Garrick at the top of the main stairs, but their conversation stopped when she approached. He looked stern, and she wondered if he ever smiled. When she saw the collar and cuffs dangling from his hand, she paused, moving no closer. Her body was still buzzing; shock, arousal, and a million wild thoughts vied for attention. She had just witnessed her best friend pleasure a man, a scene that would be burned into her brain forever.

Gage handed Garrick the wrist cuffs and addressed her brusquely. "Come here."

Without meeting her eyes, he lifted a few strands of her hair out of the way and buckled the collar. Once again, she wore the *Bad Girl* tag. Garrick was fastening one cuff when Gage impatiently reached for the other. He buckled it onto her wrist and clipped the chain to the front of her collar. He tugged the other end and snapped, "Let's get this bloody show over with."

He kept a firm grip on her leash as they walked down one level to the open play area. Brynne refused to make eye contact with anyone and focused her eyes ahead. When she saw the wide array of punishment equipment, her eyes widened like saucers. It was a cross between a jungle gym and a gothic dungeon. If she'd seen it beforehand, she might have run for the hills. *Too late now.*

In her peripheral vision, she could see a crowd gathering to witness her spanking. Could she reconcile these feelings of anticipation mixed with fear and trepidation? Maybe by the end of the night, her mind would catch up to what her body wanted?

Gage looked around the playroom and cursed himself for concocting this public spectacle. When he decided on this punishment for Brynne, he believed she would quit before ever submitting to it. Christ, she goaded him at every turn! There was no doubt she deserved a spanking, but by avoiding taking her over his knee, he brought on this debacle. *Talk about getting hoisted by his own petard!*

Brynne looked flushed and nervous, but he refused to let that sway him. He led her over to one of the custom spanking benches, choosing the one that would allow her to retain some measure of modesty. The other spanking bench was designed to spread the sub's legs wide apart. But he didn't want her exposed that way. *Bloody hell, I am getting soft.*

She silently followed him to the red trestle-style bench and kept her eyes down. He tugged on the chain to get her attention. If looks could kill, he would be dead on the spot.

"What is your safe word?"

"Dickwad?" she whispered low enough that no one else heard.

Gage took her chin in his hand. "What did you just say?"

"Red. It's red." Before she could hide it, he saw the little smirk on her face.

So that's how she wanted to play it. Good! Because he had no interest in playing a scene with a martyr.

He pushed her forward, so her thighs pressed against the legs of the trestle and her stomach rested on the padded platform. He clipped the chain from the collar to a ring in the floor so she couldn't rise. Next, he buckled each forearm and wrist into the cushioned rests on either side of the platform and fastened leather straps around her slender waist. He could hear her breath hitch in her throat as she twisted against the bonds.

He leaned down close to her ear. "Going somewhere, sweetheart?"

Perhaps she was realizing the seriousness of the situation?

Gage secured her ankles into cuffs affixed to the base of each leg of the bench. He trailed a hand up her leg and casually flipped up her skirt. What a surprise to see a pair of frilly black satin knickers. His mouth twitched at her blatant attempt at adding extra padding and coverage.

As he tucked the skirt into the belt at her waist, he asked, "Did you honestly think I would allow you to keep those on?"

"I guess I wondered how much of a bastard you were going to be."

"The sooner you realize what a bastard I am, the better."

She grunted in response.

Gage shook his head, amazed that she was still back-talking when he was controlling how much she would suffer tonight. Was she pushing his buttons on purpose, or was she just oblivious to the rules of the game?

He leaned down to whisper in her ear. "I assume you have been without a proper master for too long, or perhaps the last one wasn't able to control your rebellious nature." He watched her clench her fists, but she remained silent.

Gage decided a grand gesture of dominance was required, so he took her ruffled panties and tore them apart at the seams. The crowd reacted with cheers when he ripped the material off and pocketed the remnants. She had layered the knickers over her sheer tights on top of a thong, and yet the scent of her arousal was impossible to ignore. His cock, which was already pulsing, throbbed against his fly.

He toyed with the idea of tearing the nylons off. Instead, he slowly drew them to her knees, leaving the lacy black thong, which was stark against the pale globes of her ass.

A few more leather straps and he would have her immobilized. The crowd was getting restless, and so was he. One thing became clear: he needed to get laid soon, or he could lose this game of cat and mouse. Tonight, he had to teach his little hellion a valuable lesson. *Don't taunt the tiger.*

Brynne groaned low, and his cock responded like it was a siren's call. A moment later, his hand landed hard on her right cheek.

"Oh fuck," she murmured.

"This is just the warm-up, Red."

Smack. "Uh."

Smack! "Nngh."

Smack! "Ow!"

"That's better!" someone yelled from the crowd.

Smack! "God damn!" she squealed.

"Thank me for warming you up for your punishment."

She didn't answer for a few seconds. *Smack!* "Thank you for warming me up. Sir."

Her tone was a far cry from deferential, but he let it go. Next to Garrick stood Rory, the first one on the list.

"Rory, you're up." Gage turned to the rack of spanking tools and chose a deerskin flogger. He handed it over and said, "You get a total of five strokes," then he stepped back so he could watch Brynne's face.

"What a sweet tush she has!" Rory could barely contain his excitement.

Whoosh. The first blow landed. She made a noise and looked surprised. She probably expected it to hurt more. He took his time and swung the flogger harder, making Brynne gasp. Two more landed hard on her hamstrings, and she jerked in response. Finally, Rory took aim at the delicate flesh where her legs met the curve of her bottom and got the response he wanted. Brynne squealed and let out the breath she'd been holding.

Garrick called up the next man. "Douglas, you're next."

The man she'd served in the lounge shuffled forward. Brynne didn't see him; she was staring at the floor. Gage watched her biting her full bottom lip, and he imagined nibbling on it, tasting it, and rubbing the head of his cock over it.

He noticed Douglas mooning over her bare backside and shook himself free of those pointless musings.

Gage chose a wide leather-covered paddle that would thud rather than sting. He waved it in front of her eyes. "This should wake you from your little trance, Red."

"Bite me."

She was playing right into his hands.

"Oh, we will make sure the next one bites."

Douglas was almost eighty, so he wasn't likely to have a lot of power in his swing. He nodded in approval and asked Gage, "What did the wee lass do to incur your wrath?"

"Would you believe she tainted the ice bucket in my office with salt, expecting me to ruin a glass of my rarest scotch?" It was loud enough for the crowd to hear it. There were murmurs of excitement around the room.

The old man shook his head. "Sacrilege! The willful chit deserves what is coming to her!"

"Aye, she does. Justice must be served, Douglas," he said with a wink.

Brynne wriggled as best she could and spoke up. "Oh, please be merciful, sir. He's made my life so difficult since I got here!"

Douglas, who was deaf in his right ear, asked Gage, "Did you hear something?"

"Just the whining of an impertinent sub. Carry on." Gage handed him the paddle and watched him admire his wiggling target, certain this would be the highlight of his year.

Thwack! Dougie's strength and aim surprised Gage. Brynne hissed through her teeth and turned to glare at him. He was pretty good at reading lips. She'd just called him a bastard.

Thwack, thwack! Douglas put his hand on her lower back to steady himself and took a moment to appreciate his handiwork. Gage knew her skin must be glowing, but he stayed where he was, watching her face for any sign she wanted it to stop. She hadn't cried out, but the pace of her breathing had picked up and he swore she was mumbling to herself.

Two more hard and fast thwacks, and Brynne let out an angry growl. Douglas looked like he was on cloud nine. "Christ, I feel like a new man. We should do this every Saturday night!"

Gage chuckled and took the paddle from him. "Thank you for your help, Douglas. I'll take that under advisement."

Garrick came up to Gage and pulled him aside. He spoke low. "Martin Ridgeway is next on the list, and he wants to use the crop."

"I'm not sure that's a good idea."

"How's our little novice doing?"

"Feisty as ever. Either she hates me, or she's out to prove something. Bottom line, she isn't giving in yet."

"Mind if I have a word?"

"Be my guest." While he spoke to Brynne, he retrieved a couple of bottles of water and a straw from the nearby cabinet.

Garrick returned and leaned close. "She said she's totally fine. As long as the guy is experienced, she's ready for the crop."

Martin was one of the longest standing members at Dominus and a good friend. He had trained countless Doms in the art of impact play. He knew his way around every single item in their collection. In fact, he helped outfit this space and all the themed rooms upstairs.

Martin came up and shook his hand. "Long time no see, Gage. Where have you been hiding?"

Gage didn't explain that he'd been taking cover in his office and tormenting a little redhead every chance he could get. Instead, he nodded and said, "Too much paperwork these days." He took the purple-and-black-braided riding crop down off the rack and handed it to him.

Martin admired her pale pink skin and asked, "Where did you find this one?"

"Long story, which I'll tell you later over a drink." Lowering his voice, he added, "She claims to be a sub, but I have my doubts."

"Let's find out if you have an actress or a masochist on your hands, old man."

Gage nodded and went back to his post. He looked forward to seeing how she would react to the crop.

Martin tapped his hand a few times and touched the leather keeper as he walked around her bound form. Gage knew this would unnerve her, not knowing where he would strike. When it landed with a whoosh, Brynne's mouth opened in shock, and she recoiled against the leather straps. Before she caught her breath, he struck again, and she screeched, "Ow, god!"

Another stinging blow caught her tender thigh, and she made a yowling sound like a cat in heat. When she turned to look at him, he saw her dilated pupils were glassy with unshed tears. Martin caught her by surprise when he finished with two rapid-fire strikes on the fullest area of her buttocks. Brynne was gasping for breath when Gage bent down to put a straw to her lips. "Here, take a few sips."

She ignored him and sucked in a big gulp of water, so he squeezed the straw closed. "You can have a little more later."

"You're an ogre. I hate you," she said through gritted teeth.

"Careful, Tink. I warned you what the consequences are for a naughty mouth."

She glowered. "Then it's a pity you left that *thing* all the way down in your office, isn't it?"

His reaction was immediate and instinctual. "Mm. I have something just as good right here." With a wicked grin, he pulled her torn panties from his pocket and waved them in front of her. Brynne tried to shake her head no and pressed her lips closed but he took a handful of her hair and tugged her head back. When she gasped, he stuffed the material into her mouth.

"Spit that out and I will put something much more unforgiving in its place."

Shock was written all over her face, and he mentally put a win on the scoreboard. His erection came back with a vengeance. Somehow, she kept upping the game, and he was enjoying it so much more than he expected.

Unfortunately, the next man who walked up was the goddamned Russian. Garrick and Gage exchanged a look when he approached.

Gage broke the silence. "Another guest has the fourth spot on the list, Ivanov, so we will honor that."

He interrupted Gage. "Nyet. Tomas relinquished his place to me. He drank too much tonight and would not have passed the sobriety test."

It wouldn't surprise Gage if Dimitri either bribed him or got him drunk so he could take his place. He stalled for time. "I will need to gain her agreement for the substitution."

"Isn't she a submissive in your club, and subject to *your* decision on this?"

"We employ Tink as a waitress, not a sub. This is not part of our regular curriculum, so she must agree to continue."

Dimitri rolled his eyes and smirked. "Ladno. *Okay.*"

Gage leaned down and whispered into Brynne's ear. "Dimitri got on the list—do you consent to him taking a turn?"

She looked at him, seeking confirmation that it would be all right.

"I'll be right here. You raise two fingers or make three loud sounds in a row, and it stops."

She nodded her agreement.

He half hoped she would decline. Allowing Ivanov to have his way put Gage on edge.

Dimitri pointed to the black-and-white elk skin thumper on the rack. It was a specialized flogger with six braided leather strands, unique because of the evenly spaced knots, which ended with soft leather tassels. It delivered a thudding sensation, not a sting.

He handed over the flogger and stood next to Brynne so she could see him in her peripheral vision. Meanwhile, Garrick inconspicuously shifted closer.

Dimitri swung the flogger and let it hit his own thigh. The second time he hit harder, testing the impact, and nodded to himself.

Brynne was grinding the fabric in her mouth. She shut her eyes, preparing for another sensation. Gage had to admit, she seemed determined to make it through without surrendering.

Judging by the muted sound of the elk skin strands hitting her bottom and Brynne's murmur, the first strike was not very hard. Perhaps he was not familiar with this style of flogger, which was designed for longer punishment scenes. Dimitri raised his arm and just before impact, he flicked his wrist, causing a loud snap that was heard around the room. Brynne shuddered and whimpered loudly into the satin in her mouth. Dimitri repeated the action and struck her other vulnerable cheek, causing her to groan and jerk against the cuffs. The Russian moved closer and put his large hand on her flushed skin, lightly caressing the spot he had just punished. "Only two more, Devushka. I don't want to bruise your lush bottom—too much."

Gage clenched his fists, itching to remove the man's hand.

Dimitri took his time, while the audience looked on with bated breath. He struck her left hamstring hard—and followed it with one more on the right. The muffled squeals she made reverberated along Gage's cock, and he let out a sigh when it was over.

Dimitri handed the whip to him and nodded. "Spasibo." His mouth twisted in a fake smile, then he turned and started toward the group. They parted automatically to let him pass.

Michael Richmond was the last person on the list. He was a newer member of Dominus, but Gage's best friends and business partners knew him well and vouched for him. Aaron and Cole were longstanding members of Lucifer's Eden, the most exclusive BDSM clubs with locations in New York, Miami, and Houston. Michael had sponsored their memberships, and when he'd interviewed, Gage found out they had several mutual acquaintances in the scene, including one submissive Gage spent several months with before he moved back to London. He was fastidious in the way he dressed and carried himself, and when it came to bondage and discipline, he knew exactly what he was doing.

They shook hands, and Gage greeted him warmly. "Good to see you, Michael. I trust you will show Tink what happens when a good scotch is trifled with."

He laughed and winked. "It will be my pleasure to teach her a lesson she won't soon forget."

"Aye. And what were you thinking of using?"

Michael winked. "The cane would be my first choice."

If it were anyone else, he would have declined, but he'd seen Michael use the cane and knew he was precise and controlled. It was obvious Brynne wasn't traumatized by this experience. In fact, she may not have learned her lesson yet.

He nodded and handed the brown-haired man the quarter-inch rattan cane, then returned to his post beside the head of the bench. Gage knew that pacing and rhythm were crucial, and it took the body about five to six seconds to process the pain. If a Dom moved too fast, it would inhibit the pleasure that typically spread following the strike. Brynne would either love it or hate it.

Michael tested the spring in the rattan, ensuring it was to his satisfaction. Then he tested it on a nearby leather bench. The whistling sound and piercing *thwack* caused Brynne to flinch.

He positioned himself and took a practice swing, not unlike a baseball player before the first pitch. The cane stopped just short of her warmed flesh, and she rattled against the restraints.

The first stroke landed squarely across both rounded globes, and Michael held it there to let her skin absorb the sensation. Brynne reacted seconds later, her head jerking up in shock and coming up hard against the chain on her collar. Gage watched closely for her "stop" signals.

The second stroke landed less than twenty seconds later, and judging by the sound, it was slightly harder. Brynne screeched and squeezed her eyes shut. A few errant tears dripped to the floor.

Michael waited a little longer before landing the third, this one above the first—where a faint red line had appeared. He held it there and let the sting radiate. She sobbed, and the sound thrummed along Gage's senses, making him wish he was the one administering the punishment.

Brynne wriggled as much as the straps would allow and sniffed hard as she coped with the pain. Michael admired the marks and adjusted his stance. When he landed the last two strokes in rapid succession on her upper hamstrings, she lost it. A high-pitched wail pierced the air, and she shook in reaction. Gage reached down and pulled the soaked satin out of her mouth, and she drew in a deep breath and wept like a baby.

"Shhh, it's all over now, Red." He undid the collar, unbuckled all the cuffs, and deftly released the rest of the straps on the bench. She mumbled something he couldn't make out.

"What was that?" he said, handing her his handkerchief. She quickly wiped her eyes and blew her nose.

She sniffed, hiccupping a little, "I said, th-thank you, sir."

His mouth twitched. Garrick brought a blanket over, a knowing smile pasted on his face. Gage covered Brynne and carefully lifted her to stand, but she couldn't hold herself up. He picked her up in his arms, and she made a feeble protest.

"I've got you." Gage felt her hand grip his shirt as he made his way to the elevator.

When they entered his office, he flipped on the gas fireplace to warm up the room. She was looking up at him now, her eyelashes still wet, and little tracks of mascara staining her pale cheeks. He put her down carefully next to one of the large leather club chairs.

"I want you to kneel on the cushion and rest your arms on the back of the chair. I'm going to put some arnica gel and a cold compress on you." He waited for the inevitable protest, but it didn't come. Instead, he watched her position herself as instructed. She rested her forehead on her arms, hiding her face from him. Gage got the compress from the fridge and the ointment from the cabinet above. He drew the blanket off and lifted her skirt to reveal her punished flesh.

"Brace yourself. It will be cold, but you will feel better soon. This will also help prevent bruising." He squeezed a generous amount into his hands.

She gasped in shock when his hands touched her. "Christ, it's freezing."

"Aye, your skin is still very hot," he said, as he rubbed the cream into her skin. With herculean effort, he tried to remain unmoved by the sight, but it was futile. He couldn't deny the truth anymore. He wanted to fuck this little hellcat. So, the sooner she was gone from his club, the better.

He finished coating her cheeks and upper legs and then laid the cold compress across her backside. She pulled forward and groaned, "This is worse than the cane, for god's sake!"

He chuckled and she looked back at him, her eyes narrowed.

He brought over a cold bottle of Gatorade and a couple of ibuprofen. "Here." He handed her two pills, showing her the bottle. "Take two now and another two before bed."

"I'd rather have a gin and tonic."

He returned to sit at his desk, where he didn't have to see her tempting ass. "No. Alcohol is not a good idea. Your body needs time to recover."

She stuck her tongue out at him but swallowed the pills and gulped half the bottle of the sports drink.

Gage shook his head, picked up the phone, and called the kitchen. "George, could you whip me up a pepperoni pizza? Medium. Yes, please. My office. Thanks."

When Gage looked up, he found she'd laid her cheek on her hands and was snoring lightly. Up to this point, he had tried to ignore what was happening. The combination of her fire and vulnerability appealed to the Dom in him. Her soft voluptuous body and its tantalizing scents were constantly whispering to his cock and tripping all his circuits.

He carefully removed the compress and lifted her to the couch. She mumbled, but barely stirred when he laid her out on her stomach. He put the compress back on and covered her with the blanket.

He still didn't know if she was truly submissive or just willful and stubborn. There was no doubt it aroused her when he tied her down to the bench. Her body was humming in anticipation before the first strike. He wanted to ask Garrick or John what happened at the party and guessed it was an evening of firsts.

To distract himself, he checked his email and replied to a note from Cole, who was flying in for the fetish party. He had business in Ireland and would stop in London afterward. They hadn't seen each other since the Houston club opening ten months ago. His friend wanted to hear all about the mess with Sierra.

A knock at his door interrupted his thoughts. "Yes?"

"It's Garrick. Safe to come in?"

Gage opened the door, his face stern. "Of course, man. You know better than that."

Garrick grinned. "I wondered if she was showing you her appreciation for taking such good care of—"

Brynne let out a loud snore followed by a moan. Garrick chuckled and looked at Gage.

"She's a special little lady. Will you be seeing her home?"

"No," he said, a bit too abruptly. "I've ordered some food. I'll put her in a taxi once she's rested and eaten. Aren't you the one who said she's a tough cookie?"

Garrick snorted. "I did, but she's just had her first public scene and it was a doozy."

Gage scowled at him, annoyed that his judgment was being questioned. "I've got this, G. Shouldn't you be back up on the floor? The club is busy—and I'm sure our guests need your attention."

He nodded. "Sure, boss. I'll catch you later."

Gage sat back down at his desk when another knock sounded. "What?" he barked.

"It's Ronnie, sir. I have your pizza."

"Come in, Ronnie."

The waiter came in and couldn't help but notice the lady snoozing on his couch. He paused a moment too long.

"I'm over here." Gage's tone was imperious, and Ronnie hurried over and handed him the tray. "That will be all."

"Yes, sir." He scooted out the door.

The food smelled divine, and his stomach reminded him of how famished he was. After devouring two pieces, Gage took a plate over to the coffee table and tried to rouse sleeping beauty.

"Hey Red. Wake up, the pizza is here."

She moaned and licked her lips, but her eyes remained shut. He lifted the blanket and removed the now-thawed ice packet, and that jolted her awake. "Ow, what the? Where am I?"

"You are in my office, snoring on my couch. Now, sit up carefully and eat something." He tried to sound less like a dick than usual. Didn't she realize how hard that was?

"Oh. God, that smells divine." She wrapped the blanket around her arms and swung her legs off the couch, cringing as she sat up. "Ooh wow, that smarts!" Taking the plate eagerly, she said, "Thank you for this. You didn't have to."

He ran a hand through his hair. "You are my responsibility when you are in my club. Aftercare is as important as your safety during a scene."

"Okay," she said, covering her mouth as she chewed a big bite.

When she had polished off the entire piece, she looked at him playfully. "So, how did I do? Bet you thought I would cry uncle after the first five strokes."

"I know you have a stubborn streak a mile wide, and you were out to prove something. I'm just not sure what it was."

Her smile faded, and he felt like a heel.

"I wanted the experience. And yes, I guess I wanted to prove I could handle anything you could dish out."

His eyes narrowed. "There you'd be mistaken, Brynne. You endured a carefully orchestrated spanking, but you wouldn't last a day as my submissive."

Her chin tilted up, and she looked poised to argue, but she stopped herself.

He rose to leave the office. "Finish your pizza, and when you're ready, I'll take you home."

11

A Little Defiance & Dimitri's Pursuit

*Y*ou *wouldn't last a day as my submissive.*

"What the fuck ever. I don't need a babysitter or ride home. I won't allow him to ruin the most amazing night of my life."

Brynne stood up and almost tipped over. Her tights were still down at her knees. She hurried to pull them up and gasped as the material abraded her tender skin.

Ignoring the discomfort, she grabbed a slice of pizza and the Gatorade and rushed to get changed. She scarfed down the other piece and almost choked when she glimpsed herself in the mirror. Raccoon eyes stared back. Her face was pale, and her lips bare of any color. There was no time to repair the damage. She needed to get the fuck out of there.

As the taxi pulled away, the impact of the night hit her. She started giggling uncontrollably, which might have given way to tears, except she noticed the driver kept checking his rear view mirror. He thought she was daft. Her cell phone started buzzing the moment she turned it on. Jared had sent three messages, which she ignored. He would press her for details, but the conversation would have to wait until she'd processed everything. Her phone buzzed again, and it was a number she didn't recognize.

Unknown: *Where the hell are you?*

Brynne: *Who is this?*

Unknown: *Your boss. Where are you?*

Brynne: *In a taxi. Thanks for the pizza.*

Unknown: *I said I would take you home.*

Brynne: *Not necessary. I'm good. Thanks for the enlightening demonstration and the aftercare. Much appreciated. Good night, Boss.*

Unknown: *This conversation is not over.*

Brynne: *There isn't anything else to say. I learned my lesson. You should be very pleased.*

Unknown: *I am not pleased. You disregarded my direction. Again.*

Brynne: *I was only thinking of you—the club needs you more than I do.*

Unknown: *You don't decide what I need.*

Brynne: *OK, true. But in my vulnerable state, I might have tried to seduce you. It's best that I saved us both from that embarrassment.*

Unknown: *Good submissives don't seduce. They do as they are told.*

Brynne: *Whoever said I was good?*

It was easy to be cheeky when he wasn't in the same room. She could imagine his shock when he found her gone. God help her, she loved provoking him. Pushing his buttons was the only way to get him to drop his resting dick face and reveal some of his true self.

When the taxi driver pulled up to her flat, he asked if she was okay. She laughed and assured him that life was grand. Once inside, she made herself a tea and ran a bath with Epsom salts. She sank into the hot water and hissed at the sting. She would be tender for a few days, but it was worth it.

Brynne closed her eyes and smiled, feeling incredibly proud of herself. She had not only witnessed a private scene that shocked her to her core, but also survived a public spanking without using her safe word! Gage wasn't willing to admit she was tough, but it didn't matter. She had endured it and barely cried...well, not until the white-hot sting of the cane. That searing pain shocked her, but it soon gave way to a warmth that radiated straight to her core. The key to letting go was seeing Gage right beside her and knowing she was safe. Even if he didn't like her, he took his duty seriously and wouldn't allow any harm to come to her.

Reading about it or seeing it happen to someone else would never have given her the insight she now possessed. Being strapped down and helpless was so erotic. Those same tantalizing sensations assailed her during the scene with Mistress Patricia. She felt ashamed of these dark and disturbing desires. But that didn't stop her from wanting to explore more. He'd opened a Pandora's box of deviant thoughts, and there was no way to lock them back up. Maybe she needed someone to show her because she wanted to know everything.

She reached for her new vibrator. The clerk promised Mr. Boss was waterproof, and she hoped so because it had a job to do.

Three exhilarating orgasms later, Brynne was certain she had exorcised Gage. For the moment. She donned her pink flannel nightdress, crawled under the covers, and fell immediately to sleep.

The jarring ring of her cell phone woke her the next morning. It wasn't on the bedside table, so where did she leave it? She stumbled bleary-eyed into the bathroom to pee and found it on the edge of the sink. The missed call from Aunt Josie brought on a wave of guilt. It had been more than a week since they last spoke. Brynne made it a point to call her every three or four days. She was from the era of handwritten cards and the telephone, so she hated email and texting. Even after Brynne set up her iPhone so they could FaceTime, she refused to turn the thing on, insisting the cell signal on Skye was too weak. She was fiercely independent and stubborn, but Brynne admired that more than anyone.

She turned the thermostat up and jumped under the covers to call her back.

"Helloo!"

"Auntie Josie, it's me Brynne. How are you?"

"Brynnie, my love, it's so good to hear your voice! I've missed you."

"Me too! I'm sorry I didn't call this week. I took a second job in the evenings and I'm finally getting noticed at the paper for more than finding typos."

"That's wonderful, darling. But a second job? If you need money, you only have to ask."

"It isn't for the money, Auntie, it's actually for research." She paused and took a deep breath. "You know how devastated I was when your agent told me the book just wasn't realistic enough."

"Yes, but I was rejected many times before someone took a chance on me. You are a talented writer, and I know you won't give up on your dream."

Brynne smiled, feeling buoyed by her aunt's unyielding belief in her. "True, I'm not giving up, but I figured out a way to understand my subject matter a little better."

"Oh, that sounds intriguing, do tell!"

Brynne giggled, happy to hear a liveliness in her voice that had been missing the last few times they spoke. She told her a little about Gage, the tall, dark, and disagreeable bastard who owned the club. "I'm getting quite an education, Auntie. I got to witness a woman get spanked in front of a crowd."

Josie whistled into the phone. "Too bad it wasn't you in the hot seat! That would give you fuel for the book!"

"Yes, well, if I get on the bad side of the boss, it just might be me one of these days."

They talked for a while until Brynne could sense she was getting tired. Josie assured her that everything was good, and she wanted for nothing. A housekeeper visited every week and Declan, one of her many old flames, had gourmet meals delivered to her almost every night of the week when he wasn't there cooking them himself. She told Brynne not to worry—she was being pampered. The only thing she complained about was not being able to drive her '66 MGB Roadster. The doctor hadn't cleared her to drive the stick shift since she broke her hip last fall. Thankfully, she'd recovered from the surgery, and things were finally getting back to normal.

Maybe Brynne could take a break from work and visit. She hung up and went to brew a pot of coffee. She didn't feel human without a few cups in her. A quick glance in the fridge confirmed her suspicions. Half a loaf of bread, one old egg and some coffee creamer.

While toast and marmalade would sustain her, she needed to get to the market soon.

Jared had texted two more times, demanding to know that she was okay. She assured him she and her "sorry ass" were fine—albeit a bit tender—and that her night had been unbelievable and eye-opening. She promised to call him later.

After breakfast, she curled up on the couch and wrote her feelings about the night in her journal. Then she spent the balance of her afternoon editing her manuscript and completely lost track of time. If only she could call in sick and spend the afternoon writing.

Forget it. The ornery master of the club would read that as weakness.

Brynne arrived ten minutes late, winded from running from the train. She got changed, freshened up her hair and face, and ran up the steps to the lounge. Thank goodness Sunday was traditionally slow, and Bettie had three tables well under control. They met at the side station.

"Hi Tink, how did your night go? I overheard some fellas complimenting you on how well you did—and the cuteness of your butt!"

Brynne blushed. "I did okay, I guess. Until the last guy used the cane. That was insane!"

"It can be… But Mr. Richmond is a master in every sense of the word!" Her eyes went dreamy, and she smiled wistfully. "I have a bit of a crush on him."

"I never saw his face. Is he handsome?"

"A dreamboat. He looks like a young Tom Berenger."

"Who?"

Bettie's mouth dropped open. "Haven't you seen the movie *Someone to Watch Over Me*?"

"No, I don't think so. When did it come out?"

"Shit, probably before you were born. Late eighties."

She laughed. "I'll see if I can find it on Netflix."

"I think you'll love it. Oh, I almost forgot. I have some tips from last night's party for you." Bettie dug into her bra and peeled off £275.

Brynne shook her head, shocked. "You did all the work to set that up. I only covered it for a short while. That's too much!"

"No arguing. They were extremely generous, and this is your share." She pushed the money into her hand.

The dark-haired beauty wouldn't take no for an answer, so Brynne gave in. "Okay, thank you. I appreciate it. It got me out of Dimitri's sights."

"Yeah, that man has it bad for you."

"Speak of the devil," Brynne whispered, looking over Bettie's shoulder. *Dammit, why couldn't he have drinks somewhere else?*

He and a dubious-looking character sat down at his corner table. The other guy was oversized in every respect, his massive neck stretching the wool of the black turtleneck he wore under a black leather peacoat. Dimitri wore a dark-gray pinstriped suit that fit him to a T. Brynne took a deep breath and headed over.

"Good evening, gentlemen. May I bring you something from the bar?"

He ignored her question. "How are you feeling after your punishment, Kiska?"

"Fine, thank you. Just a little sore." Brynne hoped he would leave it at that.

"Good." He sat back and loosened his tie, his eyes never leaving hers. "Did you like being punished in front of everyone?"

Brynne swallowed a gasp. "No. I, no, it was embarrassing." Heat crept up her neck.

"I think you are lying, Devushka. I think you enjoyed being the center of attention."

She shook her head but couldn't form a reply.

"I could tell by the sounds you were making, and the air was ripe with your sweet scent."

Brynne's teeth ground together. She lifted her chin, then asked again, "What would you like to drink?"

The corners of his mouth curled in a way that made her shiver. "I would like to lap at the honey between your legs."

She cut him off, stamping her foot. "That is quite enough, Mr. Ivanov. If you continue to speak to me that way, I will not serve you."

"Oh, so fiery." He smiled fully now, enjoying her anger. "Da, Malishka. I will stop…because I want to enjoy your company tonight." He looked mildly chastened. "I will start with the best scotch you have, straight up. My friend will have a double Stolichnaya on ice. And bring the wine list. Spasibo. *Please.*"

She nodded curtly and turned for the bar. Bill could see they'd agitated her, but she waved him off and relayed the order. When he confirmed the Macallan 1948 was the best scotch in the club, she punched it in. The man had more money than sense.

He got the drinks ready and said, "Never let them see you sweat, Tink."

Bill was right. Ivanov was enjoying her discomfort.

Garrick arrived and asked her how it was going.

"He's trying to get under my skin, but it's nothing I can't handle."

"All eyes are on him, so you have nothing to worry about."

How could she explain it wasn't a physical threat that worried her? It was his Hannibal Lecter-style questioning. No one could protect her from that.

Garrick glanced over her shoulder in their direction. "They are ready to order. You just let Bill know if he gets out of line."

"Sure. Thanks, Garrick." She headed back to the table.

"Have you decided what you want for the main course?"

Dimitri stopped studying the menu and looked up at her. "I'm looking for a new submissive. Are you available, kitten?"

She choked back a laugh. "No. I am spoken for."

His eyes narrowed. "Really?" His lips compressed into a hard line. "Has he collared you yet?"

The game is on. "No, *she* hasn't yet. Our relationship is quite new."

"She? You are with a woman?" he said, skepticism blazing from his eyes.

"Yes. Not that it's any of your business."

Dimitri scoffed, and his friend cleared his throat loudly.

"What would you like to order?"

He continued to watch her, his hand rubbing the stubble on his square chin. "I'll have the escargot, and my comrade will have the French onion soup."

"Certainly."

"I will choose the wine when you come back." The other man spoke, and Dimitri turned away, effectively dismissing her. She wished she could understand Russian.

Gage was nowhere to be seen, and she was a little disappointed. After her cheeky text messages, he was probably ignoring her. Which was what she wanted, right? He couldn't be the one to show her the ropes. Hell, neither could Dimitri. That dude wanted ownership. So where did that leave her? All revved up with no place to go.

When Brynne got to the table with their appetizers, Dimitri rose with the wine list and edged close to her. His big body dwarfed hers and she fought to hold her ground as he invaded her personal space.

He pointed to a line on the menu. "I want a bottle of this." She saw the price and her eyes almost popped out of her head. He continued, unfazed. "We will both have the sixteen-ounce ribeye, medium rare. You can choose the sides."

Nervous to tell him no, Brynne cleared her throat. "Uh, I must confirm I can serve those items. They are on the dining room menu. I'll check on that right away."

"Da." His blue eyes glittered. "I expect you can make that happen."

Brynne hurried over to Bill. "He wants the '88 Richebourg Grand Cru and steaks off the main dining room menu. Can we do that?"

He shook his head, his mouth a hard line. "That bastard always likes to push the envelope. Punch it in and then go find Gage or Garrick to approve it. I'll hunt down that bottle."

"Okay, got it." Off she went.

Garrick wasn't in his office, so she reluctantly knocked on Gage's door.

"Yes?"

"It's Brynne, I mean Tink. May I come in?"

The door opened, and she was momentarily speechless at the sight of him. He wore a snug-fitting black cashmere sweater and faded blue jeans that were molded to his muscular thighs.

"Have you come to finish the conversation you started last night?"

"Um, no, not now. I need your approval for Dimitri, who wants steaks off the dining room menu. And he ordered a very expensive bottle of wine too. Bill said I should check with you."

"He's always testing my limits."

"That's what Bill said," she said, wringing her hands.

"That's fine. I'll let it go this time. Is he behaving himself otherwise?"

"Not exactly. He's just trying to make me uncomfortable, but I can handle it."

"Don't let your guard down."

"I won't. Gotta go!"

She was halfway through the door when she heard him say, "Don't think I've forgotten your disobedience or those brazen texts."

Her stomach fluttered as she took the stairs two at a time.

Bill was wiping down the rare bottle and had retrieved a decanter. He followed Brynne to the table and presented it to Dimitri, who nodded his approval. She was glad it was him handling the exceptionally rare Pinot Noir. The consequences of spilling a four-thousand-pound bottle of wine didn't bear thinking about.

The young sous chef had already plated the meals and blew her a kiss when she picked them up. She thanked him profusely and hurried to the elevator.

After she put his plate down, Dimitri grabbed her wrist. "I find it hard to believe a woman fully satisfies you."

Brynne started, "She is very special."

"If you were mine, you wouldn't have to work another day. I would take care of you. You could live in the lap of luxury, like a pampered pet."

"That's very sweet, but I'm not interested in being a *pet*."

"If you wanted a woman, one would be provided for our mutual enjoyment."

Her face suffused with heat, and she tried to pull her wrist free. "Your food is getting cold, Mr. Ivanov."

He reluctantly let her go and she escaped to the back for some water. His approach was so intimidating, it made her pulse race with fear and, if she was honest, a bit of excitement, too.

Bettie interrupted her daydreams when she came back to complain about how slow it was. "Lucky for you, Tink, you landed a whale tonight. He's on his way to spending a few thousand."

"That whale is throwing all that money away on wine—it would pay my rent for three months."

"I think he's letting you know he could just as easily spend that

kind of cash on you. I admit, he is sexy in a scary mafia kind of way."
Bettie giggled.

"Yeah, but when he tires of you, you disappear into the
English Channel."

They laughed and Bill poked his head in the back. "Ladies, back
to work. Bettie, you have a new table, and Ivanov is looking for you,
Tink. Get going."

They both hurried out to the lounge. Brynne reached the table
and asked, "Is everything to your liking, Mr. Ivanov?"

"The food is fine. You've been neglecting your duties. My wine
needs topping up." His voice had an icy edge to it.

"Of course, my apologies." Brynne carefully lifted the decanter
and refilled his glass. She looked at the other guy, and he nodded, his
glare making her nervous. She filled the bald man's glass and put the
decanter down. "May I get you anything else?"

"Da. You may answer another question for me."

Brynne sighed and gritted her teeth. "What if I don't feel obliged
to answer your questions?"

"What if I pay you to answer them?"

"That isn't appropriate or allowed." As far as she remembered,
that wasn't in the rulebook, but it sounded legit.

His head tilted to one side, and he looked her over. "I will
conceal it in your tip, so no one will have to know."

She pinched the bridge of her nose. "I don't think that's a good
idea. Are you trying to make me uncomfortable?"

A rumble came from his throat. "Da." He chuckled wickedly. "I'd
like that. In fact, I can think of many *uncomfortable* positions for you,
Kiska." The tone of his voice deepened. "I've imagined tying your
beautiful body to my bed, spreading you open to be smacked and
licked and fucked within an inch of your life."

Brynne shivered. If she heard those words from a different man, one she trusted, they would be music to her ears. But from Dimitri, they were just unnerving. "Mr. Ivanov, I am sorry, but I am not interested. I'm happy in my relationship."

"It's a pity you are afraid of what we could have together. I could fulfill your dark fantasies—in a way that I am sure your *mistress* cannot."

"My mistress knows what I need. Now, please, if you're finished, I'll take these plates."

"You can run, little kitten, but I see the pulse hammering at your throat, and the way your eyes have gone dark."

"Curiosity won't kill this cat," she fumed.

He laughed. "I knew you were curious. At least you admit that."

He was hoping she would lose her cool and give them another reason to punish her. After a few calming breaths, she went back with the dessert menus. He motioned for her to top up his glass by pointing his finger imperiously at the carafe. He was watching her for a reaction, but she remained calm and managed the task without dumping the wine over his head.

"We have a wonderful tiramisu tonight. Would you or your *friend* like to try that?" she asked sweetly.

He sat back and his eyes burned with impatience. "Nyet. I only want one thing for dessert, but you are denying me that."

She looked down at the floor demurely. "Sorry to disappoint you."

"If only I believed you meant that, Pchelka."

"What does that word mean?" she asked, trying to ease his darkening mood.

"It means *little bee*—because you sting me with your words." He handed her the menu and poured the last of the wine into his glass. "I've had enough of this game; I'll take the check now."

"Of course." She expelled the breath she had been holding and scurried to the bar to close out the order and print the check.

Ten minutes later, he was gone. He paid with a black American Express and left her a £1,500 tip. She should be thrilled, except it felt like dirty money.

Bettie was happy to stay and close so Brynne could head out. She returned from her break with a message from Gage, and Brynne rolled her eyes. Sparring with him was the last thing she needed.

She changed into her street clothes before going to his office. That should give him a clue that she was in a hurry. The door was ajar, and she poked her head in. What a stroke of luck—he wasn't there! She backed up to leave and collided with a tall, warm brick wall.

"Going somewhere, Red?"

"I was looking for you. But you, uh, weren't there."

Up went the eyebrows, and her cheeks heated.

"Please…" He pointed to his office and her shoulders drooped in defeat as she preceded him into the room. "Have a seat. We have a conversation to finish."

Brynne sat in one of the club chairs and stared at her hands.

Gage made a sound between a growl and a bark to get her attention. He was holding a drink out to her.

"Hendricks and tonic is your chosen poison, if I recall?"

Brynne nodded and took the drink from him, her eyes wide. She watched him fold his tall, lean frame onto the couch.

"How did it go with Ivanov tonight? Did he behave?"

"No!" she snapped. "He tormented me the entire time. Asking me all kinds of personal questions and he told me in gory detail what he would like to do to me!"

His lips turned white, his jaw rigid. "Did he try to touch you?"

"No, but his words were…" She trailed off.

"His words were what?" Gage's voice was like sandpaper across her nerves.

Brynne took a swig of her drink before answering. "Too much. They were just too much."

Gage stared at her. "I will speak to him."

"It's fine. I can handle it. I was just tired today." Brynne leaned back and sighed. "I would rather not have him thinking he got under my skin." She considered telling Gage about the tip, but thought better of it.

"Fine, but if he continues, I want to know about it."

"Fine," she huffed out.

"Would you care to tell me why you left yesterday when I told you I would see you home?"

Brynne took a fortifying gulp of her drink to buy herself a minute. He sat back and swirled his scotch like he had all the time in the world.

"I was feeling very off kilter and vulnerable." She took another sip.

"Go on."

"I didn't want to inconvenience you. I don't imagine you drive staff home, even after an intense scene."

He drew his finger over the rim of his glass. "This situation was quite different." His voice sharpened. "You are not one of our regular subs. I'd wager you've never experienced a scene like that before. You were under my care; therefore, it was my duty to escort you home."

"I was fine. Especially after the pizza…and the catnap."

"Are you sure there isn't more to it?"

He will not let this go. Resigned, she sank back into the cocoon of the chair. "Upstairs, in the private party, it was enlightening and bloody erotic. Then the whole spanking thing intensified those feelings."

"What happened at the party?" His voice was a low, his accent more pronounced.

"Oh, you know, just the erotic torture of two beautiful slaves, and the blow job of the century, delivered by my best friend. Who doesn't have any idea that I witnessed it!"

Gage's eyes widened. "Ooch."

Before he could say anything, she rushed on. Her voice went up an octave or two. "Since you seem hellbent on getting me to bare my goddamned soul, I'll tell you. I left because I might…I *would have* begged you to fuck me."

His brow furrowed, and he shook his head. "I wouldn't have allowed that to happen."

"No, of course you wouldn't!" She let out a strangled-sounding laugh. "So, I saved you from having to spurn my advances, and saved myself from a mortifying rejection." She put her empty glass on the table and stood. "I think that's enough therapy for today, doc. Now, if you don't mind, I need to get home. Tomorrow is a workday."

Gage went to stand, but she put her hand up, barely holding on to her composure.

"No, please don't."

She dashed out of the club without looking back. No taxis waited in the lane, so she headed for the subway. The walk would do her good and the streets were filled with people coming out of the theaters. Along the way, she avoided looking at the candlelit tables and couples making googly eyes at each other. It only made her cynical about the fake displays of affection.

Maybe she should have kept her mouth shut. Blurting out her thoughts usually got her a shocked but honest reaction. *You got your answer, Bree.* He made it crystal clear that even if he was interested, he wouldn't pursue it.

Brynne kept her gaze ahead, dodging all the people hurrying in the opposite direction. A car horn blasted right behind her, and she nearly jumped out of her skin. She noticed a flashy Range Rover with blacked-out windows and fancy black and red rims with a taxicab riding his back bumper. It was driving slowly; in fact, the vehicle was keeping pace with her. The taxi flew around them and honked again as it passed. As she approached the entrance to the underground, Brynne had an odd sense of unease. Her self-defense instructor taught her to trust her spidey senses and pay attention to her surroundings.

She considered stopping in the brightly lit pharmacy, but that felt silly. As she reached the subway entrance, Brynne abruptly turned and raced down the steps. She scanned her pass and flew through the turnstiles without looking back. The train pulled into the station a minute later and she tucked herself into a corner behind a couple of tall guys with backpacks. The balance of the trip home was uneventful, and she dismissed the experience as paranoia and exhaustion.

12

Blue Monday

Luckily, Jared was on assignment in Bristol for the day, so she wouldn't have to face him and his questions about Saturday night.

Brynne slept badly and left the house in a foul mood with an empty stomach. The line at her coffee shop was long, but she couldn't face the day without an Americano and a warm scone.

Monday passed in a blur. She reviewed four lengthy articles, which had to be submitted before the end of the day. At four forty-five, she finished and sent them to Nigel. Thank god Margaret was out today, so she didn't have to deal with her.

Tonight, she would have some much-needed time for herself. She had to get groceries, make a decent meal, and work on her manuscript. A perfect, if somewhat boring, night at home.

After heating a pre-made shepherd's pie, she opened a bottle of wine then sat at her computer. She had some juicy ideas to add to her book that would turn up the heat for her female character. The villain would now drive a tricked-out Range Rover with tinted windows.

Her phone dinged.

Jared:	Hey Bree. Finally headed home. Long effing day. How are you?
Brynne:	Good. Me too. I'm wiped but trying to do some editing.
Jared:	I can't wait to hear about Saturday. Are you working tomorrow night?
Brynne:	No, I'm on the schedule for Thursday. You?
Jared:	I'm on Wed and Sat for the big party. Fetish night will give you plenty of juicy stuff for your story.
Brynne:	I'm nervous. Haven't seen the outfit yet… :-o
Jared:	You'll look amazing, don't worry. Let's have dinner tomorrow. I'm in the mood for Mexican.
Brynne:	Sounds good. I'll meet you there after work.

Brynne downed half a plate of nachos and a large margarita while waiting for Jared to arrive. She sat in their favorite booth, stealing glances at the door every few minutes and wondered how the hell she was going to tell him what she saw at the club. As the waitress delivered her second cocktail and his mojito, he came through the front door.

They hugged, and he took the seat opposite. He raised his glass and looked at the desecrated plate. "Jesus, girl! When did you get here?"

"I've been here about half an hour. You can have the rest. Do you want to split some chicken quesadillas?"

"That sounds good!" Leaning close, he whispered, "Now, tell me everything!"

Brynne waved their server down and ordered their meal, then took a deep breath and told him about the bad girl collar and cuffs and Gage's threat to make her wear a gag. She rushed through the altercation with Dimitri, almost beating up the handsy customer. Then, skipping the entire dinner party, she went straight to the spanking scene on the third floor.

Her face heated. "I should have hated being objectified, but I didn't. Was it wrong to bask in their admiration of my bare butt?"

His eyes twinkled. "Not at all, babe. I know how amazing it can be—and impossible to describe to someone how it feels to be an erotic object d'art."

"To be honest, I felt more attractive than I have in a long time. I've always been self-conscious about the size of my butt and thighs, but I overheard people admiring them." She shook her head and shrugged. "My self-esteem got a boost, and that calmed my nerves."

Jared tucked into the remaining nachos, his eyes not leaving hers. "Go on."

"So, there I was, my ass on display, only a thong covering my hoo-ha. The prick took his sweet time strapping me down so I could barely move. And…" Brynne looked down and fiddled with her straw. "I loved it as much as that first time with Mistress Patricia. It was liberating to be restrained. Somehow, it freed me to let go and enjoy. I could have ended it any time, but that never crossed my mind. Besides, not a chance was I going to let that arrogant bastard win."

He chuckled. "He is testing you—and seeing what you're made of. How many guests signed up?"

"There were five altogether. Oh, and Dimitri stole someone's place. He told them the guy had had too much to drink and gave him his spot. Gage asked me if it was okay first. He wasn't letting him get away with it."

"And you agreed?" Jared's eyes widened.

"Hell yes! I don't want either of them to think I'm a wimp. Especially Gage. And I can't say for sure, but I think he was a bit impressed."

Their food arrived, and she was glad to take a breather from the story. Those erotic memories were making her warm and twitchy all over.

He wasn't about to let up. "What did they use on you? Have you got bruises?"

"Yeah, I have some bruises, but it wasn't as bad as I thought it would be. I don't know what anyone used. Gage chose each one himself, and they all felt very different. Until the last dude on the list came up. He asked to use a cane."

"What?" Jared's brows flew up. "Are you serious?"

"Yup. Is that a big deal?" It sure as hell felt like a big deal. The memories were still vivid.

"Uh yeah, it is. It's the hardest thing to take. Some people say there's worse, but I haven't experienced it."

"Gage knows him, and I heard he's a pro with the cane…if there is such a thing. Anyway, he lit my ass on fire. The pain was intense, and I lost it. Started bawling like a baby."

She remembered the tears of release. The anxiety, the shock, and the arousal had gushed out of her like a broken fire hydrant. She felt full and empty, hot and cold, strangely safe and a little afraid.

Jared leaned forward and grabbed her hand. "Bree, I wish I could have been there. You should be so proud of yourself!"

She nodded. "I am. Could have done without losing my shit, though."

"Sometimes that's exactly what you need. That's the ultimate release a Dom can give you. And he knows he brought you there." He wrinkled his nose. "Well, he watched while others did it. But I bet he wished he'd been the one delivering the blows."

"You think so?" She played with the stem of her glass, her mouth a little downturned. "I wished it was him, too."

Brynne shared how he carried her down to his office and put the chilled ointment on her tender bottom and made her drink Gatorade. "Somehow, I fell asleep. When I woke up, I was lying on his couch, and he was looming over me."

"Well, I'm glad he took care of you after that scene. Not everyone is that thoughtful, believe me."

"I know. But I just couldn't stick around. I was conflicted." She paused. Her hands flew to her temples. "I wanted him, and I hated him. Does that make sense?"

Jared smiled, his eyes drifting off for a moment. "Completely."

"So, when he left his office, I grabbed my stuff and ran out of there."

"Oh boy."

"Yeah." She giggled. "Look, he was planning on driving me home, J. I couldn't risk it. I would have…I could have jumped his bones and he probably would have fired me right after that."

"Maybe. Then again, you might have had the experience of a lifetime!"

"*You* are the one who told me to steer clear of him. He's out of my league, and that hasn't changed."

"I guess, but the *situation* has changed, Bree."

"You think so? He was pretty pissed that I left. He texted me."

"Lemme see!"

Brynne fumbled to unlock her phone and searched for the exchange, while he tapped the table impatiently.

She handed it over and gulped the balance of her second

margarita with a loud slurp. Jared shushed her as he read the messages. While he focused on the screen, she grabbed a swig of his drink.

He looked up from the phone, eyes wide and glowing. "Oh my, girl. I think you've intrigued him."

Brynne rested her chin in her hands and sighed. "That makes two of us." Then she sat up suddenly and almost knocked over her water glass. "That's not the best part. After my Sunday shift, he cornered me and demanded to know why I took off."

"So, what did you say?"

"I told him the truth…that I would have begged him to take me to bed."

"Holy hell."

"Look, it was the best way to get him to back off. And I think it worked. He said he wouldn't have allowed it to happen, and blah blah blah."

"You're playing with fire, Bree. You know that, right?"

Jared asked their server for the check and a to-go box.

"Hey, I wanted another drink."

He shook his head at her and then nodded at the girl. "Just the check." When she left, he added, "I'm gonna take you home. You are toast. You can tell me about the rest on the way."

They split the bill, and he led her outside to the taxi stand. Brynne was tipsy, but she needed liquid courage to ask Jared about his night.

On the ride to her flat, she filled him in on Dimitri's full court press. "I lied and said I was in a relationship." She paused for effect. "With a woman."

Jared snorted. "And you think he believed you?"

"Doesn't matter. It was the only way to make him back off. Fuck, I might have to produce Mistress Patricia if he doesn't stop."

They arrived at her place, and Jared paid for the taxi. Once inside, she plopped down on her couch and kicked off her shoes. She put her legs on his lap when he joined her.

"Now, it's your turn, J. How was your night?"

Jared looked everywhere but at Brynne. "It was uneventful compared to yours. I would have loved to witness your spanking, but I was working a private party upstairs."

"What goes on in those rooms?" she asked innocently. *Come on J, spill your guts so I don't have to ask!*

He shifted in his seat and pushed his hair back nervously. "Bree, you know I can't really tell you that. Not until they clear you to work up there."

"Right, I get it—I wouldn't want you to breach the NDA." She pretended it didn't bother her.

"I'm sure they will let you serve a party sometime soon. But listen, I am exhausted, and we both have to work tomorrow, so I'm off."

He shifted her legs off his lap and stood. She cursed her weakness; there was no way to bring it up. Not tonight.

She walked him to the door, and they hugged. He grinned. "You're swimming in the deep end now and I can't wait to read the revised draft of the book!"

Brynne chuckled. "True. So much juicy material, and I've only been there two weeks!"

She locked up her front door and rested her head on the worn wood, lamenting her lack of courage. She didn't bring up the party, and he didn't volunteer anything either. So, neither of them was ready to talk about it.

13

Turning up the Heat

Gage had been to the lounge twice already, checking on the plans for Saturday's fetish night. The Arabian harem theme had been Garrick's brainchild and the members he met in the dining room were talking excitedly about it. Members could dress up in Middle Eastern garb, and some planned to don the traditional white robes and keffiyeh headdresses. All the subs, whether they were part of the extended team or accompanied by a member, would be fully dressed while in the public areas, but once in a private room, their clothing became optional. Sonya was putting the finishing touches on the harem uniforms, and she would deliver them tomorrow. He opened the list on his computer to double-check what each of them would be wearing. He told himself it was purely to ensure nothing was missing.

Bettie would wear burgundy and gold, Melinda's outfit was royal blue and silver, and Brynne would be in deep purple with shimmering gold accents. He had Sonya create a second one in sage green for Tink, but the deep shade of violet won out. Maybe he had gotten carried away, but as an added adornment, he had also ordered special jeweled metal cuffs for their arms and wrists.

Gage sat back in his chair and closed his eyes. Why did he keep picturing a gorgeous and defiant redheaded slave girl, brought to kneel before him? The imagery in his mind's eye was vivid. And alluring. And a problem.

A knock at his door jolted Gage out of his daydream. He pulled his chair forward to conceal his tented pants.

"Aye?"

"It's Garrick. I have the menus for you to review."

His club manager knew not to walk in unannounced and he was glad to have a minute to compose himself. "Come in."

Gage feigned interest in the menu and gave Garrick the nod. "Looks good, man. Food fit for a sheik."

Garrick grinned. "Right. We have an array of choices from Persia, Lebanon, Armenia, Arabia, and Turkey. Servers will pass around the appetizers, then we will set the buffet up around eight. The key is to keep everyone well fed, so no one gets too smashed."

"Agreed. Sounds like you've got everything covered."

"That we do." Garrick nodded. "I've also hired extra security—four new guys will come in for training tomorrow."

"Good. We'll need to keep a close eye on Brynne and Dimitri."

"Speaking of our rebellious little redhead, I see she's not here until Thursday. It's been rather boring around here. Wouldn't you agree?"

Garrick was goading him, and he refused to play. "I hadn't noticed."

His friend snorted loudly, unable to conceal his amusement.

Gage glared at the big man, whose shoulders shook with laughter.

"Don't you have somewhere to be?"

"Aye, that I do, boss. Cheerio."

Alone at last, Gage went to lock his door and poured himself a scotch. He told himself he didn't miss her, he just enjoyed sparring with her. If he had taken her home, what would have happened? Would his willpower have remained steadfast against the temptation? He wasn't sure. There was something fresh and innocent about her one minute, and willful and fiery the next. She was a contradiction. A siren and a virgin. Which one was real?

It was difficult to conceal his shock when she boldly admitted her desire to invite him to bed her. In his experience, women played games. One minute they flirted, and the next they played hard to get. If they said what they wanted, there was always an agenda.

She would not play him for a fool. One way or another, he would find out what she was up to.

Gage closed the party files and tackled his Venture Capital email inbox. His assistant had sent him four messages, and the last one was rather terse. Fiona didn't like being ignored and told him so. He realized his preoccupation with the club was adversely affecting his team in Edinburgh. He had a strong COO to handle the day to day, but large acquisitions needed his explicit approval. She was asking for his signature on several documents related to land purchases, so he fired off a reply and told her he would review all of them before tomorrow. When his phone buzzed, he sighed audibly. *No rest for the wicked.*

"Hello, Mother."

"Darling, why don't you sound happy to hear from me? Never mind, don't answer that. Tell me when you're coming back to Edinburgh. Haven't you had enough of London and that sordid club?"

"No Mother, I haven't. I can't leave the business right now."

He heard her huff on the other end of the phone. "It's time you found a nice girl and settled down. I just wish you hadn't given up on Sierra. She was good for you."

"Mother, I have no intention of rehashing this with you. It's over with Sierra. She was not right for me. The furthest thing from it, in fact."

"Fine, then let me introduce you to—"

Gage interrupted her. "This is the last time I'll say this: Butt out of my life. If I want to hire a submissive, fuck the women's volleyball team, or torment an annoying redhead, there's nothing you can do about it."

She sputtered, "Good heavens, son, you don't have to be so vulgar!" She quickly picked up the scent, though. "Who is the annoying redhead? Anyone I know?"

"None of your business, Mother. I'll be in Edinburgh sometime next month and will let you know when." He punched the hang-up button and slammed his fist on his desk. "Bloody hell."

If it wasn't one thing, it was another. He could see why Cole preferred to hire professional submissives to fulfill his needs—sexually and sometimes socially. The idea looked more and more appealing. He wouldn't have to listen to any family drama. He could enjoy himself and send the woman home in a taxi afterward. *Thank you, miss, your shift is over. See you Friday at six o'clock sharp. Wear the red corset and heels. Say nothing unless I give you permission.*

His cock twitched at the thought. The problem was he could only imagine one feisty redhead being his beck and call girl.

Disgusted with his train of thought, Gage dialed one of his two best friends. It was time to set a plan in motion.

"Mack! How are you?"

Gage smiled at hearing Cole's distinctly Southern drawl. "I need your advice." *No sense in beating around the bush.*

"Wow. Since when do you need advice from me? Unless it's about a woman? Who is she?"

Gage laughed, but it sounded strangled. "She is an employee and therefore off limits."

"Ah fuck, that's funny."

"No, I promise you it's not. It's highly problematic."

"No, I meant it's funny because I have a similar problem. I hired a woman who I'm not sure I can trust. She's got a fake social security number and looks like she's on the run from something or someone. And being the knight in shining armor that I am, I let her move into my coach house."

"Okay, maybe I should have called Aaron. You probably can't help me."

"Ouch, that hurts, Mack. Aaron is a workaholic and a hermit, and he has more commitment issues than you and I put together."

"I can't argue with that."

"Can't you just fire the girl and then fuck her?" Cole always had a way with words.

"The thing is, I don't believe she is submissive. She's got an agenda, and I can't figure out what it is. But she's defiant and mouthy and not my type at all."

"Uh-huh." Cole cleared his throat. "She sounds fun. The exact opposite of that plastic blonde you almost married."

"That's a low blow."

"The truth hurts, my friend. It sounds like y'all need to figure out if she is for real. And the only way to do that is to show her who's boss." Loud laughter rang in his ear and Gage considered hanging up, but Cole continued. "You're long overdue to get laid, man. Pent-up sperm is clouding your judgment."

"On that, you might be right. We should fly over to Berlin next week. I haven't been there in ages."

"I can probably swing that, but I must be back stateside by Thursday. Can't leave my little runaway filly alone for too long. She could take off with the silverware."

Gage chuckled, shaking his head. He missed his friends and their easy camaraderie. They certainly had some great times at university. Cole and Aaron were the only two people in the world he trusted. They came from very different backgrounds, but quite by accident, they found they had similar predilections for BDSM. Had it not been for Harvard's annual sex week—and a dare from their fellow fraternity brothers to go to a "munch" club meeting for students with kinky interests—they might never have known. That was their first and last munch meeting, but it wasn't long before their reputations became known around Cambridge. They moved off campus in their second year and their house parties were legendary. Any woman who wanted to try a little bondage or submission could get an invitation.

Gage suddenly felt lighter now that he had an escape plan. "I'll have Fiona alert my crew to put a flight plan together. I'll see you Friday at the Mandarin. Eight sharp."

"Sounds good. And Gage, I'm looking forward to meeting your little hellcat."

Click. Gage scowled into the phone.

Brynne was eager to see Gage, but two hours into her shift, he was nowhere in sight. It was slow for a Thursday—she and Mel had four tables between them. She had just finished serving four flirty guests when Bill waved her over.

"Gage has ordered dinner, Tink. It will be ready in about ten minutes. You're to fetch and deliver. And he will have wine tonight. I'll open the bottle."

She hid her excitement and went to prepare the tray. When Mel came in, she told her, "I'm on delivery duty again, love. Can you watch my tables for a few minutes?"

She nodded. "Sure, Tink. Don't let him get under your skin, okay?"

"Nothing to worry about, Mel. I am immune to his charms, considerable as they may be."

Mel bit her lip to stop from laughing. "Sure you are, doll."

Brynne smirked and got to work preparing the tray. She added warm rolls and butter and set down the glass of wine before sprinting upstairs to get the entrée. *Tonight, he will have nothing to complain about.*

When she reached his office door a few minutes later, she was very proud of herself. She tapped the door with her foot and waited.

"Aye."

"It's Tink. I have your hot dinner. Could you please open the door?"

She thought she heard him groan. He opened the door and turned away from her without so much as a glance. *The asshole is in residence tonight.*

Gage pushed the papers to the side and stood back so she could place the tray down.

"Is there anything else I can get for you?" Her voice sounded weirdly high pitched to her own ears.

"Yes. There are three packages over there. Open them and dispose of all the paper wrapping." He pointed at the far end of the office, without so much as a glance. She gritted her teeth and thought about curtsying. *Dumb idea, girlfriend.*

"Okay."

"Pardon?"

Brynne rolled her eyes. So that's how he's going to play it. Turning back to face him, she coated her words in honey. "I meant, I would be happy to, sir." And added a curtsy for good measure. She spun around and waited for his reaction. The scrape of his knife and fork on the plate meant he wasn't going to play.

Brynne hurried to rip the wrapping off the first piece. She noisily scrunched up the brown paper and dropped it on the floor. The frame faced the wall, so she left it that way and uncovered the second and third pieces. After rolling all the garbage into a ball, she faced him.

"I should get back; Mel is on her own."

"Mel is fine." Glancing at his computer monitor, he added, "There are no new tables."

"You can see the lounge on your computer." It was more a statement than a question. Jared had told her he had cameras everywhere.

"Yes, I can see almost every room in the club. For security reasons." He cut a piece of steak and waved it toward the paintings. "Show them to me."

Her fists clenched, and she whirled around and flipped the frames, so they faced him. Brynne's breath caught in her throat. Keeping her back to him, she stepped back so he could see them, too.

"Aren't they beautiful?" His voice gave away nothing.

It was a minute before she managed a reply. "Yes. Quite stunning."

Brynne could not tear her gaze away. Her hand reached for her neck, sure that her racing pulse was visibly fluttering just beneath her hot and clammy skin.

Gage cleared his throat, and she turned to him. "Come here."

His eyes were the darkest she'd ever seen. The way they glowed, they could have been lit from behind. She felt like a small rabbit targeted by a hawk, its intention clear, its power unmistakable. If she was quick, she might get away.

He took a sip of wine and pointed to the chair opposite his desk. The silent command raised goosebumps on her arms.

Brynne took a seat and clasped her hands together to keep them still.

"You seem quite taken with my new photographs."

"Yes. I've never seen anything quite like them before. Do you know that woman?"

"Yes. She is well known in the scene. I've seen her in bondage before, but nothing like these. The photographer is very talented."

"Mhmm." She nodded.

Gage sat back and ran a hand over his jaw. "So, you like them?"

Brynne hesitated. She turned back and pretended indifference, but it was impossible. She was growing more captivated by the second. "Yes. I like them."

"What specifically do you like, Red?"

"They are very elegant and erotic, the way the light hits her body. Her skin looks burnished. There are so many intricate layers of rope…and everything is symmetrical."

"Do they turn you on?"

Brynne considered her response and reluctantly turned back to face him. Her eyes studied him. "What do you think?"

"I can see your shallow breathing and your skin is flushed pink."

Her chin jutted, and she threw caution to the wind. "It's true. I'd like to be her. What are you going to do about it?"

His eyes glittered. "Nothing. Get back to work."

She didn't need to be told twice. Brynne huffed out a curse and made for the door, half expecting him to call her back to pick up the garbage. *Smug bastard.*

After sprinting up the stairs, she needed a minute to compose herself before going back out to the lounge. Those images were burned in her brain.

If only she had the balls to ask him if that's what he does with his submissives. She swallowed a moan and forced the thoughts out of her mind. The trouble was, she couldn't conceal the way her eyes had dilated, and the heightened color on her cheeks.

Mel came over to where she stood. "No new tables. It's been slow." Her eyes roamed over Brynne's face, and she tilted her head in a way that reminded Brynne of Aunt Josie, who could spot a *situation* a mile away.

"What's the matter? Did Gage get you all hot and bothered again?"

She wrinkled her nose at Mel, who most would disregard as a bubble-headed blonde, but she knew it was just an act. "I am not hot and bothered. Well, okay, I might be, but it's not about him. He is being a prick tonight—all cold and demanding. But he had me unpack some new artwork, and it was seriously erotic."

"Ooh, I hope he hangs them up where I can see them."

Brynne smiled. "Fair warning, you won't be able to concentrate if you do."

Mel sighed. "I would love the distraction. But hey, we'll have plenty of excitement on Saturday night. Since this is your first fetish night, I'll show you what the plan is."

Half an hour later, Brynne was fully briefed and quite wigged out by what she learned. This was going to be a full-on sex party. Mel assured her that nobody was going to be having sex in the lounge and most of the guests would keep their *parts* covered—until after midnight. The rooms upstairs were all booked for private scenes—some allowed observers and some didn't. In the Pareo playroom where she was spanked, it would be a free-for-all sheik's harem. If luck was on her side, she might get to deliver refreshments up there. Extra security would ensure nobody took liberties, but the alcohol would flow, so everyone needed to keep a close eye on all the patrons and report anyone getting out of hand.

This was her big break. A chance to see people who lived the lifestyle and some who just played in it. Mel offered to stay so Brynne could cut out early; she welcomed the chance to get home. She remembered to get a taxi chit from Garrick and sneaked out without seeing Gage again. The next time she saw him would be Saturday. Hopefully, he would be in a better mood.

The black cab pulled up, and she got in, taking an extra look around. She forgot to tell Jared about the Range Rover. No matter—it was probably nothing.

14

Arabian Fetish Night

Fetish night had finally arrived. Gage couldn't help feeling on edge, even with extra security stationed in every corner on every floor. As soon as Cole arrived, they would head up to the lounge. He wanted to be on the floor to monitor everything—especially Brynne.

Paperwork remained unread on his desk as he watched her on the video monitor. God help him. She looked more stunning than he could have imagined in her harem outfit. She was laughing and flirting with the patrons. The timid girl was gone. Now when someone tried to take liberties, she laughed and swatted away their wandering hands.

So much for devising ways he could push her buttons. Instead of scaring her off, she met his challenges and managed to turn the tables on him. They hadn't spoken since she flew out of his office on

Thursday. He knew he'd been contradictory, drawing her in, then pushing her away. Why couldn't he stay away from her?

Last night Cole teased him about his fascination with Brynne. Part of him wished he wasn't coming to the party tonight. The tall Texan had an effortless charm and charisma that attracted women like bees to honey. Together with Aaron, they had been quite the team during university. Work first, women second, sleep third. They spent countless sleepless nights perfecting a software program to detect anomalies, fraud, and patterns in trading. The results of their hard work led to a patent which set them up for the rest of their lives. Cole invested in oil and gas and commercial property development. Aaron built a New York-based VC firm and invested in real estate, publishing, and broadcasting. His own VC firm had netted strong profits since he founded it seven years ago.

During dinner, he finally told Cole what happened with Sierra, and how much it had affected him. He was no longer interested in trying to find a *suitable* girlfriend, especially one that his mother approved of. They were all looking for money, social standing, and a big house in Mayfair. No, thank you. He was content to stoke the fires of his inherent distrust of women.

Cole suggested he find another outlet, even if it meant hiring a professional or going to Germany to get back into the club scene. When he admitted he hadn't had sex since breaking it off with Sierra, Cole nearly choked on his drink.

It was galling but true—he hadn't hooked up with anyone or sought any revenge sex. He tried to convince Cole he couldn't go fucking his way around London when his mother was up for a judicial appointment. A mocking face stared back at him.

"That's a lame excuse. Good thing I'm here to rescue you. And thanks to your wonderful assistant Fiona, we have the jet booked to Berlin tomorrow afternoon. Garrick can run this joint for a few days." Then he told him, "It's only been five days and my balls need emptying."

Gage knew he was right. The trip was exactly what he needed.

Cole texted ten minutes later that his car was pulling up. Gage told him to have Miles bring him to his office. He wanted to show him his latest artwork, which now hung over the fireplace. Anyone who stood at the door to his office wouldn't see it. Only those allowed into the inner sanctum would get the full impact.

When he arrived, Gage handed him a glass of scotch and suggested he take a seat while he finished up an email.

Cole raised his glass. "Cheers, my friend. Take your time." He sat on the long leather couch that faced the fireplace and Gage watched him as he took in the view.

"Jesus H Christopher, where did you get these?" He rose and went over so he could study them more closely. "Fucking stunning. Where can I order some? Who is the photographer?" He turned to Gage. "And who is *she*?"

Gage laughed. "I'll give you the number of the studio; the photographer works here part time. I've seen the model before, but not like this. These are one of a kind."

"That is some serious ropework. Makes me itchy to play."

"If you want to play tonight, I can arrange it. I'm sure there are a few subs with room on their dance card."

His friend downed the rest of his drink. "What are we waiting for? Let's go upstairs so you can introduce me to your little redhead. I'm dying to see who's got your dick in a twist."

Gage's jaw clenched.

Cole looked at him with mock innocence. "What's the matter, Mack? You can't have your wicked way with her. She's your employee, but there are no such rules where I'm concerned."

Gage gripped the glass in his hand. "She is off limits."

"You're no fun and I am. She'll recognize that right away. That must be what worries you." Cole chuckled as they went upstairs.

"Not worried. She's not your type."

"Really? What is my type?"

"You always went for the tall, athletic blondes at school and at the clubs. Brynne is none of those."

"Maybe I'm due for a change."

"Keep it up, mate. I can still throw you out of my club."

Cole slapped him on the back and winked. "I'd like to see you try."

They entered through the main doors of the bar and took in the scene. Most of the chairs on the right side of the lounge had been replaced with low curved couches, with multi-colored pillows in bright orange, purple, and green silk. Low round tables sat in front of each seating area and colorful Persian rugs covered the dark hardwood. The lighting was muted, accented by dozens of flameless candles. The scent of sandalwood and patchouli incense wafted from each corner of the room.

Gage pointed to an empty table near the bookcases, where they could see the entire room. "Have a seat there, Cole. I need to talk to the bartender. What are you drinking?"

"I'll have a Jack and Coke."

Gage made his way across the crowded room, his eyes searching for the harem girl in purple. Bill was finishing an order when Gage signaled to him. "How are things going so far?"

The gray-haired man grinned and nodded. "So far, so good. Although the night is young."

"Damn true. I'll have a Macallan 18, and my friend will have a Jack Daniels and Coke on the rocks." He scanned the room again. "Has Dimitri shown up yet?"

"Not yet, but he called ahead to ensure he gets his usual table in the corner, and he demanded that Tink look after him."

"Aye. I figured. Have her bring the drinks over. We're by the wall over there."

"Will do, boss."

Gage sat down and briefed him on Dimitri. "This Russian prick has been pursuing her—pressing her hard to go out with him. She swears she can handle him, but I'm not so sure. He's got a reputation for being ruthless and he found out a few months ago that without my political connections, he would have won the bid and opened his own club here. I wish I'd never allowed him to become a member."

"Where is this no-good swine?" Cole sat forward, looking around the room.

"Not here yet." Gage saw Brynne approaching with their drinks. "Now behave yourself."

Cole looked up and grinned. "I always do…" He stopped midsentence when Brynne reached them.

"Good evening, gentlemen. I believe this is for you." She handed Cole his drink and bent down to place a cocktail napkin on the table.

Gage attempted a casual smile when she nodded shyly at him. His voice froze in his throat. She was a vision. Multiple layers of lavender chiffon swished around her legs when she walked. He'd heard the jingling of her decorative belt, with its dangling coins. The bikini top left nothing to the imagination. It shimmered with beads and crystals sewn into the purple material. He wanted to toss her over his shoulder and walk out of there.

Cole interrupted, "Aren't you going to introduce me, Mack?"

Clearing his throat, Gage took his drink and pretended a calm he didn't feel. "Of course, Brynne, I'd—" Her eyes widened at his use of her real name.

Christ, that was stupid. He checked their surroundings. The only person within earshot was a security guard standing a few feet away.

"Right, I mean Tink, short for Tinkerbell, I'd like to introduce you to an old friend of mine, Cole Bradford."

She grinned, and Gage realized she had never bestowed that kind of smile on him. "Very nice to meet you, Mr. Bradford."

"Please call me Cole." He rose to his feet and took her delicate hand in both of his. The bastard was pouring on the charm, making a spectacle of his height. In university, he would tell the girls he had several inches on Gage—and advised them to make an educated choice about whom to go out with. He towered over Brynne by more than a foot.

"The pleasure is all mine, darlin'. Where have you been hiding all my life?"

Gage snorted. "I should have warned you. He's a lecherous Texan, and you can't believe a word he says."

Brynne giggled and pulled her hand out of his. "Not to worry, *sir*. I know how to handle lecherous Texans, depraved Russians, and *cantankerous* Scotsmen." She winked at Cole, and he laughed loud enough to draw the interest of the other guests.

Gage leaned back and took a sip of his drink, his eyes glinting like ice. "You want me to take you over my knee, don't you?"

She leveled a look at him. "You know I do. I'm not sure why you insist on denying us both when I've done plenty to deserve it." Brynne turned to Cole. "Have a lovely visit, Cole. I must run. I have tables to get back to."

She turned and fled in a flurry of tinkling beads. Cole sat down and grinned at him. "Now I understand what the fuss is about, man. She is ripe for the picking."

Gage ran a hand roughly through his hair. "You see what I mean? She's not submissive. She wants to play around—and fulfill her fantasies of what she thinks BDSM is."

"Well, if I were in your shoes, I'd toss her into the deep end to see if she's all talk or not."

"I have no interest in training a novice, only to find out later it isn't what she really wants." He looked at Cole and saw sympathy reflected in his eyes. "Sierra pretended for months to love it and she had me fooled."

"I get it, man, but not all women are as dishonest as that witch. And don't take this the wrong way, but you fell for a cold-hearted bitch, who was just like your mother."

Gage swore and stared into his glass of scotch, swirling the amber liquid. "That's pretty fucked up."

"Yeah, it is. Bottom line, we have to get you laid. But right now, you should show me the sights. What is happening in this Arabian den of delights?"

Gage shook himself free of his dark thoughts. He finished his drink and rose. "Let's go up to the second floor. I'll show you the sheik's playground."

Brynne arrived at the club an hour early so Mel could help with her hair and makeup. She used extra smoky eye shadows and black kohl to make her eyes stand out and curled and styled her hair in a way Brynne could never do herself. She stood staring at her reflection, admiring how the pretty colored jewels on her top shimmered in the light. When she moved, the dangling beads on her waist and ankles jingled so everyone could hear her coming. Sexy didn't describe how she felt. It was far more powerful. The outfit would draw attention to her curves. It made her feel exotic. Wanton. Carnal.

When she delivered the drinks, Gage had looked strange—like he was in pain. His friend was charming and handsome, but she only had eyes for the broody motherfucker who wouldn't make a move. Brynne had made her desires clear enough and held out hope that he would act on them.

There was no time to worry about it now. She had tables to serve, and the *depraved Russian* had just arrived with his entourage.

Brynne could see him searching for her as he made his way to his table. Unfortunately, he didn't bring any subs with him. Her hopes of him focusing his attention elsewhere were dashed. She wanted to see how he treated them—and what he might make them do. Instead, he brought two massive bodyguard types with shaved heads and glowering faces. They were out of place in the sumptuously decorated room.

When Dimitri saw her, his eyes lit with a feral gleam that caused her to falter. The fancy beaded mules didn't help—she almost tripped twice over her own feet.

Brynne took the drink order for Rory and his friend and went over to the bar. She needed to take a breath and center herself before dealing with him.

"Look out for me tonight, Bill. I feel like a rabbit amongst a pack of wolves!"

"Don't worry, Tink. Every security guard in the room will watch you and your fellow harem gals closely. You will be safe."

Brynne kept her eyes on the floor on the way to Rory's table and delivered their drinks without her usual flair. Rory took her hand as she was turning away and asked, "Sweet Tink, will you be getting into trouble tonight?"

"I hope not, Sir Rory. I'm planning to be on my best behavior." She winked at him.

"Mores the pity." He kissed her hand and let her go, a wistful look in his eye.

She took a deep cleansing breath, her head held high and walked to the corner booth. Dimitri's eyes devoured her, but she refused to let him unnerve her.

"Good evening, gentlemen. May I get you something from the bar?"

The beefy henchmen looked to Dimitri, not daring to speak first. His lips were white, his jaw stiff. *Why does he look so angry? Nobody grabbed my butt on the way over.*

"If you were mine, I would not allow you to dress this way in public. This would be for my eyes only, Kiska."

"It's not that bad." She looked down at herself. "I am totally covered."

Despite her assertions, it did not placate him. "Nyet. Every man here wants to fuck you because of the way your body is on display."

Brynne shook her head, sensing this situation could easily unravel. "It doesn't matter what every man wants. I am not interested and plan to leave here as I came—alone."

"You should leave with me, moy angel. But I have the whole evening to convince you of what I can offer."

"What can I get you to drink?" she asked, avoiding his searing gaze.

"Bring a bottle of Stoli on ice, and three glasses. I need something to calm me."

She nodded and headed for the bar, searching the room for Gage and his friend. Their absence made her feel more vulnerable.

Bill smirked when she gave him the order.

"I put the vodka on ice an hour ago." He placed the bottle on her tray with the glasses. "This should calm the beast."

She sighed. "I hope you're right."

Brynne wanted to enjoy tonight, not run back and forth for Ivanov's amusement. She hoped to watch people enjoying the playroom, which they said was decorated like a sheik's lair. For now, she was stuck serving his table.

After she poured the vodka, he grabbed her hand in a firm grip. He looked at her, his chin raised. "Aren't you forgetting something, Tink?"

She scanned the table. "The ice bucket. I'm so sorry. Bill had the vodka in the freezer before you arrived. I'll be right back with it."

He held on for a moment longer and smiled, baring his perfect white teeth. "Perhaps I will keep track of your mistakes tonight. And hope for the chance to punish you later."

She dug her fingernails into his hand and tried to pull away. He looked surprised and amused. Finally, he let her go and chuckled. "My kitten has claws. I'll count that as another strike."

Brynne whirled around, causing all her dangling coins to sound like a penny slot machine that just paid out. She stalked toward the kitchen and almost lost a shoe. "Stupid shoes. Stupid Russian." She seethed under her breath, ignoring the stares she was getting.

Mel met her in the back when she was scooping out the ice. "You look fit to be tied, Tink. Please don't put salt in the ice bucket." Mel knew how to lighten her mood.

"You know how badly I want to, but it would play right into his hands." She turned to Mel, her eyes lit with an idea. "Hey, if you get a request to deliver anything upstairs, could I take it? I'm dying to see the playroom." She lowered her voice to a whisper. "And see who's doing what to whom!"

Mel laughed. "For sure, Tink. I've seen it all. I will ask Bill to give some of my deliveries to you."

"Thanks babe! I'm off. Wish me luck. Let's hope I don't trip and drop this bucket on him and his goons!"

Dimitri's mood did not lighten as the night wore on. Just the opposite. He ordered a second bottle of vodka and a different appetizer each time she went to the table. He repeated his wish to take her away from all this drudgery, and she rebuffed him as gently as she could.

So far, she hadn't seen any juicy action. To add to her irritation, Gage hadn't returned either. Maybe he was upstairs having his wicked way with a submissive!

There was a lull in orders, so she told Mel it was time for a fast look upstairs. "I'll take some bottles of water up. People need to stay hydrated, right?"

Mel nodded and winked. Before heading up, Brynne popped down to the locker room to pee and freshen up.

Cole and Gage entered the lounge and took a seat at the same table they occupied earlier. Gage scanned the room, but Brynne wasn't in the lounge. Annoyed, he excused himself from Cole and strode to the bar. "Where is Tink?"

"I believe she took a break. Ivanov has been running her off her feet."

"Okay. Can you send her over when she returns? Same order as before."

Bill nodded, and Gage turned to find Martin sitting at the table beside them. Gage introduced the two men. Martin introduced his sub, Cara, who kneeled on a pillow at his feet. Her silky black hair was braided down her back and woven with gold strands. She wore a very short white skirt and a beaded bikini top that was stunning against her glowing brown skin. Her wrists and ankles were cuffed, and Martin held a leash, attached to a decorative gold choker around her neck. Cara looked up and acknowledged the men with a nod.

Cole was talking to Martin when Mel brought over the drinks. Gage stood and asked her privately where Tink was.

Melanie nibbled her bottom lip. "She was going to take water up to the playroom to see what was happening. But she's been gone a while."

Cole overheard and stood. They looked at Dimitri's table and back at each other. "Cole, you check the playroom. I'll check downstairs; she might have gone to freshen up."

They left by the main doors and split up. Gage started down the stairs, unease twisting in his gut. He was almost at the lower level when he heard her scream. His blood curdled as he reached the corridor in time to see Brynne sprinting barefoot toward him. Her hair had come undone, and her eyes were wide and glassy. He grabbed her and pulled her to his chest. "Where is he?"

She spoke into his chest, her arms wrapped around his torso. "In, in the locker room. Bleeding. Nose." She trembled against him, her breath coming in shallow gasps. He held her tight and patted her back, as much to calm her as himself. He felt capable of murder.

Cole came bounding down the back stairs with two security guards. Dimitri emerged from the women's locker room, holding a bloody towel to his face. Cole grabbed him by the lapels and pushed him up against the wall. "What kind of animal are you, preying on innocent women?"

The Russian ignored him and turned toward Gage and Brynne. "Malishka, I'm sorry if I frightened you."

Reining in the urge to smash his face to smithereens, Gage gritted out, "Ivanov, you have crossed the line. I want you out of my club. *Now.* Your membership is revoked." He should have trusted his instincts about Dimitri; now he had the opportunity to be rid of him once and for all. His security team and all his rules failed Brynne. He failed her. Garrick and John approached from the back stairs.

John looked at Gage, a heated look passing between them. "Does she want to press charges?"

Brynne turned her head slightly and spoke in a whisper. "I don't know. No, I don't think so."

Gage addressed Garrick. "Show Mr. Ivanov out—collect anyone he brought with him and escort them off the premises."

Cole left with them, and Gage knew he would help ensure they delivered the three pieces of garbage to the curb.

Brynne loosened her grip and backed away from him. She stared at the marks her mascara had made on his dress shirt and bit her lip. "I'm sorry about your shirt."

"Come," he said—and he led her down the hall to his office and gently settled her on the couch. He poured her two fingers of scotch on ice and brought it to her. When she didn't take a drink, he sat down beside her and put the crystal glass to her lips. "Drink."

A little fire returned to her eyes. "So bossy." She took a swig of the scotch and closed her eyes and moaned.

"I cannot help it where you are concerned." He looked her over and saw red marks on her arm. "Can you tell me what happened?" His voice was deceptively calm.

She took a deep breath and swished the amber liquid round and round. "He…he followed me down here and cornered me in the locker room. I've told him repeatedly that I'm not interested and that I have a mistress." She looked at him for a second, her face heating. "He was in a bad mood when he saw my outfit and it just got worse the more he drank." She sighed, her breath shuddering. "I don't normally get shaken up like this, it's just…" She paused. "He's unnerved me from day one."

"Did he hurt you?"

"When I tried to get around him. He grabbed my arm to pull me closer. He was begging for a kiss." She looked down at her wrist and paused. "I took self-defense classes last year. I knew I couldn't let him get my other arm, so I tried the twist maneuver, but he was too strong. When he leaned closer to kiss me, I bashed his nose with my forehead."

Gage was stunned. He lifted her hair and saw the golf ball-size bump on her forehead.

"Jesus fucking Christ," he snarled. He went to the sideboard for ice and a cloth napkin. He placed the cold pack on her forehead as gently as he could. Brynne sucked in a breath.

"I think we should get you checked out at the hospital."

She took a gulp of the scotch and shook her head. "I don't need the hospital. It's just a bump. I'm fine." She swallowed another sip and looked at him with a little smile. "I could do with some more of this, though. If I'm not mistaken, it's the real good stuff." Giggling, she added, "I'll be good as new in no time."

Gage went to his phone and rang the lounge. "Bill, please locate Doc McCaffrey and ask him to come to my office." He turned and lowered his voice. "Aye. Ivanov and his thugs are gone. Make sure security is in place when you leave the bar."

15

Fit to be Tied

Gage's face was as forbidding as she'd ever seen. She had finished the scotch and lay back on the cushion waving the glass. He took it and filled it with water. She tried to lighten the mood. "Hey, he didn't hurt me. I got away before he could…do anything."

"I am sorry. This should not have happened." He repeatedly clenched his fists.

"It's not your fault. I should have alerted security that I came downstairs. I just wanted to check out the playroom but needed to pee. He caught me by surprise and was pressing me to quit the club so men couldn't ogle me in outfits like this." She waved a hand at her costume. "He didn't really hurt me." She clenched the glass, trying not to think about what might have happened.

Before Gage could respond, the doctor arrived. He was wearing flowing white robes with a sheikh's headdress. Brynne wanted to apologize for interrupting his evening, but he was all business and asked her if she had any headache, imbalance, or confusion. After checking her pupils and examining the bump on her head, he suggested they continue the cold compresses and, seeing the glass, added, "Nothing alcoholic to drink, and in a few hours you can take two painkillers before bed. You don't appear to have a concussion."

Gage thanked him and walked him to the door. When he turned, his lips were compressed in a solemn line. "Get your things. I'm going to take you home now."

She shook her head. "Your party is still going. I can take a taxi."

"No arguments. I'll carry you out if I have to."

"Good grief," she huffed. When she got to the door of his office, she paused. "I would rather not go to the locker room alone."

He was beside her in an instant, his protective hand on her back the whole way. She didn't change, wanting to get out of that room as quickly as possible.

They exited the club from the lower level into an underground car park she had never seen before. A big man, dressed from head to toe in black, waited beside a gleaming silver Bentley sedan. The guy reminded her of a Hollywood mafia enforcer with his thick goatee and bulging arms. He tipped his peaked cap to Gage and moved with lightning speed to open the rear door. For a guy built like a tank, he was fast on his feet.

The warm leather seat enveloped Brynne, and she let her head fall back. The car smelled like new leather, and Gage—an intoxicating combination for her already addled brain. She watched him exchange words with his driver. Moments later, they were both seated in the car, gliding toward the exit ramp. Sharing the enclosed space with him made her stomach flutter, and she absently played with the silky material of her pantaloons.

Gage was staring out the window, brooding. She had to break the uncomfortable silence. "I wish we brought the scotch with us."

"The doc said no more alcohol."

"Just because you're taking me home doesn't give you the right to boss me around."

"I beg to differ." His jaw tightened.

"Well, I appreciate the ride home, but I'm really fine and could have taken a taxi."

He turned to her, his eyes narrowed. "You don't get it. Dimitri is one of the wealthiest men in Russia and he has an unhealthy obsession with you." Gage ran a hand roughly through his hair. "He's ruthless in business and *acquires* women like other people do cars."

She sat forward. "What does that mean? Am I in danger?"

"This is London, not Moscow, so his powers here are not above the law. But I want you to be extremely careful over the next few weeks."

Brynne tried to make light of it. "He doesn't know my real name. There is no *Tinkerbell* in the phone listings and my next shift isn't until Wednesday."

"Regardless, take a taxi to work, not the train. The club will reimburse you."

Brynne took in his hard expression and wondered aloud, "I never gave him the impression I was interested." She was getting herself worked up. "I only smiled at him because it's in the job description!"

He took her hand in his and hissed, "Jesus, you're freezing. Give me your other hand." His hands were hot, as usual, and she let him warm her icy digits, enjoying his rare display of affection.

"Russian men have a reputation for taking the tiniest display of interest and blowing it out of proportion." Gage turned her chin so she was facing him. "I won't let anything happen to you."

His eyes dropped to her mouth and lingered. Brynne licked

her lips and waited. But instead of doing what she knew they both wanted, he dropped her hands and sat back in his seat. *Psych!* His iron control won out again.

She looked out the window and didn't recognize the area. "Where are we? Don't you need my address?"

"I have it from your file. We are taking a detour, in an abundance of caution."

She crossed her arms over her chest and fumed. "Christ, if you're trying to scare me, you're doing a fine job of it!"

Ten minutes of awkward silence passed and finally they turned into her street. She didn't want the night to end like this. He was closed off again.

The car glided to a stop in front of the old fourplex and she unclipped her seat belt. He followed suit. Brynne tried the door, but it wouldn't open. He and the driver got out, looked around, and then he came around to help her out.

Gage said something to the Tank, to which he grunted in response and got back in the car. Brynne asked, "Was that Gaelic?"

He nodded and took her by the arm. She fished out her keys and decided she had nothing to lose except a little of her pride. "Would you like to come in for a cup of tea?"

He loomed over her while she fumbled with the two locks. She assumed he would deposit her and leave, so it was a surprise when he stepped in ahead of her and felt the wall for a switch. "Sure, why don't you do that while I look around?"

"Wait, a second!" She ran after him, realizing too late that her place looked like a bomb hit it. Gage stood there looking totally out of place in her tiny sitting room. Springing into action, she closed her laptop and gathered all the stray papers into a pile. Out of the corner of her eye, she saw him walk toward her bookshelves, sending her heart banging against her ribs. Just what she needed—him prowling around her dirty book library and making judgments.

She cleared a space on the sofa and squeaked, "Why don't you sit down and relax while I put the kettle on?"

At his silence, she grew more anxious. "I have been working long hours and my place has gotten a bit out of hand. It's not usually like this. I'm normally very tidy…" Her voice trailed off.

"You have quite an eclectic taste in books." His gaze traveled up to the top shelf. "And erotica."

She rolled her eyes, exasperated. "It's for research. I'm writing a novel, and so I've been studying the craft."

He laughed. The sound was gravelly from disuse, and it reverberated along her nerve endings. Collecting herself, she filled the kettle and found some clean cups. When she turned to ask him how he took his tea, he was gone.

"Jesus," she said under her breath and hurried toward her bedroom, plowing into him in the doorway. He steadied her, and she caught sight of something bright pink in his hand. She blushed at the roots of her hair. "Give me that! How dare you touch my things? Have you no manners?"

Amusement twinkled in his eyes. "Just trying to unlock the mystery."

"No mystery. Just a red-blooded woman with needs!" She held out her hand.

He ignored her and kept studying the thing. When she grabbed for it, he held it up out of her reach. He was grinning, and the sight of his smile knocked the breath out of her.

"Explain to me how this works," he said playfully.

She made an unladylike snorting sound. "You mean you can't figure it out?"

He turned it over and found the switch. Fortunately, nothing happened. He lifted an eyebrow. "Och." He grinned at her. "Did you wear it out, Red?"

Brynne noticed his accent became more pronounced as he teased her. He had found her broken Womanizer sex toy. She stuck her chin out and lit the proverbial match. "If you must know, I rode it to death."

His eyes darkened as he stalked toward her. She backed away until she was up against the refrigerator. He stopped just short and looked down at her. "You like playing with fire, don't you, Brynne?"

The way he said her name kick-started her pulse. "I know what I want, if that's what you mean."

He planted his hands on either side of her head. "Tell me what you want."

"For you to stop playing games. If you want me, then take me to bed." *There, she'd said it.* This chemistry had been building since the first day she laid eyes on him. He might be unwilling to admit it, but she was past caring.

He took another step and pressed his whole body up against hers. She gasped when he maneuvered a foot between her legs and nudged them apart. The heat from his body seared her skin; his distinctive scent of citrus and sandalwood overwhelmed her senses. He took a fistful of her hair and pulled her head back, forcing her to look at him. "Will you do exactly what I tell you to do?"

She responded by grinding up against the muscular thigh wedged between her legs.

His grip tightened. "I need you to say it." His deep, gravelly brogue ignited her like a tinderbox.

She glared at him. "Yes. If that's what it will take. Anything to get you out of my system!"

Brynne saw the muscle twitch in his cheek. She sensed his control was slipping by the minute, which was exactly how she wanted him. Slowly, his head descended, his mouth hovering over hers, just out of reach. She tried to close the distance, but his grip on her hair was unyielding.

He spoke in a strangled whisper against her mouth. "You think one night will be enough?"

She brazenly stuck out her tongue and licked his bottom lip. "There's only one way to find out."

His eyes burned into hers and the hand that imprisoned her suddenly cradled her head, and his mouth was on hers. He kissed and licked and nibbled at first. She wanted more, her fingers clutching his shirt. She opened for him, and their tongues met and danced. Still, he held himself back, like a starving tiger chained just out of reach of his prey. She wanted him to pounce and devour her.

He stepped back, and she almost sank to the floor, a whimper escaping her lips.

"Give me your wrists."

She tentatively put her hands together and extended them toward him. He grabbed one of her tea towels and twirled it at the corners to make a long band.

His face had changed, all playfulness gone. "Turn around and put your hands behind your back."

Brynne shivered and pleaded with him. "Couldn't they be in front?"

"That's one."

"One what?"

"One act of defiance to be punished." His voice came out rough, and it vibrated along her nerves. She spun around and clasped her hands behind her.

He crossed her wrists and bound them tightly with the towel. Heat built between her legs when he secured her hands; it was the strangest sensation.

"This will have to suffice, unless you have some ties around?" He took hold of her shoulders and turned her around. Brynne looked up at him, her eyes begging him to kiss her again.

She licked her lips. "My raincoat, it's by the front door, it has a belt. My robe does too. It's hanging on the back of the bathroom door."

His green eyes glittered. "One might think you want to be tied."

She looked away, flushed with embarrassment. "I have a fantasy or two."

"I've seen your reading material, Red, so I know you're lying. That's two."

"Oh, come on, that's not fair," she whined until his squinty-eyed look quelled her to silence.

"Never said I play fair." He bent down and tossed her over his shoulder.

"Ooh, ow!" She gasped.

"Shhh," he said as he smacked her behind.

He grabbed the raincoat and yanked the belt out of it. Then he carried her into her bedroom and laid her on her unmade bed. Rolling her off the coverlet, he pulled the spread down to the footboard and folded it into neat layers.

She watched, fascinated, and said, "You're a bit OCD, aren't you?"

His eyes bore into hers. "That's three."

"Oh, for fuck's sake!"

"Four." He shook his head. "Tut, tut, do I need to gag you?"

Brynne clamped her lips shut and shook her head. He went into her bathroom and retrieved the tie from her bath robe. When he came out, he was holding up her new vibrator, a wicked gleam in his eye. It, too, was hot pink, had six fabulous speeds, and was fully charged.

"What? That fine piece of German engineering prevents good girls from taking bad boys home with them."

The look on his face was pure amusement. She rolled her eyes and sighed heavily.

Gage stared at her as he took the belt out of his pants and threw it on the bed. She saw it and worried her bottom lip. Squirming against the bonds, she moaned with need, "Please, Gage…" She was losing her mind, and he had hardly touched her.

Finally, he crawled onto the bed and lay beside her, his head propped on his hand. He placed a hand on her bare stomach, and she chewed her lip to keep from talking.

"Before we go any further, we need to get a few things out of the way."

"Yes, I want this. Yes, I consent to you touching me, tying me, and fucking me!" She should probably stop babbling but couldn't stop herself. "Haven't you made me wait long enough?"

He put a finger to her lips. "You need to hush, or I *will* find something to silence you."

She whispered against his finger, "Promise?"

"First, I'm going to punish you. Then I'm going to strip you naked. I might fuck you. I haven't decided."

She nodded, giddy with excitement.

"Your safe word is *red*. If you need me to slow down, or your fingers get numb, for example, you say *yellow*. Do you understand?"

"Yes!" She nodded excitedly.

He placed a kiss on her nose and shifted himself off the bed. She watched in a trance as he fastened his belt around her thighs, just above her knees. He rolled her onto her stomach to undo the buttons and hooks on her harem pants. He pulled them down to mid-thigh, along with her panties. She moaned into the sheets when his hands ran over her ass, squeezing and pinching until she flung her feet in the air to deter him.

"With each little defiance comes one more level of restraint."

She tried to roll away, but he leaned his heavy torso over her legs and made quick work of securing her ankles with one of the cloth belts. The restraints made her feel more helpless and more aroused than since...well, ever.

When he rose and pulled her legs toward the edge of the bed, she let out a squeal of pain. He stopped and turned her over. "What's wrong, Brynne?" Concern creased his forehead.

"My top, it hurts. The beads are digging into me."

In a split second, he unhooked the clasps, ripped the straps and threw it on the floor, his eyes dark with purpose.

"Oh no!" She pouted. "It was so beautiful, and you ruined it."

He looked down at her bountiful breasts and laid feathery kisses where the underwire had marked her delicate skin. "Sonya will make you another one that doesn't hurt you."

Her nipples hardened under his attention, but he concentrated everywhere but there. Finally, he captured her breasts in his large hands, cupping them with his fingers and pressing them together, his eyes dilated with desire. Her areolas were dusky pink, hard little points jutting from the centers, begging for attention.

He rolled her nipples between his fingers until her mouth opened, her breathing ragged. "You should have said something sooner."

"I didn't care. I'm out of my mind waiting for you to put me out of my misery. Please, god..."

He bent low and used the point of his tongue to flick and torture the hard peak, making her moan. His mouth sucked and nibbled one and then the other until they were glistening and aching for more. Her head was buzzing, and her pussy swelled in anticipation.

"First things first," he said, picking her up effortlessly and laying her over his lap.

"Oh god," she breathed, squirming on his hard-muscled thighs.

"No screaming, we don't want your neighbors to call the police," he said as he pulled her bound hands higher on her back.

"How can I promise that?"

Smack! The first blow on bare skin caught her by surprise, and she moaned loudly.

"That was nothing. Surely you are tougher than that?"

"Bite me," she blurted without thinking.

"Aye, lass, that's five, or was it six?" She heard the amusement in his voice.

Smack! His hand came down hard. She whined and pressed her lips together, refusing to be a wimp. Again and again, he smacked her cheeks and her upper thighs. Heat was spreading, and she squirmed to avoid the next blows, but he had her pinned. She realized by grinding herself against his thigh, she might be able to bring herself off. She struggled to bring his leg into contact with her mound and smiled when his hard cock pressed up against her stomach.

"Don't you dare." His tone was dark and threatening.

She was not averse to begging. "Oh please, I'm so close."

"I decide how and when you come, my sweet, and it won't be wasted on my leg." His tone was serious as he laid her carefully on the bed and stood. "My god, you're a beautiful sight, all trussed up for me. I'm going to devour you."

She stared up at him in awe, her body drunk on helplessness. He started stripping off his clothes. Her mouth watered and her lady parts followed suit when he revealed his muscled chest and washboard stomach, lightly covered in dark hair.

He undid the button on his pants but stopped and rolled her onto her stomach. "That's long enough to be tied this way. You are probably oblivious to the numbness in your arms." He made quick work of releasing her wrists and rubbed her arms and hands to restore full circulation.

Brynne moaned when he turned her back over. "Ooh god, that's better—they are tingling a bit!" Then shyly she looked at him. "I, I liked it. Being tied that way, it did something to me."

"It did something to me, too." His jaw was rigid as he untied the belt at her ankles and fumbled with the last tie. "Now get those pretty pants off, unless you want them ripped to shreds."

Brynne finished undoing the belt and dragged the flowy harem pants off, then sat in rapt fascination as he stripped off his pants and boxer briefs. His long thick cock jutted out from his body, and she marveled at how beautiful it was—dark, shiny, and rock hard. She licked her lips in anticipation. He saw and responded in a low dark voice, "Lay back on the bed and spread your legs. I want to look at you."

Brynne blushed deeply, unable to meet his gaze, but did as she was told.

"Wider."

His voice had dropped deeper than she'd ever heard it. She swallowed a whimper.

"Look at me," he ordered. "Now, use your fingers and spread yourself open." He ground the words out between gritted teeth.

Brynne looked at him in stunned silence, but his eyes warned her not to disobey. She slowly put her hands on herself, tempted to conceal her arousal.

"I'm waiting," he rasped, impatiently. She was trembling in anticipation as she trailed her fingers over her mons. Her legs twitched in reaction when she inadvertently grazed her aching clit.

Gage raised an imperious eyebrow. "Did I say you could touch that?"

She shook her head and watched him grasp his hard length and squeeze. The beautiful plum head of his cock glistened with pre-cum.

"Spread those luscious lips and show me how hard your clit is."

Oh, dear god, I will do anything you ask. Her brain processed his commands, and she fell more completely under his dominant spell. He made her feel beautiful and safe and willing to do anything he asked.

"Keep them there. I'm going to taste you."

He pulled her body closer to the edge of the bed, so that her feet almost touched the floor—then he kneeled between her spread legs.

"So pink," he whispered before his tongue circled her clit, causing her to shudder. "So wet." His fingers spread her wetness up and down while he continued to tease and lick her engorged flesh. She was panting and concentrating on not begging, afraid he would stop before giving her what she needed. His tongue lapped at her core, then two fingers entered her slowly, but not nearly deep enough. She was at her limit; her legs were shaking, and she was about to grab his head and pull him to her.

Sensing her desperation, he spoke in the scariest voice she had ever heard. "Don't let go, or I will not let you come."

"Jesus," she pleaded, "I'll do anything you ask, please may I come?"

"When I decide, and not before."

"Yes, sir." She sighed heavily, signaling her surrender to his will.

His tongue returned, circling at first, then softly sweeping back and forth over her clit. His fingers dipped into her vagina, then out, in a little deeper, and out again. Brynne's legs tensed; her fingers stayed holding her swollen flesh open for him. Finally, when she was certain she couldn't take any more, he latched on and sucked hard on her swollen nub, thrusting his fingers into her as she came apart. A keening cry came from somewhere deep within and her hands let go to cover her mouth as she cried out and shuddered against him.

Slowly, the little tremors eased, and her breathing returned to normal. Gage dug a foil packet from his pants and donned a condom. She sat up and looked at him, her mouth in a pout. "I wanted to return the favor."

Shaking his head, he ground the words out. "I can't wait one more second to be inside you."

He climbed onto the bed and pulled her into his arms, his mouth devouring hers in a kiss so intense it stole her breath away. She tasted her juices on his tongue, and it sent her heartbeat into overdrive. The head of his cock pressed at her entrance, and she wiggled impatiently. He held himself still and through clenched teeth said, "Don't move."

Brynne held her breath as he pressed forward excruciatingly slowly, stretching her, filling her inch by delicious inch. She sucked on his tongue and yanked on his hair but kept her hips as still as she could. It would be easier if he'd tied her down, so she could not move a muscle.

When he finally sank his full length into her, Brynne sobbed into his mouth. He stopped kissing her and brushed her hair out of her eyes, looking questioningly. "Did I hurt you?"

"No. I just…it's been a while. It feels exquisite. Don't stop… please don't stop." She felt her face flush and closed her eyes, suddenly shy.

His hand encircled her neck, "Look at me, sweetheart." The playful curve of his lips vanished, replaced by an intensity that darkened his eyes. His whole demeanor shifted. "I'm going to fuck the living daylights out of you."

"Please, yes!" She pulled him down to kiss him, hungry for his mouth.

Gage withdrew slowly, leaving the head inside her. This time, when she raised her hips up to him, he drove it home like a tiger unleashed. One hand grabbed her wrists and pinned them over her head, the other grasped her jaw possessively, angling her mouth so he could deepen the kiss. He was as deep as he could go—his tongue in her throat and his cock buried to the hilt. She exulted in feeling totally possessed. Brynne wrapped her legs around his waist and tilted to receive him fully, stunned to feel the delicious ache of another orgasm building. When his grip on her tightened, she knew he was close, as if he feared she would try to escape. When his pace quickened, she heard a wail in the distance, unaware that it was coming from her. She screamed into his mouth as light exploded behind her eyes.

She was still shuddering and twitching, her legs having fallen to the bed, when he lifted himself up slightly, and thrust deeper still. He stilled, every muscle rigid. His mouth was open, but no sound came out. As his cock swelled and pulsed inside her, his body was like a statue, as if every ounce of blood and breath and cum left him petrified.

When he sank down on top of her, he buried his face in the crook of her neck. Their bodies were still joined, and she couldn't tell if it was her heart or his pulsating on her chest. Her eyes opened in shock when he continued to twitch inside her. It took every ounce of her willpower to let him go when he carefully withdrew and rolled onto his back.

He rose and said, "Be right back. Don't move."

Where the hell am I going? I feel like a bowl of Jell-O.

Gage turned before reaching her bathroom door, leveling a glare meant to intimidate, but all she could do was laugh.

He shook his head and tried not to smile. "Impossible brat."

Brynne lay there, her head spinning with what this night meant.

Would he let her keep working for him? Would he be willing to do this again? She was loath to ruin the moment by telling him the earth moved. Women probably gushed all over him, literally and figuratively. She would not be one of those. But god help her, it was the most amazing sex she had ever had.

During college, she learned how to maintain her distance and perfected the art of indifference. It was better to be the one who left first. She watched her girlfriends try to sink their teeth into the men they fell for, only to be dumped a couple of weeks later. Brynne learned from an early age not to get attached to anyone. Sex could be fantastic without all the gooey emotions that her friends fell prey to.

With Gage, she had to be careful. He didn't seem like the attachment type. However, that wasn't the most worrisome problem. She just might want him beyond her three-date limit. In fact, she wanted him again right now—and it wasn't just about writing better steamy sex scenes.

Nothing sent a man running faster than a clinging female post coitus. No choice but to play it cool. There was only one way to pull that off. She grabbed her pillow, turned over, and pretended to be asleep.

Gage stared at himself in the pitted mirror of her little bathroom and asked his reflection what the fuck he was thinking, taking a vulnerable, inexperienced member of his staff to bed?! He couldn't lay the blame solely on the harem outfit, although it was a factor. No, it started long before that. He knew he wanted her from the moment she dropped the ice cubes in his office. Tonight, he'd let his guard down and succumbed to playing knight in shining armor.

He was more content and sated than he had been in months. The self-imposed celibacy was obviously to blame. When she dared him, with that pouting bottom lip begging to be kissed, he should have turned around and left. But he didn't. How the fuck could he? Cole was right. She was begging to be taught. And god help him, he wanted to be her teacher.

He was hard again just thinking about it. If he didn't escape right now, he'd bury his cock between her sweet thighs again. Determined to make a quick exit, he washed up and returned to find her sound asleep. He smiled, hearing her soft breathing and intermittent snoring.

He pulled the covers up and tucked her in, unable to stop himself from touching a lock of her silky auburn hair. *Leave now, Mack.* He grabbed his clothes off the floor and went into the living room to get dressed. She lived modestly; her bedroom was the size of a broom closet, and her entire apartment could fit into the living room of his penthouse. He sat down on the rickety couch to put his shoes on and took in the clutter. Piles of handwritten pages littered her coffee table.

He was tying his laces when he saw the Limits list, which she must have filled out for Mistress Patricia. Against his better judgment, he took out his phone and snapped a picture of the two pages with all her ticked boxes. On the front were two sticky notes, one with the names of several kinky websites and the other with the web address of a BDSM chat room. Christ, he hoped she didn't think that was a safe way to meet people! He took that sticky note and put it in his pocket. A justifiable act of protection.

Taking a closer look at the list of websites, he wondered what the hell she was researching: Hogtied.com, PornHub, Sex&Submission, plus one he had not heard of—Badgirlsbible.com. His little pixie was quite the online adventurer.

He texted Angus that he was coming out and then perused her

bookshelves one more time. She obviously didn't want him to see her library of vintage Black Lace books, *The Story of O*, Anne Rice's tales of Sleeping Beauty, plus two shelves of historical romances. He would have to dig a little and find out what she was writing. She refused to tell him, but he could hazard a guess.

On the way back to the club, Gage checked his phone. Garrick said the party was winding down. Everyone was having a great time, and the bar was humming with the news of Dimitri's ousting.

He saw that Cole had tried calling him a few times, and he read a string of text messages.

> **Cole:** *Trouble back in Houston. Sorry man, I'm on my way back stateside. Will take a rain check on Berlin. I hope your harem girl is okay. And if you haven't properly bedded her, you're a fool.*
>
> **Gage:** *Properly bedded, but it changes nothing.*

If only he believed that.

16

A Very Persuasive Proposal

The plan to fake falling asleep backfired spectacularly. Brynne woke up just after six a.m. with a headache and a furry mouth. She brushed her teeth, took two painkillers, and crawled back into bed. Her mind shoved the ordeal with Dimitri under the rug so it could focus on all the delicious things Gage did to erase him. She would never look at her tea towel the same way again. And the spanking! It was a dream come true when he finally took her over his knee.

He came to her rescue, in more ways than one. And she fell totally under his spell. Remembering how he commanded her to touch herself made her blush and giggle. So did the realization that she would have done anything he asked.

One night was definitely not going to be enough. Now she had to convince him they should do it again. An offer of casual sex with no strings…maybe a little rope? Hopefully, he wouldn't insist she leave her job at Club Dominus, but if she had to quit, so be it. With him as her teacher, she would no longer need the club.

After a nice soak in the tub, Brynne called and left a message for her aunt. Next on her list was Jared, and he answered on the first ring. She told him what happened with Dimitri, how Gage threw him out of the club and accompanied her home. He squealed in delight when she shared what had happened afterward. On her way to Dominus, Brynne decided how she would persuade him to throw his rules out the window.

His office was empty when she stopped by, so she headed to the lounge and got busy. The patrons were still talking about Saturday night and Dimitri's departure. She and Mel exchanged glances. There was no time to talk because they both had several tables.

As the evening wore on, she grew more anxious. Gage hadn't sought her out, and there was no request to deliver his dinner. By the end of the night, she had worked herself into a state. Once the last table signed the check, she headed to his office.

His response to her knock was gruff. "Who is it?"

"Tink. Do you have a minute?"

"The door is open."

He was sitting on the large couch with his legs sprawled and a scotch in his hand. His hair was disheveled like he'd repeatedly run his hands through it. The ticking muscle in his jaw had her doubting her ability to convince him of anything.

She perched on the arm of a chair and wiped her damp hands on her skirt. "I would like to talk."

"There is nothing to talk about. Last night should not have happened."

"Maybe not, but I'm glad it did." She took a deep breath and continued, "I want to learn from you, submit to you. And if that means I must quit the club, just say so."

Brynne grabbed a throw pillow from the couch and kneeled on the floor at his feet. She lowered her eyes and placed her palms on her thighs.

"What do you think you are doing?"

"Proving how badly I want this." She met his gaze head-on. "Please let me show you how much."

Minutes passed. Gage got up and walked to the door. She was certain he was going to ask her to leave. Instead, she heard the clicking of the lock. When he sat back down, she remained still, staring at the floor, waiting for direction.

"Are you bloody sure about this, Brynne?"

"Yes."

"Yes, what?"

"Yes, sir, I am bloody sure."

He sat forward and lifted her chin so she could look at him. "You are a novice. I don't believe you have any real experience, even though you wrangled a glowing reference from Patricia Valentine."

"I don't know much. That's why I need you."

She licked her lips, and he made a strange sound deep in his throat.

"Aye, you need a teacher—a benevolent Dom to show you the ropes—but that man is not me. I'm a mean motherfucker who expects obedience. You haven't shown me anything but defiance."

"I know. I'm sorry for my rebelliousness, but I promise to follow all your directions to the letter from now on. Couldn't you give me another chance?"

"You have no idea what you are getting yourself into."

"What I lack in hands-on experience, I've made up for with intensive studying." Her eyes pleaded with him. "Will you please show me?"

Gage stood up and unbuckled his belt, and Brynne fought to contain her smile. He noticed. "Let's see if you are still smiling when I'm finished with you. Put your hands at your sides."

Brynne immediately complied. Gage wrapped his belt around her—pinning her arms to her hips. Then he buckled it snugly under her breasts.

"This is your last chance to change your mind. Tell me now if you want to leave, otherwise I'm going to put my cock in your mouth."

"I'm not leaving." She ran her tongue over her bottom lip in invitation and prayed he didn't change his mind.

He shook his head and drew his pants down. "Let's see what you can do with that pretty little mouth—besides get yourself into trouble."

Holy hell! Everything was riding on this. In a weird, fucked-up way, this was a job interview—only it was a blow job interview!

She took him into her mouth and swirled her tongue around like she was French kissing the head. Licking lightly, she coated him all over the crown, savoring the pre-cum gathering at the tip. Then she began nibbling and lapping at the sensitive underside. He sat back and his breathing hitched, giving her a surge of confidence. She refused to meet his gaze, afraid to lose focus. She used her lips and tongue to wet the shaft, starting at the base and moving up slowly. Pretending he was an ice cream cone, she sucked on the plum and moaned against him while taking the head fully into her mouth.

His hands gripped his thighs, and he growled. "Enough playing."

She rose to her knees so she could take him deeper into her mouth, each time pressing a little further. When she felt him bump against the back of her throat, she held him there, getting accustomed to it. She took a breath and pushed deeper, subduing her gag reflex. He groaned and took her head in his hands. His fingers sank into her hair at her temples and held her still for a moment. "I'm going to fuck your mouth. If you need me to stop or slow down, shrug your shoulders twice."

She nodded and let him take over. He leaned forward and pulled her slowly back so that just the head remained held by her lips.

"Don't let me slip out of your mouth." His voice was so rough, it made the hair stand up on her arms.

Brynne wondered what would happen if she failed to hold on. But she refused to fail. She wanted to surprise and impress him. The next time he drew her down, she forced her throat to relax, and when he pulled back, she wrapped her lips tightly around him and sucked hard. Judging by the noises he made, she was succeeding. His large hands cradled her face as he controlled the pace, deliberately slowing down and driving it deeper each time. Brynne moaned and looked up at him before propelling herself farther still. His jaw was rigid, like he was trying to stay in control and losing the battle.

He let go of her head then, and through gritted teeth said, "Show me."

It thrilled her to take over, and she threw herself into the task, taking him deep, swirling her tongue like she was strumming a guitar string. In her head, a heavy pounding drumbeat kept the rhythm of her strokes. She lost track of everything but her task until she heard his breathing getting uneven and heavy. Gage let out a guttural moan from deep in his chest, and his hands gripped the cushions of the couch. She felt him swell in her mouth. His legs jerked on either side of her, and he threw his head back and rasped, "I'm going to come—"

She appreciated the warning, but she wasn't about to stop now. When she felt his cock twitch, Brynne took a deep breath and pushed herself down deep enough that her throat held him in its thrall. She swallowed on it repeatedly and her throat gripped the head, milking every drop without a trace touching her tongue. He groaned loudly and swore, his entire body shuddering in reaction.

She slowly drew back, letting her tongue lightly trail a path to the top. Then she sat back and tried not to smile. But Christ, she was proud of herself!

Gage stayed as he was, resting his head on the sofa, staring at the ceiling. When he finally raised his head, he avoided eye contact and ran a hand through his hair. She swore he was suppressing a smile. He rose and stepped aside to fasten his pants, then reached for her. After helping her stand, he unbuckled the belt and guided her to the couch while he tucked his shirt in.

Brynne didn't want to be the first to break the silence. She watched him go over to the sideboard, enjoying the warmth he'd left behind on the leather cushion.

He poured two tumblers of scotch on the rocks. Handing her the drink, he tapped her glass and took a drink. Brynne did the same.

Fighting to contain an impish smile, she asked, "Was that okay?"

He shrugged and replied, "Not bad."

Brynne's mouth dropped open until she saw a twinkle of mischief in his eyes.

"Bha thu do-chreidsinneach." At her questioning look, he added, "You were incredible."

She beamed, all shyness forgotten.

"I don't want to ask how you…? Och, never mind."

Brynne giggled and shrugged. No one needed to know she had been practicing on fudge pops and cucumbers since watching Jared the week before.

She seized the moment. "So, will you tutor me in the art of submission?"

He closed his eyes and sighed.

"To put your mind at ease, I'm not looking for anything serious," she went on. It was time to lay all her cards on the table. "I want to explore my submissive side, and I think this could be a lovely diversion for both of us."

One eyebrow lifted. "What makes you think I need a diversion?"

"Seriously?" She grinned. "You are uptight, grumpy, focused on work all the time, and you get your jollies from making me run up and down the freaking stairs with your food."

"You really aren't a very good submissive, are you, Red?" His eyebrow lifted imperiously.

"No, but I don't know all the rules yet. With the right guidance, I can only get better."

"Don't you mean the right *punishments*?"

Her body and face warmed at that thought. "Um, yes, I imagine that will make a difference."

"This isn't a game, Brynne. If I take you on, you will do as you are told or suffer the consequences. I expect deference, not defiance. Obedience, not rebellion. I am accustomed to getting what I want—when I want. We will review your hard and soft limits and then discover all the things you don't even know you like—or dislike."

Brynne nodded and nibbled her lip. "I'm ready. I have done plenty of research."

He laughed harshly. "That can only take you so far. In your head, you might think you like restrictive bondage, for example, but until you experience it firsthand, you won't know. It will be my job to help you explore and understand your limits, while I train you."

"I understand." She could barely contain her excitement.

"We will see if you do. Get changed and meet me back here. I'll take you home."

Brynne nodded and hurried to change. She was in a state of euphoria and totally freaked out at the same time.

Angus nodded to her when he helped her into the Bentley. He

drove another long and convoluted way to her house and Brynne considered Gage's warnings about Dimitri. She stayed quiet and scanned her email while Gage did the same. When they reached her front door, she fumbled to open the lock, while trying to think of something witty to say. He snatched the keys and opened the door.

She stepped inside, expecting him to follow. Instead, he stood under her dim porch light and said, "Text me your personal email address. I will send you a document to review and sign."

"What kind of document?"

"An NDA, plus my medical report, and a referral to a clinic for tests. After that, we will discuss my expectations and your hard and soft limits."

"Oh." She felt awkward now and disappointed with his official tone.

"Nothing more should happen until those are complete."

He was all business, and she hated it. She thrust her chin out. "Is that all?"

"You can always change your mind. I'll understand."

"Do you want me to? Change my mind, I mean?"

He paused for a moment, his eyes narrowing. "No. But these formalities are in place to protect us both."

"I have no intention of changing my mind and I don't give a rat's ass about the paperwork. I would, however, like to discuss you fucking me into next week."

She saw his eyes darken, and his mouth twitched. "A rat's ass?"

"Please don't make me beg, but if that's your *thing*, I will." *Careful, Brynne.*

He pushed her into the flat and kicked the door shut behind them. His massive hand clamped around her neck, the warmth of his unyielding palm pressing against her hammering pulse. His fingers slid beneath her hair, tilting her head back until she felt the old dresser digging into her back. He buried his nose in the crook of her neck, inhaling deeply. A sharp nip at her ear sent a jolt through her, and he growled against her exposed neck, "You really like to test me, don't you, Red?"

"Yes," she breathed. It gave her a thrill to push the boundaries of his control. She wanted him to let go.

His grip on her hair tightened, and he nibbled her bottom lip. "If you were mine, you would quickly learn the consequences of disobedience."

"Don't hold back. I want to experience *everything*."

Gage stared at her, and it felt like time stood still. She knew it was a gamble, but there was no stopping now. In essence, she'd just said, "Do with me what you will."

His mouth devoured hers in a ferocious kiss. Their tongues met and dueled until they both had to come up for air. He abruptly pulled back, yanked off her coat, and tossed it on the floor. He frog-marched her to the couch and pulled her sweater up and over her head, trapping her arms in the sleeves behind her. Next, he dragged the cups of her pretty lace bra down, exposing her breasts so they swelled above the crushed material.

"I will fuck you into tomorrow, but you will not come." He rolled her aching nipples between his fingers as he continued, "In fact, you may not come until you've signed the documents and gotten tested—and then, only when I'm present to give you permission."

"That's just cruel," she whined.

"I warned you. Good girls only get to come when they do as they're told."

His body was up against her back, and Brynne could feel the hard line of his erection against her rear. She pushed her backside into him and maneuvered her hands so she could caress the bulge in his pants. In response, he tormented her nipples until she cried out.

"You're lucky I don't have a crop here to punish you properly."

Brynne knew one thing: He knew how to make her body sing. There was nothing contrived about his dominance. It was as natural as breathing to him. And it caused her insides to melt.

He pulled her head back so it rested on his collarbone. His gravelly voice vibrated against her ear. "Don't move." Then his teeth closed on her earlobe.

He shoved her legs apart with his foot. She moaned plaintively when his hands worked the button and zip on her jeans, quickly unfastening them. Heat radiated off his hands. She bit her cheek to keep from whining when his fingers burned a path south until they sank between her swollen folds and found her soaking wet.

"All for me." His hot breath bathed her ear as he played, caressed, and painted her skin with her juices. He was avoiding her throbbing clit and Brynne shifted her hips to aim his fingers. When that failed, she considered pleading.

His teeth still held her captive when he brought his hand to her mouth and smeared her wetness all over her lips and under her nose.

Brynne whimpered, and a tremor went through her body.

When he released her ear and turned her face toward his, she saw raw hunger radiating from his eyes. His gaze was full of fire and triumph. His fingers sank into her mouth, and she instinctively sucked on them with wild abandon. Holding her jaw in his iron grip, Gage licked and nibbled on her lips. If he wasn't holding her up, she would have sunk to the floor. His mouth covered hers and she tasted scotch and herself on his tongue.

He yanked her jeans and panties down to her knees and bent her over the arm of the sofa. She was helpless, exposed, and loving every single second of his power over her.

She floated somewhere between shame and excitement. The yearning to surrender to his control drowned out the voices whispering that it was wrong. Her heart soared when she heard the condom wrapper, and his harsh intake of breath. A moment later, he was spreading her cheeks wide, and she lurched in fear that he had another avenue in mind.

"Be forewarned, Red, you will take me there. But not until I have prepared you."

Brynne whimpered as he moved the head of his cock methodically back and forth, coating it in her arousal, taunting her clit.

"Please," she begged, hardly recognizing her voice.

Whether he was answering her prayers or giving into his own need, she didn't know and didn't care. When he entered her, it was sublime deliverance. He drove his full length slowly and deliberately until he buried himself balls deep.

Brynne squeaked in awe of the exquisite fullness, but before she could savor it, he grabbed hold of her hips and started plunging in and out, faster, and harder. His thighs smacked against hers over and over, making her dizzy. She heard his breath hissing between his teeth, then he dragged her up by the shoulders, so her back was up against his chest. She laid her head back, reveling in her helplessness, and he took advantage of her exposed neck, nipping and sucking on her hammering pulse.

"Look at me." It was a command, pure and simple. When she turned toward him, his hands seized her breasts forcefully, making her gasp. His mouth was on hers to take her breath into his. It was then, with their mouths fused, that he came in a violent torrent.

Gage expelled a harsh breath and carefully withdrew. The intensity of his release stunned him. If he wasn't careful, she could become as addictive as heroin.

Pulling up his pants, he made his way to the bathroom to dispose of the condom. After quickly cleaning himself, he returned to the scene of the crime. Brynne looked ravished and radiant—her lips swollen from his kisses; her breasts flushed pink from his rough treatment.

"You like to bring out the beast in me."

She had the decency to blush. Her playful smile disarmed him. He placed a kiss on each breast and pulled up the lace cups to cover the temptation. She wiggled her arms but couldn't get the sweater off without his help. Once free, she yanked up her jeans and glared at him. "I don't understand why you want to deny me an orgasm. It could take a week for me to get to the doctor."

"It is to teach you that I am in control of your pleasure, not you. You're accustomed to getting what you want, when you want it, through manipulation and misbehavior. Your submission allows *me* to decide what is best for you. And with it, I get the pleasure of delivering your long-awaited release."

"Oh."

"Where is your vibrator?"

Her mouth dropped open in shock. "Seriously? You don't trust me?"

"I'm removing unnecessary temptation." He searched the bedroom, then remembered the bathroom was the last place he'd seen it.

"Found it."

She wrinkled her cute nose in fury. "I can't believe you."

"Hmm, I'll enjoy thinking of you like this. Pent up, angry, needy, and waiting for me to deliver you from sexual purgatory."

"I didn't know you were a sadist!"

He smiled and winked. "I thought you wanted to learn about the B, the D, the S, and the M?"

She huffed out a breath. "Touché. I do." She lifted her chin. "You don't scare me."

"Good to know, Red."

She followed him to the door and crossed her arms petulantly. Without heels, she came up to his mid-chest.

He tipped her chin up. "I will know if you masturbate, and I will be very disappointed. Let's see if you can comply with this one request, knowing it will please me." He kissed her on her nose and left.

17

Heartbreaking News

Brynne had lain awake for hours after he left, savoring the scent of him on her skin and pondering what made him tick. Maybe his grudging agreement to tutor her meant the abominable iceman was melting. She still felt a surge of pride for making him come without using her hands. And before he could freeze up again, she taunted him into breaking his infernal rules.

While Gage might desire her, she didn't believe it could be anything more. Their worlds were so far apart, and no matter how it played out, this D/s dalliance wouldn't last. She was a novelty to him, and this was a social experiment to improve her book. Nothing more. The only problem was, she might need sex rehab when it was all over.

Nigel had left three articles on her desk, with a sticky note on top. *Do your magic. We need these before two p.m. today.*

Brynne got to work and finished the first two articles by noon.

She canceled lunch with Jared and told him he had to wait until after work for all the juicy news.

She was eating a sandwich at her desk when her cell phone rang.

"Hi Auntie! What's up?"

"Brynne. This is your Aunt Josie's lawyer, Alistair Mackenzie."

Her heart dropped into her stomach.

"I am sorry I'm calling with some bad news. Josie passed away yesterday."

"What?!" She choked back a sob. "No, that cannot be. Please say this is a joke!"

The man cleared his throat. "I'm afraid not, dear. I'm here with the doctor and it appears she took her own life."

"That's impossible. There must be some mistake."

"I take it you didn't know about her illness?"

Brynne put her forehead down on her desk. "What? No, she never told me. She said everything was fine." Her mind scattered. How could she not know this?

"Cancer had spread to her bones, and her brain. They gave her three months, and she was going to need palliative care quite soon. She refused it."

She started quietly sobbing. "How can this be?"

"Josie left a letter for us to find and has named you as her executor. She didn't want a funeral or public announcements until after you spread her ashes. There are more details I can share when I see you."

"Oh my god. Okay." Brynne tried to process his words. *Executor. Funeral. Ashes.*

The lawyer interrupted her scattered thoughts. "How soon can you get to Skye?"

Brynne grabbed a tissue and wiped her nose. "Uh, I will try to get a flight out this afternoon. I should be able to get there by tomorrow at the latest. But I have to arrange the time away from my two jobs."

"I understand, dear. There is money set aside for your travel and anything else you need. Do you need me to wire you an advance?"

"No. Thank you, Mr. Mackenzie. I can use my credit card, and we can figure this out when I get there."

They arranged to meet at his office tomorrow afternoon, unless she had an issue getting to the island. Brynne hung up the phone and stared at it, her mind in complete turmoil.

She didn't want to be seen bawling at her desk, so she ran to the restroom and sobbed alone in the stall. When she heard the outer door open, she held her breath and pulled herself together. She texted Jared a brief note.

Brynne: *My auntie passed away. She was dying and didn't tell me! Leaving for Skye asap. I'm her executor. Will call u later.*

Brynne repaired her tear-soaked face and went to find Nigel. Margaret was at her desk, reminding her of a mean junkyard dog.

"I need to see Nigel. I've got an emergency."

She looked over her reading glasses at Brynne and replied in a patronizing tone. "What's the emergency? I will see if he can spare the time."

Brynne felt the rage sizzling along her nerve endings, like the fuse on a stick of dynamite. She clenched her fists hard and dug her nails into her palms.

How about you get the fuck out of my way before I clobber you with your stapler.

Nigel saved Brynne from blurting her thoughts when he came out of his office. One look at his concerned face and she promptly burst into tears.

He ushered her into his office and shut the door. She sat opposite his paper-strewn desk and explained the situation in between sobs. He looked uncomfortable but told her not to worry about the unfinished article, someone else would finish it. Brynne nodded and stood—thanking him for being so kind.

The shock of the news—and the realization that Josie didn't trust her enough to share it—felt like a punch in the gut. Her nerves were frayed to the breaking point.

After a quick search, she booked a flight to Inverness. She reserved a car and a hotel, deciding against making the drive to Portree in the dark. Those roads were hard enough to navigate in broad daylight.

Brynne packed up her things, delivered the articles to Margaret's desk, and went to find a cab. On the way home, she tried to reach her father but had to leave him a message. For a moment, she thought of her mother. Was she alive, and if so, where was she? Frankly, she didn't care. It had been twenty-four years since Jaclyn Larimore had walked out the door, leaving her husband and daughter to fend for themselves. Aunt Josie lost her own father to a heart attack when she was young and her mother remarried Jaclyn's father when she was nine years old. The half-sisters were ten years apart, and never became close. After Brynne's mother abandoned them, Josie became the only maternal influence in her life. Losing her carved a gaping hole in her heart.

She must not sink into her own self-pity. She had to pack and be at the airport in two hours. There would be time to think once she was on the plane.

Brynne called Gage from her apartment and had to leave a message. *Why the hell is no one answering their phone?*

"Hi, it's me. Brynne. I…I've had a death in the family." She swallowed. "My auntie Josie. She was like a mother to me; she was there for me when nobody else was. Anyway, I have to help with the funeral arrangements. I just found out that I'm her executor. I'm sorry I won't be at work for several days. Um, I expect to be back by the weekend. I hope that's okay." She took a deep breath. "Okay, call me when you get this. Bye."

Next, she tried to reach Garrick but got his voicemail, too. Maybe it was just as well. She didn't want to say it out loud anymore. She secretly prayed it wasn't true, and that she'd wake from this nightmare soon.

She pulled out her small suitcase and paced around her bedroom in a fog, wondering what to pack. Her black dress and shoes went in first. On autopilot she gathered enough warm clothing for a week and called a taxi to take her to Victoria Station.

Her train to Luton was delayed, so she had to run for the boarding gate. Once she got to her seat on the plane, she saw three missed calls and several text messages.

Gage: *Brynne, I'm sorry to hear about your aunt's passing. Take the time you need. G.*

Jared: *Babe, I am so sorry. I know she meant the world to you. I'm here for you. Tried you a few times. Let me know you are there safely. Sending hugs! xo*

Brynne was exhausted and fell asleep before they reached cruising altitude. The budget flight to Inverness had no Wi-Fi so her replies wouldn't go through until they landed. She didn't know what to say to Gage, except *thank you.*

The car rental only had a manual mini compact left. Thank goodness her father taught her how to drive a stick when she was seventeen. It took three wrong turns before she found the little hotel.

With a deep sigh, she dropped everything and lay on the bed. She rang Jared and filled him in before going to sleep.

The day dawned gray and drizzly. She ate a hearty breakfast of eggs, bacon, black pudding, and toast before getting on the road. There was nothing like a good Scottish breakfast. She and Josie would often go to town on Sundays for breakfast at the Imperial Portree Hotel and then go on a nice long walk around town. Brynne remembered how she would flirt shamelessly with Declan, who owned the place. She wondered why they had never gotten together.

Two and a half hours later, as Brynne crossed the bridge to Skye, a feeling of peace engulfed her. She always felt safe, cared for, and loved here. It wasn't only her aunt who made her feel that way. It was the close-knit community, too. They looked out for one another, unlike the people in London, who rarely looked up from their phones and never said hello even if you passed them every day. *I've been gone from this place too long. I forgot how this island makes me feel.*

In Skye, she felt she was coming home. The craggy Cuillin mountain range, the rugged terrain, the mercurial ocean, which could go from calm to gale force waves in an instant. As a child, she would stare at the clouds and try to guess when the heavens would open. To this day, they were impossible to predict. As she navigated the winding roads toward Portree, a small smile came to her face as she recalled countless sweet memories of Auntie Josie reading to her while they sat in front of the fire pit wrapped in wool blankets. She shared many legends of the faeries inhabiting the Misty Isle. How apropos that Garrick had named her Tink after the famous storybook fairy—

not knowing her connection to them.

Would this island hold the same magic without Josie? Brynne couldn't think about it. It was all too depressing.

Less than an hour later, she arrived in downtown Portree and parked in front of the law offices of Alistair Mackenzie.

The old wooden door creaked loudly when she entered and the bell jangled, alerting everyone to her arrival. The décor of the waiting room was dated, and she could smell burnt coffee mixed with a slightly musty odor. Nature was calling, so she ventured down the main hall to find someone.

She found the bathroom before anyone appeared and was glad to get freshened up. Alistair was waiting for her when she came out.

"Brynne. It's lovely to see you, dear. I'm just sorry it's under these circumstances."

"Me too, Mr. Mackenzie. I'm afraid I am still in shock."

He was a kindly man, tall with carefully trimmed gray hair, horn-rimmed glasses, and a pencil mustache that reminded her of Clark Gable. "Alistair, please call me Alistair. Would you like a cup of coffee or tea?"

Brynne assumed the coffee had been on the burner since breakfast. "No, thank you. I had one on the road."

He led the way to his office, which resembled her editor's. Piles of paper were everywhere, and file boxes lined the floor behind his desk.

"I'm sure you're tired after your trip, so let me get right to it. Your aunt knew she was going to die and several months ago she put her affairs in order."

"When did she find out about the cancer?"

"About six months ago. She sensed it had come back because of pain in her hip and back. That's when she came to see me."

"I see." Brynne's shoulders slumped. "I should have noticed.

And I should have visited, but she always convinced me everything was fine."

Alistair looked her sternly in the eye. "Josie didn't want you to know. When she put her mind to something, nothing and no one could stop her. You know that."

"Yes, I suppose I do." Brynne nodded. Now it made sense why she insisted on putting Brynne on the deed of the house not long after she broke her hip.

"Josie left an additional codicil, in her own handwriting, which details her wishes. I'm here to help you with this. Her body is still with the coroner since they recorded it as a suspicious death."

Brynne nibbled her bottom lip. "Do you have an idea how long that will take?"

"A couple of days at the most. I don't want you to worry. Josie took care of most of the decisions for you. She prearranged with the funeral home for her cremation, and even booked Geordie Freeman to take you out on his boat to spread her ashes."

"Wow, she thought of everything, and I'm so grateful for that. You mentioned on the phone about not letting anyone know. How are we going to keep this secret? Everyone in this town knows everyone's business."

"That's the truth. But we will do our best. Only Declan knows, plus the doctor and the coroner. They are all sworn to secrecy."

"Did she have special wishes about the announcements or the obituary?"

"Oh yes. She wrote them herself and posted them to me a week ago."

"Of course she did." Brynne couldn't help but smile. That was the way her aunt did everything. With precision and good planning.

"She registered her last will and testament here with me. I have a copy for you." He handed her a sealed envelope, Josie's clean bold script on the front: *For Brynne.* "As her sole heir, and favorite niece, she left everything to you."

Brynne's mouth dropped open. "Oh my. I knew she wanted me to have the cottage, but do you mean the rest of her assets as well?"

"Yes. It is a substantial estate and will take time to get through probate, but you will be quite a wealthy woman, Brynne."

She sat back in the chair, holding the unopened envelope in her hands. The shocks just kept coming. "I'm stunned."

"It shouldn't come as a huge surprise. You were the daughter she never had."

Brynne's eyes filled with tears. Josie was her mother in every way except by birth. Remorse filled her because she hadn't been to the island in over nine months. Now it would never be the same. Her lighthouse keeper, the one who guided her through every storm, had gone dark.

Alistair handed her another envelope with the keys to the cottage and to Josie's car. "The car runs. Declan took her out in it every week and will continue to do that if you like. I presume you aren't staying long?"

"I need to get back to London by the weekend, if possible."

Alistair nodded. "I understand. We don't have to talk about this now, but if you want to sell, there is keen interest from the owner of the adjacent property."

"Okay. Good to know. I can't think of doing that right now but I appreciate knowing it's an option. Thank you for everything, Alistair."

"You're very welcome, dear. I'm here if you have any questions. I'll call you when I hear from the coroner, and we can proceed. For now, mum's the word."

Brynne nodded. She put the unopened copy of the will in her purse and hurried to the car. Ominous rain clouds had rolled into the harbor, mostly dark gray, some edged with silver. Her phone had been buzzing for the last hour, and she had multiple messages to answer. Before anything else, she needed to figure out where to stay the night.

She couldn't bring herself to sleep at the cottage alone. She needed a hotel, and the obvious choice was just around the corner. Declan was Josie's closest friend, lover, and often her caregiver. He owned the best inn and restaurant in town. She was tired and hungry and would benefit from his calm presence.

Brynne made it inside before the rain started. She booked a room and went to the inn's cozy bar and grill. Once seated, she let the hostess know she wanted to say hello to Declan.

He was not due back for about an hour, so Brynne ordered and checked her phone.

Jared: *Bree, let me know you reached Skye and that you are okay.*
J.

Brynne: *Hi J. All good. Made it to Portree. Met the lawyer. Going to stay in a hotel tonight.*
So much to tell you.
I'll call once I'm checked in.
xoxo

Gage had texted, which was a nice surprise.

Gage: *Let me know you've arrived and if there is anything I can do. Your shifts are covered.*
G.

Brynne obsessed over her reply, typing and erasing three messages. Finally, she settled on one:

Brynne: *All is okay. Already met the lawyer. I've got a hotel for tonight and will go to my aunt's house* *tomorrow. She made most of the arrangements in advance. I have to wait for her body to be released. I appreciate your offer. I'm doing okay. Brynne.*

A few minutes later, he responded.

Gage:　　*Good to hear.*

Brynne:　*I forgot to give you my email address. BALarimore89@gmail.com.*

Gage:　　*Thank you. I'll send the docs. No rush.*

Brynne was finishing her fish and chips when Declan walked in. His light blue eyes met hers and she saw pain reflected there. She stood when he reached the table, and they hugged for a long time. The lump in her throat threatened to choke her.

He took the bench opposite and covertly wiped a tear from his eye.

"It's good to see you, Brynnie."

His thick accent made her smile. He was a salt-of-the-earth Scotsman. His hair and beard had gone grayer since she last saw him, and he looked weary.

"You too, Declan. I really can't believe she's gone. I never got to say goodbye."

"I know, but she wanted it this way. She left a couple of letters at the house for you, which should help explain." His weathered hand reached for hers and squeezed.

"I don't think I can go there alone. I booked a room here tonight. Do you think you could come with me tomorrow?"

"Of course. I can take you after breakfast."

She put her other hand on top of his and smiled. Then she spied the redness on his forearm. "Is that a new tattoo?" Brynne lifted the cuff of his shirt to reveal the top of it. Below a beautiful drawing of angel's wings were the words *Josie, my Angel* in an old English script.

"It's beautiful! I love it." She spoke low, not wanting any attention. Declan had tattoos on his arms and chest, plus a few on his calves, which were visible when he wore his kilt. He looked pleased that she liked it.

"She put up a fight when I told her about it. But in the end, I convinced her." He winked suggestively when he said it, and Brynne blushed. "Okay lass, I must go. You call me if you need anything tonight." He kissed the top of her hand and stood. "I'll fetch you from the lobby at eleven tomorrow."

"Okay. See you then. And Declan, thank you for everything."

The waitress came over and talked her into trying the homemade Cranachan and a wee dram of whisky, compliments of Declan. Brynne was easy to convince, and she devoured the creamy confection of raspberries, whipped cream, and toasted oats, drizzled with malt whisky. She was pleasantly buzzed by the time she got to her room.

She avoided opening the will and instead ran a hot bath. Reading that document would make the nightmare real, and she wasn't ready for it.

Once she tucked herself into bed, she opened the envelope and finally read the contents. Alistair had given her a hint, but seeing the list of assets in black and white was another thing entirely. It mentioned the house, noting that she was already on the title. She would assume the taxes and upkeep beginning in six months. Josie's treasured '66 MGB was not to be sold, but if Brynne didn't want it, she should gift it to Declan Fraser.

There were several pages of legal jargon regarding her pension fund, and royalties from her books would continue to be paid by the publisher into an investment account, which would not be accessible until…

"What the fuck?!" Brynne screeched aloud. She read the last page of the document, and her mouth dropped open in shock. It laid out the conditions surrounding the inheritance in four bullet points:

- *Brynne must complete her revised manuscript within six months of my death.*
- *Brynne must open her heart to a loving relationship and banish the three-date rule from her vocabulary.*
- *She must endeavor to sustain a relationship with a suitable* man for a year.*
- *Finally, Brynne should spend at least four months a year on Skye for the next two years.*

*Suitable: Intelligent. Kind. Successful (this doesn't mean money). Honest. Preferably Scottish. Preferably Dominant.

Brynne blew out the breath she was holding and sank back into the pillows. So, this is what it came down to? Conditions! Stipulations! Clauses?! Josie knew her better than anyone and knew damn well she didn't like to be controlled. Yet she was trying to manipulate her from the grave? Not cool!

I love you Auntie, but this little plan of yours will not work!

Brynne would not go along with any of these bloody directives. She had two jobs, providing a steady income with a bit of extra cash to spare. God knows she had her hands full obeying a tall, annoying bastard back in London.

Brynne punched the pillow, turned out the light, and tried to get some sleep.

18

Storm Clouds in Skye.
Lightning in London

The hot fresh scones with jam only slightly improved Brynne's mood. Declan met her at eleven on the dot, and they headed to his truck. He broke the silence as they pulled out of the parking lot. "Did you not sleep well, Brynne?"

"No, actually, I didn't. I read my dear auntie's will last night. Seems she is having a laugh at my expense. She put some pretty ridiculous conditions in it, which I will not be following."

"Ooch."

Before he could reply, she plowed on. "For starters, she expects me to find a *suitable* man and hold on to him for at least a year!" Her temper was gaining momentum. "Oh, and she did me the favor of listing some *suitable* characteristics!" Each time she said the word suitable, her upper lip curled in contempt. "Suitable!" she repeated and laughed harshly.

Declan was silent. When she turned to look at him, his shoulders were shaking as he tried to stifle his laughter.

"It's not funny, Declan. *Suitable* men are fucking impossible to find. And she's one to talk! She could have opened her heart and gotten together with you, instead of keeping you at a distance all these years."

Oh, shite. I probably shouldn't have said that.

His face turned solemn. "It's more likely she didn't want you to make the same mistakes that she made. She couldn't take risks with her own heart, and I have a feeling she regretted that."

"Pfft. That doesn't mean it's okay to manipulate me like this." Brynne turned to stare out the window, glad to see the sun trying hard to escape the clouds' embrace. They turned into her aunt's road and Brynne immediately noticed a change.

"When did they pave the road?"

"That would be your new neighbor. The name is MacCallum. He didn't like the dust and gravel on his fancy cars, so he had the whole lane done."

"So strange not to hear the pebbles popping under the car." It annoyed her that this guy had altered the landscape of her childhood.

"Aye, wait until you see the massive house he built. They finished it last month. I'm sure you'll meet him at some point."

As the house came into view, Brynne gaped at the two-story stone-and-timber mansion.

"Jesus, are you sure it isn't a hotel? There are three chimneys!"

"Nope, it's definitely a single-family home, and he doesn't strike me as the type to let it, so don't worry about it becoming a bed and breakfast."

"Thank god. He certainly found himself a million-dollar view. You can see the outer islands from this spot." She snorted and looked at the front of the mansion as they passed. It was equally impressive, with a large balcony off the second floor and a ton of windows.

They drove down the winding lane and pulled in behind the modest cottage that her aunt had lived in for the past twenty-two years. Brynne looked up the hill, relieved that she could only see the roofline and a small row of windows from the center dormer of the huge house. She didn't like the idea of a stranger looking down on her little slice of heaven.

Taking a deep breath, she took in the stunning water view. The large flagstone deck ran the full width of the white stone house. Her favorite memories were of them snuggled up there in front of the fire pit.

As soon as Brynne walked in, she could smell her aunt's distinctive scent. For years she wore Bal à Versailles. She used to say it was a perfume created to attract a man, with the right mix of floral elements blended with sandalwood, leather, and sex. She would respond rather haughtily to anyone who questioned the choice, "If it's good enough for Elizabeth Taylor and Bianca Jagger, it's good enough for me." Brynne always thought it smelled like warm caramel and spices.

Memories of the last time they were together in this sanctuary by the sea came flooding back. Josie was her hero and had been since the day she welcomed the remote, angry little girl into her home so many summers ago. She was an independent, financially self-sufficient woman who didn't need a man to complete her. Unlike her own mother, she was thoughtful, nurturing, and she loved children. She was comfortable by herself, which was good, because writing was a solitary pursuit, especially in this remote part of Skye. Josie never wanted to come back to London or Edinburgh. She'd say, "Those people are gray and colorless, Brynnie. They dress in blue suits every day, ride the tube to work, come home and stare at the TV, until the next day when they do it again. Don't ever be one of those."

Brynne would reply, "No way Auntie, I'm going to be an adventurer like you!"

Even though she loved living in the Highlands, she traveled around the world countless times. Josephine Lamond did countless book signing tours, African safaris, Southeast Asia island getaways, spa retreats in Switzerland, ice hotels in Norway, and cruises to Greece and Italy. She went abroad every year for at least two months to replenish her imagination for her books.

Josie renovated the one-and-a-half-story crofter's cottage when she first came to Skye. She added a second bedroom and bath on the main floor and created a laundry and mudroom. In the harsh light of day, Brynne saw it looked rather tired. She considered how long her aunt was unwell, and guilt swept over her at not visiting more in the last few years.

Declan interrupted her thoughts. "There are a couple of letters on the kitchen table for you. I'm going to take a walk, and I'll run the car so you can have time to yourself."

"Thanks, Declan."

She went up to Josie's second-floor retreat and sat in the cozy window seat that overlooked Cuillin Sound. The sky was moody and dark, like her thoughts. She wasn't ready to stay here tonight, especially if this was where Josie died. She would ask Declan.

Brynne believed steadfastly in the soul and the Universe and Heaven and destiny. She wondered, not for the first time, if Josie messed with her destiny. Then again, perhaps she was supposed to leave with dignity and intention.

Hopefully the letter would help her understand.

Dear Brynnie, my love,

I am sorry that I didn't tell you of my impending demise. There was nothing anybody could do, so I decided the only course of action was to depart before the illness could overwhelm me. The end would be ugly, and I was having none of that.

Don't you dare think that I gave in without a fight. I sought second, third, and fourth opinions. I investigated treatments from all the best minds in medicine, but this disease had too tight a hold on me and my important bits. While I still had my faculties, I knew I had to get my house in order.

You know I wanted you to have this little hideaway. Whether you live here full-time or only spend the summers, it will be your bolt hole when the world gets to be too much. Just promise me you won't ever stop living, writing, loving, traveling, and adventuring.

By now you have read my will and you're pissed off. Good. That is the reaction I wanted. I intended it to snap you out of your melancholy and into another primal emotion. That's not to say I didn't mean it. I chose those conditions— and in time, you will understand why.

Repairs need to be made to the house. I've let things go the last few years. But you can fix it up to suit yourself. This is the place where I wrote my best stuff: the wildness of the sea, the howling winds, the rain you'll swear has teeth. They all kept me sharp, and they will do the same for you. Just don't underestimate Mother Nature. She can be a fickle bitch in any season.

By now, you're probably wondering where I did it and how. Please rest easy knowing my spirit was carried swiftly away by gusts from The Minch to the North Atlantic. I took a conglomeration of pills, wrapped myself in a blanket, and sat at the firepit. It was one of my favorite places on this earth because of the times we shared. When you sit there, I will always be in the chair beside you. No, I won't haunt you, dearest. I hope I can float in when you need me. And when you bring a man around, I promise not to stick around and watch!

I love you, my Brynnie. You were, in every way, the daughter I always wanted. God brought you to me when we were both lost, and you were a gift that enriched my life.

Live life juicy, my peach!

xoxo Josie.

Tears traced a path down Brynne's face and dripped onto the page. She felt some measure of comfort knowing she couldn't have changed the outcome. Josie died outside, in her favorite spot, not in the house. That thoughtful decision was one of many her aunt planned to ensure Brynne was okay.

She put the letter back in the envelope and noticed the writing on the second: *Do Not Open for 8 Weeks.*

Brynne shook her head. Josie was still orchestrating mystery and intrigue from the great beyond. She went in search of a tissue to blow her nose and rescued Declan from hanging around waiting for her. She would spend one more night at the hotel, then come to the house tomorrow.

Thunder and lightning began their heavy metal concert around three a.m. Gage loved the penthouse, but there was no escape from the deafening sounds of an intense spring storm. He normally slept deeply, but tonight he had lain awake for hours.

He was not easily shocked, but Brynne managed to surprise

him. She set out to convince him, and by god, that blow job was bloody amazing. It was more remarkable because she didn't seem very experienced. Then again, maybe he was losing his ability to read women. He had been totally wrong about Sierra. Could he be off base regarding Brynne, too? When she returned, he would find out what she was made of—and how far she would go in her pursuit of BDSM knowledge. Whether it was in business or personally, he prided himself on discovering what a person's true motives were. Brynne remained a mystery.

It felt like he had just dozed off when the alarm jolted him awake. Then he realized it wasn't an alarm. His phone was ringing.

"What the bloody hell?" he groaned as he stretched to reach the night table. He glanced at the screen.

"Garrick, what's going on? Is the club on fire or something?"

"No, but this could be just as bad."

Garrick never got rattled, but his voice sounded off. Gage sat up, a sense of foreboding coming over him. "What the fuck is it?"

"I couldn't sleep with the storm, so I was scanning the news on my phone. There's a goddamned story about the club. Not only does it reveal your name as the owner, but it lists key members, including John, Martin, Dimitri, Judge Marchand, two members of Parliament, and a member of the House of Lords. My email has blown up in the last half hour. The print edition is landing on people's doorsteps as we speak."

"How is this possible? Who the fuck wrote it?" Gage was up and fishing his tablet out so he could read it.

Garrick swore. "*B. Larimore*. Oh my god. Brynne?!"

A million thoughts warred for supremacy in Gage's brain. "That conniving little bitch. She disappeared just in time. In fact, I would bet there was no death in her family." *How could I be so wrong? So stupid?*

"Gage, this doesn't seem right. Why?"

"To get a promotion, to get famous. Who the fuck knows! But when I'm done with her, she will be lucky to get a job washing dishes in this city."

"Fuck." Garrick sighed heavily into the phone.

"Get in touch with everyone who is named and let them know we are working on a retraction. I need to speak to the owner of that rag they call a newspaper. They have no idea the powerful people they have pissed off. It will cost them some serious advertising revenue."

Gage pulled up the article and swore.

Club Dominus: Who is behind London's kinky private men's club for affluent misogynists?

Gage MacLeod, Scottish club owner, runs this hideaway for the immoral. Members of this exclusive men-only club include high-ranking officials from Scotland Yard and London's Parliament. Inside this den of iniquity, you might run across judges, CEOs, and the sons of London's wealthiest families. So, what goes on in the unassuming Georgian in London's West End? All kinds of kinky sex games. Just last week, they put on a racy Arabian nights party, with sexy harem girls wearing collars and chains. If you want to paddle your partner, you need only go upstairs to access the punishment room. Head to the top floor if you want to hire a themed room to have sex with a male or female slave. It's London's best kept secret brothel.

She listed six members by name and had the audacity to suggest the place be shut down.

"I'll meet you at the club in an hour. Send an email to all our members to say the club will be closed for a couple of days. And add that we'll be in touch as soon as possible with more information. I'll ask John to meet us there as soon as he can. We need to discredit her and the paper."

"Got it. See you there." Garrick rang off and Gage jumped in the shower.

Thirty minutes later, his driver passed in front of the club where several paparazzi were staking out the main entrance. Gage was glad he had an underground garage linked to another building, so no one would know when he entered or exited.

His mother had tried him three times, but he ignored the calls. Until he had a plan, he wouldn't speak to her. John answered on the first ring and Gage worked to calm him down.

An idea took shape while he was getting ready. John could tell his superiors that Gage asked for his advice about a member he suspected of dirty deals, and they met to discuss it in the lounge. Hopefully, Brynne knew little more than his name and that she'd seen him. Since the article mentioned nothing about the private party, he hoped it was safe from exposure. Especially since her best friend was the star attraction. The worst-case scenario would be the exposure of John's sexuality when he had not come out to anyone, including his family. Gage needed to call her friend Jared and warn him to keep his mouth shut.

Once in his office, he called the editor of the *Mirror*. Garrick gave him Jared's cell, and he called him too. Gage expected the voicemail message would scare the shit out of him.

"Jared, if you value your business and reputation, you will speak to no one about my club. Ever. You can, however, tell your friend that her career as a journalist is over. She has crossed the wrong person, and so have you. You're both fired."

Next, he crafted an email to the members he surmised had large ad budgets and gave them instructions to threaten full withdrawal if the paper did not retract the story.

The editor called him back within the hour. Nigel Linkletter sounded like a complete wimp. He spent ten minutes apologizing, and Gage had the distinct impression he didn't know about the article before it landed on his front page.

Gage used his scariest Dom's voice. "Listen Linkletter, I expect a full retraction of this story. This woman got a job in my club under false pretenses. She collected information about some of the most influential people in this city. By now, I imagine you have received multiple emails demanding a retraction and an apology. Unless, of course, you and the paper's owners don't care that your ad revenue is disintegrating as we speak."

Nigel cleared his throat, but Gage kept going. "Furthermore, what happens in my club is nobody's business. Nothing illegal goes on at Dominus, and we practice safe, consensual activities in complete privacy. You should also know that my next call is to the CEO of the *Mirror's* parent company. I am sure Mr. Knight will be interested in knowing you published a story that embarrassed his father and several of his close friends."

Gage heard a choking sound through the phone. Linkletter cleared his throat. "Mr. MacLeod, I am very sorry for this. Give me until this afternoon. I need to speak to my superiors about a retraction and get back to you."

"When you see the ramifications of this ridiculous story, you'll see that is your *only* course of action. Expect to hear from my lawyers before noon today."

Gage hung up and threw his phone down on his desk. Garrick did some digging and found out that the *Mirror's* owner was none other than Roger Knight. His father, Douglas, was one of the first members of the club. That little discovery might turn the tide in their favor.

Now his mother was texting him. She never texted.

Mother: *Where are you? Call me ASAP. Have you seen the news??*

Gage needed a coffee before he rang her back. He made an espresso and sat down at his desk.

She picked up before it had the chance to ring. "It's about time! Would you care to explain what the hell happened, son? The only thing that saved us is them not knowing your real name or your relationship to me."

"Mother," he began.

"Don't *Mother* me. I was afraid of this. That club is going to destroy your reputation, and by association, it will damage mine." Her shrill voice assaulted his ears.

"I'm taking steps to get it retracted. They won't find out who I am. And if they do, you can publicly disown me. I'm tired of sneaking around. I am who I am. That will not change just because you're a judge."

"Well, I may not get the appointment with this scandalous story around our necks. Who is this B Larimore, anyway? How did they get those members' names?"

"It's a long story and not one I want to get into with you. I have taken steps to remove her as well. She won't be writing another word."

"She? A woman wrote that story?"

"Yes. Look, I must go. There are members calling for my head on a platter, and some want refunds. I'll call you on the weekend."

"Okay, dear. Good luck. I hope to Christ you can fix this."

"Goodbye, Mother."

John arrived forty minutes later. He and Garrick sat down and the three of them formulated a plan that Scotland Yard would buy.

By midday, they had appeased most of the members. Two demanded to exit their contractual membership and get their fees back. Gage quietly freed up one million pounds and arranged wire transfers. The club's bank account was buried under a numbered company, which was registered under a second numbered corporation that Gage used for investments he didn't want tracked to his London identity or his Edinburgh venture capital firm.

Once he calmed down, he dialed Brynne. Lucky for her, it went to voicemail.

"You have crossed the wrong person, Ms. Larimore. I don't know what you thought you would accomplish with that story, but what you've got instead is the obliteration of your journalism career. If you even had a career. And as far as your bullshit submissive games are concerned, you are finished in the London scene too. It's a pity you didn't realize how far my connections run. This may sound cliché, but mark my words, you will never work in this town again."

He stabbed the hang-up icon. Instead of feeling better, he felt more out of sorts. He wanted to punch something. *How could he have been so stupid? How could he have trusted her—fucked her?*

19

Misfortune & Meltdown

Brynne almost kissed the ground when they got back to the dock. She rarely suffered from seasickness, but the channel between Skye and the Isle of Eigg was very rough and the engine of the fishing boat cut out three times, requiring Geordie to go below and tinker with it while she turned green up on the deck. He insisted on a life vest and hooked her to the railing. His excessive precautions made her nervous, but today was the only day he could take her out. Brynne was thankful when the coroner released Josie's body for cremation yesterday morning. Now she could return to London tomorrow.

He took the fishing trawler into the middle of the channel and assured her it was the best spot because the currents were strong, and they would whisk her adventurous aunt to all the far-off places she liked to visit. Geordie didn't strike her as the fanciful type, but she was glad to have his company when she sprinkled Josie's ashes into the dark teal waters of the Sea of the Hebrides. The winds had their own plan. As she finished shaking the urn, some ashes flew up into her face and hair. She smiled to herself—perhaps that was her aunt's last kiss before departing.

Three layers couldn't keep the wind from chilling her to the bone. She was looking forward to a bath and a hot toddy when she got home. As she turned into the lane, her phone started buzzing in her handbag. A signal here meant her rich new neighbor probably bumped up the cellular antennae in the area to ensure he was never without service. The vibrating and pinging didn't stop, so she pulled to the shoulder and fished it out. The screen showed multiple missed calls and eight text messages.

What on earth?

Jared had texted all eight messages.

Jared: *Bree—call me as soon as you get this.*

Jared: *Where are you?*

Jared: *All hell has broken loose. Why did you do this?*

Jared: *What were you thinking?*

Jared: *They fired me.*

Jared: *WTF?!*

Jared: *Now I'm sick with worry*

Jared: *Are you okay?*

There was a missed call from Gage, another from Garrick, and Nigel had called four times.

Since the signal was strong there, she rang Jared.

"Bree, what the fuck! Where have you been? What were you thinking?"

"J, what are you talking about? I've been on a boat all morning spreading my aunt's ashes. What the hell has happened?"

"Oh, my god. Are you serious? The article. They published your article. Why didn't you tell me you were writing that?"

"Jared, I don't know what you're talking about. What article?"

"The article that ran in the *Mirror* this morning about the club. The article naming clients, revealing what goes on there. Are you saying you didn't write it?"

"What?! No! I have no idea what you're talking about—text the link to me. I'll put you on speaker so I can read it."

"Bree, listen. This is fucking serious. Gage fired me, and he warned me not to speak to anyone. The club is closed for the next few days. And Nigel is looking for you. He asked me where you were. He looks like he could have a heart attack any minute."

The phone dinged, and she opened the article.

"Oh. My. God. Who would do this? How did my name get on it? J, I didn't write this. I would never do such a thing. You know that, don't you?"

She continued to read and started shaking, her heart thumping in her ears.

Jared broke into her scattered thoughts. "Babe, this looks really bad. You work at the club, you work at the paper. If you didn't do it, it's a perfect frame job."

"I need to call Gage back."

"You need to call Nigel first—explain to him you didn't write it."

"Okay, right. I'll call him. I have a ton of missed calls. Let me listen to the messages."

"God, if you have a message from Gage that sounds anything like mine, it will flay you alive. Just know he thinks you betrayed him."

"I'll call you after I speak to them. I have a flight booked tomorrow and should be home by two o'clock."

"Okay. Good, I will see you tomorrow. But call me later."

"I will. J, I'm sorry he fired you. That's ridiculous. We had nothing to do with this. I'll sort it out."

"I know. Don't worry about me. I'm okay."

Brynne accessed her voicemail. Nigel sounded like a man losing his grip on reality. She had never heard him swear, but his messages were littered with *fucks* and *shits* and a few *Christ-almightys*.

She had to leave a message. *God damnit!*

"Nigel. It's Brynne. Please call me. I was out on a boat and missed your calls. I did not write that article. I don't know how this happened or who put my name on it. It was not me. Please call me."

Next, she listened to Gage's message. If she could describe the devil's voice, it would sound like his. Ferocious, dark as pitch, flames licking at the edge of every syllable. *My god, he hates me.* She burst into tears.

It took her a few minutes to catch her breath. How could he believe she did this? She had to explain this was a mistake. A horrible mistake. She dialed his mobile; it rang once and then a message played: "The caller you are trying to reach is not available."

A sense of dread settled in her stomach. Had he blocked her number? She tried texting.

Brynne: *Gage, please call me. I did not write that article.*
             I would never do such a thing.

It wasn't delivered even though she had four bars. *This cannot be happening.* In desperation, she tried calling the club. Garrick answered.

"Garrick, it's Brynne Lar—"

Click.

She tried again, and it kept ringing until the automated voice said the mailbox was full. Her hands started shaking. The phone slipped out of her grip and disappeared between the console and the seat. Tears ran unfettered as she pounded the steering wheel in a total meltdown.

"Fuck!" she screamed in the confines of the little car. She scraped the top of her hand raw fishing the phone out, then searched for Garrick's email address.

> Garrick, please—you must believe me. I did not write that article. I don't know who did. But I didn't betray any confidence and would never do that. Please call me back.

She sent it and took a deep breath. How could this happen? Who would do this to her? Margaret hated her, but she knew nothing about the club. That was a dead end. Someone who worked at the club could have provided information, but how did it get published? And why?

She drove to the cottage and stumbled inside, her mind numb. She was hungry but felt sick to her stomach. The cup of tea and toast she made went untouched.

The phone rang, and she fumbled to hit the right button to answer.

"Nigel. Thank god."

"Listen, Brynne. I have no choice but to fire you. You gave the sub-editor a story that wasn't vetted or approved. You put me and the paper in an untenable position. MacLeod wants to sue us."

"Nigel, I don't know who did this or how it happened, but it wasn't me. You must believe me; I've been in Skye dealing with my aunt's death."

"I am sure you regret writing it now, but you should've thought of that before you submitted the story for publishing." He had never spoken to her in that harsh tone. "Margaret will pack your personal things and leave them at security. You should find a new line of work. No paper or magazine in London will give you a job. Gage MacLeod has made sure of that."

"What?"

"I'm sorry, Brynne. I liked you and you did a good job copy editing, but I will be lucky to keep my job after this."

Click.

Brynne took her head in her hands and started sobbing. How could she prove her innocence if they barred her from the paper? If she was unable to reach Gage or Garrick, she had no way to defend herself at the club, either. What was she supposed to do?

She went upstairs, crawled into bed, and cried herself to sleep. It was dark when she awoke to the ping on her phone.

Jared: *Any update?*

Brynne: *No one believes me. Garrick wouldn't speak to me. Gage has blocked me from calling or texting. Nigel fired me and there's no way for me to prove my innocence.*

Jared: *Oh, babe, I am so sorry. What are you going to do?*

Brynne: *I don't know. I can't think. There's nothing for me in London. Nigel said Gage told every paper that I'm persona non grata. I will make a few calls on Monday, but I doubt I'll find a job anywhere.*

Jared: *Maybe you should stay in Skye for a while? Let the dust settle.*

Brynne: *You might be right. Eventually I'll need some more clothes, though. I didn't bring much with me.*

Jared: *Why don't I come up next weekend and bring you what you need? How far is the drive?*

Brynne:	*Oh J, it's a twelve- or thirteen-hour drive. I couldn't ask you to do that.*
Jared:	*It's the least I can do. I feel partially responsible. I got you into the club.*
Brynne:	*That wasn't your fault! I wanted it and dove in headfirst. Who could have predicted this?*
Jared:	*No one. It makes no sense—who would want to hurt you?*
Brynne:	*I don't know, but they succeeded in destroying my career. My reputation is mud.*
Jared:	*Hang in there. I'll see what I can find out. You stay put.*
Brynne:	*Okay. I'm going to cancel my flight and figure out a plan tomorrow.*
Jared:	*Okay, babe. Night. Xo*

Six days blurred into one another. Brynne didn't leave the house, and no one knew she was still in Skye. She was running out of basic necessities and would need to go to the store soon. The rental car was due back too, but she couldn't summon the energy to do anything. Her meals consisted of toast, coffee, and eggs. All the crackers and cheese were gone. That morning, she found a few tins of soup in the pantry, so she didn't have to go out. Instead, she lay back on the couch and closed her eyes.

Jared texted each day to make sure she was okay. She hadn't opened her laptop or looked at her email since Friday when her world imploded.

The sound of tires on gravel had her jumping off the couch. When the garage creaked open and she heard the MG start, she knew it had to be Declan. She checked herself in the bathroom mirror, stunned at the pale face and sunken eyes that stared back. Her hair looked like a rat's nest. She hadn't changed or showered in a couple of days. Or was it longer? She should fix herself up or Declan might worry she had lost her mind. Not her mind, just everything else.

She put on a pair of wellies and an old hat and headed out the back door.

He was looking under the hood of the car and jumped in shock when the screen door slammed. "What the hell? Brynne—what are you doing here? I thought you went back to London?"

She shook her head, unable to utter a word. He took one look at her forlorn expression and hurried across the yard. When he pulled her into his arms, she struggled to catch her breath.

"Shhh, there lass, dinnae fash. It's going to be all right."

She refused to give in to another bout of tears. Her body stiffened and she pulled back to look at him. "No, it's not, Declan. But it doesn't matter."

"What are you talking about? Josie wouldn't want you to wallow in sadness for her."

Brynne shook her head. "It's not that. I've lost both my jobs; someone framed me, and I have nothing to go back to in London."

They went inside, and Declan whistled in shock. She cringed seeing the mess. Dishes were piled in the sink, the garbage was overflowing, and crumpled tissues littered every surface.

Brynne tried to tidy up, then gave in and shrugged. "It's been a terrible couple of days."

They sat on the couch where she had been sleeping, eating, and crying for countless hours, and she told him everything.

He sat silently until she finished. "Listen up, Brynnie, you need to snap out of it. You may not be able to prove your innocence, but you can't let them win."

"But—"

"No buts. I've got an opening at the inn, in the bar. The best thing for you is to get out of this house."

Brynne sat there nodding, unable to produce a good reason not to take him up on his offer. Sure, she needed the money, but she had no desire to be around anybody. "I need a few days to pull myself together."

"Fine—you have until Friday. I'll expect you in for the lunch shift. You can work alongside Myrna."

"Okay." She sighed, letting him win this round.

"I'll see you there at eleven a.m. And Brynnie, I'm going to leave, and you need to get in the shower. You look like something the cat dragged in."

She blushed to the roots of her ratty hair, which was sticking out of the wool hat. "I will. I need to go to town for groceries and maybe get a haircut."

"That sounds like a right good plan, dear."

He hugged her goodbye. His parting words made her smile. "You have a book to finish and a life to create, Brynne. Josie is tsking from up above and you know she's saying, 'No more moping. What's for ye will no' go by ye.'"

After a long hot shower, she felt restored, and better able to think. She could stay in Skye for a while and work on the book, but what about after that? Perhaps she was destined to disappear into the woods like the fallen angels? The Highland legends say the faeries hid in the forest after being driven out of Heaven with the devil and the sounds of their cries can be heard in the wailing wind. Brynne remembered when Josie read to her from Otta Swire's book about the Skye for the first time. She cried when she learned the faerie angels were never restored to God's favor.

Brynne shook herself free from those melancholy thoughts. If she wasn't careful, she would be back in bed, buried under the covers. She booked a haircut for that afternoon and made a list for the supermarket.

Gage hung up from his lawyer and went to find Garrick. He decided they should sue the newspaper for defamation of character and libel. It was a long shot, but he hoped other members would follow his lead and intimidate them. Usually newspapers were careful to say "allegedly" when they gave no proof sources. Brynne had called his club a brothel, which was patently untrue. If he had to, he would also sue her for reckless intent to smear his name.

Garrick also made calls all afternoon. He confirmed that five of their members were sending emails to the *Mirror's* owner and threatening to pull their advertising. Gage was intent on a front-page retraction and admittance of negligence by the paper for allowing a false and damaging story to run. He showed Garrick the email he crafted to Roger Knight, which would follow the delivery of his lawsuit against the newspaper.

"I suggested they admit a person inside the paper circumvented the process and was subsequently fired for cause. They can prattle on about the procedures they will change so that nothing like this can ever happen again. Then they can apologize to me and the members whose reputations were tarnished by their incompetence."

Garrick nodded. "I like that approach. If they feel enough heat, we should get the retraction. And Dominus will live to see another day."

"I won't go down without a fight." He sat on the couch and ran his hands over his face. "I could use a drink. What have you got handy?"

"Courvoisier XO?"

"Perfect. Will you pour me one?"

Gage was never more thankful to have Garrick running the club with him. He was a solid manager, always fair and hard as nails when needed. In all the years they'd known each other, he'd never seen him lose his cool, even with the assholes.

Garrick handed him the tumbler of cognac and clinked it with his own glass. "Slàinte."

Gage looked at him, his eyes solemn. "Slàinte Mhath, mate. I could not have survived today without you."

"I've always got your back, man. On that score, you never have to worry. Now, tell me what your mother had to say about today's fiasco?"

Gage rolled his eyes and took a swig of the amber liquid. "I put her off for now. Nobody has figured out my real name, so they cannot link her to the scandal. Thank god I revealed nothing else to that little bitch. I'm glad she wasn't around long enough to do more damage."

Garrick sat back and rubbed his chin. "I don't know, man. Why would she do this? I'm an excellent judge of character. How could I be so far off?"

"You are not the only one she fooled, Garrick. It seems Tink is quite an actress in her own right."

"She emailed me and insists she didn't write the article. However, from what we know, no one else had the access to get that story into print."

"Exactly. She had the means and the motive." He shook his head, his jaw set. "Enough pondering the why, I will not waste another second on her. I think we should remain closed this weekend and see what our campaign nets. The best-case scenario is we have a retraction on Monday. If not, we go to Plan B."

"What's Plan B, boss?"

Gage smirked. "I have no fucking idea."

20

Starting Over

Brynne opened her eyes and groaned, "Oh. Wow."

The hairdresser's smile faltered when she saw her face. "Please say you like it. I think it looks amazing. You suit a pixie cut!"

Brynne forced herself to smile at the girl. After all, she got what she asked for.

Cut it all off. Those words came back to bite her.

"I like it, really, I do. It's just a bit of a shock, that's all." Brynne examined her new look and took a deep breath. *Okay, it's not so bad. I can style it a few ways, and it'll be easy to care for.*

The girl had a mirror in her hand, but she stood there biting her lip nervously. "It's always an adjustment when you do a big change like this."

"You're right. You did a great job. I needed this. Thank you." She smiled fully to put her at ease. "I love it."

She headed into the grocery store, feeling lighter than she had in days. She loaded the cart with all her favorite comfort foods and a few vegetables because her conscience told her to. At the checkout line, she was debating a chocolate bar when a headline stabbed her between the eyes.

Who is the Real Owner of Club Dominus?

Her stomach dropped. The hounds were out for blood. It was obvious that this disreputable excuse for a paper wanted to keep the story front and center. They were capitalizing on the mystery surrounding Gage. She hated to give that gossip rag any money but added it to her order, then hurried to the car with her bags.

> We have not yet uncovered the identity of the elusive owner of London's poshest BDSM club. It's buried in several numbered companies.

Her head fell back to the headrest in relief. They hadn't uncovered any information on Gage. He might hate her right now, but she hoped to one day exonerate herself and have his forgiveness. *Fat chance.*

They also speculated that Russian mafia money backed him. That was a ridiculous way to sell papers. Then her eyes zeroed in on her own name near the end of the page. *Fuck!*

> Brynne Larimore, a lowly copyeditor who worked at the paper, allegedly wrote the article to punish MacLeod for dumping her. The *Mirror* fired her, and she has not responded to requests for an interview.

"You have got to be kidding me!" Her screech was loud enough to draw the attention of two people walking by. *Gage had to be the source of that made up shit!*

She dialed Jared as she reread the lies, getting increasingly agitated.

"Have you seen the tabloid? That bastard told everyone a story about me to cover his own ass! He basically said I made the whole thing up to punish him!"

"Calm down, Bree. I don't think it's such a terrible thing."

"Not terrible? In what universe, J?"

"The sooner this thing dies down, the better for all of us. You included." His placating tone was annoying as shit.

"So, you think it's better I look like a woman scorned than a journalist writing an exposé that angered London's kinky elite?" As she said it, she could see the logic, but it still pissed her off.

"Yep. It will take the sizzle out of the story. And Gage got a retraction printed on the front page on Tuesday. Didn't you see it?"

"No. Today was my first day off the couch. I guess I should be glad." Her harsh laugh was devoid of humor. "Maybe now he won't put a hit out on me."

"Not funny. Oh, I almost forgot to tell you. Nigel took a leave of absence. I don't know if he'll be back."

"Oh great, one more horrible thing they're laying at my feet. They need to figure out who did this so innocent people don't get blamed."

"I agree, but everyone just wants it forgotten." Jared paused, then added, "The club reopened yesterday."

"Do you think they'll let you back?"

Jared paused. "Not likely. There is a member who might go to bat for me, though."

Brynne bit her lip. It must be John. God, she hoped nothing bad happened to him because of the story. "I hope so. I know you loved it as much as I did. Too bad it put an end to my sex education."

"Speaking of that, how is the editing going?"

Brynne snorted. "It's going nowhere. I could barely summon the energy to walk and talk last week, let alone write. But I'm pulling myself together. And I cut off all my hair today. I'm taking a job in town and will try to summon the energy to do some editing next."

"What? Send me a picture! I want to see!"

"Hang on." Brynne snapped a selfie and texted it to Jared. "I expect you to lie to me if you don't like it. I'm in a very fragile state."

His squeal burst though the phone. "Oh my god, I love it! It's sexy and feisty—like you."

"You really like it?"

"I do. I think it's fabulous. The men of Skye will be all over you."

"Dude, there are like eight eligible men on this entire island. Besides, I'm not ready to put my rod in the water. I'm liable to catch myself a toothless fisherman."

Jared couldn't stop laughing. "Oh my god, you mean your line, not your rod, babe. But I'm going to steal that phrase."

"Be my guest. It suits you more than it does me."

"I think you should get back on the horse, or the boat, as soon as possible."

If only it were that easy. Jared didn't know how hard she fell for Gage MacLeod. "I'll take that under advisement. I've got to go now; my butter pecan ice cream is melting."

"Okay. Talk to you tomorrow. Ciao, bella!"

"Ciao, J!"

Brynne returned home and got to work cleaning up the evidence of her meltdown. She collected all the debris, washed the dishes, stripped the bed, and threw a load of laundry in. At some point, she would go through Josie's closets, but that project could wait. For now, she put her things away in the main floor guest bedroom.

She set up her laptop at her aunt's beautiful antique writing desk, which faced a window with a picturesque view of the water. It sat near the big wood-burning stove, so she would be toasty when the colder weather came.

As her old laptop whirred to life, she looked for the Wi-Fi network. It never occurred to Brynne to ask Alistair about it, since she hadn't planned on staying. It was another expense she had to take over in six months. Without Declan's job, she would have run out of cash well before that.

First, she needed the internet, especially since she had no other sources of research. Two networks popped up, both protected by passwords. Brynne started looking through the old desk and found Josie's day timer in the bottom drawer, under a sheaf of her personal letterhead. She'd stuffed loose papers and sticky notes between many pages and tied it with a ribbon. Brynne carefully released the bow and flipped through it.

Behind the last calendar, she found an address book filled with all her handwritten contacts. She shook her head, recalling Josie's distrust of technology. When she reached the Ps, she found a list of passwords, including one for *Wi-Fi Guest*. It was *LLJ1952!*

Brynne smiled. Josie's favorite saying was "Live life juicy!" and she always signed off her letters *LLJ, Josie*. Since there was no password for the main Wi-Fi network, she signed in as a guest, and expelled a breath when the emails started downloading.

Ten minutes later, a strange grinding sound started coming from the back of the house. Brynne rushed to the mudroom to find the shuddering washing machine hemorrhaging water. Suds were drifting across the floor.

She turned off the machine and ran upstairs for towels.

Soon every towel in the house was drenched. However, that

wasn't the worst of it. The washer had shifted away from the wall to reveal rotted floorboards beneath. It was a miracle that the machine hadn't fallen through the wet planks. Now she had a major repair job to deal with, not to mention two loads of soaking wet laundry.

Of all the shitty luck!

She called Declan, who gave her the number of a local tradesman who could do plumbing, carpentry, and just about everything else. Declan added a warning that he was handsome and incorrigible with the ladies, so she needed to beware. Brynne laughed at his concern and said, "Declan, there's nothing to worry about. I am immune to those kinds of boys."

She was still smiling as she dialed the number. As she listened to his greeting, she considered the possibility that a bad boy with a sexy accent might be just the cure-all she needed. If only there was a cure. She doubted it very much.

The club was getting back to normal. Since the retraction, the majority of members had calmed down and come back. Thank Christ there were no more requests to cancel and divest. John told him that his superiors at Scotland Yard seemed satisfied with his explanation for being at the club. He assured them nothing illegal was going on. They also supported his plan to drop in occasionally to ensure things continued that way, especially since London's most influential players were members.

These days, Gage rarely left his office except to get his dinner, and Garrick was giving him grief about being a hermit. He didn't care. He was taking extreme care not to get his photo taken until after his mother's appointment came through. As an extra measure, he was going to Edinburgh to focus on his VC firm's new projects.

Before he left for the day, he had one last appointment. Patricia Valentine had written two days ago requesting to meet and discuss a new business proposition. Curious, he agreed to the meeting, provided she came to him. Gage sent his driver so she could enter discreetly from the underground garage.

He could hear her laughing down the hall at something Garrick said just before he delivered her to his door. He went to take her hand, but she pulled him into an embrace and kissed his cheek. She looked resplendent in a designer cream suit.

She stood back and looked at him, her eyes sharp and assessing. "It's been too long, Gage. I've been worried about you with all that rot in the press."

"I'm relieved to say it has died down and we've had a satisfactory retraction. There was no lasting damage to our reputation; in fact, inquiries have picked up."

Her head tilted, and she hadn't let go of his arms. "Then why do you look so tired, darling?"

He smiled at her perceptive comment. "Just working too hard. But you'll be happy to know I'm heading to Edinburgh and will follow that up with a week off."

"That's wonderful news! The timing couldn't be better. I want to ask your advice on a new business venture I'm looking to develop— and coincidentally, the property is in Edinburgh."

Gage poured her a gin and tonic and they sat down to talk. Patricia's face lit up when she told him of her plans to open a private club for women.

"I believe there is a market for a club like Dominus for women, Gage. I'm conducting market research in the UK and more broadly in Europe. There are plenty of women who would come to a club that caters exclusively to their whims. We won't have a punishment room like yours, but there will be a state-of-the-art spa where a woman can have a massage with a happy ending."

Gage chuckled at that thought, but he couldn't help but question the viability of her plan. He tread carefully, not wanting to discourage her. "This is an interesting concept. Are you looking to attract single or married women? Husbands might object to your special services unless they think it's just a health spa. You'll need a good base willing to pay the entry fees, and the percentage of single wealthy businesswomen in the UK is quite low."

"I'm still working on the numbers and deciding whether we should have a high membership fee or keep the initial costs lower and have the restaurant and spa services be pay-as-you-go. You are right about the lack of independently wealthy women, but if we can draw people to the club as a destination, that could make the difference. It will be a place they save up and escape to for girls' weekends, birthdays—where they won't see anyone they know. What do you think?"

"I would need to see the property specs and review the costs to convert it. What is the building used for now?"

"It's a twenty-four-room hotel and decent-size spa leased on the top floor, so it would convert well to what I want. It's listed for 2.2 million pounds and would need about a million in renovations."

He ran his hand over his chin as he considered the numbers. "Why don't I put you in touch with someone from my office who can help you dig into the details? Armand has done multiple conversion projects for me; he can get access to building code info, construction costs, and a ton of market research. Then you'll know exactly what is required."

"Oh Gage, that would be amazing! I need a strong business case to take to prospective investors." She paused and winked. "Like you."

He laughed. "I had a feeling it wasn't just advice you were looking for."

"You are always so perceptive. I want more than your brains; I need you for your experience in running an enterprise with all these service elements. The Hellcat Club will be one of a kind."

His eyes widened. "The Hellcat Club? That name should raise eyebrows. I love it."

"Did I mention that all the waiters will be astonishingly hot and very submissive?"

"Of course they will. I expected no less from you, Madame Valentine." He grinned and went to his desk. "I'll email him and make the introductions." Gage welcomed the distraction, so he told her he would go see the property with Armand.

Patricia rose to give him another hug. She held his hands and caught his gaze.

"I cannot thank you enough for your help, Gage. But I have one more favor to ask."

One dark eyebrow rose.

"I know you think Brynne wrote that story and put it in the Mirror, but I just don't believe it."

His jaw hardened, and he stepped back from her. "You're wrong. Just like I was wrong. She is a conniving little liar, trying to make a name for herself."

"It makes no sense. She wants to be a novelist, not a reporter. I cannot fathom why she would do anything to harm you. There could be another person behind this. Have you hired a private investigator to prove it one way or the other?"

"No. There was no one else with the means to get the story published, and she had access to our members' names."

"I've been studying people and their motives my whole life and I would bet a substantial sum of money that something else is at play."

Gage stared at her and shook his head.

She put a hand on his arm. "If I'm right, will you become an investor in The Hellcat Club?"

Gage ran a hand through his hair. "And what if you're wrong?"

She considered that for a minute, then smiled. "If I'm wrong, I'll settle for you being an advisor and I won't ask you to invest."

"That doesn't seem like a very palatable wager for you. If you're right, I will give you half a million pounds in seed capital and I'll be an advisor—provided the business case works. And if you're wrong, you come to my club and let me lay my favorite flogger across your bare ass."

Her eyes widened. "Christ, you drive a hard bargain. But I'll take that wager. For one, I want your help and your money, and two, I think you're wrong about that girl."

After Patricia left, he sat for a while contemplating what she'd said. Would it be worthwhile to have an investigator look into it? Only to prove that he was right about her. Angry at the dredging up of old wounds, Gage pulled out Brynne's employee file and read the reference letter.

> *Brynne is a natural. She became aroused the moment the restraints went on her wrists; however, she continued to fight her submissive nature. Her endurance and threshold for pain were not fully tested, but I believe elements of her personality drive her to seek more intense punishments. The strap shocked her initially, but she let herself go and came hard with the last few blows.*
>
> *She can be willful and struggles to obey explicit directions. It appears she wants to be pushed past her limits and rebels against fully submitting, as one way to up the ante. It is my conclusion that she would be suited to a*

male Dom with a firm hand, one with whom she has an emotional connection.

Her hard and soft limits were surprising—in that she will try things she has no experience with. This stems from a need to prove her worthiness and her strength. Her fantasies are about being forced to comply, not submitting willingly. In the wrong hands, it could get her into trouble.

He slapped the folder shut, intending to dismiss Patricia's suggestion, but he couldn't. He wanted the truth, so he rang John and asked him to recommend a private eye. Then he packed his briefcase and went to see Garrick. The club would be in excellent hands, and he looked forward to getting out of London. It had lost a bit of its luster in the last week.

21

Hot Handyman for Hire

The handyman hadn't called back by the next morning. Brynne filled two garbage bags with wet laundry and took them to the launderette in town. Aunt Josie had fallen in love with clothes dryers during a visit to Canada. She imported one and then created a laundry room outside of the kitchen. Many considered her to be eccentric, but Brynne knew she was a trailblazer.

The repairs could be costly, and she had very little money in reserve. She stared out at the islands in the distance and nibbled on her bottom lip. The old stone house was over a century old. It was bound to have some issues. She called Jared and talked him out of making the twelve-hour drive to Skye. After explaining the saga of the washing machine, he suggested she pay the plumber with sex and kill two birds with one stone.

"You are assuming I'm good enough in bed to get all the flooring, plumbing, and god knows what else fixed in this house!"

"I have the utmost faith in your abilities, Bree!"

She laughed, then abruptly yelled, "I've got to go. He's calling!"

Logan sounded as sexy as his voicemail and offered to come over at nine on Saturday morning to look at the job. Brynne gushed her thanks and forgot to ask anything about the cost. It didn't matter. It had to be fixed, and if she needed a loan from the estate, she'd speak to Alistair. That settled, she checked her email and searched online for estimates to ship boxes of clothes from London to Skye. Jared offered to pack her clothes and courier them, so she didn't need to fly back for a while.

Eventually, she would need to decide what to do with her apartment in Brixton. If there was no work in London, Edinburgh could be another option.

Brynne wished she had more time to enjoy the tranquility of the cottage. The last few months had been frenetic, and she was glad to be off the treadmill. Unfortunately, it made her realize she was bone weary and adrift at sea without a rudder. Friday came too damn fast, and she was due at the restaurant in less than two hours.

The place was cozy and casual, with sage green walls and dark wood tables. The bar lined one end, a stage for live music at the other. Myrna showed her around and explained how the POS system worked.

"Our slang is the hardest thing to learn. It can be a wee bit hard to hear when the music is blaring. Cook will do a couple of specials for lunch and dinner, and you'll get used to it in no time."

The kitchen staff was friendly, and Brynne was secretly relieved to be around regular folks. They were not likely to get any stuck-up billionaires demanding forty-year-old whisky. She looked forward to brushing up her bartending skills on Monday night.

Two men came in after the lunch crowd had thinned. One of them was too handsome for his own good. He had a full beard and wore his blonde hair tied back in a man bun. She never thought that look was sexy—until now. He was a cross between a sun-kissed surfer and a biker from *Sons of Anarchy*.

Myrna went over and took their order while Brynne finished clearing dishes. Soon after, Myrna announced she had put the *coinneach's* fish and chips order in and she was going to take her break. At Brynne's questioning look, she said, "It's Gaelic for cute hunks." Myrna winked conspiratorially.

The cook's bell signaled their food order was up. Up close, surfer boy had a deep tan that showed off his baby blues, and those superhero muscles were hard to miss.

"Is there anything else I can get you, gentlemen?"

The dark-haired man shook his head and started popping chips into his mouth. The blond turned his gaze on her. "You must be new around here, Red?"

She froze. When she finally spoke, her voice had a serrated edge. "Yes, I am new around here. And my name is not Red."

She could tell her hostile reaction surprised him. Undaunted, he asked, "Well, sweetheart, tell me your name, so I know what to call you?"

Right, she didn't have a name tag yet. She didn't want anyone to connect her to the article. "Bree. My name is Bree."

He took his time studying her. "Nice to meet you, Bree. I'm Logan, and this is Fergus." He winked. "I'd like another Caledonian, please."

She nodded and hurried to the bar, berating herself on the way. His name was Logan. Knowing her luck, he was probably *that* Logan. How many hot handymen could there be in this small town?

She delivered the beer and pasted on a smile. "Are you Logan Mitchell, by chance?"

"The one and only." He grinned, clearly pleased to be recognized.

"Declan referred you to me—you agreed to come and look at my pipes tomorrow."

His friend Fergus made a strangled sound. The man's face was beet red, and she thought he was choking, so she pounded his back until he raised his hands in surrender. She didn't get the joke until she looked at Logan, who was desperately trying not to laugh.

He tried to look serious and failed. "I'll be over to inspect the, um, pipes."

They couldn't stop laughing. She shook her head and walked away in disgust.

Myrna returned and asked what had her so flustered. "Those two infantile twats are laughing at my expense."

She made a tsking sound. "My dear lass, that one is as cute as a dumplin' in a hankie. If I were your age, I'd be wheedling and fawning for his favor. He's single, built nice and burly, and they say he's quite a braw lover."

"They say that, do they?" Brynne made an unladylike sound. "I don't go for pretty boys. Besides, my last relationship recently came to a screeching halt, so I'm not interested in sampling the town's tastiest tomcat with a tool belt."

Myrna burst out laughing. "We'll see how you feel in a few months when the weather is dreich and you're needing something warm and muscley in your bed!"

Brynne tried not to laugh but couldn't stop herself. She would get on well with Myrna. She reminded her of Aunt Josie.

Myrna collected their payment, and when they got to the door, they waved and blew kisses to them both. The flirting gave her a fleeting lift, but the reality of going home alone to the cottage brought her back down with a depressing thud. She never minded being on her own—she was used to it from an early age. It was more the absence of *him*. She missed the angst-ridden anticipation she felt before seeing Gage, the excitement of their furtive attraction, and the thrill of playing with danger. She'd fallen unwittingly into his thrall.

Declan came in as they were setting up for dinner. He reminded her to order a meal from the kitchen to take home. She agreed to work again tomorrow for karaoke night, which was always wildly busy. She gave him a hug and thanked him for looking out for her, staving off the stupid tears that threatened to spill.

Before she left, she asked him to make her name tag Bree, not Brynne. "New name, new hairdo, and new beginning."

"Right! We'll see you tomorrow, Bree." He winked.

Brynne stopped at the market for a bottle of wine to go with her takeout spaghetti. She came out with two bottles of wine, a bottle of Glayva liqueur, one apple crumble, and a can of whipped cream. At this rate, she would find all the pounds she lost last week. She scoffed at her reflection in the rear view mirror. "Do you give a flying fuck? Nope! 'Cause nobody's going to see you naked!" She put the car in gear and headed home in a dark mood.

Bam. Bam. Bam.

Brynne's head was pounding. It sounded like someone was hammering nails right next to her. She opened one eyelid and quickly closed it when sunlight pierced her eyeball. It wasn't her imagination; someone was banging somewhere. On her door. Who the hell would be here this early?

She squinted at her mobile phone and saw the screen said 9:10 a.m. "Oh god," she groaned. "Why did he have to be all that, *and* punctual?!"

She got up from the couch and felt woozy. Ouch. Polishing off half a bottle of wine with her dinner, followed by a tumbler of sweet liqueur, was a bad idea. She pulled her robe tightly closed over her nightie. One look in the mirror, and she wanted to cry. No time to fix the hot mess staring back at her.

He was almost to his truck when she yanked open the back door and called out. "Logan, please wait! I'm so sorry I didn't hear the door."

He turned back, annoyance written all over his face. He slowly took in her appearance, and his eyes went from cold to amused. His mouth twitched. "You look like you were in a fight, princess."

She nodded and rubbed her forehead. "In a manner of speaking, I was. The Glayva won."

He chuckled. "Ooch no, that stuff is lethal. It'll put you into a sugar coma." He reached the steps as Brynne backed away and tried to wipe the caked mascara from under her eyes.

She stood back as he examined the floor and the pipes connected to the washing machine, taking notes in a little book as he went.

"Either the machine has been leaking for a while, or there's a problem behind this wall. I won't know until I rip up the floor and get into the crawl space."

"My aunt did this addition about twelve years ago, and I think she replaced the washer around then. I can't be sure."

"I'm no appliance expert, but repairing it will probably cost more than a new one."

"And what about the floor?" She braced herself for the answer.

He got down on the floor with his flashlight to check the space beneath the boards.

"I'll need to replace this entire section to ensure you don't get mold."

She laid on the puppy dog eyes and wrung her hands nervously.

"I've just moved here and don't have a lot of savings. How much will this all cost?"

"With labor and materials, it will be around 850 pounds. It will take about a week, provided there are no surprises."

Brynne chewed her bottom lip and sighed. "Okay. It's got to be done. I pray critters don't come climbing up through that hole in the floor." She shivered just thinking about the spiders and other vermin under there.

"From what I can see, they sealed the crawl space well. I can put a sheet of plywood down in the meantime because I can't start until next week."

"That would be great. Thank you."

"Okay, I'll come by tomorrow. What time will you be up tomorrow, princess?"

She blushed. "I have to work late tonight, so could we say after twelve noon?"

"Sure. I'll see you then." He winked and added, "I like your Scottie dog PJs."

Uh oh, flirting. "Thanks," she said. "And thanks for not taking off."

"Of course. Declan said you're a good friend. Besides, I would never leave a beautiful damsel in distress."

Once he was gone, she went to the front room and surveyed the mess. Gross. She scraped the plates and filled the sink to soak the crusty dishes. She got coffee on and put some raisin bread in the toaster. Her stomach wouldn't handle much else.

Josie's agent emailed to confirm that they would release the death announcement to the public today. It would be in the newspaper, online, and on Twitter and Facebook. Josie wrote under the pen name Joyce McLennan, and from the very beginning, she guarded her privacy tightly. Her stories were very risqué for their time. Using a pseudonym protected her from overzealous admirers and adoring fans alike. In the small community of Portree, a simple obituary ran in the local newspaper a week ago. Her dear friends knew her secret identity, and everyone in town protected her when fans came snooping around.

Brynne decided she needed a pen name for herself. It would free her to write the wildest material imaginable, without fear of judgment. Josie used to tell her that publishing a book was like walking down the street naked. It took guts to reveal what your imagination conjured up. It was more important than ever to create a new identity since her name had been dragged through the mud.

She arrived ahead of her shift to find Myrna tidying up. They went over the dinner specials, and she introduced her to the bartender and other servers.

By nine thirty, the place was packed. This would be like her university days—fast, loud, and exhausting.

A girl got up and sang "Girls Just Want to Have Fun" by Cyndi Lauper. Her friends cheered and Brynne wished she had friends to go out on the town with. If Jared visited, they could do one of their favorite duets. Ever since she started dating Ross, they hadn't gone out partying. Wow, she hadn't thought of him at all. Gage had monopolized her thoughts more after a few weeks than the man she spent over a year with. What did that tell her? That she never loved Ross—she'd just found a safe place to hide.

A group of people stayed until the house lights came on and the karaoke operator started packing up his stuff. The work was exhausting, but it kept her hopping and her mind off the depressing state of her life.

When she got home, Brynne barely had the energy to wash her

face and brush her teeth. She was dozing off when she remembered to set her alarm. No way did she want to be caught in her pajamas again.

Sunday morning dawned sunny and warm. She sat on the deck outside to have her coffee. The breeze was crisp, so she opened the windows to let the ocean air freshen the house. After breakfast, she went to take a shower. The water pressure was oddly light. She cranked the dials all the way to the max and suddenly brown water started sputtering out of the faucet. "You've got to be kidding me!"

Cursing, she stomped upstairs to the ensuite bathroom, which had an old clawfoot tub. The water was clear, and it was warm—there just wasn't any pressure. At this rate, it would take a day to fill the tub, so she stuck her head under the faucet, soaped up, and splashed the rest of her body in three inches of water. Afterward, she moved her things up to Josie's room, so she was out of Logan's way.

As promised, he arrived at noon. She watched him covertly from the back window as he unloaded the plywood from his truck. His faded jeans hugged his mouthwatering butt like a glove. That body was hard to ignore. She prayed his plumbing skills were as impressive.

She opened the door before he could knock. "Hi."

"Good morning, beautiful. Looks like you had a better sleep last night?"

His smile was infectious, and she smiled back. "Yeah, I slept great, but I'm wondering if I'm cursed. I've got another plumbing problem." She showed him the brown water coming out of the bathroom taps. "When I tried the bath upstairs, there was hardly any pressure, but at least it was clear."

"Oh boy, that's not good. There must be a problem behind these walls. I'll see if I can close off pipes in the newer part of the house and divert water upstairs for you."

"I hope that works."

He rested his hands on his tool belt and tried to look serious. "You can always come and shower at my place."

She smirked. "That's very sweet of you, but I'm sure I will manage."

"Have you got a boyfriend, then?"

The bluntness of his question took her by surprise. "No. I just broke up with my boyfriend and I'm not ready to date yet."

His mouth quirked up. "The best way to get over a breakup is to have fabulous revenge sex."

"I'm not sure it's revenge I need."

His face lit with mischief. "Even better. Sex for the fun of it. I'm happy to volunteer my services. Just say the word."

Brynne laughed. "I appreciate the offer, truly, but could we stick to plumbing for now?"

"All right. But I hope we can expand the scope of work at a later date."

She watched Logan single-handedly carry the washing machine out the back door and questioned her sanity. The man was sex on two legs, and she was letting him walk. In her twenties, she moved effortlessly from one man to the next without remorse, revenge, or regret. There was no reason she couldn't erase the lingering thoughts of Gage with hot sex. Maybe that was exactly what she needed.

Brynne left a message for Alistair, asking for an advance from the estate. She sat down at her computer and opened her manuscript. It had been over a week since she had written a word, and it was time to recapture the momentum. This book had to sizzle, and she would do whatever it took to get it back on track. She searched through her backpack, looking for the sticky notes with the websites and BDSM chat rooms. If she was lucky, she would find a real Dom online, willing to answer her questions.

22

First Right of Refusal

On Monday morning, Alistair returned her call and suggested she drop by his office so they could discuss the matter in person. She wondered why he wouldn't just tell her on the phone. Whatever, she was going into town for her first bartending shift that night, so they agreed to meet around four thirty.

Brynne knew something was amiss. Alistair was always put together, but today his tie was gone, and his hair stuck up all over the place.

"I received a call today about your aunt's estate. There has been a development that I must share with you."

"You're making me nervous Alistair, what on earth is going on?"

"Let me get right to it. The man who owns the property surrounding yours is claiming Josie made promises to him."

"What? What kind of promises?" she tried to keep her voice calm.

"The first was gaining access to dig a trench from the main road down to the shoreline. And second, he said she gave him the first right of refusal to purchase the property. He learned of her death on the weekend and sought me out."

Brynne's stomach dropped, and she felt lightheaded. "Does he have any proof of these so-called promises? She meant for me to have the house, that's why she put me on the title. Doesn't that mean it's my decision whether to sell it?"

"Yes. It's totally your decision. And I don't believe he has written proof. He said they had discussed it at length but never got the agreements signed."

"Wow. That's crazy. She mentioned nothing about selling—or this trench thing."

Alister pulled pages off his printer and stacked them neatly in front of Brynne. "After a rather heated discussion, he asked that I present an offer to purchase the whole parcel."

She scanned the paperwork and noticed they made it out to *The Estate of Josephine Lamond.* She stopped and frowned at Alistair. "I don't want to sell right now. Josie took steps so I would own it, knowing how much I love it."

"I believe that too, Brynne. When you moved to London and began pursuing your dream of writing, she knew one day you would need a place away from the city. Like she did."

She scanned the rest of the document. When her eyes landed on the numbers, her mouth dropped open in shock. "Five hundred thousand pounds! That's crazy, isn't it?"

"Not that crazy. It sits on two and a half acres, which includes the beach. I don't think the buyer wants the house, they want the land and access to the water. Something about running underground pipes or cables."

"Christ, that's a lot of money." She stared at it and shook her head. "I can't decide this right now. My whole life has turned upside down and this is the only place I feel safe."

"I understand. I will convey your decision not to sell— understanding that if you change your mind, they will be the first to know."

"Okay. Thanks Alistair." She stared at the paper. *Magnus MacCallum.* "Who is this guy? What do you know about him?"

"I believe he owns a communications company and has purchased land on Skye, Rum, Eigg, and Uist, and you know he bought all the land around your place and just finished building the house at the top of the hill."

She wrinkled her nose. "He probably wants to tear down Josie's house so he has a clear view of the water."

One gray brow lifted. "Funny thing is, Josie really liked him. He was always very kind to her. So, I don't think he's all bad."

Brynne wasn't buying it. "If he was so *nice*, why didn't she tell me about him?"

"That, I'm afraid I cannot answer, dear. But it's good to know that if you decide to sell, you have a buyer ready."

"I suppose that's true, but right now, it needs serious repairs. The contractor came on the weekend to survey the water damage. I need to know what I can borrow from the estate."

Alistair took off his glasses and rubbed the bridge of his nose. "There was money set aside for your travel and such. We can immediately access 3,500 pounds. And I can stretch it to another 1,500 pounds. Just bring me the written estimate on the repairs and send me any receipts."

"Okay, that's a good start. I'll get that for you as soon as possible. Thanks, Alistair."

Brynne left his office and walked to the hotel, mumbling

to herself about the mystery neighbor. *Who the hell does this guy think he is?*

Brynne quickly changed into her white dress shirt, tartan bow tie, and matching apron. Declan used the green Hunting tartan of Clan Fraser throughout the hotel. The uniform was simple, and she could wear her own jeans and comfortable black combat boots.

An hour later, the dinner crowd filtered in. It was steady, but nothing she couldn't keep up with. She hit her stride, serving several customers sitting at the bar and filling the orders for the servers. It kept her from focusing on her neighbor and his outrageous offer.

It was after one a.m. when she collected her purse from her locker. Jared had texted to say he got reinstated at the club and he was staying at a friend's tonight, so he would call her tomorrow. That sounded promising! Brynne hoped the *friend* was John.

Another surprise was a text message from her father. He and his new wife were in Prince Edward Island and had just picked up her message about Josie's death.

Once home, she dialed him on FaceTime. When she told him Josie committed suicide, he was speechless. For as long as she could remember, he had avoided all difficult subjects and swept them under the rug. After her mother left, he never mentioned her name again. Today was no exception. He changed the subject and asked about her job and that *nice boy*, Ross. *Oh geez.*

"Uh, I guess we haven't talked since last month, Dad. Ross and I broke up, and I left my job at the paper to come to Skye. Josie left me the house, and I'm going to spend the summer here."

He looked surprised; his brow creased with worry. "Oh, sweetie, are you sure you're okay? I thought you and Ross were serious?"

"He was not the man for me, and it's good I figured it out. I'm doing great, and I've got a job at a hotel in Portree. I'm going to take my time before deciding where I want to work next—plus I'm almost finished with my first novel."

"Oh, that's wonderful. I always thought you had a special way with words."

That remark caused a lump to form in her throat. "Thanks, Dad. That means a lot." She kept peppering him with questions about the trip and where they were going next. When he yawned, she jumped at the chance to get off the call. "Well, Pops, it's super late here, and I've just come from work. Send me a postcard when you get to Newfoundland, and be careful."

He winked. "I will, sweetheart. Look after yourself. I love you."

"I love you too, Dad."

Tears came without warning. What the hell was wrong with her? In the last ten years, she had cried maybe four times, and now she couldn't keep them at bay. This was becoming annoying. Sure, she missed her father…or rather, she missed the man he was before her mother left. The in-between years were not worth remembering. At least he'd found happiness and someone to share his life with.

The next morning, Alistair's phone call woke her out of a deep sleep. She swore and rolled over to grab her phone.

"Brynne, I'm sorry to wake you." He cleared his throat. "MacCallum was not pleased that you declined his offer, and he is threatening to contest the will."

"What?!" Brynne bolted upright.

"There are only a few ways to do that here in Scotland. He could sue under the grounds of facility and circumvention."

"God help me, Alistair. What the hell does that mean?"

"It means he might petition to have the will overturned if he can show Josie was vulnerable as a result of her illness—insinuating you coerced her to leave you the house."

She sank back into the pillows in utter shock.

"Brynne, are you there?"

"I'm here. I just can't believe this. That claim is ridiculous. I never asked Josie for anything."

"I know that, dear."

"So, what does this mean? I don't have money to fight this. Who has the burden of proof?"

"They would have to prove the undue influence, but you have to pay your own legal fees."

Brynne felt sick, then fury took over. "What a bastard. And he was supposed to be her friend?"

"I believe this is a tactic to get you to sell. This chap is used to getting his own way. Since you didn't take the money, this is a way to frighten you to reconsider."

"Pfft. He doesn't know me very well. Back me into a corner, I'll come out fighting. In fact, I'd like to burn his monstrous house to the ground."

"Jesus, Mary, and Joseph, Brynne, please don't say things like that."

"I'm only joking. But a girl can dream, can't she?"

"Not dreams of arson, no."

"I think we should set up a meeting, Alistair. Tell him I would like to negotiate."

"Oh, dear. Do you think that's a good idea?"

"Yes. I will not cower and wait for him to make the first move. Doesn't he know hell hath no fury like a woman threatened, scorned, and ruined?!"

"Okay, Brynne. Leave it with me. I'll see what I can arrange."

Brynne called Jared, desperate to vent. *Fucking voicemail. Story of my life! When I need a man, they're never there for me.*

"J, it's your pathetic friend whose life is unraveling. I am wondering if someone made a voodoo doll of me, and they're sticking pins in it. Call me when you get the chance."

Fresh air was what she needed, and some exercise. Her jeans were tight, and her bra felt like bondage—and not in a good way. As she stomped down the worn path to the water, she imagined all kinds of ways to annoy the dickhead at the top of the hill. If only she had a dog, she could put shit at his back door. Better yet, a giant horse turd.

When she arrived at the rocky shoreline, her mood was much improved. The wind off the water reminded her of a cold granny smith apple: fresh, tart, and crisp. The sounds of water lapping against the beach always calmed her down. She sat on a boulder to contemplate the world and her place in it.

How had she gone from a simple existence to disaster and chaos? Throughout her life, Brynne struggled with maintaining attachments, and it only worsened after the experience in Toronto. She'd lost touch with her friends from school, and if not for Jared and his larger-than-life personality, she might never have come out of her shell. She also knew that without her aunt's faith and encouragement, she wouldn't have started the book. It was her lifeline now.

So, she had to deal with an overzealous neighbor making threats and a little house needing some TLC. Was that enough to make her run for the hills? "No!" she yelled to the wind.

She had more things to be grateful for than freaked out about. Her house had stunning water views. Her job allowed her time to write. Plus, she'd found a handsome handyman who could do countless projects. Maybe if she dated him, she could get around the stupid stipulations of the will. *OMG, what a brilliant idea!*

She would not run away anymore. Instead, she would be rational *and* spiritual to get through this mess. She would fight the claims because the truth was on her side. If she needed reinforcements, she would pray for Auntie Josie to come and haunt that motherfucker. It was settled.

When she reached the cottage, she had a stitch in her side. Her phone dinged, and she realized the signal didn't go beyond her front porch. Jared had returned her call, so she rang him back.

"Bree! How are you, babe? What the heck is going on?"

She sighed. "Nothing a little hike to the beach wouldn't cure, my friend."

"Your message was kind of intense! What of voodoo dolls and pins?"

"Where do I start? King shit of turd hill is threatening to sue me, the repairs to the house are probably going to be in the thousands, and my aunt's will won't pay out until I find the man of my dreams."

"Oh my god. Wait, what? First tell me who is king shit?!"

"He's the guy who wants to buy my house." She sighed heavily into her fists. "I didn't know it sits on almost three acres and goes all the way to the water. He claims Josie promised to sell it to him or let him dig a trench right through it. Since I refused the offer, he's considering contesting her will." She paused, thinking, then sat forward. "Wait, I just thought of something! I think I know how to win! This brute plans to try to prove I influenced Josie to leave it to me when she was sick and therefore susceptible to influence. But she put me on the title of this place over a year ago. She wasn't sick then." Grinning, she asked, "Do you know what this means?"

"Honestly, I'm not following, but it sounds like you don't have to worry about that part."

"Exactly. He's assuming I pushed her around so she would leave it to me. When I meet him, I'll tell him where to go and where to stuff his five hundred K."

"What did you just say?"

"Yeah, he's willing to pay five hundred thousand pounds for it. How crazy is that?!"

"Holy shit! Are you sure you don't want to take the money and come back to London? It's so goddamned remote out there, babe."

"I know, but I love this place. Even if I never find love, I'll have enough money to live comfortably."

"What the hell are you talking about? I seriously cannot keep up."

"Auntie Josie said I won't collect the bulk of the estate unless I find a suitable man, give up the three-date rule, and meet other ridiculous conditions. Ha! I have a way around that, too."

"Wow. I'm gonna need some popcorn. God, I miss you, girl!"

"I know, I miss you, too. I'll come to the city soon, I promise. In other news, the contractor I hired is smokin' hot, and he's going to do all the repairs. If I date him, I might be able to get around that *other* clause. He seems keen."

"Jesus. A shit ton has happened these last few days. But you sound good."

"I am not going gently into that good night. Hell, I've been through worse."

"You are a warrior! I'm so proud of you. And how is the writing going?"

She grimaced. "Okay, so I got a bit off track, but I'm going to dive back in and join a BDSM chat room. Oh, and I need to come up with a pseudonym."

"Okay, wow. Lesson number one: Do not go into any chat room with your real name. Can you hide your location and use a VPN?"

"A what?"

"Oy vey. Hang on." She heard muffled voices in the background. "I'm sorry I have to run, babe. But don't go joining anything online yet. I'll get you set up and we'll talk about the pen name. Call me later tonight?"

"Can't tonight. I'm working the bar. How about tomorrow? I'm off in the evening."

"Perfect. I love you, and I miss you so much."

"Me too, J. Just realized I never asked you anything about yourself. I'm an awful friend."

"Stop it. You are not. We will talk tomorrow night."

"Okay. Love you."

She hung up and checked her email. There was a note from Alistair advising that MacCallum's legal firm was requesting a copy of the will and they would be available for a meeting in Portree next Monday. She begged him to take his time responding and to wait until the last possible minute to provide the will. He agreed and suggested they black out Josie's special conditions for the inheritance. Brynne was grateful he thought of that. It would be bloody mortifying if they saw those.

In an abundance of caution, she asked him to minimize the use of her full name in the correspondence and instead refer to her as the beneficiary, the niece, or the estate of Josie Lamond. Alistair didn't know the details of the London scandal, only that they had wrongly accused her of something horrible. It was best if they didn't make the connection and paint her in a worse light.

Gage missed Edinburgh. With its stunning skyline, ancient castles, and cobbled streets, the city had a unique personality, unlike the never-ending sprawl of London. He loved that it had plenty of green space and a much slower pace. The best part was being able to walk from his place to the office in ten minutes.

His townhome had a much warmer feel than the London penthouse because he'd kept many of the original architectural features. Not long after taking possession, he'd left for London to open Dominus. In a moment of weakness, he'd given the interior designer carte blanche. They created a spectacular combination of contemporary style while keeping the original charm of decorative cornices, lead-paned windows, and working fireplaces in every room.

Fiona had the fridge stocked, and the place aired out before his arrival. After being cooped up for days hiding from the press, his only desire was to walk to his favorite pub for a beer and some fish and chips. After he dumped his case and changed into jeans, Gage walked with a spring in his step, relishing the crisp night air. As he made his way up to George Street, he saw the sun setting behind the majestic castle on the hill. It was good to be home.

He sat at the bar and enjoyed a cold draught in the pub's relaxed atmosphere. His phone buzzed. It was an email from the private investigator with a preliminary report on Brynne.

- Born in Inverness on August 9. Family moved to Canada when she was eight.

- Mother left eight months later. Father became an alcoholic and eventually lost his job. It was five years before he found full-time work.

- Brynne won her first writing contest at age sixteen. She was accepted into a local college for journalism because of her entry essay, not her marks.

- In the middle of her second year, her father was diagnosed with cancer, and she dropped out to look after him. She attended night school to complete her degree at the age of twenty-six.

- A year or two of odd jobs and then she landed an internship at a Toronto magazine which turned into a junior copy editor job. Two years later, she was fired or quit because of an affair with the CEO of the media group. There was a link to the articles about his scandalous divorce.

- At thirty, she moved back to the UK and got the job at the *Mirror*.

Gage processed this info while he finished his meal. Did Brynne make a habit of sleeping with her bosses? Could she have been conspiring with the bumbling editor, Nigel? He would ask the investigator to get more detail from Toronto and see if there had been any attempted extortion.

They had no information on her mother's current whereabouts. He found it strange that she abandoned her daughter. The PI said he would dig into her relationships and employment at the *Mirror* next and had some interviews lined up with friends from her college days. As he walked back to the townhouse, Gage suppressed the irritating pangs of sympathy he felt for her lousy childhood. Instead, he considered her motives for the story in the *Mirror*. It was obvious her career had not taken off. She was thirty-two and had nothing to show for it. The other alternative was that someone offered her money or a position if she could get an exclusive on the club. He would get to the truth—one way or the other.

23

Game, Set, Match

Logan, boy-toy with a tool belt, showed up Wednesday as scheduled and started the demolition of her little money pit. He flirted with her whenever she came downstairs. While eating his lunch at her kitchen table, he asked if she was ready to go out with him.

"Not yet," she replied with pursed lips.

He countered, "When you fall off a horse, it's crucial to get right back on."

The next day, as he was preparing to leave, he tried again. "Everyone needs a transitional fling to help them get over the end of a bad relationship."

She laughed at his suggestion. "If I change my mind, you'll be the first to know."

Maybe she should give Logan a chance…if she could only stop thinking about Gage's commanding green eyes and the power they had over her. Despite everything, she still found him irresistible.

Realization struck—he still had her vibrator! She had half a mind to write and demand that he send it back, or at least reimburse her. The moment he fired her, that stupid requirement of no masturbation without permission went out the window.

There were no *toy* shops nearby, so she had to search for a replacement online. That shopping expedition led her down the rabbit hole of toys, bondage gear, and x-rated videos. It was his fault that dark and deviant thoughts plagued her. She had to figure out how to banish them—and him—forever.

Since the whole first floor was a disaster, Brynne spent her days in the window seat of the master bedroom with her laptop. Logan diverted the water so she could bathe upstairs, but her kitchen and all taps on the main floor were out of commission. Repairs would take weeks. Thank god for Declan, who let her bring her laundry to the hotel and invited her to take meals home from his kitchen. He was her knight in shining armor, just like he'd been for Josie.

Sunday night, she found it impossible to sleep, worrying about the meeting. MacCallum and his team would be there at two o'clock. Brynne struggled to zip up the only dress she brought and groaned at her reflection. The simple black sheath was ridiculously tight. She'd always had curves, but her weakness for Scottish pastries and other rich carbs from the restaurant had taken their toll. She was stuck unless she found something in her aunt's closet.

A thorough search confirmed Josie's clothes were too big, unless she kept up her unhealthy habits. On the bright side, she found fabulous accessories to enhance the outfit. Josie had expensive taste—and the Hermès scarf and Yves Saint Laurent clutch turned her ensemble from a mediocre to a wow. She took special care with her makeup and hair, and a pair of patent knee-high boots completed the ensemble. With little time to spare, she raced to town in the MGB praying the seams of the dress would hold up.

Brynne's confidence faltered when she walked up to Alistair's office and saw three fancy cars lined up out front. Few people in Skye drove these kinds of posh cars, so she knew they belonged to MacCallum's well-paid legal team. A silver Range Rover, a black Mercedes, and a sporty blue BMW gleamed like they had just come out of the showroom. *Whatever. They will not intimidate me.*

Taking a deep breath, Brynne walked in. She could hear muffled voices coming from the boardroom and was glad Alistair was right there to greet her.

He grabbed her hands in his. "Brynne, you look lovely."

"Thank you, Alistair. I wanted to look unruffled, no matter how I feel on the inside."

"Well, you succeeded. Listen, there are three young lawyers with *MacCallum.* He arrived a couple of minutes before you. I will go in now. Take a minute, then make your entrance. You're sitting at the head of the table. He is at the other end."

"You're brilliant. I like knowing the layout and where I'm sitting. I'm going to freshen up, and I'll be right in."

In the small bathroom, she stood with her hands on her hips and spread her legs as far as the slit in the dress would allow, and she prayed.

"You've got this, Brynne. Auntie Josie—I am calling on you to be with me. I will not show weakness. I will face this entitled dickwad and will not let him push me around."

A little touch-up of her plum lipstick and she was ready. She swung open the door to the boardroom and stopped dead in her tracks. All five of the men stood and their eyes turned toward her, but she only noticed one pair. Her legs froze and her heart started stuttering. It was as if time stood still. She and the man at the end of the table spoke in unison.

"What the fuck are you doing here?"

His lawyers looked disconcerted and unsure what to do. The young man closest to where she stood pulled out the chair for her. She ignored him and turned to look at Alistair. He'd leaped forward as if preparing to catch her if she fainted. To him alone, she whispered, "I don't understand."

Before he could respond, Gage spoke.

"Your aunt was Josephine Lamond?"

From somewhere within, she found her footing. She turned scathing eyes on him. "No shit, Sherlock." A million questions swirled in her brain, but she couldn't put them together.

Fury blazed from his eyes, and she wondered if his teeth would shatter from how hard he was gritting them. She seized the pregnant pause. "I guess you didn't read the two hundred pages your crack legal team provided, Mr. MacCallum." Her voice dripped with so much venom, one of the young lawyers audibly gulped. They looked like college boys dressed up in their Sunday finest. "Is Gage your stage name for the devious games you play in London?"

His upper lip curled in contempt. "It's a shame, but I have to protect my identity from bad actors like you, Miss Larimore."

Alistair touched her arm and looked on worriedly, urging her to take her seat. He must think she was going to tip over. Once the adrenaline stopped coursing through her veins, she just might.

Gage continued to stare at her, then finally spoke. "I'd like a moment alone with Miss Larimore."

The trio of suits looked ready to flee. She turned to the lawyer at her immediate right, who was staring at her. "Please stay. I do not wish to have a moment alone with Mr. MacLeod—I mean MacCallum." She stopped herself from calling him Master Gage, the king of turd hill.

They looked wide-eyed from her to him and back again. Gage smiled, the way Lucifer might smile as he welcomed you through the gates of Hell. She imagined horns and fangs springing out of his face any second. He spoke in that voice that burned her eardrums with its disdain. "Allow me to let you all in on the joke. Miss. Larimore worked in my London club as a cocktail waitress until a few weeks ago, when I fired her for breach of trust and confidentiality. She was behind the libelous article in the *Mirror*."

More quiet intakes of breath. And some serious fidgeting from Alistair. She sat down and leaned forward, gripping the worn table. "So, you still think I wrote that article?"

"Indeed, I do."

"Well, that settles it. You really are a self-absorbed bastard."

His eyebrows shot up. "Excuse me?"

She tucked her trembling hands in her lap. "You believe I came to work at your club solely to meet you? And that I put up with all that crap to get some juicy gossip to publish and get myself fame and fortune?" She paused for a breath. "Only a conceited prick would make it all about him."

Gage sat back in his chair. Every muscle in his face was rigid. "Are you quite finished, Brynne?"

The raw hostility in his gaze seared her skin, but Brynne refused to look away. She squared her shoulders. "No. I'm afraid you came all this way for nothing, gentlemen. My aunt put me on the title of the house over a year ago when there was no question as to her health or sanity."

She was pleased with herself. It was time for this to be over, otherwise she might need a paramedic.

The cutest lawyer, whom she thought she'd won over, cleared his throat. "Actually, the house is of little consequence. Your aunt's investments and royalties from her catalogue of books make up the bulk of the estate's value."

Brynne felt the blood drain from her face for the second time today. She looked over at Alistair, her eyes pleading. *It's up to you, big guy, don't fail me now!*

He pushed his glasses up his nose and began. "I will easily prove that Ms. Larimore did not influence her aunt's wishes. She was the closest relative to Josephine for the last two decades. Furthermore, she had no other family members to leave her estate to."

The lawyer, whom she was fast beginning to hate, cleared his throat again. She sighed in annoyance at the nervous tic, and they all waited for him to speak.

"There is one other familial party who would stand to inherit some of the estate."

"What? Who?" Brynne burst out.

He had the decency to look sheepish. "Your mother."

Brynne made a harsh, unladylike sound and clung to the edges of the table for support. Her eyes narrowed at Gage and then the young lawyer. "You've got to be kidding me. She is a ghost. No one has heard from her in years."

Gage rested his elbows on the table and steepled his fingers to his lips. His eyes bore holes into hers. "We will endeavor to find her."

Brynne raised her chin. "Like I said. Good luck. I think we're done here." She pushed her chair out and leaned down for her purse.

"Not quite." Gage's voice was low and quiet and deadly calm. "We requested the will last week, but only received it today."

She pinched the bridge of her nose. "What of it?"

"There is a portion omitted. We need the redacted section."

Brynne thrust her chin out. "It's a personal note from my aunt, and not relevant to this discussion."

"Everything in the document is relevant…unless you will consider a revised offer."

They placed a piece of paper in front of her and Alistair. She scanned it, her eyes glossing over all the legal mumbo jumbo. It was an offer of 85,000 pounds for the right to dig on her land, bury fiber optic cable, and a commitment to return the land to its pre-construction state afterward.

Gage cleared his throat and spoke. "Perhaps that is a compromise you can live with. And if you change your mind about selling, I will up the offer on the entire property to 650,000 pounds."

Brynne looked up, her eyes glittering. "You think after the way you've bullied me, I would do anything to benefit you?"

"If you accept this offer, I will withdraw the contestation of the will."

"I'll take my chances in front of a judge. And you, Mr. MacCallum, can kiss my ass."

She ripped up the paper and headed out of the stuffy room. Brynne heard him call after her, but she flew out the front door like the hounds of Hell were chasing her. She ran to the hotel without looking back. Out of breath and dizzy, she hid in a booth in the back of the bar.

Myrna came over. "My, don't you look the spiffy girl!"

"Thanks, Myrna. I need a drink please—a Hendricks and tonic. Is Declan around?"

"He's in the kitchen. I'll let him know you're here, love. You look pale. Are you sure you don't want some food?"

"I'm sure. Thanks." She tried to smile but knew it didn't hit the mark. Myrna's creased brow gave away her doubt.

Declan arrived shortly after she got her drink.

Brynne held the glass with both hands, willing them to stop trembling. Declan sat opposite her and waited for her to speak. He was a good and patient man. Brynne took two more large gulps of her drink and met his concerned gaze.

"Gage MacCallum is Magnus. I mean Magnus is Gage. He...he's the man I worked for in London. The one I...I fell for, who hates me. He's here. He wants Josie's place. He wants to pay me a ton of money to disappear off the face of the earth. Either that or a pile of cash to let him put cables in the ground. Did I mention he hates me? I told him to kiss my ass. I channeled Josie and basically told him no. Nobody tells him no." She took a breath and held her face in her hands. "I'm not feeling good. I might need to puke."

"Breathe, lass. You stood up to Goliath. I'm proud of you, and Josie would be, too."

She peeked at him through her fingers. "Thank you, but all I did was wave a bright red cape at a furious and unforgiving bull."

Gage watched Brynne fly out of the room and forced himself not to chase after her. He'd lost the upper hand the moment she walked in, looking gorgeous and furious. That dress accentuated her hourglass figure, and every man in the room took notice. It shocked him to see her with short hair. Now she was truly a pixie like Tink, with a fierce temper.

How the fuck did he miss that she was the niece? *Because you walked in here, not having read the package, asshole.* He'd shown up to the meeting cocky and ill-prepared, certain that Josie's niece would back down and accept the very generous offer for the land and then kiss the old house goodbye. Why the hell didn't his lawyers connect the dots when the same firm was handling both cases?

Alistair was a nice man, but he was out of his depth. Gage needed to exploit his weakness and find a way past her stubborn resolve. When he pushed for the redacted section of the will, she looked down to the right. He knew in his gut she was lying.

"Mr. Mackenzie, I think it's safe to say that emotions are running extremely high under the circumstances. The fact that Brynne and I shared a personal relationship back in London has not helped matters. I wish I'd known she was Josephine's niece. We could have avoided this misunderstanding."

Alistair looked at him, his gray brows raised. "You were dating?"

"Yes, we were seeing each other before she came to Skye. Things ended rather suddenly between us, but I would never wish her any harm. I would like to try to resolve this—to her benefit and mine."

Alistair nodded, processing that new piece of information, so Gage continued.

"I don't want to tie up the estate needlessly. I think you can agree that what I am offering is very generous."

He mumbled, "Yes, quite generous, but—"

Gage interrupted him. "I suggest we let Brynne calm down. After all, it was a shock seeing me. I won't take any action for the next week, and I hope that she will see reason."

Alistair fiddled with the large stack of papers in front of him, then he looked at Gage like a father would when a boy came to take his daughter on a date. "I will speak to her about the options you have presented; however, I hope your intentions are honorable, Mr. MacCallum. Brynne is a special girl. She was like a daughter to Josephine."

"I understand. Rest assured, my intentions are honorable. I only wish to access the land so that we can provide reliable and affordable cellular and internet services to even the most remote inhabitants of the islands. This has been my dream for a long time. Many of these investments in infrastructure are funded by me personally."

"I see." The old man looked surprised, and Gage knew his plan was working.

"Do you mind if we use your boardroom for a few more minutes?

I would like to consult with my team before we head out."

"Certainly. Take your time. Good to meet you, gentlemen."

Three heads nodded and mumbled their thanks as he left the room.

Gage waited for Mackenzie to be out of earshot before addressing his legal team.

"Jeremy, I need you to get the unredacted will before you leave here. I don't care how you get it, even if you have to seduce his secretary."

The young lawyer gawped at him. "I am sure that won't be necessary, sir. I will make an official request under Section 57.5, Lodging of testamentary documents and filing of evidence. They must provide it if we plan to submit it to the court."

"Whatever. Just get it. We will give her five days, and if she hasn't caved by then, I want to turn up the heat."

"Sir…" The one who had been mooning over Brynne was angling to speak.

When he continued flipping through the package, Gage glared at him. "Spit it out, kid."

"Sir, we assembled everything to make this look solid and daunting to Miss Larimore, but you must know the case itself is very weak."

"I am aware of that fact. What's your name?" Gage pinned him with a steely-eyed stare.

"Benson, sir."

"Benson, I know we won't win this case, and I don't expect it will ever get to a judge. I'm glad you took your eyes off Miss Larimore long enough to make a few salient points."

He blushed. Gage shook his head, wondering if this was his first case out of law school.

"Yes sir. I just wanted to—"

"Just get me the document. I'll be in touch." He grabbed the stack of papers and strode out.

He considered stopping for a drink but thought better of it. His housekeeper would have stocked the bar and pantry for his arrival.

As he passed the hotel, a flash of auburn hair caught his eye. Brynne was facing away from him, but he knew her lush shape a mile away. She was embracing a man who looked old enough to be her father. He recognized Declan Fraser, the owner of the hotel. *What are they doing together?*

Gage turned back and hit the brakes hard, almost running a red light. His hands gripped the steering wheel. Had she already moved on to a new guy? *Why do I care?* He didn't. It was a lingering annoyance at how she'd upended the meeting and refused the money. A glance in the rear view mirror showed them standing on the sidewalk. Declan's arm was still around her. The investigator needed to hurry with the next report. He wanted to know everything. *Too bad it didn't come before the meeting today.*

A loud honking woke him up. The light was green, and he was sitting there preoccupied. He hit the gas and headed out of Portree. He needed to burn off this anger and negative energy. Maybe the punching bag hanging in his loft would do the trick.

He pulled in behind the house and walked to the front deck to admire the view. The sun had drifted toward the horizon and the sky was a vivid swirl of oranges, reds, and purples over the darkening gray. This house was a passion project he'd started fifteen months ago. It was supposed to be a relaxing holiday home for him and Sierra. He snorted in disgust at how wrong he had been about her. None of that mattered now. They finished it and he planned to enjoy it as often as he could.

His deep connection to Skye went back to his childhood.

Growing up, he'd often questioned why he had no father and no family here. At thirteen, Gage pressed his mother for the truth. She was twenty when she got pregnant by a married man who owned a company in Fort William, where she worked as a secretary. He seduced her, and although he could not—or would not—acknowledge her son as his own, he set her up in a home on Skye. The company had a large fleet of fishing boats in Portree, and he visited every week. However, when Gage was five, he died and left them with no support of any kind. She fought hard to hold on to the house and eventually went back to school to become a family lawyer. He admired her tenacity, but she was never an affectionate or nurturing presence in his life. Most often, he was left to his own devices while she worked two jobs to keep a roof over their heads.

She had a modern house near Elgol Beach, which sat empty most of the time. It was his temporary home during the construction of his place. The lack of decent network services was not just annoying, it was detrimental to business development and tourism on Skye, and he wanted to change that. The project's success depended on getting access to the only viable path to the shore. Josie's parcel of land was one of the few without layers of sedimentary rock and basaltic lava. Stunning rock formations were part of Skye's rugged beauty, but you couldn't bury cables in them.

Gage's phone pinged. The email subject read *Unredacted Will*. He opened the message from Benson and read the attachment. His mouth dropped open in shock. He could not believe it and read it a second time.

- Brynne must complete her revised manuscript within six months of my death.

- Brynne must open her heart to a loving relationship and banish the three-date rule from her vocabulary.

- She must endeavor to sustain a relationship with a suitable* man for a year.

- Finally, Brynne should spend at least four months a year on Skye for the next two years.

Four insane conditions, two of which struck him as hilarious. Her definition of suitable made him laugh out loud.

* Suitable: Intelligent. Kind. Successful (this doesn't mean money). Honest. Preferably Scottish. Preferably Dominant.

Dominant? He'd known Josie was a firecracker and liked her the moment he met her. But why did she think her niece needed a dominant Scotsman? Yet another mystery to unravel.

They shared many a cup of tea while discussing their mutual love of travel, books, and the Isle of Skye. He only wished he'd discovered sooner how critical her land was to his plans—and that she was terminally ill. In April, he noticed how quickly she tired, but she dismissed it and told him she'd just gotten over the flu.

Imposing those requirements on Brynne was highly manipulative. He could just imagine her reaction. Josie had unwittingly given him the power to get what he wanted. Brynne was in for thousands of dollars of repairs and couldn't access any real money.

The sun had almost set when he saw the MG fly past his house and down the hill. He smiled, knowing she was as shocked as he was today. It was only a matter of time before he regained control. He went into the house to pour a drink and plan his next steps.

24

Advantage: MacLeod

Brynne navigated her way to the front porch entrance using her phone's flashlight. Since Logan had torn the drywall off, the back door was impassable. She needed a drink but had to get out of the tight-fitting dress and killer high-heeled boots first. It was time for flannel Scottie dogs and a double gin and tonic. After changing, she poured herself a tumbler-size cocktail and made some crackers and cheese.

She needed the fire pit and a talk with Auntie Josie. Declan had prepared the logs and kindling when he came to run the car. What would she do without him?

She lit the fire, wrapped herself in a blanket, and stared up at the stars dotting the black night sky.

How could you do this to me? Why those stupid conditions? I can't fix this house without surrendering to that bastard up the hill. How could you have trusted him?

She stared into the darkness and waited for the answers she knew wouldn't come. To the spirits, she muttered, "How do you expect me to find a suitable man on this tiny island of thirteen thousand people? If I couldn't find one in London, there is no chance of finding one here."

Brynne had to consider her options. Did she want to live down the hill from the bane of her existence? Seeing the hatred in his eyes today had cut her to the bone. How could she still want him? Unless she really was a masochist? She remembered when he asked that very question.

Maybe I am, since I choose unsuitable men who inevitably hurt me. Not the good hurt like an erotic spanking, but hurt like "you're sick" or "you're fired, and you'll never work in this town again."

Lights suddenly glowed on the ground beside the house. Brynne heard the car engine and jumped up, her heart hammering in her throat. She grabbed an old canoe paddle to use as a weapon. The interloper came around to the deck and she prepared to swing.

Gage raised his hands in defense. "Whoa, it's only me. I saw your lights on."

"You scared the hell out of me. Why are you here? I have nothing to say to you."

"I thought we could talk and find a compromise."

"How do you plan to do that? Your trio of suits aren't here to help you bulldoze me—like you want to do to this house."

"Brynne, I don't want to bulldoze the house. I just want to bring decent network capabilities to the islands. Can you not see the benefits of that?"

"I might have if you hadn't threatened me. Instead, you want to tie me up in court and suck all the money out of my inheritance." Her face heated at the double entendre, and she hoped he couldn't see it in the firelight. He smirked, but it was gone so fast it might have been her imagination.

"Your aunt agreed to let my company lay cable down to the shoreline. We talked about it in the spring, but I hadn't gotten the chance to bring her the paperwork."

She stared at him and shook her head, regretting the gin and tonics that had scrambled her thoughts.

His tone turned softer. "I didn't know she was sick. And I wanted to tell you how sorry I am for your loss."

"Don't. You don't get to say that. I don't want your sympathy or your stupid money."

"It seems you need my money. The house needs extensive repairs."

"I'll find a way. And how do you know that? Are you digging into all my business?!"

"Relax. Your contractor Logan helped build my house and is still finishing a project for me. He told me about your plumbing issues."

She looked at him and sneered. "How can I possibly trust you? You want to disinherit me and dig up my pathetic excuse for a mother—after you blacklisted me all over London."

His eyes widened at her scathing tone, but he thundered back. "Your betrayal of my trust brought on your exile from London. Let's not forget how you faked your way into my club and wrote a sordid news story."

Brynne raised the oar higher. "I think you should go before this paddle finds its way to your head." Her voice gave away her near hysteria. "Get off my property and don't come back. Ever."

He shook his head, his mouth a hard line. "You will be sorry, Brynne. I'm trying to find a solution that benefits both of us."

"Oh well, *Magnus*, I guess you will just have to find another place to lay your goddamned cable."

His temper bubbled like volcanic lava about to erupt. Gage felt the top of his head tingling when he got into his car and peeled out of her driveway. She was impossible! Unreasonable! How dare she speak to him that way?

She looked like a wild pixie in the amber light, wielding a paddle and threatening his person. The urge to grab her caveman-style and carry her off to his bed was too real. He should not want someone he hated. Right?

She was a challenge. That's all. He wanted to bend her to his will. Bend her over his bed. Bend her over his knee. Or bend his leather belt over her ass until she begged for mercy.

Except there would be no mercy.

Fuck. What was wrong with him? He had planned to mention the clause in the will, but totally forgot. Pain emanated from her wide eyes when she spoke of her mother. That woman had done a number on her daughter.

Gage refused to feel sorry for her. Everyone had to deal with some shit in their childhood. In middle school, the boys would mock him for not having a father until he learned how to box. They broke his nose only once, and after that, no one touched his pretty face again. The principal expelled him three or four times for fighting— then his mother sent him away to boarding school. The teasing didn't stop there, but he learned how to close himself off and ignore the snide comments.

He was unbeatable in the ring and vicious when crossed. By the time he reached university, the girls flocked around him like bees to honey. They couldn't get enough of his aloof confidence. He was a challenge they wanted to conquer, but he did the conquering. He commanded respect, and by the time he was twenty, he'd discovered an affinity for bondage and discipline.

In his third-floor fitness room, he punched the heavy bag until his body ached. He had to regain the upper hand. The plan to entice her with money had failed. Threatening her inheritance only made her furious. Tonight, he tried convincing her of the merits of his project, but she was past caring and wanted to bean him with a paddle. And yet, she still expected him to believe her lies about the article.

After a hot shower, Gage poured a scotch and checked his email. Benson's latest note suggested they move to contest, then take full advantage of the conditions in the will. The kid tested his patience today, ogling her from the moment she walked in. But he was the only one to add value. When Brynne ignored his request to speak in private, and smiled warmly at him, he wanted to punch his face.

He typed his reply: *Do not file any formal actions unless I give you explicit direction.*

Garrick sent an update on the club. Requests to join Dominus had been steadily increasing since the story broke. The retraction received more social media attention than the original story. Ironically, the unwanted publicity garnered a positive effect. Several of the members no longer cared if the press knew they belonged to the club. In fact, they said it gave them a *cool* factor they hadn't had in years. Patrick Knight posed for the paparazzi, tipping his hat to them as he entered through the front doors. Garrick assured him that things were returning to normal. Only John was still taking advantage of the underground garage entrance.

The last email contained his cable and internet bill from SkyeNet. In a month, he would be the company's controlling shareholder. In the meantime, he still had to pay the exorbitant bills. His eyes widened when he saw the alert that he'd exceeded the download limit in the last two weeks. How was that possible? Josie was the only one with guest access to his network. Unless…

He used his stellar hacking skills to access the Wi-Fi network. A few clicks later and he displayed the usage, downloads, and all the websites accessed.

Jesus H. Christ. It was no wonder the bandwidth was maxed out! Brynne had been surfing an array of bondage video sites and Pornhub for several hours each night. Her Google searches were eye-opening too… And she had bookmarked four BDSM chat rooms.

It was time to cut her off. With a wicked smile, he changed the guest password and wished he could be a fly on the wall when she tried to get online. The reaction would be like detonating an explosive device.

All he had to do was wait until she figured out that he held the key to all her services, including a decent cell signal. With any luck, she would run back to London.

25

A Delicious Conquest

Y*ou will be sorry, Brynne.*

What exactly did he mean by that? He said he wanted to find a solution that benefited them both. More likely, he wanted her to take the money and leave Skye. She grabbed her cell phone and pulled the covers up to ward off the chill. Jared was the only one who could be her sounding board. She needed his wisdom.

The screen looked like it was dialing, but nothing happened. She opened her email and there were no new messages. The Wi-Fi signal was strong, but she wasn't connecting after two attempts. *Goddamnit.*

Throwing her robe and slippers on, she went downstairs to check her aunt's notebook for another password. Access denied. WTF?! After a thorough search, she realized she had no modem or router.

What she did have was a landline hanging on the kitchen wall. Thank god! The receiver cord hung to the floor because Josie used to love to walk around while talking. Brynne looked up Alistair's number and dialed.

"Hello Brynne."

"Hi Alistair, sorry to bother you, but do you have the number for the internet provider? I realize the utilities aren't transferred yet, but my Wi-Fi is down, and I don't have an account number or anything to reference."

"Hang on, I have a file here with all the recent invoices."

She chewed on her fingernail while she waited.

"Sorry dear, there is nothing current for the internet. About six months ago, Josie closed her account with SkyeNet, so you'll need to open a new one."

"But I've had services up until today. I used the password Josie had written down."

"Maybe they didn't disconnect it until now, although that seems odd."

"It does. Do you have their number? I can't even get a signal to Google it."

Brynne took the number and thanked Alistair, ready to hang up.

"Oh, Brynne…"

"Yes?"

"I am sorry MacCallum's lawyers now have a copy of the unredacted will. By law, I had to provide it."

"Oh god! He'll see those absurd conditions." She blew out her breath. "What happens next?"

"If they make a formal filing, they will notify us. So far, they haven't."

"No, he's still hoping I will cave and give him what he wants."

Alistair cleared his throat.

"What? Is there more bad news?"

"No, it's nothing like that. I was, um, surprised. Magnus mentioned you and he dated back in London."

Brynne's mouth dropped open. She gripped the receiver, not believing her ears. That bastard. "We had a very brief... It was... Yes, we dated."

"It's none of my business, dear. It's just too bad it didn't work out. Maybe then—"

She cut him off. "Yes, unfortunate. Well, I must go. I can't survive here without the internet. Keep me posted on their next move."

"Will do."

Brynne beat the receiver against the old Formica counter in a rage before slamming it into the metal holder. She wanted to kill him. How dare he? Obviously, he had a cozy little confab with her lawyer after she left!

"Bastard!" Screaming only made her feel marginally better.

After an hour of pacing up and down the kitchen, she was unwilling to listen to SkyeNet's horrid hold music a second longer. Logan was due anytime, and she decided her best bet was to work from the library.

Jared texted his full support of her plan to date Logan. He was a firm believer in diving back into the pool, assuring her it would help her forget the demon, Gage.

She hadn't asked a guy out in forever. What if he said no?

Logan arrived right on schedule and gave her a warm and twinkly-eyed hello as he carried an array of equipment into the house. She smiled and stood there, fiddling with the strap of her purse.

He looked at her quizzically. "What's up?"

"Not much. I'm going to the library. My internet is down."

"Okay." He looked down at his phone. "Oh shit, no signal.

Magnus has probably called and, knowing him, they're on the way to fix it."

"Okay, well, that's good." Brynne watched him unpacking his stuff and took a deep breath. "I wondered if you wanted to go out sometime. Um. Thursday, they are having a karaoke night at the Whistling Oyster Bar, and I thought, I wondered—"

He grinned, showing off his dimples. "I'd love to. I can't sing worth a damn, but it sounds like fun."

"Okay great, cool." Her cheeks turned pink.

"I can pick you up around seven p.m. on Thursday. Does that work?"

"Sounds good. Okay, I'm off. Coffee is made if you want some."

"Thanks. See you later."

She waved awkwardly and left.

As she drove past Gage's fortress, she threw up her middle finger in salute and hoped he was watching.

The public library was decent. She found a quiet corner on the second floor to set up. She did an online application for internet services and then tried to settle into editing. Each time she reviewed a sex scene and tried to turn up the heat between her characters, it was Gage's face she saw. Finally, she ran with it and allowed her thoughts free rein. It worked. She wrote a 1,200-word scene before breaking to grab lunch. It was a frustrating process; her second draft needed more erotic content, and she had minimal firsthand experiences to draw from.

If she was honest, forgetting Gage wasn't her only reason for dating Logan. If things worked out, she could show the hot handyman what she wanted in bed. Meeting the "boyfriend" conditions of the will would be a bonus.

Thursday came quickly and Brynne tried on three different outfits before finally settling on a pair of jeans, a simple white button-down blouse, and her navy blazer. She found a cute pair of blue suede ankle boots in her aunt's closet. The best thing to happen this week was the discovery of Josie's designer shoe collection. And learning they both wore a size seven.

Logan looked very handsome when he came to fetch her. He wore a pair of dark jeans, a pale blue chambray shirt paired with a worn leather jacket and sexy cowboy boots. He told her how pretty she looked when he helped her step up into his truck.

On the drive to town, Brynne broke the awkward silence by asking him about his work. Logan was happy to have something to talk about and started regaling her about the last nine months spent working at Gage's house. Brynne ooh'd and ahh'd at the right times while he told her about the imported slate in the bathrooms, the two-story stone fireplace, and the amazing gym in the third-floor loft with its own luxurious spa bathroom on one end and a massage room on the other. Brynne was relieved when they arrived at the restaurant, even though she'd been devouring every damned detail about the house.

Over dinner, Logan finally asked her about her own career and seemed surprised she wasn't a full-time waitress. She told him about her journalism degree and the book project. When he asked what kind of book, she called it a mystery romance. She was happy he didn't ask more questions, saving her from making something up. The karaoke started, and they ordered another round. She admitted needing liquid courage to get up to sing.

It started to get loud, making conversation difficult. Brynne went and grabbed a copy of the song book. The guy working the machine was the same one who ran karaoke night at Declan's bar, so she knew he had a broad selection.

"You sure you don't want to sing?" Brynne asked Logan as she considered her choices.

"Hell no. My voice would empty this place. I'm looking forward to hearing you. What are you going to sing?"

"I'm thinking of a song by Jefferson Airplane."

"Nice—I like classic rock."

"They were one of my aunt's favorite artists. She introduced me to them, the Moody Blues, and the Stones."

"So which song, 'Somebody to Love'?"

"Either that one or 'White Rabbit.'"

"Oh, that's a killer tune. Do that one."

Brynne gulped down more of her cocktail and put her name on the list. There were two other names before hers—a cute couple did an old country and western duet and then a group of friends sang Journey's "Don't Stop Believing." She was up next.

"Wish me luck!"

The drinks helped her nerves, but as she neared the stage, she wondered if this night was a bad idea. If it didn't work out, he wouldn't finish the repair work. First dates were always awkward. She needed to calm down and get through the song. It had been ages since she did this—and never without Jared. She walked up to the microphone and was glad the lights were so bright that she couldn't see Logan or anyone beyond the dance floor.

The song began with its distinctive bolero-styled bass notes, and when the crowd heard the military beat of the drums, they cheered. Brynne started tentatively, but then got absorbed in the song and belted out the last verse—with the audience singing along.

"Feed your head! Feed your head!"

The clapping and whistling reassured her, and she received some high fives as she made her way around the tables to their booth. Brynne felt elated that her voice hadn't cracked when she stretched to reach the highest notes.

When she got back, Logan was nowhere to be seen. What the

hell? Did he miss her performance? She noticed he had left her purse unattended, and that pissed her off. A quick check confirmed her phone and wallet were still there.

She turned to search the crowd for him and was startled by a six-foot-two mass of testosterone staring down at her, a dangerous glint in his eyes.

"What are you doing here? Where is Logan?"

"I sent him home."

"You did what?! You had no right!"

He moved to sit in the booth beside her, and she scrambled back and put her purse between them.

"Keep your voice down, Red."

"I will not. Besides, no one can hear us over the music." She crossed her arms and scowled at him.

"I caught most of your song. You were great."

"Pfft. Why are you here, Gage? Or should I call you Magnus?"

"Why don't we get out of here so we can talk?"

She shook her head. How did she forget how big and imposing he was up close? His distinctive scent drifted over her, causing her heart to pound like a bass in her ears. She stuck her chin out. "Not until you explain why you scared off my date."

"He doesn't know what you need."

"How dare you! And you think you know?"

His eyes bore into hers. "I do. Let me drive you home."

"I can get a taxi after I have another drink and sing another song. Like, 'You're So Vain.'"

His unexpected laughter took her breath away. She was in deep trouble.

"You've already had plenty to drink, and it's too loud to have a conversation."

"I have nothing to say to you."

He shook his head, amusement dancing in his eyes. "I can easily carry you kicking and screaming out of here, or you can be civilized."

"I am so past civilized, it's not funny, Mags. Was that your nickname as a child?"

That last cocktail had made her reckless. She watched in fascination as he looked around, as if measuring the reaction if he tossed her over his shoulder and waltzed out.

He leaned close to her ear. "Be careful what you wish for, Brynne. If you keep teasing the beast, you might find yourself caught and devoured."

She considered her options when he rose and held out a hand to her.

"Do you always get your way?"

"Yes."

She shook her head and took his hand. "Fine. I'll come with you, but only because I'm ready to leave and you scared off my ride."

He helped her into the luxurious SUV, and she couldn't help but run her hands over the rich leather seat. Gage got in and started the Range Rover. Then he reached over to clip her seatbelt.

She blew out a sigh. "Thanks, Dad. I would have done that, I was just captivated by all the pretty lights on the dash. It looks like an airplane cockpit." When he didn't respond, she said, "You better not have made Logan mad at me. I need him."

"He's not mad. I explained that you and I have some unfinished business."

Brynne snorted. "That's one way of putting it."

They drove through the darkened roads in silence. But when they pulled into his drive and the garage door opened, she sat up. "What are you doing? I thought you were taking me home."

"Your place is a construction zone. I'll take you home after we talk."

She huffed. "I hate that you know my business!"

"You seem to forget this is a small town. Everyone knows everyone's business."

He came around to open her door. She was struggling to unclip the seat belt, then turned pleading eyes to him. "I'm stuck."

Gage put his foot up on the running board and leaned into her space. "I do enjoy seeing you like this. Trapped and unable to escape."

Up to this moment, she never understood what romance writers meant when they described the hero giving the heroine a smoldering look. She knew it now because she was melting under his gaze. She licked her lips—whether it was inadvertent or because her body was inviting him to kiss her, she couldn't say. Gage stared at her mouth for what felt like an eternity. His thumb caressed her bottom lip, then pulled her mouth open slightly. She closed her eyes, thinking a kiss would follow, but it didn't. His warm breath tantalized; his fingers spread over her cheek and held her there, just below her ear. He nipped her bottom lip and then licked it. Lips brushed lightly across hers but were gone as she lifted her chin in a silent plea for more.

When his hand encircled her neck and tilted her head, her eyes flew open and met his.

"Do you want this?" His eyes pinned her in place.

"Yes." Her voice squeaked.

The word "please" was lost when his mouth met hers. His hand moved to cradle her head and his tongue sought entry, darting in and out, until she moaned and grabbed onto his shirt to pull him closer. His tongue played with hers, gently at first and then harder and deeper. She met his ferocity with her own until he stopped and withdrew, just out of reach. A flush of satisfaction warmed her at the sound of his ragged breathing. He was just as aroused as she was.

Suddenly, he unclipped the seat belt and pulled her forward so he could hoist her over his shoulder.

"Oof!" It knocked the wind out of her, but that didn't stop her from wriggling and playfully pummeling his backside.

A hard smack hit her bottom. "Stop squirming or I might just fuck you over the hood of the car."

She was still trying to catch her breath and had no snappy comeback.

Gage headed into the massive country kitchen and put her down on the counter. He spread her knees and stepped in between. Brynne put her arms on his shoulders and entwined her fingers in his hair, which had grown past his collar since she'd last seen him. He allowed her to kiss, lick, and nibble his mouth while he pulled her jacket off and started on the buttons of her blouse. With three buttons to go, impatience drove him to rip the shirt open, sending the little pearls flying. Brynne gasped when he spread open her blouse and yanked it partway down her arms. He moved in to kiss her neck and drew the straps of her pale pink bra off her shoulders.

Into the crook of her neck he drawled, "Did you wear this for Logan?"

"Maybe I did."

He pulled back and stared at her. "How many dates before you send him packing?"

"Thought I might keep him around. He looks like good boyfriend material."

"Ha!" he barked. "He is as vanilla as they come. You'd be bored in a week."

"How do you know? Have you slept with him?"

Gage suddenly leaned back and grabbed her wrists. "Don't think I will tolerate this impertinence. For once, are you going to do as you're told?"

Brynne grinned impishly and fluttered her eyelashes at him. "What do you think?"

"I think by the end of this night, you will understand what obedience is. That is, if you don't run home."

She giggled nervously. "I'm not afraid of you."

"You should be." He smiled so wickedly, her stomach did backflips.

He dragged her arms behind her, holding them pinned against her back. Heat blazed from his eyes. "I've warned you enough times what I expect, yet you continue to play games."

Brynne pressed her lips together and stuck her chin out. "You hate me. How can you want this?" *I need the answer because I should hate you, but I can't deny this unquenchable need.*

"My cock doesn't care if I hate you. Now is your chance to leave, because if you stay, I'm going to take everything I want from you until I've had my fill."

The truth was Brynne had never wanted anything so badly. But she couldn't bring herself to submit completely. "I won't surrender willingly. I want you to make me."

He rocked back on his heels and looked up at the ceiling. "That should go against all my principles, but for tonight, I'll make an exception. And if you cannot take it, say your safe word and it all stops."

Brynne thought to herself, he doesn't know me very well. She never backed down from a challenge and he just double-dog dared her.

He stood back and yanked her boots and socks off and tossed them into the corner. She found herself carried like a sack of potatoes through the great room to the master suite. Half expecting to be dropped onto the Viking-size four-poster bed, she was surprised when he walked into the adjoining bathroom and put her down. She felt the heat coming from the stone floor and was admiring the gigantic bathtub when he spoke. "You have five minutes to do what you need to, because for the rest of the night, you will be chained to my bed."

He turned and shut the door.

Holy fuck. Brynne was glad to have a few minutes to collect herself. She needed to pee, then searched and found a clean facecloth. No way did she want him to know she was already soaking wet. The washcloth did the trick and, against her better judgment, she used his toothbrush. Knowing him, that could tip him off the deep end. Whatever, she knew he could can afford a new one.

One loud knock made her squeal and jump. "You have two minutes to get out here. Naked."

Naked. Pfft. She took a minute to breathe and center herself. This was a dream come true. She would remember every detail of the night; it would fuel her writing, and she would get over wanting him.

His voice bellowed through the door, "Anything you don't take off will be shredded if I have to remove them for you."

"Okay!" she yelled back. Bastard.

The door opened when she was pulling her jeans off. She hopped on one leg and started to tip over. The hard floor was coming up to meet her. Just her luck, she'd get knocked out and miss the whole damn night!

Gage caught her before she hit the floor. She looked up with a weak smile. "My hero."

"Christ, woman, the only way to keep you safe is to tie you down."

He sat her on the closed toilet and pulled her jeans off, then helped her to stand.

"Cute panties. It will be a shame to destroy them."

"Wait no! I was going to, before you came barging in here."

He held out his hand for them, and she rolled her eyes angrily, then yanked them off and handed them to him. Rebellion shone from her eyes.

"Do you plan to keep them as a souvenir?"

"No, I will keep them close by. If you can't stop talking back, you know where they will end up."

She crossed her arms when he motioned for her to exit the bathroom. The bedroom was toasty and cast in a warm glow from the gas fireplace. She eyed the canopy bed that dominated the room. On top of each carved wood column was a wrought iron design with four scrolls that doubled as hooks. Thick metal posts extended the columns to well beyond seven feet and supported the forged metal canopy above. She shivered when she saw the restraints on the bed.

"Get on your knees." His eyes were gleaming.

She met fire with fire. "Make me, Mags." In her head she wondered if she had a death wish.

One hand gripped her by her hair and forced her over the side of the bed; the other pressed down between her shoulder blades so she couldn't move.

"Fight me all you want. It will make your eventual submission all the sweeter."

She groaned in response and tried to wiggle free, but his body was on top of her, and she could feel his erection through his jeans.

He grabbed the padded leather cuffs and buckled them snugly on each wrist. Then he dragged her arms up over her head and clipped them together by a short chain.

He lifted her up and maneuvered her to stand facing the post at the foot of the bed. One arm gripped her around the waist and the other pulled her arms up over her head. Before she could react, he pressed her forward against the post and hung her wrists over an iron hook. She struggled for purchase on her tiptoes and watched him cross the room to his closet. He returned with several scary-looking implements and laid them on the bed where she could see them.

"See anything you like?"

"You've seen one flogger, you've seen them all." She tried to sound flippant and failed.

He laughed, a low gravelly sound that skittered across her skin.

"First, let's ensure you can't kick me." He grabbed another set of cuffs and fastened them around her ankles. Brynne's pulse thrummed hard in her ears and wetness pooled between her legs. She was helpless to his whims and the truth was inescapable; she would give him anything he wanted.

She felt the heat from his body right behind her and tried to press herself against him. Bad idea. He smacked her ass hard. Slowly, his hands trailed a path up from her hips. With a feather-light touch, he caressed the undersides of her breasts. All around he went, playing close to her hardened nipples, but never touching them.

"Please," she whined.

"Please, what, Red?"

"Please touch me, let me feel you up against me, inside me… anything."

"Punishments first. Rewards later."

"Do it then! Punish me—just stop teasing me!" Her body flooded with need. Desperate and impatient, she turned her face into her arms and moaned, "Just get it over with."

"What is your safe word?"

"Red."

Gage picked up the flat two-inch-wide leather strap with the braided handle. He smacked his hand, and she jumped at the sound.

Thwack! The first strike hit the fullness of her bottom. *That wasn't so bad.*

Thwack! Thwack! Thwack!

"OMG that stings!"

He took his time and spanked every single part of her ass, then her thighs, then back up to her already tender cheeks—all the while acting oblivious to her whining and moaning.

"Oh! Ow! Ooow!" she screamed. Her backside was on fire; strange electric currents were thrumming over her clit. In her head, she could hear the intense bass line of "The Chain" by Fleetwood Mac. It vibrated across all her nerve endings.

She lost count of how many times that infernal strap hit her tender flesh, aware only of the prickling burn that zinged through her body—equal parts pain and arousal. Her hips pressed forward, trying to rub against the bedpost, but he noticed immediately and wrapped his arm around her waist. His mouth was next to her ear. "Don't even think about it."

With little effort, he lifted her off the hook and laid her face up across his bed. Brynne groaned when her tender flesh touched the cool sheets. She felt him detach the clip holding her ankle cuffs together and flushed in embarrassment when he dragged her left leg toward the foot of the bed. He tugged it wide and chained it there, leaving her totally exposed. She drew her other knee up and rolled to conceal herself from him. His low and wicked chuckle mocked her as he captured her right ankle and fastened it to the head of the bed. She covered her face with her arms and called him a bastard under her breath. The chains held fast, but she still tried to draw her knees together.

A hard smack on her inner thigh made her gasp and jerk against the cuffs.

"Keep your legs open. I want to see how wet you are for me."

"You've got me where you want me. What now?"

"What do you want, Red?"

Letting him know how much she wanted him was not an option. "You have a cock and I happen to want one." Lifting her head up, she stared him down. "You ran my date off—and I almost forgot, you stole Mr. Boss!"

"What?"

"My vibrator—you took it with you, remember? I want it back."

"So, any phallus will suffice right now?"

He moved to the other side of the bed, out of her sight. She paused, not sure how to answer. "Yes… No! Please, I'll do anything."

Silence.

"Fine, it's your cock that I want. Is that what you wanted to hear?"

Warm hands grasped her cuffed arms and drew them over her head, where he had another chain ready to secure them. She tested the give and found none. When he placed a blindfold over her eyes, a whimper escaped. The bed dipped beside her. Then he grasped her just above her waist and pulled her toward him until her legs were stretched taut and her arms were pinned to the bed.

"Are you afraid I will escape?"

No reply: just footsteps moving away, shoes being kicked off, the sound of a zipper followed by the jingle of his belt. She squirmed in anticipation. A drawer opened and closed. Then the sound of leather hitting his hand. *Uh oh.*

"I told you I wanted to see you writhe and pull against these restraints. I control everything, sweetheart, including when you come, and when you get released."

Brynne sighed dramatically. "If you don't let me come soon, I may perish."

"Mmm. So impatient." The bed dipped again, and she could feel the heat of his body next to hers. Her hands reached out, but the tether was too short.

His fingers grazed her breasts like before, except both hands teased her simultaneously, alternating between squeezing and then lightly caressing them. Then finally his palms abraded her nipples, back and forth, making them engorged and achy. One hand grasped her flesh and plumped it—she hoped for his mouth, but it was the shocking sting of leather instead.

"Ah, god!" she screeched just before his mouth was there to soothe and bathe the tortured nipple. He repeated it with her other breast, and even though she knew what was coming, it still made her jerk against the bonds when the leather tongue bit her. He lapped and kissed and grazed the tips with his teeth until Brynne was panting. Again and again, he punished and then soothed them until they were swollen and throbbing.

"Open your mouth."

No hesitation, just total compliance. Much, much later, she would question her blind obedience. Right now, she wanted to scream, *Oh yes, please!*

Gage kneeled over her head and lowered his cock to her mouth, dragging the tip across her waiting tongue. Brynne raised her head so she could wrap her lips around the head, her tongue stroking in circles, swirling the sensitive underside, reveling in the sounds that came from his chest. She licked and sucked as much as he would give her and was so engrossed in the task that she hadn't noticed he had moved down her body—until he settled himself on top of her, with his mouth poised above her spread thighs.

She felt his warm breath first, then his fingers on her most intimate parts, exploring her folds, dipping into the source of all her pent-up desires. His fingers penetrated and withdrew, once, twice, three times until she was writhing beneath him. On the verge of a climax, she screamed a desperate plea, which was muffled by his shaft. Suddenly, he pulled back, raising himself above her. His accent was stronger than she had ever heard it. "No coming yet, sweetheart. I'm going to fuck your throat first."

Brynne was close to the edge—one touch on her clit, and she would come. But the bastard had other plans. "I hate you," she whispered.

He chuckled. "Good things come to those who wait. And obey."

In response, she dropped her head back on the bed and stuck her tongue out before opening to him. He slowly slid his shaft in deeper until the head tapped the back of her throat. As he withdrew, she used her tongue and lips to enthrall him. He allowed her to lavish the head like a lollipop before pushing down, deeper this time. It thumped against her soft palate, and she tensed. He withdrew a few inches and held it there. "Relax your throat for me. I'll take it slow." His voice sounded strained.

Brynne forced herself to breathe so that the next time he slid deeper still, she was ready for it. He established an unhurried pace, leaving her enough time to inhale and focus solely on the rhythmic pulsing of his cock owning her throat. It thrilled her to hear his breath becoming labored, and each time it kissed the back of her throat, he made a noise like he was enduring rapturous torture. She felt him swell further and his whole body tensed. Gage groaned, "Fuck," and pulled himself out of her mouth.

"What's wrong?" She couldn't hide her pleased little smirk.

It took him a minute to answer. "Nothing. I got too close to the edge. And I intend for you to go over when I'm coming down your throat."

She swallowed a shiver. "Oh."

Gage straddled her body but kept his cock out of reach. She felt him between her legs, his fingers spreading her open, and then his warm, magnificent mouth began worshipping her. She shuddered when his tongue lapped back and forth, waking her clit back to full attention. His thumbs stroked, one finger delved into her vagina, then two, all the while his wicked tongue teased and tormented until her legs tensed up and she began tilting her hips back and forth in near madness. "Please don't stop. I'm close, s-so close."

"Open," was all she heard. She did, surrendering to his command. His thickness filled her mouth, and she gloried in the moment. Her lips enveloped him, and her tongue laved him as he thrust in and out. Her orgasm was building, but she wanted to hold it until he was there with her. She knew the moment had arrived when he groaned, and it reverberated on her whole mound. When he latched on to her clit and sucked, she shattered into a million pieces. Her entire body shook. Her keening wail was muted by the head of his cock, which was poised at the back of her mouth and starting to pulse. She thrust herself up and started swallowing around him, milking it straight down, until he finally stopped shuddering.

26

A Diabolical Arrangement

So that's a magnitude ten on the Richter scale?

Brynne's heart was still thumping against her rib cage as he slowly lifted himself up and rolled onto the bed beside her.

Words were beyond her. She sure as shit would not tell him the earth moved. The power dynamics, the bondage, the punishment—set off a cataclysmic reaction that defied description. An involuntary shiver shook her body, which jangled the chains securing her to the bed. Gage reached over to unclip her arms and legs, and she automatically pulled herself into the fetal position. He laid the comforter over her and spoke in a low and soothing tone. "Stay right here. I'll be back in a minute."

Brynne couldn't move if she wanted to, so she stayed in her cocoon and replayed the entire scene in her head. *Holy hell Dorothy, we are not in Kansas anymore.*

Rain pelted the roof, and the sounds of thunder permeated her muddled brain. In the distance, she heard bath water running and the faint tinkle of dishes. Gage returned and sat on the bed. He slipped the blindfold off and brushed her hair gently back from her face. She was grateful only the glowing embers of the fireplace lit the room. He methodically removed all the cuffs and carried her into the bathroom.

The bath was still filling when he stepped in, and they sank together into the hot, scented water. She smiled at him. "How did you know my legs wouldn't carry me?"

His mouth tilted up at the corners. "I've seen you almost face-plant twice now and I take your safety seriously." He leaned back in the enormous bathtub and positioned her between his spread legs. She was facing him now with her feet on either side of his muscular thighs. Brynne was so busy ogling his naked body, she didn't notice all the goodies laid out on the ledge of the picture window.

"Here, eat." He handed her a plate loaded with an assortment of cheese, grapes, and crackers. He poured them both a glass of ice water and helped himself to some cheese.

Brynne was thankful for the snack. "This is delicious. I'm starving."

When she looked up from her plate, he was studying her.

"What? Is there something on my face?"

"No, you look properly ravished. And very beautiful."

Color bloomed on her cheeks, and she got flustered. "Um, thank you. You don't have to say that."

A crease appeared between his dark brows. "I don't *have* to say anything, Brynne. You are a beautiful woman."

She looked away, embarrassed, and piled another cracker with the creamy brie.

He turned off the water and leaned back to watch her, while sensuously popping grapes into his mouth like a sultan. She shook her head and smiled shyly while her body responded with a mind of its own. Her nipples beaded under his gaze, and tingles started between her legs. She grabbed the glass of water and took a few gulps.

He leaned forward and took the plate and the glass from her. "Come here." He slid forward and pulled her onto his lap, wrapping her legs around his waist. "You pleased me very much when you stopped fighting your own desires."

"I didn't want you to think I was easy."

He chuckled low. "You are the furthest thing from easy that I've ever met."

She pouted and tried to pull back, but he linked his arms around her.

"I'm not done with you yet." He pulled her closer with one hand on the small of her back and the other encircled her neck so he could plunder her mouth.

She wound her arms around his neck and melted into the kiss. His hands gripped her hips, and she felt his cock nudging at her entrance. When a loud thunderclap burst overhead, she jerked forward. He took advantage and thrust into her slippery heat.

"Oh god," she cried into his mouth. She couldn't move easily with her legs crossed behind him, so she tensed her muscles and squeezed him repeatedly.

"Christ, that feels good," he said. Lightning lit the sky and the night lights under the vanity flickered. Brynne barely noticed.

"Can you come this way?"

She shook her head. "Mmm, I don't think so. I need to lie on top of you with my legs straight."

"Do it." He braced on his arms and lifted his hips out of the water so she could straighten her legs. He managed to stay embedded inside her while she maneuvered around and got herself situated. She heard him chuckle and looked up to find him grinning.

"Are you laughing at me?"

"No, I'm enjoying watching you get comfortable on your mount." His expression turned wicked. "Now shut up and ride me."

After tucking his sleepy initiate into bed, he returned to the scene of the tsunami. He gathered the pile of wet towels and threw them in the tub, knowing he would never look at the jacuzzi the same way again.

His brain wasn't ready for sleep, so he poured himself a scotch and sat in his favorite chair out in the darkened living room. What the fuck just happened? Why was a woman he supposedly loathed asleep in his bed? The rain came down in torrents and the generator was still running, so it was reasonable for her to stay rather than venturing out in the storm.

Five orgasms she wrested from riding him—while splashing a few gallons of water all over his bathroom floor. He wondered if she could have kept going but watching her *in flagrante delicto* pushed the limits of his control. He ended up ravaging her up against the bay window with her legs wrapped around him. A whimper of pain escaped when he propped her on the ledge, but she'd insisted that he keep going.

When did he lose control of the situation? Fucking her bareback while perched on one leg in the bathtub had insanity written all over it. He'd completely disregarded his own rules about unprotected sex. She told him she was on a birth control shot, but he had not seen the proof. He'd let his guard down, and that pissed him off more than anything. Where did that leave him? Besides wanting to make her cry and scream and come again, he wasn't sure. Gage drained the glass of scotch and decided he could figure it out in the morning.

He woke at dawn to the sound of the bedroom door clicking closed. The space beside him was still warm, so he bolted out of bed to investigate where his little captive had gotten to. She was in the kitchen, putting on her blouse and looking for her boots.

"Going somewhere?"

She screeched and jumped in shock. "Christ, you scared the hell out of me. I was going to head home."

"Did I give you permission?" It was all he could think of in his groggy state.

She started giggling until she saw his serious expression. "You're funny. Listen. I had a great time, but I should go."

He walked over to the coffee maker and flipped the switch. "We still have some matters to discuss. Stay for a coffee and hear me out."

"I don't know. Nothing has changed just because we had some fabulous sex."

"Fabulous?"

She rolled her eyes. "I take my coffee with cream. Unless you have some, I am not staying."

"I do." He pointed to the counter with stools. "Sit down and I'll make you some toast."

She pursed her lips. "Butter and marmalade?"

"My god, you drive a hard bargain."

"Said the kettle to the pot."

He laughed, feeling an ease he hadn't experienced in a long time. He pulled what he needed out of the fridge and set two place settings.

"You live alone." She waved at hand at her surroundings and asked, "Why do you have a fridge the size of a Sherman tank and a bathtub that can fit four people?"

That struck a nerve he wasn't willing to acknowledge, so he feigned nonchalance. "Blame the designer. I was too busy running the club to be involved in those decisions."

In truth, he and Sierra chose everything in this house, but she didn't need to know that.

He poured her a cup of coffee, and the toast popped a moment later. Brynne took a tentative sip and closed her eyes. "Oh wow, that's good coffee."

He poured himself a cup and took a deep breath.

"I have a proposition."

"I'm listening."

"I've seen the conditions your aunt placed on you."

She bristled and bit into her toast.

"You have substantial repairs to make to the house livable and money is in short supply."

"We've already established that you've unearthed every detail of my life. I told you—"

He stopped her with a hand. "Must I gag you so I can finish?"

"You'd like that, wouldn't you? Then you could lecture me uninterrupted."

"I would do a lot of things. Lecturing is not among them."

She bristled, but he saw the heightened color on her cheeks.

"Shall I continue?"

"Yes please." That sounded sarcastic as fuck. A punishable offense.

"I had a gentleman's agreement with your aunt, which is a moot point now, but the fact remains, my company needs access to this strip of land. In exchange, I'm offering to pay for the repairs and improvements to your house. I'm sure there are things you'd like to modernize."

"Go on."

"You need to finish your book. You've said you want an education in BDSM, which you will not get from surfing kinky websites or joining dangerous chat rooms."

She looked at him over her mug. Her eyes were first questioning, then incredulous. Her face and neck reddened in shock. "How? What the hell? You hacked into my Wi-Fi?!"

"It's *my* Wi-Fi, Brynne. I put Josie on my plan months ago, so she didn't need to deal with those idiots at SkyeNet. Imagine my surprise when I received an invoice for 980 GB of data usage."

"Oh my god. I can't believe this. I've heard enough." Brynne hopped off the stool and grabbed her jacket.

"Sit down and hear me out." His tone brooked no argument. She stood for a few seconds staring at him, before plonking down and crossing her arms in a huff.

"You seem to have an avid interest in bondage. I happen to be rather skilled in the field. You need firsthand experience for your book, which I am guessing is erotic in nature. And you need to show you're capable of a relationship that exceeds three dates."

"You are a bastard, you know that?" Her eyes were glittering, and her bottom lip stuck out adorably.

"Indeed, I am. Simply put, you give me what I need, and I'll give you what you need."

"How can you suggest this? It's not that simple."

He ignored her and continued, "You become my submissive for a month. You follow my rules, and you get a proper education in bondage and discipline. And I'll pay for all your renovations."

Brynne's eyes went wide as she chewed on her thumb. Clearly his offer impressed her. "I don't think that's a good idea."

"After last night, tell me it doesn't intrigue you?"

Her chin lifted. "Just because I am intrigued doesn't mean I should do it."

"Chat rooms are not safe. This will be safe and consensual. There will, of course, be rules for you to follow. You will have the power to stop any time with your safe word." He calmly took a sip of his coffee. "I will, however, push your limits."

"Following rules is not my strong suit."

"I'm well aware, but in time, you'll get better." His mouth quirked. "Because I will punish the defiance out of you."

Her head tilted, and he was sure he'd convinced her. She spoke softly, "You don't trust me."

"I told you; I don't care. And a month should be long enough to get *this* out of our systems."

"So, I'll get an education while you get kinky sex and access to my land?"

"Exactly. You will move in here."

"Wait, what?" Her eyes widened.

"Your place will be under construction. It makes sense."

"Where will I sleep?"

"You'll have your own room for sleeping, unless I decide otherwise."

He could see the wheels turning in her head. "I need to think about this."

"Of course."

"How much money exactly are we talking about?"

"One hundred thousand pounds."

Her eyes widened and she couldn't conceal her shock. "What if we can't get along? Or one of us quits before the month is up?"

He contemplated his answer. "If I quit before the end of the month, you still get fifty for the access. If, for example, *you* quit after a week, you'll receive twenty-five thousand. Fifty thousand for two weeks, and so on."

"That's not fair. I want seventy-five, regardless of how long we both last. I should get a bonus if I can put up with you for the entire month."

Her eyes gave away her excitement. He admired her sweet attempt at negotiating the terms and shook his head in amusement.

"That could backfire on you, Red. It might make me a harsher taskmaster if I'm paying more the longer you stay."

Gage knew without a doubt that his libido dictated this negotiation. What if he tired of her in a week? *Not bloody likely.* "If you make it to thirty days, I will give you a bonus of twenty-five K for a total of 125,000 pounds."

Brynne nodded, not quite smiling, but looking pleased with herself. "Okay. I think we have a deal." She started giggling uncontrollably.

"What's so funny?" he asked.

She could barely get the words out. "The only thing that goes in the agreement is the one hundred K...for you to lay your pipe."

Gage dropped her at home with explicit instructions to arrive at his door on Saturday by eleven a.m. sharp. He was going to prepare a simple agreement and NDA. If anyone asked, they had put aside their differences and reconciled.

She dragged her tired butt upstairs and lay on her bed. Staring at the ceiling, she questioned her sanity. She'd made a deal with the devil. The devil who still thought she published a libelous article about his secret sex club. *Could she afford to pass on the opportunity, and the money?*

That was some serious cake he was offering, and it would enable her to fix up everything in the house. Did that make her a prostitute? *No, it's just a business transaction!*

This *arrangement* would give her more juicy experiences that she could use to make her story more compelling. That was a win. To the outside world, they would seem like a regular couple.

She plugged in her dead mobile and waited for it to get a pulse. Jared might call her five kinds of crazy for doing this, but wasn't this exactly what she hoped would happen in London? She would need to explain it to him.

Brr-ring. Brr-ring. Brr-ring.

The landline was ringing downstairs, but she heard a muffled ring in the bedroom too. She rolled to the other side of the bed, followed the sound, and found a cute pink princess phone tucked in the bottom drawer of the bedside table.

"Hello."

"Brynne! Where have you been, woman? Are you okay?!" Jared sounded peeved.

"J! Yes, I'm fine. Sorry! I was out last night without my charger, and my cell phone is dead. I was just about to call you! Do you have ESP or something?"

"You know I do. Dammit, I tried the house multiple times. Oh wait, did you go home with the hunky contractor last night?"

"No, not exactly."

"Start talking. My photo shoot got delayed. Spill the details now!"

"I had a date with Logan, but Gage interrupted it."

"Oh boy."

"Yeah. He sent Logan packing when I was up singing, and when I came back, he basically insisted on driving me home."

"Uh-huh."

"We stopped at his place, since mine is a mess right now. And anyway, one thing led to another…"

"And you went to bed with him?!"

"You could say that."

"Holy shitballs!"

"There's more."

"Wait, don't tell me. Is there a red room?" Jared sounded like a kid in a candy store.

Brynne laughed. "No! Well, not that I know of. But he has an insane four-poster bed and a seven-foot bathtub."

"My guess is you christened both! Am I right?"

"Yup. Anyway, there was a wicked thunderstorm, so I stayed over."

"Wow. Well, I was worried."

"Why? Skye is the safest place on earth."

"That may be, but two weird things happened that I've got to tell you about. It could be nothing, but my spidey senses say it's not a coincidence."

"What is it?"

"When I left the paper on Monday, a super fancy Range Rover was parked by the front doors. I saw it again when I came out of the drugstore."

"Did it have blacked-out windows and red and black rims?"

"Bree, how the fuck did you know that?"

"I saw it too! It felt like it was following me after I left the club— it was driving slowly behind me before I raced into the underground."

"That's not all. When I went to your flat to pack your suitcase, I saw it again."

"Oh my god. That means they have my address. Who do you think it was?"

"I don't know, babe. Maybe Dimitri? After all, he had an unhealthy attraction to you. And god knows he has the money for a car like that."

"Jared, this is unnerving!" She paused and chewed her lip. "What did you do with my suitcase?"

"Nothing yet. I didn't want to ship it until I talked to you."

"So, whoever it was, was following you to get to me? Fucking hell."

"Listen, don't worry. There's no way they can track you to Skye. I'll figure out a way to get it shipped. I'll ask my friend John for help."

"John, from the club?"

"Yes. He works at Scotland Yard, and I trust him with my life."

"Ooh, that sounds interesting! Are you guys seeing each other?"

"Sort of. On the down low. And he's the one who got me reinstated at the club."

"I'm thrilled for you, J. But please be careful."

"I am. We have to. No one can know about us. But what about you? I don't like that you're all alone out there."

"Well, here's the thing, I won't be alone. I'm moving into... Um, that is, Gage and I are going to spend the next thirty days together."

"Say what?!"

"We struck a bargain. I spend a month following his Dom rules so he can teach me the ins and outs of...*you know*. He'll fund the renovations I need done at the house and, in exchange, I let him bury this fiber optic cable through Josie's land."

"Bree, are you sure about this? I mean, does he believe you didn't write the story now?"

"Well, we haven't talked about that in a while. He probably still thinks I did it. But that's the beauty of this. It's a business arrangement."

Jared said nothing, so she continued, "My heart will be safe. He believes I sold him out so he will remain cold and aloof. This is the best way for me to get my fantasies fulfilled and inside knowledge so I can fix my book!"

"You make it sound so simple. It's anything but. You are hugely attracted to him!"

"Only slightly attracted, and that is surely going to change when he starts bossing me around for real."

"Except if you like it."

"J, you are a worry wart. Don't worry. I know what I'm doing."

They said their goodbyes and agreed to check in by phone or text every other day during what she called her *incarceration.*

Brynne tamped down the worries that Jared stirred up. Dimitri was a thousand kilometers away and she couldn't worry about the Russian's obsessive crush right now. Her first concern was how to navigate living under Gage's roof.

Why did he ask me to stay at his house?

What does he have planned?

How can I prevent my heart from falling for him?

Saturday morning arrived, despite her wishes to the contrary. The snooze button didn't help. She felt trapped on a runaway train without working brakes. Declan was not happy when she told him she and Magnus, a.k.a. Gage, were rekindling their romance. She poured on the excitement about putting aside their differences and starting again, but he still looked skeptical.

"Oh, the tangled web I'm weaving! It will be the death of me!" It was never a good sign when she talked to herself, and she'd been doing a lot of that since coming home yesterday.

She started the bath and pulled out her suitcase. "What does one wear to meet her new warden?" All she had were casual clothes and one tight black dress. *He cannot possibly plan to keep me naked all the time. Can he?*

It was ten minutes past eleven when she got to his door and rang the bell. Like an idiot, she dragged her suitcase up the hill, leaving her winded and sweaty. She should have driven the car up and taken it back later. She was brain dead.

He made a show of looking at his watch, then back up at her. She waited for the reprimand, but it didn't come. If he wanted to keep her on edge, it was working.

He motioned her in and took hold of her suitcase, looking outside before he closed the door. "Where did you park?"

She blushed. "I walked up. It's a nice day, and I just thought…I don't know what I was thinking."

"I see." He didn't look overly amused. "Let me show you to your room."

Great, Mr. Cold and Aloof is in residence.

Bree slipped off her sneakers and padded after him. There was no time to take in the amazing view of the water as they passed through the great room. She followed him past the double doors that led into the master suite and continued down the hall to the end.

He put her small suitcase on the purple velvet ottoman at the foot of the bed. "This will be your space. It has an adjustable standing desk so you can write here." He pressed a button, and the blinds rose to reveal a door to her own private deck.

Brynne's mouth hung open. "Oh, that's a beautiful view."

"If you want to sit out there, I'll have some furniture brought up from downstairs."

"Okay. Thank you." Why was he sounding so businesslike?

He showed her the ensuite bathroom, then the tablet that controlled the lights, TV, and window shades.

"I'll leave you to unpack and settle in. Meet me in the kitchen at twelve thirty for lunch. We will go over a few things."

"Okay." He left her standing there, and she wondered if she had entered the twilight zone.

At least he didn't install you in his dungeon! Too bad, so sad.

The guest room could feature in a design magazine with its vaulted ceiling and timber trusses. The bedding on the Empire-style four-poster had little purple and green thistles and a rich purple velvet coverlet for chilly nights. Her toiletries took up one drawer in the sumptuous bathroom and her pathetic wardrobe of T-shirts and jeans fit into two shelves of the big closet. It was high time she shopped for clothes with her imminent financial windfall.

She set up her laptop and told herself she would avoid all porn sites for the next few weeks. He must have changed the network password back because it connected automatically.

It was only eleven forty-five a.m. Too much time to kill, so she texted Jared.

> **Brynne:** *Checked in to Gage's five-star hotel. He didn't put me in the cellar. ;-) He's acting as cold as ice, and I still have my clothes on. Maybe I was worried for nothing. I'll check in with you later—if I still have the use of my hands. lolz*

No response. He must still be sleeping. After an internal debate, she took her laptop to the living room. Gage was nowhere to be seen, which gave her a chance to look around. The enormous stone fireplace was the focal point of the room, as were the floor-to-ceiling windows overlooking a deck that stretched from one end of the house to the other. The room had vaulted ceilings and big beams, giving it a rustic feel. She got comfortable on a loveseat that faced the water.

Gage emerged from his office a little while later with a bunch of papers.

"All settled in?"

"Yes. It's a beautiful room. Thank you."

He nodded. "I've drawn up a simple NDA and the agreement for the exchange of land access for home improvements. It's better if I pay any contractors directly, so you can avoid tax implications for the whole one hundred thousand."

"Okay, but I'll need some of that money for me. I've used up most of my savings paying the rent on my place in London. The lease is up in September. My waitressing job doesn't pay enough unless I get some more shifts."

He handed her the contract and sat opposite her in one of the two wingback chairs. Brynne took the two-page contract. "I want to keep the apartment in case I find another job back in the city."

"You plan to go back to London?"

"Yes, unless you turned my career to dust. Did you really tell every newspaper not to hire me?"

"Brynne, you turned your own career to dust."

"Wow, so I guess you did." Her shoulders dropped. "I can't prove my innocence, but it's stunning that you can't admit someone might have framed me."

"Who the hell would want to frame you? You were a junior copy editor and a waitress! What kind of fool do you take me for?"

"I don't take you for a fool. Just a total asshole who doesn't want to open his eyes."

"Calling me names is a punishable offense." His jaw was rigid.

She rolled her eyes. "Are you going to keep tabs?!"

"You can bet on it. Anyway, I'll ensure your rent is paid through September, so you don't have to worry. I don't want you working extra shifts at the bar. There are duties for you here."

"Duties?" Her brows creased.

"Yes."

"Such as?"

"One of them is finishing your book. You will learn the other tasks as we go."

"How can I prepare if I don't know what to expect?"

"That's one of the goals of this experiment. Not only will we see if you can submit to my wishes, but we will determine if you are truly submissive."

She nibbled on her lip and wondered the same thing.

"We will start with demands that aren't all sexual."

"Oh. That's disappointing." At the question in his eyes, she huffed. "You took Mr. Boss. I assumed you were going to be his replacement."

"Cute. No, you'll need to earn orgasms through good behavior."

"That sounds fucked up and totally unfair."

His eyes sparkled. "That's how we'll get you focused on my pleasure and less on your own."

"I'm betting it will backfire on you, professor. I'll be so horny that I'll be thinking only of my own release!"

"We'll see. The key to your release will be your devotion to my satisfaction."

"Jesus, what have I agreed to? You're a sadist."

"You agreed to learn and be open-minded. For the record, I'm more of a voluptuary. Admittedly, one who enjoys turning your ass a pretty shade of red."

"I'll be looking that word up."

"Come to the kitchen. It's time for lunch." He led the way to the kitchen, and Brynne saw two large salads garnished with grilled jumbo shrimp and avocado.

"Are their little elves hiding somewhere doing your bidding?"

He chuckled. "No. A local caterer delivers fresh cuisine every morning." He pulled the stool out for her. They sat facing each other and his proximity made her jumpy.

"This looks delicious. I'm relieved you weren't planning on making me cook. I'm not very skilled in the kitchen."

"Your mother never taught you?"

Her eyes speared his, and she clenched her knife and fork. "My mother taught me nothing. Wait, that's not true. She taught me that blood is not thicker than water, that all mothers aren't nurturing, and being in love is for idiots."

He looked taken aback at her bitterness and then his gaze turned sympathetic.

"Don't do that. Don't feel sorry for me. Truthfully, it was the best thing she could do for me. Her leaving made me stronger."

"Understood. New subject. One of your first assignments will be to tell me about your book."

Brynne's eyes widened in shock. She covered her mouth, which was full of lettuce. He poured her a glass of Sauvignon Blanc and continued, "I want to understand the premise, the characters and what you are trying to accomplish. So, you'll read it to me."

She finished chewing and swallowed a big swig of the white wine. "I don't know about that. It's very personal."

"I thought you wanted to publish it? If so, you'd better get used to feedback—good, bad, and indifferent. To build your following, people will want to get to know you."

"I've decided to publish under a pseudonym."

He laughed. "Regardless, you will receive feedback, which could be mean or judgmental. Are you ready for that?"

She fiddled with her fork. "I'm not sure."

"A pen name is a good idea, but it doesn't solve your issues of shame. Is that why you didn't make it as hot as you could have?"

"Okay doc, I think that's enough psychoanalysis for one day."

She tried to make light of this, but her brain was spinning. How did he uncover all her deepest fears in one sitting?

"It's time for you to take responsibility for your writing, your desires, your needs. You need to stop being bad to get spankings and bondage. And start being good because that's what I expect from you this month."

She made a harrumph noise, then swallowed the lump in her throat.

"What? Did you expect it to be all fun and games?"

"No. Not exactly. I thought it would be more of what we did the other night."

"As I recall, you did very little submitting. I took what I wanted, and you seemed to enjoy it. What I expect for the next several weeks is for you to follow my instructions to the letter. And if you do, I will reward you. If you choose to be a *brat*, you won't like the consequences."

He pushed his plate away and stood. "Since you lack cooking skills, you will handle the clean-up. And before you lose your mind, that means scrape the plates and load the dishwasher. My housekeeper will do the rest on a weekly basis. Your first assignment is to look up the term *brat* in your BDSM dictionary. Tonight, you will read me the sexiest scene in your book. Dinner is at seven. I will provide your outfit later today."

27

Dominance & Submission

Gage paced back and forth, wearing a path from one end of his bedroom to the other. What the fuck was he thinking, having her under his roof for four weeks? He should be keeping her at a distance, but that plan went out the window when she looked up at him from the car with a pout on those lush lips.

If he unleashed his demons, she might give up after two weeks and run home. She wanted to understand the power exchange, and he would deliver a crash course in submission. Teaching her wasn't his goal. He planned on peeling away the layers to reveal the real woman beneath—not the fake one she presented to the world.

It was imperative that he not let his guard down during this little experiment. He would keep her talking about herself and her book, revealing no personal information about himself. Once he succeeded in *mastering* her, she would be out of his system for good.

Brynne tidied the dishes from their lunch and poured herself another glass of wine before grabbing her computer. She went to her room to hide.

It took her several hours to choose the scenes to share with him. She spent another hour editing and then lay down on the luxurious bed and fell asleep.

The room was dark when she woke up. She breathed a sigh of relief when she saw it was only four forty-five p.m. Gage must have closed the blinds and covered her with the throw. She flipped on the bedside lamp and saw the designer clothing bag hanging on the closet door. Beneath it was a pair of sexy-oh-my-god-Jimmy Choo shoes with an envelope on top.

Brynne hurried over to unzip the bag and saw the gorgeous black Marilyn Monroe-style halter dress. The monogrammed slingbacks were stunning with a two-and-a-half-inch angular kick heel. At least she wouldn't break an ankle walking to the dining room.

The card bore his distinctive scrawl.

Be in the dining room by seven.
No panties. Just the dress and the shoes.

M.

Whew. Okay, Mags. Or did he mean M for Master? Either way, she'd be there before seven. She ran herself a bubble bath and took the time to pamper herself for a change. Ninety minutes later, she was ready. Fingers and toes painted the color of champagne, important bits shaved smooth, hair tousled, eye makeup dark and smoky, and lips painted pale pink.

When she entered the dining room, her heart was racing as if she'd run up from the beach. She didn't want to choose the wrong seat, so she stood waiting next to the beautifully set dining table. A moment later, he walked in, followed by a middle-aged man dressed in a fancy waiter's uniform. Gage pulled out her chair and the server poured champagne for them both, then quietly disappeared.

"Did you follow my instructions?"

"Yes, of course."

"Show me."

"But he…" she stuttered.

"Show me." His voice deepened.

Flutters danced in the pit of her stomach, and she imagined a little x marked in the ledger. She stood back up and twirled so the dress would fly up, then she flashed him her bare hip.

He shook his head, his lips compressed. "Lift the front of the dress."

She gritted her teeth but did as she was told, keeping her legs pressed together.

"Hiding from me now will only get you tied and spread wide later." He motioned for her to sit down. The waiter, as if on cue, returned with a platter of oysters on ice and refilled their glasses before disappearing. Gage explained the three varieties which he had flown in today from Loch Fyne in Cairndow. "Have you had oysters before?"

"Yes—back in Toronto. Although, the last time I had them, I swallowed a bad one that ruined me."

"I assure you, these are the freshest you'll ever taste. Try it with a little of the mignonette sauce." Gage dressed it and raised it toward her. "Ready?"

When she nodded, he tipped the concoction into her mouth and the tangy delicious flavors burst on her tongue as she chewed.

"Wow, that's incredible."

Gage prepared his own oyster, and she watched him savor it, sipping her cold bubbly.

"So, tell me the premise of your novel."

Brynne prepared another oyster to buy herself some time and took a deep breath.

"It's a dark romance. The heroine of the story finds herself destitute after her husband embezzles millions of dollars from his employer and disappears. The Italian billionaire he stole from comes calling—certain she knows where he's hiding. They met several times before at company events, and he found her shyness intriguing. She insists she filed for divorce before the theft and tells him she is selling everything to pay their creditors. Dante, the story's anti-hero, expects her to reveal her husband's whereabouts and threatens to hold her responsible for the debt. Then he suggests she come to work for him. She used to be a personal assistant before she got married and became a pampered society wife. He wants revenge, and he wants her, so he devises a plan to get her to his remote estate in Italy. If she doesn't come willingly, he threatens prosecution."

"Interesting. And how does she feel about him?"

"She denies her attraction to him, but he appeals to her because he's everything her husband was not. Confident, intelligent, comfortable in his own skin. But that quickly changes when she receives some rather harsh treatment."

"Is she submissive?"

"Yes, but she has never explored it. She thought her husband was dominant, but he was just a bully."

The server brought warm lemon-scented cloths for their hands and cleared the dishes. Gage opened a bottle of red wine and asked how she liked her filet mignon cooked.

"Medium rare, please. And I would like to thank you for the dress and shoes. They're gorgeous." She wanted to ask how he knew her sizes, but when his eyes locked on hers, she fell silent.

"You're welcome. They are as much for me as they are for you. Everything I choose is because I want to see you in them. Until I don't."

Brynne blushed and sipped her wine. Dinner passed in a blur. He asked her more questions about the plot and what the agent told her to work on. As the evening wore on, she became more relaxed and open about her novel.

The waiter had removed all the dishes and disappeared. Gage reached over and pulled both sides of the halter dress open, baring her breasts. Her eyes flew to his, and she bit her bottom lip, panicked that the server would walk back in.

"Did you look up the meaning of brat in your erotic dictionary?"

"Yes."

"And?"

"It's when someone seeks discipline by being naughty and not following directions—hoping to trigger their Dom to take action."

"Mmm, indeed."

"I come by it honestly. A therapist told me it's because I didn't get enough attention as a child. I had to misbehave to get my parents to notice me."

Gage sipped his wine, his eyes darkening as they stared at her hardening nipples. "Take the dress off."

"What?" Her eyes flew to the door. "Your butler might come back in."

"He might. This is one of your first tests. Are you going to defy me?"

Brynne knew this was it. Stay and submit or run home like

a coward. Her inner voices were warring with each other, but she shut them up and stood on wobbly knees. She undid the clasp at her neck and let the two parts of the bodice drop. He sat back in his chair and adjusted his pants, which emboldened her to continue. She reached behind and unzipped the skirt, and it fell to the floor, baring her completely.

"Did you intentionally defy me in London so I would punish you?"

She nodded and looked at the floor. "I wanted to see how you would react."

"I suppose that's understandable. After all, you don't know me. You don't know that I'll enjoy disciplining you, even when you're perfect. You will want to ask what you did wrong, and it might just be because I get off watching you writhe and cry and fight your body's responses to what I'm doing."

Oh god, his words were winding her up like a tightly coiled spring. He stood and took their wine glasses over to the sideboard.

"I'm going to help you onto the table so I can see all of you."

A whimper escaped her throat. "Oh, please…"

"Please what? Are you worried Colin is coming back with dessert?"

"Yes." She clasped her hands tightly to calm her fidgeting.

"Don't worry, my sweet. You're going to be dessert." He lifted her onto the cool wood surface, so her knees were bent at the edge. "Lie back and make yourself into a star."

Brynne obeyed, while trembling in anticipation. He would see her—and know her body was ready for him.

From a drawer in the sideboard, he took out two coils of black rope. She watched as he unwound the first and looped it around her right wrist several times, then ran the lines over her palm so she could hold them as he tugged her arm back over her head. He bent down and fed the rope under the table and then tied it around her left ankle, spreading her leg wide. With the other length, he bound her left wrist and right leg, so she was spread-eagle on the table.

A sultry smile lit his face when he leaned over her. Brynne stared at him and let her eyes convey acceptance and trust. *God help me, I want this.*

Gage stood near her head and laid the palm of his hand over the small triangle of red curls on her mons, his fingers whispering against her bare lips. Then he bent down and kissed her mouth, lightly teasing at first and then more insistent. When his tongue delved deeper, his fingers followed suit, sinking into her wetness. Brynne moaned her need, and he pulled back, rationing his attentions, grazing her mouth lightly with his tongue, and using his fingers to torment her clit by circling it with her juices.

"Please…" she whined.

Just as quickly as he began, he stopped and rose. "I will be back soon. Remember, patience will be rewarded."

Brynne gazed up at the ceiling and daydreamed about making snow angels in the yard under a dark night sky. Her amusing thoughts took her to a place far from her very vulnerable position. Sounds from the kitchen brought her back to the present. She tested the bonds, and the lack of give caused a visceral reaction between her legs.

Shhh. You're safe. Displayed as an object for his pleasure.

Gage returned, rolling a trolley of goodies. The heavenly scent of warm donuts and cinnamon teased her senses.

He positioned the trolley so she couldn't see what was on it, but she saw a lit flame in her peripheral vision. Candlelight? Or a warmer for something?

"Did you know cinnamon has been used for centuries to treat illnesses?"

She shook her head, her mouth salivating at the smells so close by.

"Not only was it used to treat sinus conditions and indigestion, but it also increases blood flow and raises body temperature on contact. We're going to have it on our bolinhos de chuva."

She lifted her head to see what he was doing. "What are those? They smell divine"

"I discovered them in Portugal, but they originated in Brazil. It's deep-fried sweet dough—made in the shape of a raindrop."

"May I please have one?"

"That's not a good idea—you might choke in that position. I'll be right back." He returned with a small bolster pillow to put under her head. "That's better."

He moved the cart a little closer so she could see everything. "We have bolinhos, hot butter, and cinnamon sugar."

"I'll be careful. Can I at least have one?" she begged.

"You've been a good girl. But you must chew it completely."

"Oh, I will, I promise."

She watched him dip one of the crispy teardrops into the butter, then he coated it in cinnamon sugar and held it over her breasts until a drop of the mixture landed on her nipple. He fed it to her, and she savored the concoction with a long moan. "God, that is amazing!"

"My turn." He coated his dough, but instead of popping it into his mouth, he dragged the sugary confection across her areolas one by one. The coarseness of the sugar was stunning. He ate his bolinho and then his head dropped to lick and suck on her rock-hard nipples. More sugar from his mouth abraded the tender skin and had her squirming in reaction.

Next, he took a brown bottle and shook it up. "This is pure cinnamon, which I've carefully mixed in a base of almond oil. The ratio is important, so it doesn't irritate the skin."

Brynne trembled in reaction. "I'm going to put this on your lips and tongue first." He put two drops on his fingers and coated her lips then put both fingers in her mouth. She licked them tentatively at first, unsure of what would happen.

The heat began to increase immediately. Her lips felt swollen, tingling, then hot. The same for her tongue. His mouth was on hers a moment later, and he groaned as their tongues intertwined. He must have felt the same heat. Using the dropper, he filled her belly button with five drops of the oil. "Don't spill this." He tried to sound stern, but she could tell he was enjoying himself.

His fingers dipped into the makeshift cup, and he glazed her nipples with the liquid.

It took about ten seconds. Her eyes widened and her head raised off the pillow. "Oh, god, that stings. Wait, no it itches. Please, they're on fire. Do something!"

He dipped a donut into the cinnamon sugar and tortured the over sensitized tips. "Is that better?"

"Oh god, no!" Brynne tried to stay still, but it was impossible. His fingers dipped again, and he painted her outer lips with the oil.

"Somebody is soaking wet. I am going to need more oil."

"Oh, no, you can't."

"I can. Your body will douse the flames."

The heat was spreading between her legs, causing her labia to heat and tingle. Again, he dipped into her belly button and this time touched the hood of her clit with it. Brynne started squirming and moaning, begging him to stop but not meaning it. She turned imploring eyes on him. "Please Gage. My clit is on fire. I'm dying."

Next, he anointed one of the dough balls in warm butter, followed by a generous coating of cinnamon sugar, and held it over her mouth. "Savor this one—when you finish it, I want you to come for me."

"Yes, please. I want to come!" She pulled against the bindings on her wrists and forgot they only tugged her legs apart. "Fuck!"

"Shhh, I will make it all better."

Brynne held the donut in her mouth and sucked on it as Gage positioned himself between her legs. He leaned down and began licking her everywhere except where she throbbed the most. His tongue circled all around her swollen clit. If it had a voice, it would be screaming for his attention. His other hand dipped into the pool of wetness, then entered her—leisurely pushing in and out while his tongue danced and lapped and nibbled. Finally, his warm mouth kissed her there—then he licked and sucked until she could not hold on any longer. She swallowed the donut and let out a loud keening wail of ecstasy as her bound limbs struggled and twisted. Just as she caught her breath, Gage's mouth started strumming her sensitive flesh again. He ignored her pleas, and a second violent orgasm took her by surprise, making her cry out in shock.

He grabbed scissors out of the sideboard and cut all the ropes to free her. She sat up and inched toward the edge of the table while watching him strip off his pants and don a condom with shaking hands. "Next week you see the doctor." His words were ground out with effort. He picked her up and impaled her in one stroke. Brynne gripped his shoulders, wrapping her legs around his waist. When his mouth found hers, his kiss carried an undercurrent of raw unrestrained passion that took her breath away. She tasted the divine combination of cinnamon, sugar, and herself on his tongue.

Gage carried her like she weighed nothing, bouncing her up and down on his prick as he strode into the master bathroom. In the walk-in shower, he set her down to put the water on. "I feel sugar everywhere." He groaned.

When the temperature was right, he took the handheld shower

head and washed the residue off her and then himself. Then he turned her to face away from him and handed the sprayer to her.

"Brace yourself and spread your legs."

She wordlessly complied. He grabbed her hips and pulled her back against him, straight onto his cock.

"Ooh uh!" she squeaked as he slammed fully into her.

"If you can aim that stream of water and give yourself another orgasm, you are welcome to try. But I warn you, I won't last long."

He began fucking her hard and fast, and Brynne braced herself with one hand on the wall and aimed the shower head with the other. She was close, but his thrusts were becoming more ragged. Then he suddenly pulled her torso up so her back was flush to his chest, his hands kneading her breasts, his mouth biting her shoulder. She aimed the water and found the spot by accident and held it there, losing her focus on everything but the pounding in her ears and between her legs.

His mouth was on her neck. "Come. With. Me." Her body obeyed before her mind could catch up. She felt her legs would not hold her up and had no concept of time—until she felt him slowly pull out of her.

"Are you okay?"

She nodded. "More than okay."

He wrapped her in a plush bath towel, then grabbed one for himself. As he disposed of the condom, he said, "Make an appointment for bloodwork so I don't have to use those bloody things anymore."

"I will." She dried herself while he loaded his toothbrush. "I need water. Is that guy gone?"

He grinned. "He was gone after clearing the dinner plates."

"You let me think he could walk in at any moment." She pouted.

"Aye. And yet you managed to do what I asked."

"Be glad I have nothing within reach to lob at your head."

He laughed and went on brushing his teeth.

Brynne put on the T-shirt he wore earlier that day, inhaling his distinctive scent. On the way to the kitchen, she saw the wild state of the dining room. Her beautiful dress was on the floor, shoes discarded under the table, and the scattered black cords reminded her of coiled snakes lying in wait. She blew out the warming candle and began tidying up. It would not do for the housekeeper to see this mess. She tucked the ropes back into the drawer and grinned. He was certainly imaginative.

The cinnamon oil was a wicked surprise and one worth repeating, so she tucked it way back in the spice cabinet. She packed up the rest of the delectable Brazilian donuts, loaded the dishwasher, and cleaned up all the cinnamon sugar. Anything to delay the daunting task of reading him her story.

He had dimmed the lights, and he was lying in bed asleep, the sheet drawn to the sexy dimples in his hips. She stood there, admiring his muscular chest and his flat stomach. A sexy swirl of hair charted a path downward to her own carnal Sword of Damocles.

"There can be no happiness for one who is under constant apprehensions."

The one thing she'd managed to avoid her whole life was staring her in the face: a man she could fall for. She'd eagerly accepted the proposal, ignorant of the dangers that came with it. When it was over and he walked away, she would never be the same.

Brynne tiptoed out of the room. She needed some space to think, and she wouldn't get that sleeping next to him. It might piss him off, but she would deal with the consequences tomorrow.

Gage rolled over and felt the empty space next to him. *What the fuck?* The bedside lamp was still on, and she was not there. The last thing he remembered was her going to the kitchen for water.

A quick check of the living and dining rooms confirmed she cleaned up the evidence of their cinnamon sugar orgy. The kitchen was neat as a pin. He grabbed a bottle of water and headed to her room. She earned herself a serious punishment for not following through and reading to him. It was clear from her agitation and excuses that she found the idea of reading to him unnerving. That just made him more determined to hear it.

Moonlight streamed in from the window. He could see she was wearing his T-shirt. Her legs were tangled in the sheets, and she had wedged a king-size pillow between her thighs. Part of him wanted to drag her over his knee right then and there, at odds with the part that wanted to tuck the covers in and leave her to sleep.

He mentally shook himself. *This was not the time to go soft.* She wanted the full experience, and he planned to give it to her.

Decision made, he dragged the covers off and picked her up. She stirred and started struggling in his arms.

"Stop wiggling."

"You," she whispered.

"Who did you think it was, Red?"

She didn't answer, instead turning her cheek into his chest and nuzzling him.

God help him. His dick was getting hard again. He laid her

down on his bed and she turned to her side and grabbed a pillow to curl into. Before pulling the sheet up, he decided a little extra lesson was in order.

He retrieved two cuffs—one for her ankle and another for her wrist. Chains would be noisy, so he used rope to tie the ankle cuff to the post at the foot of the bed with about three feet of give. He did the same with her right wrist since she was sleeping on that side. In the morning, he would deliver another surprise. It was time to turn up the heat.

28

Truth or Consequences

Something felt strange. She couldn't close her legs; something was restricting her movements. Heat engulfed her clit, but she couldn't figure out why. Oh, wait, maybe it was the cinnamon oil? That must be why she felt so warm and tingly between her legs. But she hid the bottle, didn't she? Where was Gage? He could make the aching go away.

She tried to reach between her legs, but for some reason her hand wouldn't reach. Her wrist was tethered to something. Was she still on the table? No, it was much too comfy.

Gradually, she came awake and realized she was not in her own bed. Cool air tickled her breasts, and she shivered as the sheet was drawn away. Teeth scraped her nipple. A tongue followed. It wasn't a dream. Fingers caressed and teased but it was not enough to make her come.

"Mmm, that feels good, but I need more. Please, I need to come." His hand stilled and she moaned in response.

"No coming for you today."

"Ooh," she whined, "but why?" She opened her eyes to find him looming over her.

He looked more menacing than usual, with his dark beard and messy hair. "You should've woken me up last night."

"I—you were sound asleep and looked so peaceful."

"Doesn't matter. You figured out how to avoid reading your book to me." While he spoke, he shifted her to the middle of the bed and climbed between her legs. She came fully awake when he dragged the head of his cock back and forth through her juices and, without warning, thrust deep.

Brynne tried to reach for him and wrap her legs around his torso, but she met with resistance. "You tied me to the bed?!"

His eyes glittered. "You were not where you were supposed to be."

"Oh!" To hammer the point home, he lifted her untethered leg up to his shoulder and slowed down his thrusts. His thumb found her clit, and he teased it until she writhed and tilted up to meet him. "Are you close?" he asked.

"Yes!"

"Good, because *close* is as far as you're getting today."

"Motherfucker!"

"That's going to cost you." He took his hand away and picked up the pace, his face contorted with his impending release.

Brynne took advantage of his eyes closing and used her free hand to play with herself. Her hitched breathing must have given her away because he caught her in the act. He let her leg drop off his shoulder and pinned her arm to the bed as he came with a roar.

His body dropped onto hers and he pinned her there until his breathing returned to normal.

She wiggled, but he didn't budge. "You're crushing me, and I have to pee; let me up!"

"I beg your pardon?"

Could he sound more imperious? Calming her fury, she schooled her voice and asked again, "Please Gage, I really need to go."

"That's better." He lifted himself and unbuckled her wrist. "I left one hand free so you can get these off. The buckle is quite easy."

Swatting his hand away from her ankle, she quickly undid the cuff herself and ran to the bathroom. She slammed the door and locked it.

So, that bastard planned to keep her on the edge all day? Ha! She would find a way. *Let the games begin.*

He was gone when she came out. She heard him whistling in the kitchen and found him making the coffee.

"I expect you to be ready at ten for a workout. There is a fitness room on the third floor. We will have lunch at one and you'll read me those passages. You can write when my massage therapist comes over at three. And tonight, we are going out for dinner."

"Christ, I'm not a child. Are you planning every waking moment for me?"

"Get used to it. You should know, in many D/s relationships, the Dom is in total control, and he takes over all aspects of his sub's life. Her food, what she wears, how much exercise, sleep schedule, orgasms, and so on."

"Well, I wouldn't want that kind of arrangement. That's a bit much."

"Lucky for you, it's not my cup of tea either. But I warned you there would be consequences for every rebellion."

Brynne put the bolinhos in the microwave to warm them up. "Maybe you should explain the ground rules, so I don't get into any more trouble?"

"Good point. We never discussed your hard and soft limits. I should have insisted on that before we drew up our agreement."

"True. There are things I won't do."

"Such as?"

Brynne could feel her face heating. "I have a list that Mistress Patricia gave me. I could draw from that."

"Fetch it."

She scowled at him. "Can't I get a cup of coffee in me first?"

"I'm counting every one of your little fits. If I were you, I'd go now."

She huffed at him and stalked out. In her bedroom, she pulled the paper from its hiding spot in her backpack. A quick scan had her rethinking some of those choices. She searched for a pen to make some adjustments.

"What is taking so long?" he said from right behind her.

Brynne jumped out of her skin with a screech. "What the hell?! You scared me to death!"

"Why are you so jumpy?"

"I'm used to living alone. Stop sneaking up on me."

He saw the papers on the bed. As he leaned over, she turned to grab them, but he was quicker.

"What are you afraid of, Brynne? Is there something you want to remove?"

She put her hand out, and he gave the sheets back to her. She pulled them to her chest defensively and her shoulders sagged in relief.

He smiled mischievously. "Let's review and discuss the parameters of this truce."

He poured the coffee and put the warm donuts out. "I'll go first. The ground rules are very simple. When I ask you to do something, you obey immediately. Of your own free will, you submit to my physical and sexual demands. You accept punishment for not following the rules—the ones you know, and the ones you don't."

She bristled and was about to reply, but the look in his eyes stopped her.

"You keep me informed as to your physical health—if you are under the weather or have your period, for example. While you are with me, you don't flirt or lead any other man on. And when you call out or signal your safe word, I will stop everything. Red is a full stop and yellow is slow down and check in."

Brynne sipped her coffee and digested what he said. "What kinds of physical and sexual demands?"

"That's where your list comes in. But in short, sucking, fucking, bondage, and discipline."

Wow. That's one way of putting it.

She looked at the list and didn't know where to begin.

"May I see?" He put his hand out. "I assure you there are things on that list that don't interest either of us, but Patricia is always inclusive, so she probably covered all the bases."

"Okay." Brynne handed it to him and took the pen out.

He scanned the first page and popped a donut in his mouth. "Shall we go section by section?"

She stammered, "Fine."

"I can see you are open to various types of bondage, nothing too extreme—no hoods and no suspension upside down. Got it."

Brynne cleared her throat. "I don't know how I feel about wearing any kind of gag."

"In your interview, you said you had been in two D/s relationships. How can you *not know* how you feel about that?"

Oh shit. "I might have exaggerated a little. They were dominant, but neither were into restraints and stuff."

Gage's mouth pursed, and he tilted his head like the headmaster at school when he wasn't buying the story. "Exaggerated? I knew you were overstating your experience to get the job."

She looked at him sheepishly. "Um, maybe a little."

"Perhaps that means one of your *maybe*s should change to a yes. For me."

Her stomach dropped. "Like what?"

"I'll know when we get to it. Let's continue."

They went down the list and he explained the things she put question marks next to. Together, they crossed out a bunch of items that did not interest him and totally unnerved her. She agreed to try some other *maybe*s to see if she liked them.

When he got to the sexual activity list, things got interesting.

"I see you marked anal sex with a *no / don't know*. Have you had a bad experience?"

"I haven't tried it. And frankly, I can't see you going *in* through the *out* door with that monster you call a penis."

Gage choked on his coffee. He took a few minutes to stop coughing and collect himself, and even then, she saw he couldn't contain his amusement. "There's nothing to be afraid of, Brynne. I will ensure you are well prepared. That's what we have toys and plugs for. You are open to those, aren't you?"

"I guess so. But for now, that stays on the *maybe-one-day* list."

He nodded, but there was a twinkle in his eye, and she knew they would revisit that one. They got through the bottom half of the list without incident. She was relieved he didn't question her rejection of tickling and electricity, but her pulse raced, knowing he now had the means to push her buttons.

A box was on her bed when she went to change. Inside were a

pair of hot pink workout shorts and a white all-in-one bra tank top. Both pieces were too small, but she had little choice until she did some shopping. She checked herself in the mirror. *Holy shit, this will be interesting.*

Brynne put on some pink lip gloss and her trainers and headed upstairs. His workout room was bigger than her apartment. It wasn't only the array of professional equipment that shocked her—it was the stunning views of the water. Lined up in front of the floor-to-ceiling windows were five kinds of professional-grade cardio machines. The back wall had weight machines, free weights, and a corner for boxing. She hated working out, except for boxing, but she was badly in need of some exercise. Her clothes were tight, and she had gained at least five pounds since arriving in Skye.

She stepped on the treadmill and studied the complex dashboard, looking for the ON button.

"Looking for this?" He snuck up on her again and she screeched and stomped her foot.

"You should wear a bell, so I know you're coming."

From the devilish way he smiled, she knew his devious mind filed that away for future use. He flipped a small, concealed switch, and the screen lit up. After his quick tutorial, she started a walking program.

Brynne stepped on to the side rails and turned to him. "While I appreciate you providing me with an outfit to exercise in, you got my size wrong. It's too small and I look ridiculous."

He looked her up and down, his pupils widening. "I chose the outfit for my enjoyment. It's perfect if you ask me."

"You mean your amusement. At my expense!"

"No, Brynne. Everything I dress you in is with intention. You are not supposed to feel ridiculous; you are supposed to enjoy knowing you are turning me on. Sometimes it will be pink short-

shorts, other times it will be stockings and garters under a revealing evening gown, or a leather body harness that shows off all your assets and hides nothing."

Brynne looked off to the left and tucked a strand of hair behind her ear. "I am not used to wearing such revealing things."

He took her chin in his hand. "Are you ashamed of your body? Has someone made you feel self-conscious about it?"

She bit her lip. *God, I don't want to go there.* She nodded.

"That is unfortunate. If that person said you were stupid, would you believe it?"

Her forehead creased. "No."

"Do you hold him—and I assume it was a *him*—in high esteem, or value his opinion?"

"Hell no."

"Then he isn't worthy of your energy, and it's time to wipe those thoughts from your head. I could always arrange to have his legs broken."

She smiled. "Thank you."

"Don't thank me. Be happy I gave you something to put on. Now, start that machine up so I can watch your delicious ass while I lift weights."

Brynne worked her way up to a decent speed, dismayed to feel winded after ten minutes.

She could feel Gage's eyes on her, enjoying the sight of her skimpy shorts creeping up inch by inch. She imagined him behind her with glistening muscles as he pushed weights up and down, the steady clank of the machine keeping time with his heavy breathing. The room was warm. She recalled in vivid detail all the unbelievable things he had done to her, with her. It was only her second day, and she was falling under his dominant spell. In that short time, he made her acutely aware of her body and its carnal purpose: giving and receiving pleasure.

There was another, more dangerous aspect of this agreement she needed to guard against: the allure of having someone take care of her, to make decisions, and take over the burdens of money, food, and shelter. Could she become addicted to that? Possibly. Unless the price was too high. *Losing my sense of self and everything I have worked for. I cannot let that happen.*

The decision was simple. Play the game. Follow the rules and get the experience. *Do not let him wear down my defenses.* This whole thing was just temporary, and he could end it on a whim.

Gage sat back and started his reps, admiring the way her little shorts rode up, revealing more of her ass. It would be a challenge to deny her any orgasms today, especially when any diabolical scenes he devised were sweet torture for him as well. He switched to the leg press and realized his masseuse Kylie might expect to give him a happy ending. *Shit.* It had been several months since he'd seen her. It could get awkward if she tried to arouse him, like last time. He needed to ensure that didn't happen.

Tonight, he planned to introduce Brynne to new things marked as *maybe* and *don't know* on her limits list. He never expected to enjoy teaching her how to submit. After this was over, he would find a submissive. There was no reason to continue being celibate.

She was glowing from her cardio, and getting into the spirit of strutting her stuff. A few feet in front of where he stood doing lat pull downs, she started stretching. The windows reflected a mischievous grin on her face as she gave him a tantalizing view of her backside. She spread her legs and started doing squats. After two sets, she bent over to touch her toes, and he stopped and watched. His cock was already ready for action, but he intended to make her wait. To remove temptation from view and piss her off a little, he got on the treadmill.

He increased the speed until he was running full on. After five minutes, his curiosity got the better of him. When he slowed and turned to see what she was doing, he almost fell off the rolling track.

Brynne lay back on the weight bench. Her legs were spread with her feet planted on either side of the leather seat. She had pulled her shorts down, so they rested at her hips, and her top was rolled up, baring her breasts. With eight-pound weights in each hand, she was doing flat dumb bell presses. *Not on my watch!*

He walked over and took the weights out of her hands. "You shouldn't be doing this exercise without a spotter."

"Oh." She turned her twinkling eyes on him, feigning innocence. "Would you be able to spot me, then?"

"I don't think so. I think it's time for the punishment you've had coming since yesterday."

"Wait, what for?" She tried to rise, but he pushed her back down.

"I told you, I don't need a reason." She didn't need to know he couldn't remember what it was.

Gage yanked her shorts down. Instead of taking them totally off, he unhooked one leg, twisted the material so it tightened on her calf, and then pulled it under the bench and put her other foot back through the narrowed leg hole.

Brynne squirmed. "Were you a boy scout?"

"Ha! Maybe in another life."

Gage went to the cabinet, where he kept an array of toys. Today, she would experience a combo leather and suede flogger. It would thud with a little sting and was perfect to use on her breasts, thighs, and pussy. He also grabbed a little bottle of oil.

Her eyes had darkened to the color of chocolate, her pupils blown wide with excitement. When she opened her mouth to say something, he silenced her with a finger to her lips and a warning shake of his head. He rolled the tank top up over her head and discarded it.

"Put your hands under the curve of your back and keep them there."

She hesitated for a second and he swatted her breast hard enough to make her gasp. With wide eyes, she watched him and quickly tucked her hands underneath.

"Good girl. Now, I'm going to warm you up with my hands and then we will test out the new flogger I bought just for you."

He bent down low and kissed her lightly on the mouth. Then he moved to nip and lick her nipples, which were standing at attention.

She gasped in shock then moaned as he smacked one breast and then the other several times, turning them pink. He shocked her with a quick slap between her legs, making her jump. "Oh. My. God!"

The tops of her thighs received the same treatment before he gave another surprise swat to her swollen sex.

"Are you ready?"

She mewled and nodded.

"Say it. Do you accept this punishment, knowing it gives me pleasure?"

"Yes. I accept."

"Do you understand your role for the next month is to submit to my wishes—even when you don't like them? Dressing to please me? Deferring to my judgment in all things?"

She bit her lip. "Yes, sir."

"Good girl."

Good girl. Why do I like hearing that?

Gage circled her, and she felt like that girl on the dining table at the club: a centerpiece to admire—laid out for his enjoyment. It made her feel powerful and sexy. Any lingering self-consciousness disappeared when she saw his tented shorts. His gaze went from hooded to hard in a split second, and he followed that up with the first strike on her thighs. It took her breath away.

He took his time—letting her get used to the feel of the half-inch leather strips on her skin. At first, it felt like she was lying naked in a spring rainstorm, big droplets of water pitter-pattering on her skin. Gradually they got harder until the pelting made her squirm and moan. She fought the urge to cry *yellow*. It didn't actually hurt. In fact, it felt like every area touched by the strands heated, swelled, and preened for his attention. Her moans grew into brief gasps interspersed with growled swear words.

What's wrong with me? How can I like this?

If he hit the right spot between her legs, she would come.

The bastard must have known she was close. Suddenly, he stopped and stripped off his shorts. His cock looked ravenous, the head shiny with pre-cum. He straddled the bench and moved to stand over her face.

"Get it nice and wet." The words were ground out with effort, his accent very pronounced. He rested his hands on the bench above her head and fed it into her open mouth. He hovered there, raising and lowering his length to the back of her throat, while she coated it with her saliva.

She heard him swear, then he raised himself up and reached

between her legs. Brynne sighed audibly when his hand caressed her tender and engorged sex. He coated his fingers in the wetness that had gathered between and showed it to her.

"I'm glad you enjoyed the flogging, sweetheart. You're soaked."

She stuck her tongue out at him in response.

His eyes gleamed as he spread her juices all over his length. Then he collected more and spread it between her breasts. Realization dawned and her brows snapped together. She wanted to call him a selfish prick, but found herself admiring his ingenuity. Jared was right—he was Ph.D. level, and she was totally under his spell.

He squatted down, crushed her breasts together around his cock, and started thrusting back and forth between them. Brynne grabbed onto his thighs and watched him piston back and forth, mesmerized.

She could tell he was getting close—his jaw was rigid, and his legs vibrated under her hands. He stopped and reached for a little bottle from his discarded shorts. She watched as he dribbled a stream of oil onto his shaft. He took her hands and put them where his had been holding her breasts. "Squeeze them together nice and tight, and don't let go."

He braced his hands on his legs and thrust back and forth. The erotic sounds of the oil sluicing around their flesh filled the room. With a growl, he came, and it shot all over her neck and chin, and some landed in her hair.

No damned orgasm for her, but he got his rocks off. She lay there stunned and horny as hell, committing every single moment to memory. The flogger was shocking and amazing. No one knew she had secret fantasies about that very thing. Could he have snuck into her computer and read her dirty stories?

Gage roused her from her thoughts as he pulled her shoes and socks off and then unwrapped her legs from the shorts. He pulled her up and carried her to the bathroom that adjoined the workout space.

The shower stall was bigger than the one in the master bathroom, and it featured rows of jets lining the wall. He put her down and set the water to come from the two rain heads.

He washed her hair while she stood there in a trance. When he was done, she washed his back while he did his front. As he wrapped her in a big fluffy towel, she asked, "How long are you going to keep me on edge?"

"If you are good, I'll put you out of your misery tonight before bed."

"I'll be good. I promise."

He gave her a hard look. "I'll know if you bring yourself off. You won't like the consequences."

"Always with the scare tactics," she said, biting her lip nervously.

"Why don't you go get dressed? I'll meet you in the living room and you can read to me."

29

Playing with Fire

Reading to him made her more skittish than any threats of punishment. The only thing scarier than letting a man read her dirty novel was having to read it out loud to him!

A fire crackled in the hearth. Gage sat on the oversized sofa with a plate of finger sandwiches and crudités while she fiddled with her laptop. She closed all the browser tabs in case he looked over her shoulder.

Her stomach was in knots.

"I'm not a patient man, Brynne."

"I know! I just need a minute to find the latest version of chapter one. No one has seen this; you will be the first."

"You look like I've sentenced you to the guillotine. Relax."

She blew out a breath and shook her head. *Here goes nothing.*

Twenty minutes later, her face was on fire when she forced herself to look up from her screen. He had a crooked grin on his face. Was he trying to find something nice to say?

"Well. What do you think? Be honest."

"It is very good. It flowed well. You captured my interest and I want to know what happens to the heroine next. You've also given the reader a taste of what kind of morally gray character Dante is. Well done."

She beamed at him. "Thank you. I'm happier with this version, too. I reworked it so there's more tension between them right from the beginning."

"Thank you for sharing it with me. I'm looking forward to hearing more." His smile looked genuine, and she was relieved. He suggested she have something to eat and take the afternoon to edit. He had some work to do before his massage therapist arrived.

Brynne returned to her room to work at her desk. If she stayed on the couch by the fire, she would fall asleep and get nothing done.

After editing two chapters, she went to the kitchen for a drink. On the way back, she saw a tall, slim blonde coming down the steps. Of course, the woman was gorgeous with a perfect body. She looked ill at ease until she spotted Brynne, then her eyes turned squinty as she looked with disdain at Brynne's ratty pink robe and mussed hair.

The woman flipped her long hair and said, "You must be his latest sub. I'm Kylie, his personal massage therapist."

Brynne pasted on a phony smile and replied, "I'm Bree, the flavor of the month."

"Cute. But, you'll see, no matter who is warming his bed, he still needs a professional to work out the kinks and give him a happy ending."

Brynne laughed harshly. "Sorry Karlie, but I'm going to lay odds he had nothing for you today but sore muscles from all the fucking we've been doing. And while I'm here, he won't be needing a happy ending. You can see yourself out."

Brynne didn't wait to see her leave, but she heard the front door slam. Did he honestly think it was okay to let that bitch touch his dick? If Brynne wasn't seeing anyone else for the duration of this agreement, the same rules applied to him. How could she convey that point?

A little while later, Gage popped his head into her room. "How's it going?"

"Good. I'm a little stiff though. I could use a massage after all this computer time. Can you give me your therapist's number? I want to book myself a treatment."

He hesitated for a second, then nodded. "Sure, I will text it to you. We will leave here at six. We are going to a hotel in Sleat with a fabulous chef. Your outfit is in the closet."

"Okay." She bit her lip and wondered what he planned for tonight.

"Don't look so worried. It's perfectly respectable."

He left, and she ran to check the closet. The new dress was a silky wraparound style in dark teal. He'd also provided stockings, garters, and a matching black lace bra and panty set. She wondered how he found beautiful outfits that fit her to a T. And how much money was he spending to get them here? Crazy man!

Her phone dinged with Kylie's contact info. Brynne would book a massage to follow his, then the day before, she'd cancel it and any upcoming appointments. That bitch wouldn't be back while she was in residence. He could call her when she was gone!

At the dot of six, Brynne was excited and ready to leave. An older gentleman stood by the Range Rover, waiting for them. He nodded and tipped his cap before opening the rear door. Gage helped her into the SUV and introduced her to Hugh. They chatted briefly about his wife and grandkids, and Gage explained Hugh had been driving him and his mother for years. If she needed to go to the mainland or the airport, Hugh would take her.

When they pulled in, Brynne recognized the quaint boutique hotel. She and Josie ate lunch there years ago, after a tour of Armadale Castle.

The owner welcomed them personally and gave them a very secluded table. The staff seemed to know him, and Brynne wondered if he brought anyone else there. She didn't want to think about who came before.

The meal was delicious, and they polished off a bottle of red wine without realizing it. Gage got her talking more about her novel and her summers in Skye. Perhaps it was a ploy to keep her from asking personal questions. She still knew next to nothing about him.

When dessert arrived, he told her he needed to go to Edinburgh for a few days on business. Secretly, she was relieved to have a few days to herself.

He lowered his voice and leaned closer. "While I am away, I want you to journal about your dirtiest fantasies. Hold nothing back."

Her eyes widened and she knew creases were forming on her forehead.

"This exercise will help your writing. By delving deeper into what turns you on, you'll be able to turn your readers on."

She glared at him and leaned close to whisper harshly, "And how am I supposed to write all that stuff and not bring myself off?"

"You will save all your orgasms for me. I want to be the one to unleash them." He winked and called for the check. They were both quiet on the drive home, and Brynne spent the whole time stewing about his latest demand.

They entered through the front door and Gage helped her

coat off. "Take the dress off, Brynne. I want to see you in that sexy lingerie."

All that erotic talk over dinner together with the wine helped lessen her inhibitions. She was not used to stripping for him and fumbled with the tie that held the dress together at her waist.

He held out his hand for it and his eyes raked her over from head to toe. "There's a package in the kitchen for you. Bring it."

Brynne hurried excitedly to the kitchen and returned with the brown paper package. She found him in the bedroom getting undressed. He'd lit the fireplace and pulled a lounge chair forward, so it was a few feet from the bed.

"Go ahead and open it."

She ripped the packing tape off and pulled out the inner box. "Oh my god, you replaced Mr. Boss! Thank you, Gage. That was so sweet of you." She pulled him down to kiss him on the cheek and said, "I was going to order one this week."

"I'm glad you like the gift, Brynne. Now you can show me how you use it."

Her mouth dropped open, and she backed up a few steps. "No, please. You can't be serious."

"I'm deadly serious. You only use it when I give you explicit permission or when I can watch."

"I can't. I just can't. That's too private."

"I guess you won't get that orgasm tonight, will you?"

"Who made you such a bastard?"

"Watch it, Red. You're treading on thin ice. I'm going to pour a drink. Do you want one?"

"Yes." Her irritated tone had him turning back, one eyebrow raised. "Yes, please *sir*," she added sweetly, then scowled at his back and threw up two middle fingers.

What the hell! How could he ask this of her?

It was yet another test.

When he returned, he had two glasses of port. She took the glass and glowered at him.

"Well, are you performing for me tonight or not? Remember, I'll be gone for a few days, so…"

Brynne watched him sink into the chair and casually sip the drink. She stood there, debating her options. Fine. He wanted to play games. She could play too.

She downed the contents of her glass, deposited it on the bedside table, and started ripping open the box. How nice that he replaced the exact one he ran off with that night in London. Lucky for her, the hot pink, six-speed toy came fully charged.

He was watching her, his mouth twitching in amusement. She turned away from him and bent over to undo the delicate straps of her shoes. The lacy bra, garter belt, and stockings made her feel very sexy, so they were staying on. Slowly, she pulled her panties down and flung them in his direction. He caught them, put them up to his nose, and inhaled.

She sat on the edge of the bed and lay back, leaving her legs dangling over the side.

You can do this, Brynne. Just pretend you're alone.

She turned the vibrator on and focused on the wrought iron scrolls above the bed. Gage was suddenly standing over her. He had a pillow in his hand. "I expect you to look at me when you come." She rolled her eyes and lifted her head so he could prop her head up.

He looked at his watch. "You have five minutes."

"Five?! That's not fair. Do you want me to fail?"

"Perhaps I'm just trying to see what you're made of."

She smiled wickedly and turned the switch to a higher setting. "Don't worry, Mr. Boss always delivers." Staring boldly at him, she spread her legs and coated the toy in her juices. If she hated this so much, why was she already wet? It didn't matter why; the clock was ticking down fast. Her mind went to her darkest fantasy, then drifted to that first night on this bed—when she took his cock deep in her throat and was helpless to stop him. A blissful moan escaped her as she pushed the toy inside. In and out, she thrust it until her breath was coming in quick gasps. Short panting cries came from deep in her belly as her fingers manhandled her clit, and she forced the toy deeper until it reached the ultimate sweet spot. Brynne screamed her release and shuddered again and again, riding the waves of ecstasy to the end.

As she floated down from that amazing release, she smiled, satisfied she'd beaten him at his own game. Her eyes fluttered open to find Gage naked, sheathed and lifting her legs to his shoulders. He took the toy and threw it across the room.

"Mine."

When Gage walked into his Edinburgh office on Monday afternoon, his assistant Fiona shocked him by jumping up and giving him a hug. As a rule, she was pretty buttoned up and she ran a tight ship—keeping everyone on their toes in his absence. She was one of a select few he allowed into his personal life.

"You look like shit, Magnus. How do you intend to attract a nice woman looking like you do?"

"Fiona, my dear, I have found a woman, and she's keeping me up all night, so you needn't worry about my sex life any longer."

"I never worried about your *sex* life; it's your *love* life that needs resuscitation."

"Sorry to report that isn't about to change anytime soon."

They went to his inner sanctum and got to work. Fiona sat with him, noting action items as they went through his list. Out of the blue, she asked, "How did you convince your neighbor to let you dig?"

Gage smiled crookedly. "I made her an offer she couldn't refuse." He pulled out the signed paper from his briefcase. "Scan and file this with my lawyers. The crews can begin work on her property in ten days." His team had worked tirelessly to get the surveys and permits in place, but everything waited on clearance from Brynne.

"I am sure your powers of persuasion worked on the poor girl." She winked knowingly.

"Not quite. She fought me tooth and nail. In the end, it required me to add a sweetener."

"Oh cripes, don't tell me she is the one keeping you up all night?!"

"If I said I was doing it for the good of the poor residents of Skye, would you believe me?"

"No fecking way. I know you. She must have tweaked your interest."

"Something like that. Anyway, it's a temporary diversion while I'm in Skye. It will end when I get back to London."

"Oh Magnus," she sighed. "If you like this one, give it a chance." His expression told her to drop the subject, and she knew him well enough to leave it alone.

They worked over the next several hours on paperwork and reviewing the newest investment proposals. Armand, his COO, was due back tomorrow. He was out with Patricia again. She was close to making an offer on a castle they'd found. It was outside the city and would be the perfect private location for a destination spa. Zoning and permits were also easier to get in the neighboring county. Gage planned to invest half a million pounds, and Cole and

Aaron had agreed to do the same. His friends loved the idea when they heard about it.

He was still at the office going through files when Garrick rang him. "Hey Gage. Sorry to bother you during dinner. Do you have a few minutes?"

"No issue mate, I'm still at the office. What's up?

"Dimitri showed up today, demanding to see you. He wasn't happy to hear you were out of town."

"What the fuck did he want?"

"He asked to be reinstated as a member, claimed Brynne led him on and that he never touched her. He insisted he didn't break any rules, and that she overreacted. Then he threatened to sue us."

"Jesus Christ."

"My sentiments exactly. He pressed me on when you would be back. I said I would pass along his message."

Gage ran a hand through his hair. "Did he leave peacefully?"

"Yeah. I made him leave his bodyguards outside. We spoke in the lobby and then he left."

"Let John know. I want him to be aware he has resurfaced."

"Got it. I'll see him later tonight."

"Good."

"When are you coming back to London? We miss you."

"Not for a few weeks, at least. Things in Skye are moving along well now, and the excavation starts soon."

At some point, he would have to tell Garrick about Brynne and their arrangement, but not today. He didn't want to hear his objections, or the I told you so. They agreed to touch base again in a few days. He called the house to check in but kept it brief. She seemed a bit annoyed when he reminded her, no touching, and no orgasms.

"Sure thing, Mags. I'll save all my comes for you. I expect you'll do the same for me, right?"

"What is that supposed to mean?"

"It means no happy endings for you either."

He cleared his throat. "Watch your tone, Red. I'll give you the benefit of the doubt because you don't know me. However, listen carefully. I don't cheat and I don't play with multiple partners— although there are exceptions to that rule, which we'll discuss another time. For the duration of our agreement, my cum will go down your throat, or into one of your other orifices. And if not *inside* you, then all over you. Do you understand?"

She made an unladylike snorting sound into the phone. "Yes, sir. When will you be back?"

"As soon as I finish. Likely Wednesday. Why? Do you miss me?"

"No. I just want to be *ready*," she said cheekily.

"I may just surprise you—so I suggest you stay ready."

The cloud cover was heavy Tuesday night and sat low on the hills, so Gage's helicopter could not land at the new helipad at his house. Fiona arranged for Hugh to pick him up from the Broadford airstrip. As they flew low over the Skye Bridge, Gage wondered what Brynne was up to. He looked forward to catching her off guard, since she expected him tomorrow afternoon. The lab had processed her bloodwork quickly after he offered a generous incentive for next-day results. From now on, he could forego the condoms.

Armand and Fiona had things well in hand and he wouldn't admit it to anyone that he left early because he missed sparring with Brynne. He came in through the garage entrance and tiptoed into the living room. She was tucked into a corner of the loveseat, snoring lightly. It had been unseasonably cold the last few days, and she was in her purple flannel nightie. It was a garment that he should not find at all sexy. Except he did.

He crept behind the couch so he could see over her shoulder.

There was a massage porn video paused on her computer. *What the hell is she researching now?* He put his hand over her mouth and grabbed her wrists. She came awake, struggling and squealing.

He leaned down behind her and growled in her ear. "Shh. I won't hurt you. Unless you've been a bad girl."

She squirmed against his grip and tried to say something. He made his voice deep and raspy. "I will take my hand off your mouth if you promise not to scream. Nod if you understand."

She nodded. He helped her stand up on the cushions, then roughly turned her, so she faced him. Pinning her wrists behind her back with one hand, his other went under her nightie and started a slow path up her leg. "Have you been a good girl?"

He watched her face—reading guilt, followed closely by defiance. "Mostly."

"Tell me." He was already hard when his hand reached her hip.

"I, um, I pleasured myself."

His pupils darkened. "How many times?"

She looked at the floor. "Two."

"How many?" His voice took on a scary, grating tone.

She sighed. "It might have been three. But I couldn't help it. I was doing research, and you weren't here to *relieve* me."

His hand squeezed her hip, then he quickly turned her back around and pushed her to sit on the back of the couch. "Pull up your nightgown and don't let go." He yanked off his jacket and threw it on a chair. Standing behind her he asked, "How many dirty videos did you watch?"

She didn't answer.

He couldn't see her expression, but knew she was trying to choose the right answer. "Well?"

"I can't be sure."

"You know I can check."

She looked back at him, her eyes lit with excitement. "You told me to be ready for you."

He gritted his teeth so he wouldn't smile. "One might think you were asking for trouble."

She smiled playfully. "One might…"

His hands went to her knees and pulled them apart as he dragged his fingers lightly up her inner thighs, toward the apex. "Are you ready to pay the piper?"

She inhaled. "What does the piper want?"

Gage spread her with his fingers and found his private paradise. "Christ," he uttered. His hand cupped her, then smacked her swollen flesh lightly, causing her to squirm.

"I want this soaking wet pussy…right now."

He couldn't wait another minute to have her. Forget the teasing, forget punishing her for breaking the rules; forget all of it. He picked her up roughly, carried her to his bedroom, and tossed her onto the bed.

"Take that thing off, or I'll rip it to shreds."

Brynne quickly did as she was told, grinning at him. She then laid herself on the bed like a virgin sacrifice. He stripped off his clothes, barely able to string a thought together. He wanted her so badly.

Gage climbed between her legs and entered her in one stroke. His mouth swallowed her gasp and devoured her in a desperate kiss. He couldn't get deep enough inside her and knew he would not last. Brynne was almost feral—demanding as much from him as he was from her. Her hands were yanking on his hair, then gripping his shoulders and clutching his hips to pull him deeper.

"Please Gage, please, may I come?" She begged him so sweetly, how could he deny her?

He rolled onto his back, taking her with him. "Ride me."

She kissed him with wild abandon and straightened her legs. Perching on his cock, pubic bone to pubic bone, she started squeezing and grinding against him. Seconds later she screamed and came—her body shuddering with aftershocks.

"Again," he said against her mouth.

She lifted her torso off him, perched on her hands like a cobra pose in yoga, and closed her eyes in concentration. More grinding followed louder and louder moans until she went off like a firework again. She collapsed on his chest, buried her face in his neck, her breathing ragged against his skin. He thought she was finished, but her hips started rotating and twisting again. She nibbled on his earlobe and panted, "One more. Just one more, please."

He enjoyed being her stallion, but it was time to add a little spice. One hand gripped her ass, the other dipped between her legs and gathered her juices on his finger. When he touched it to her bottom hole, she jerked her head up and clenched her cheeks together, staring at him with uncertainty in her eyes.

He stared back. "One finger, in exchange for one more orgasm."

Her breath hitched, but she nodded. "Okay. But be gentle."

She hid her face in the crook of his neck and then nibbled and sucked on his shoulder while he wet his finger again. She rubbed herself on him, gathering momentum for another orgasm. When he tapped the tight little ring, she moaned into his neck. He waited for her to get into her rhythm and then pressed forward with the tip of his finger. *Christ, she's tight.* Her body pressed down on him harder and faster, so he slid into the first knuckle and she lost it. His shoulder muffled her piercing cry as she came apart. It seemed to last for a full minute until she finally slumped against him, panting to catch her breath.

Gage rolled her beneath him and dragged her legs up into the crook of each arm. He was a man possessed and he fucked her as if she could save his soul and banish his demons. He couldn't be sure which. Moments later, he detonated like a bomb, reaching the peak of ecstasy as wave after wave surged through him, leaving him breathless and trembling with its force.

Later, he would analyze why he didn't immediately leave her side. Instead, he pulled her body in close and spooned her while his mind struggled to make sense of this profound attraction for a woman he didn't trust.

30

Without Trust, We Have Nothing

What the hell just happened? She stared at her reflection in the mirror. Her face was red from madly kissing Gage's whiskery face. It was like they were apart for two weeks, not two days. It was a slight consolation that he appeared to feel the same.

Hunger pains reminded her she hadn't eaten since noon. She put on her nightie and went in search of sustenance. Gage came into the kitchen a short time later, fresh from a shower. He opened a bottle of red wine and poured them both a glass.

"I'll get the fire going."

Brynne put together an antipasto tray and heated some chicken satays. She brought it to the living room, where he had a roaring fire going. "Are you okay with this selection? I didn't order from the caterer today since you weren't due until tomorrow."

"This is perfect. I had a late lunch before I left Edinburgh."

They sat in silence, nibbling the food and staring into the flames. Brynne felt like she needed to fill the silence. "Did you have a productive trip?"

"Very much so. How about you—did you get a lot of editing done?"

Brynne wanted to ask him about his family but didn't know where to start. He always turned the conversations back to her, so she learned nothing about him.

"I did a substantial amount of rewriting last night and today. After my doctor appointment, I met with Logan, and we went over the plans for the house. He has done the estimates to update the upstairs bathroom with new fixtures and heated floors. I also asked him about giving the kitchen a little facelift. He will get that to me next week."

"Good. How are the other repairs coming along?"

"The house looks like a bomb went off in the hall, and the toilet and washer are on the back porch. I'm lucky to have another place to stay. Thank you for that."

He nodded and took a sip of wine. "My assistant will wire twenty-five thousand to him tomorrow for this project, so send me estimates for the other things when you get a chance."

Brynne was chewing on a piece of chicken, so she nodded.

"I have opened an account in your name in Portree at the RBS branch. The debit card should arrive in a few days."

"Thank you." God, she hated feeling like he was buying her—not just the land, but her body, too. She considered telling him this was about more than the money for her, but his cell phone started ringing and he excused himself to take the call in his office.

When he came back, she saw his creased forehead. He took a big swig of his wine.

"What's wrong?" she asked.

"That was Garrick. I have to go to London on Thursday."

"Is everything okay?"

"Ivanov is demanding to meet with me. He insists we wrongfully terminated him and is claiming that you came on to him, not the other way around. He wants his full membership fees back or he'll sue us and file assault charges on you for breaking his nose."

"Oh my god." Brynne felt sick.

"Don't worry. I'll give him his money back and this will all go away."

"I don't trust him, and you shouldn't either." Brynne told him about the Range Rover.

"Why didn't you tell me about this before?" His tone was accusing, and she didn't like it.

"I didn't think of it since I never saw it again. It was only when Jared told me it followed him to my place that I wondered if someone was trying to track me."

Gage took out his phone and left a curt message for John on his voicemail.

"Jared has already told him about it. I'm sure he's looking into it."

Gage sat back and rubbed his jaw. "I forgot you met him at the club. I gather they're still seeing each other?"

Brynne paused, not wanting to break a confidence. "I believe they are still in touch."

Gage looked like he had more to say, but changed his mind. He made a plate of food and stood. "I have to make a few calls, so I'll see you later."

Brynne hid her disappointment. "Cool. I'll finish what I was working on this afternoon before I fell asleep."

He smirked. "It looked to me like you were looking at graphic massage videos."

She leveled him with a stare. "Yeah, I was wondering if that was the type of massage Krylie usually gives you."

"Kylie is a registered massage therapist. Is that why you told me no happy endings?"

"She looked flushed when she came downstairs. I wondered what made her that way."

"Probably embarrassment. I told her I wasn't interested in any extra services."

"For now, I suppose. But when I'm gone, you can get your rocks off with her, right?"

"Why are we talking about this? I told you I am monogamous for the duration of our agreement. This subject is closed." He stalked to his office and kicked the door shut.

Brynne cursed herself for showing him how jealous she was. It was none of her business what he did before her or after her. It shouldn't depress her, but it did.

After making a plate of snacks, she gathered her stuff and headed to her bedroom. As she passed the office, she heard Gage's voice raised in anger. Curiosity got the better of her and she stopped to listen.

"I don't care who she fucked back in Canada. Did you uncover anything else about her time at the Mirror?"

Brynne froze; her stomach churned. He was having her investigated?! She was living in his house and sleeping in his bed, and he still didn't trust her! The urge to howl threatened to choke her. The sword had dropped and sliced open her heart, just as she feared it would. She stood frozen, feeling all the joy bleeding out of her.

How could she have been so stupid? She had allowed herself to dream of more, hoping the past was behind them—or that they would conveniently never talk of it again.

She needed to get out of there so she could think. After changing into yoga pants and a warm sweater, she knocked on his office door.

"Come in."

She poked her head in. "I'm going to pop down to my house for some things. I'll be back in a while."

"If you can wait a few minutes, I'll drive you."

"No, it's okay—I need the walk and will drive my car back up and park it here."

He looked placated. "Okay. Be careful, the sun is setting."

"I will." She shut the door and bit her lip to stop the words from tumbling out.

The urge to run was strong. The sky was a fiery combination of red and orange swirls tonight. It made her think of Aunt Josie and the last sunset they watched together on the porch. Josie would sip Drambuie and impart kernels of wisdom. What she wouldn't give for a visit with Josie right now.

The main floor of her house was chaotic, and Brynne wondered if it would ever be the safe haven it used to be. Would she want to stay after their agreement ended? It was impossible to say. She could ignore him and get on with her life, maybe date Logan. But running? No. Fuck no. Not anymore.

She went upstairs and dialed Jared, praying that he picked up.

"Bree! How are you, doll?!"

Her breath caught on a sob. "I'm a mess, J. I'm a bloody idiot who is falling for a man I can never have."

"What's happened? I thought things were going fabulously?"

"They were. Until I overheard him tonight on the phone. He has someone investigating me. They are digging into my background because he's still convinced that I wrote the article. I have been a fool. For him, it's just sex and nothing else. Great sex, mind you, but that's it."

"Oh, babe, that's awful."

"I don't think I can stay here under the circumstances."

"What the hell are you going to do—is your house livable?"

"No. It's impossible to be here during the construction. I was thinking of coming back to London."

"Ooh shit, I don't like that idea. John has got people tracing the SUV. I gave him most of the license plate. I think you should stay in Skye for now."

"Gage is going to London on Thursday. Dimitri demanded to meet him. He threatened to sue him and said he might press charges on me for assault! Can you fucking believe that?!"

"That's insane—and more reason for you to stay away. When Gage leaves, you'll have the place to yourself. Tell him you're getting your period and you don't feel well."

"Oh my god, you're a genius! I'll do that. It's a good reason for being cranky, too. In fact, it should arrive any day." She forced herself to take a deep breath. With a little time and space, she'd figure out what to do next.

"Perfect. I'll ask John what he's found out when I see him later."

"I'm so glad you have him in your life. You deserve to be happy, Jared."

"So do you, Bree. Could you have misheard Gage? Maybe he's trying to find out who really wrote the article?"

"No, I heard it clearly—the investigator is digging into my life in Canada. It's him trying to prove I did it so he can toss me out. Anyway, I'll stall the other renovations on the house and ask Logan to just finish the downstairs. I need to conserve the cash Gage is giving me in case I need to get away."

"That's a good plan. Hang in there, babe, and you know you can call me anytime. I'm here for you."

"I know, I will. You are my best friend and I love you."

"I love you too!"

Brynne felt marginally better as she picked out a few clothes. She grabbed her aunt's day timer and a box of tampons.

The MGB took two tries before it started. Tomorrow, she would take it for a long drive. It was time to see Declan about a few shifts at the restaurant.

Gage's office door was open when she got back. She peered in. "I'm not feeling well. I'm going to have a bath and go to bed early."

He looked overly long at her. Brynne feared he would push for an explanation, and she would shatter into a million pieces. She was turning away when he said, "Is everything okay?"

"Yes, fine. I'm just getting my period, so I'm a little tired." She forced a smile. "Good night, Gage."

"Good night, Brynne."

Wednesday morning, she woke up late and found a note in the kitchen. Gage left for London early so he could meet with his lawyers before Thursday's showdown with Dimitri. His parting line was *Look after yourself and edit without distraction. M.*

Brynne's emotions were churning like the angry waves of the North Atlantic. Waves of regret, sadness, and anger crashed into each other. Part of her wanted to confront him about his misguided beliefs, the other wanted to crawl into his arms one more time and forget what she'd heard. Stupid, stupid girl. She got dressed and headed into Portree for lunch. Declan wasn't around, so she visited the bank and saw that Gage put fifty thousand pounds into her account. All her excitement about fixing the house was gone. She had to consider what her future looked like. Her home, her career, and her love life were in shambles.

Brynne woke early Thursday after a night of tossing and turning. She was making herself a second cup of coffee when she heard the helicopter overhead. Gage wasn't due back today. If she had known, she would have made herself scarce.

She considered going to hide in her bedroom, but that was childish. When the doorbell rang, she hesitated. Why would he ring the bell unless he forgot his keys? She opened the front door and immediately threw herself against the wood to close it on the intruder.

Her strength was no match for Dimitri's. He forced it open and sent her flying backward, landing on her butt. She tried to scramble away but wasn't quick enough. His big, meaty hand grasped her upper arm and yanked her to her feet. Another giant of a man filled the doorway. He lumbered in and closed off her means of escape.

"Ow, you're hurting me. What do you want? Gage isn't here."

"I know. We have a meeting this afternoon in London. We are here for you, my elusive little pet. Now listen carefully, we don't have much time. I need you to pack a bag. We are taking a trip."

"I'm not going anywhere with you."

His eyes narrowed and his lip curled. "If you don't cooperate, I'll have no choice but to have my people burn down Club Dominus, with your boyfriend Gage inside. Or should I call him Magnus?"

31

Taken

Brynne bit her tongue so she wouldn't cry out as Dimitri dragged her along and kicked open the door of the master bedroom. "Pack your things."

"My things are in the other room."

His head tilted in confusion. "Don't you sleep in this room with him?"

"Yes, but I have my own room, too." As soon as the words popped out, she regretted them. It might have been better to deny sleeping with Gage.

His grip tightened. "Lead the way, Kiska."

With the other man hovering in the living room, she had no way to outmaneuver him. Dimitri interrupted her frantic thoughts. "I expect him to repay me for all the trouble he has caused. And you will too, my pet."

She tried to pull away. "I am not your pet."

"Pets don't talk back; you'll learn soon enough. You will write him a goodbye note, so he thinks you left him. That way, he won't come looking for you."

"You're crazy!"

He slapped her hard across the face. If he didn't have an iron grip on her arm, she would have fallen. She tasted blood where her teeth must have cut her cheek. Blood had spattered on the wall, but he hadn't noticed.

"Don't make me angry, Kiska. I am not gentle at the best of times, but if you continue to provoke me, you'll be sorry."

He opened the closet and scoffed. "This is the extent of your wardrobe?"

Any response could set him off, so she nodded.

He pulled her small suitcase out and tossed it on the bed. "Fill it up." He finally let go of her arm and she rubbed the tender area, bruised from his grip.

She scooped up her clothes and shoes and dumped them into the case. Next, she collected her toiletries from the bathroom, concealing a lipstick in her hand as she packed her makeup. After putting it into the case, she said, "I need to use the toilet."

"Fine. Leave the door open."

"Please. I can't go with you watching."

"Kiska, you will do everything in front of me. Get used to it."

She pleaded, "Please. I have my period—don't make me do that."

He stared hard at her, then nodded, his face taking on a lethal scowl. "Da. You may have a few minutes, but I will break this door down if you try to lock me out."

She sat on the toilet and forced herself to pee. Using a few sheets of toilet paper, she wrote with the lipstick, *Dimitri took me! Help! B.*

On the side of the vanity, she drew a small arrow so the cleaning lady would see it and hopefully find the paper behind the trash can. She flushed the toilet and washed her hands.

He was looking at the black halter dress she left in the closet. "You forgot this."

"Gage gave that to me. I should leave it."

"No. I will see you in it. Pack it."

She put the dress in the suitcase and zipped it up.

He took the case, grabbed her wrist, and hauled her back to the living room. The big, ugly Russian was there waiting. His cheek had a wicked scar from his ear to his mouth that she would never forget. If she lived through this, she could identify him in a lineup.

Dimitri gave him the suitcase and turned to her. "Where are your car keys?"

"Why?"

He grabbed her by the throat and growled close to her face. "Because Vlad is going to drive your car away. How else will they know you left?"

Her mind was spinning. Gage might never look for her if the MG was gone. "I don't have the keys. The mechanic has them—he takes it out for a run every week."

The Russian squeezed her throat until tears came to her eyes. He smiled in a way that made her nauseous. "You take me for a fool. My people saw you drive the car up from your little cottage yesterday. Lie to me again and you will regret it."

"I'm sorry." She tried to squeak the words out, but his hand still gripped her throat. A hand so powerful it could easily snap her neck.

He finally heeded her panicked sounds and let her breathe. "Now, get your keys, your phone, and a piece of paper. You are going to write a convincing goodbye note."

His harsh grip on her arm made her gasp as they marched to the kitchen. She handed him the keys and cell phone, and he passed them off to his henchman.

"Make it quick. I have to get back to London."

"We're going to London?"

"Not you, my pet. You will wait for me on my yacht until I get my money from the club. Then we will be together."

God help her. How would she escape if she was on a boat? She ripped a sheet of paper out of her notebook. Her heart was pounding in her chest. How could she let Gage know she wasn't leaving of her own free will? She dug out a pen from her bag. A quick glance confirmed her abductor looked capable of anything, including murder.

"Tell him you are leaving him. That you don't love him. Whatever. He needs to know you don't want him."

Dear Magnus,

I can't do this anymore. It's better for both of us if I go away.

Your investigator will eventually confirm I didn't write that article, but it will be too late for us. I don't love you anymore.

RED

Dimitri impatiently grabbed the paper and read the note. He seemed satisfied and walked her to the foyer. "Where is your computer? You have a backpack, don't you?"

Fuck. She hoped he would forget that. If she left it, Gage would know something was wrong. "It's over there." She pointed to the sitting area. "I'll pack it up."

"Hurry the fuck up."

She stuffed the laptop into the bag and put it over her shoulder. He had retrieved her overcoat from the front closet.

"Come here." He pulled handcuffs out of his leather jacket pocket and snapped a cuff on one wrist. "I will take your bag. Give me your other hand."

She tried to pull back. "You don't have to do this. I will come quietly."

He attached the other cuff. "Be grateful I did not drug you. I expect you to walk normally to the helipad. Act up and you will be very sorry."

He put the coat over her shoulders and led her out the front door to the waiting helicopter. Vlad was already there, stowing her luggage. Once they were inside the cabin, the ugly man shut the door and saluted.

Dimitri turned to her with a wicked grin. "He will make sure you didn't forget anything or leave any clues."

Dimitri buckled her in and gave the signal to the pilot. The hum of the engine increased, and the blades started turning. Brynne prayed to God that someone would see them.

Her stomach dropped as the helicopter lifted high above the house. It rose higher and higher until her little cottage was the size of a dollhouse. They flew north past the Cuillin Hills and stayed close to the coastline until they passed Dunvegan and left Skye behind. When they started their descent, Brynne couldn't see any place to touch down. Then she spotted a sleek black yacht a few hundred feet below. It was miles from shore, making it an inescapable prison. She closed her eyes, feeling an overwhelming sense of dread.

The machine landed with a thud on the deck of the yacht, and she choked back tears. Dimitri unclipped the seatbelt and waited for his crew to open the cabin door. He handed her stuff to the first uniformed man, then yanked her out of the compartment by her cuffed wrists. Once they were clear of the rotors spinning slowly above their heads, he picked her up and carried her toward the sliding glass doors of the salon. "My kitten has put on some weight. I may need to ration your food to get you down to the size I like."

She stiffened in shock at the remark. It was everything she could do to keep her mouth shut.

"I'll wait until I see you naked, before I decide."

She ignored him and tried to pay attention to her surroundings, so if she got the chance, she could find her way out. They entered an elevator and descended two floors. One of his crew was holding open the door to a cabin. The suite was over the top, like everything else she'd seen. This room boasted a king-size bed with a zebra-patterned headboard, matching the black-and-gold color scheme. He put her down and pushed her back until her legs hit the base of the bed.

"You are lucky I cannot stay, as Gage awaits. I trust my crew with my life, but many of them haven't had a woman in months. So, I must put you in the cage."

"What?" She looked around frantically and saw the large cage on the other side of the bed. "No, please," she begged.

"It is for your own safety. They will bring you food and water and I will be back by tonight."

Brynne struggled and fought, but it was no use. He easily forced her into the metal enclosure, using his massive body to pin her down. The humiliation wasn't over. He buckled a collar around her neck, which he padlocked. "This will help you understand you are my pet now."

She kicked and fought until he roughly drew her cuffed hands over her head with one hand and squeezed her chin painfully with the other. "Stop fighting me. It is futile and will only cause me to hurt you."

Tears spilled from her eyes, and she sagged against the bars of the cage. "I hate you."

He backed out of the cage and slammed the door. "You were supposed to be mine weeks ago, but you managed to elude my people. Imagine my disgust when I learned where you were all this time."

He took a blanket off the bed and passed it through the bars. "I suggest you rest. When I come back, we will begin our life together."

Gage was getting angrier by the minute. It was going on an hour past the time of their meeting. He had gone to the bank and withdrawn half a million pounds. John had suggested they mark the bills, with Interpol's help, so they could keep tabs on Dimitri after he left London. With billions at his disposal, there was a chance he wouldn't touch it, but they would track him if he did. Multiple investigations of extortion and money laundering were underway, but he had a complex set of numbered companies that couldn't be traced back to him. John confirmed the Range Rover that followed Jared belonged to a Russian who had been in the UK for three months. They were struggling to prove he was linked to Dimitri. One thing was clear, the man was a master at covering his tracks.

He had tried Brynne twice, but she was not answering. She was distant last night after going to her place, so he gave her the space she seemed to want.

As he paced up and down the library, an email arrived from his investigator. He had a lead on someone who worked at the *Mirror* with her. The woman recently took a leave of absence—after telling her co-workers that she inherited a large sum of money and was going on a cruise. He was tracing the source of the funds and her whereabouts and would advise as soon as he had news.

It was time to tell Garrick about the arrangement he'd made with Tink. He found him in his office and when he explained, his friend just shook his head and laughed.

Gage scowled. "What's so bloody funny?"

"I knew you liked her more than you were willing to admit."

"So what? How can I trust her?"

"It's easy. You just do. She's nothing like Sierra, and if you would open your eyes, you would see that."

Gage rubbed his forehead. "She only agreed to the month with me because she needs the money and the kinky sex to finish her book."

"You keep believing she has some nefarious agenda to part you with your money. What if you're wrong?"

Gage scowled but didn't reply.

"How do you feel about her?"

"She makes me crazy. She makes me laugh. And she makes me hard. All the time."

"Hmm. Sounds terminal."

Miles rang to announce Dimitri's arrival.

"Let's get this shit over with. I need to get back to Skye."

"You mean back to your girl?"

"Aye."

Gage met him in the boardroom on the first floor and Garrick remained close by. Dimitri reluctantly agreed to leave his bodyguards outside.

"I apologize for keeping you waiting. Traffic in the city is terrible."

Gage's jaw tightened. "You made threats to me and my club, Dimitri—so it was imperative that we have the chance to sit down and discuss this, like adults."

Dimitri forced a laugh. "You are correct. I want to make it clear; I believe you were hasty in kicking me out of the club. And if you are not willing to welcome me back, I am due all my money."

"I have your funds. I believe it's best for all concerned that we part amicably and permanently."

"The way you British behave so politely is baffling to me. In Russia, if you threw a person of my status out, we would burn your club to the ground. And here, we meet and discuss it like gentlemen."

Gage gritted his teeth. "Indeed." He put the paperwork his lawyers drew up on the table in front of Dimitri.

"Is Tinkerbell still working here?"

Gage stilled, giving nothing away. "No. She left some time ago."

"Ah, that is too bad. I would like to apologize for frightening her that night. And since we are coming to a resolution, I won't have to sue her for assault."

He wanted to wipe that smug smile off the Russian's face, but forced himself to ignore the obvious taunt.

"This document confirms we are refunding your membership dues in the amount of five hundred thousand pounds in cash, and you agree to release the club and all its employees from any damages, now or in the future."

"You mean you will not accept my word?"

"I am sure your word is your bond, Dimitri, but my lawyers insist upon this paperwork to protect the business from any future liability."

"Da. I will sign. Even though I should ask my lawyers to examine it."

"Please look it over. I'll get your cash." Gage rose and left the room. He nodded to Garrick, who went to retrieve the large black case.

He returned as Dimitri was signing the documents. Gage signed and gave him a set, concluding their business.

As he prepared to leave, Dimitri asked, "Are you staying in London?"

The question surprised Gage, but he answered casually, "I live here. It's one of my favorite cities in the world. What about you, Ivanov? Are you staying long?"

The Russian's mouth twisted into a fake smile. "I am here for a few days, before a brief holiday in Monaco."

Gage walked him to the front door, and two burly bodyguards flanked Dimitri and escorted him to the waiting Maybach limousine. One got in the front and the other jumped into a Range Rover idling behind it.

The hand-tailored suit couldn't camouflage the criminal he was. He was pure scum. Gage felt like he needed a shower. Garrick put a hand on his shoulder. "I'm glad that's over. And I hope to god they pin something on him soon."

Gage stared out the front windows. He hoped so, too. He would feel better when Dimitri was locked up or permanently deported. Turning to Garrick, he said, "Let John know he has left with the money and hopefully he leaves a trail of breadcrumbs. I'm heading back to Skye. Brynne has not returned my calls."

"Okay mate. I'll keep you posted if I hear anything."

He called Fiona from the car to let her know he was on his way to Northolt airport. She would alert the pilots about his ETA. Then he called Logan and left him a message to check on Brynne. Twenty minutes later, he rang him back.

"Magnus, I went up to the house and knocked. There was no

answer, and her car was not in the garage."

Gage's stomach dropped. "Did you see her at all today?"

"No man, I thought you were home though—I heard a helicopter land on your pad this morning, so I figured you were back."

"It wasn't me." *Who the fuck would dare?* "Do you remember what time that was?"

"Must have been around ten a.m. I got to the cottage around nine thirty this morning."

"You still have a key, don't you?" Gage wiped a damp palm on his pants.

"Yeah, do you want me to go in and look around?"

"Yes. Look for anything strange. Check the main floor guest room for her things. I must make a call—I'll ring you back in fifteen." Gage hung up and dialed John.

"Gage, what's up?

"John, I have a bad feeling and I need your help. Do you have people tailing Dimitri?"

"Yeah, we have been tracking him since he left the club. I put a tiny transmitter in the briefcase and layered another between a stack of bills at the bottom, in case he dumps the case."

"Good. He thinks we are stupid, but god help me, John—Brynne is not at home. She hasn't answered my calls, and someone landed at my helipad on Skye this morning. Can you find out from the CAA if anyone filed a flight plan?"

"I'll get on that right away. We will also check for any records of a heli charter. But couldn't she be out with friends or something? Was everything okay when you left?"

"It was okay—she was distant, but nothing earth-shattering. Just call it a hunch. Maybe before I go crazy, can you track her mobile? If she's on the island, I'll calm down."

400 • LUCE SUTHERLAND

"Got it. I will call you back ASAP."

"I'm getting on my plane in ten minutes. I'll text you the satellite phone number."

Gage boarded the plane and called Logan back before they started taxiing. What he said was like a punch to the gut. Her closet was empty. No sign of her computer, but the cord was still plugged into the outlet. He was checking the kitchen next.

"Hey, there's a full cup of coffee sitting on the counter. And it smells like burnt coffee in here." He heard him rummaging around. "It looks like she left the pot on."

"That is strange. She either left in a hurry or someone interrupted her before she could have that coffee. Thanks, Logan. Let me know if you find anything else at all."

"I will, and I'll check with the neighbors to see if anyone saw the helicopter or her car leaving."

"Thanks."

Gage was about to hang up when he heard Logan yell. "Wait! There's a note."

Logan read it to him, and his stomach churned. How did she know about the investigator? She signed it Red and said she didn't love him anymore? It wasn't right.

His intuition screamed that she was trying to tell him something. Could she be in danger? Gage texted John the plane's number, which would work once they reached ten thousand feet.

His mind raced through the events of the last week. How could he be so blind and stupid? Brynne was unlike anyone he had ever been with. She was fiercely independent and not afraid to tell him what she thought. Unlike most, she wasn't on the hunt for a husband, and money was not her primary motivation. No, she wanted his body more than his bank account, which made him smile.

She fought her submissive nature but loved to be dominated. Christ, he hoped they could continue seeing each other after the thirty days, because he didn't want it to end.

A text sounded.

John: *Brynne's cell signal was last online at Inverness Airport. Nothing since two o'clock today and no sign of the car yet.*

Gage gripped the phone until his knuckles turned white. Did she leave him? Was she that unhappy with the situation? Where would she have gone? He wrote back.

Gage: *Jared might know. If she left me, she might run to him.*

John: *We just spoke. She was very upset last night. Overheard you on the phone with the PI.*

Jared said it devastated her that you still didn't believe her.

Oh my god. What did she overhear? No wonder she avoided him.

Gage: *Was she going to leave me?*

John: *He doesn't think so. Not yet anyway.*

John said he would call when he got answers back on the heli charter. His team was working on it.

Not yet anyway.

Gage's heart sank. Jared obviously thought she was going to leave him. Could he still try to win her back? He would explain why he hired the investigator. And why he found it so hard to trust. If he wasn't too late.

32

Dire Straits

Brynne pretended to be asleep when a member of the crew entered the cabin with a bottle of water and a sandwich. She was starving, but she waited until he left to reach for the food.

It was dark outside when the same guy returned. He leaned down and leered at her, snaking a hand through the bars toward her leg. She scooted back as far as possible, and he laughed like a serial killer toying with his prey. He was creepy, and she was grateful for the safety of the cage. He spat some words at her before shutting off the lights and slamming the cabin door. Time passed slowly and she couldn't concentrate on anything. She took only a few sips of water, afraid they wouldn't let her use the bathroom.

The waves lulled her back to sleep until she heard the roar of the helicopter. The madman was back. She heard loud voices outside the cabin, and then the door burst open, and he flipped on the lights.

"How is my little kitten feeling?"

She refused to engage and instead looked at him with loathing. He leaned down to look at her with a fiendish smile.

"It appears you need more time in the cage. I expected you to be happy to see me."

She scoffed. "You will never get away with this."

"Pchelka, I have already gotten away with this. I have half a million in cash, and this ship can be in Russia in four days."

"Russia? You can't be serious?" Her shrill voice gave away her panic.

"Da. Deadly serious. I presumed you were bright and figured that out. I have thought of everything."

"You can have any woman you want. Why me?"

He came close to the bars of the cage. "Gage is the reason I don't own Club Dominus. Imagine my surprise when I discovered my revenge could be so sweet and satisfying. You see, I've always wanted a fiery redhead for my collection. But I will make you suffer for cutting off your beautiful hair. When I saw the surveillance photos, I wanted to cane you black and blue."

Brynne swallowed a sob.

"Don't worry, Kiska. Now that I have you, I've calmed down. I will punish you at my leisure."

"You are vile. Why take someone who doesn't want you?"

"It is the fire in you. The moment I met you, I knew I would enjoy making you surrender your will to me."

"That will never happen. I'll never surrender to you."

He laughed loudly. "Excellent. I hate easy submission. When I break you, it will be all the sweeter."

Brynne refused to show him any weakness. She wouldn't cry, either. That was probably the ultimate fetish for him.

"I will leave you now. Dinner awaits. You are not ready to share a table with me. Rude pets stay in the cage until they learn manners."

He left the cabin. Brynne lay back down on the hard pallet and prayed.

The satellite phone rang in the cockpit, and the pilot transferred the call to Gage.

"John, any news?"

"Yes. We found out who chartered the helicopter. Nikolai Seminov is an employee of Ivanov's UK holding company. He flew him from Inverness to Skye, then it landed on a yacht anchored off the coast of Lewis. Dimitri then took a jet from Stornoway back to London to meet you. The heli landed thirty minutes ago on the same ship. According to His Majesty's Coastguard, it's a seventy-two-meter superyacht called the *Russian Princess*. She has charted a course for the Shetlands, but we think they will continue to Russia."

"Jesus fucking Christ. What if Brynne is on that ship? Can we intercept it?"

"Gage, to involve the Coastguard and demand to board and search, we need some proof of a crime."

"Christ almighty. I just pray to God that she left me a clue at the house. It will be an hour before I am home. I will call you from there. Don't lose sight of that fucking boat."

"We won't, Gage. I'm working on a warrant based on our suspicions, and I hope to hear from your investigator about that woman from the paper. He tracked her to a river cruise due into port tonight. If she knows something, he will get it out of her."

"Okay, thank you, John. That's the least of my worries right now. I have to find Brynne."

Gage couldn't stomach any food, and he refused a drink on the plane. He needed a clear head. As the helicopter landed at the house, he saw a car waiting in his driveway. Two officers got out and flashed their badges.

"Mr. MacCallum, John sent us. He wanted us to dust for fingerprints and look for any evidence that could help in your girlfriend's disappearance."

Girlfriend. The word didn't do justice to what he was feeling. Maybe it wasn't a traditional relationship, but he realized at some point she had become important to him.

"Thank you. I'll go in through the garage. They probably came in through the front door from the helipad. You guys should start there."

He raced into the house and felt the chill of her absence. His heart started pounding when he saw the note and the untouched coffee. After letting the agents in, he went directly to Brynne's room.

One man followed him while the other dusted the front door handles. Her closet was empty. Logan had told him, but he needed to see it for himself. In the adjoining bathroom, he opened all the drawers, replaying the events of yesterday in his head. As he turned, he noticed a lipstick on the floor by the tub. He leaned down to grab it and saw the red line drawn on the cabinet.

"I found something!" The agent quickly joined him. "I think she left a note." Gage carefully unfolded the toilet paper, his heart in his throat.

"Fuck. He took her. Here is the proof." It was a punch to the gut.

The agent was already dialing the phone. "Sir, I'm sending you a picture. It's enough for a search warrant. Yes. I'm going to dust everything for prints in case there's other physical evidence."

Gage sank down on the bed and dropped his head into his hands. It was his fault for underestimating the Russian's obsession.

The agent tapped him on the shoulder. "John wants to speak with you."

He took the phone and watched the man bend down to examine the wall. Gage saw him shine his light on the dark red spatter and his stomach dropped.

"Hold on, John." He looked at the agent for answers.

"It's blood. I'll get a sample to the lab as fast as possible."

"Did you hear that? So help me god, I will kill that bastard when I get my hands on him."

"Gage, I've put every available man on this. We are getting the warrant and notifying the Coastguard. The yacht has not left Stornoway. They have a large order of provisions being delivered tomorrow morning before they depart."

"I should never have left her alone. If anything happens to her…"

"Listen, we will get her back. Dimitri has pursued her relentlessly; he will not harm her. We will get there in time."

Gage's fear was blossoming into rage. He would destroy Dimitri as soon as he had his woman back safely in his arms. "I want to be there, John. I will fly up to Lewis tonight."

"That's not a good idea, man. Let us handle this."

"I can't. But I won't interfere." He handed the phone back to the agent and went to change. Sleep would be impossible, so he might as well be there.

Two hours later, Gage's jet landed, and he checked into a local hotel in Stornoway. He forced himself to eat and then took a walk along the waterfront. They anchored the yacht offshore, out of the jurisdiction of the port authority. He felt completely useless, and at ten p.m., he called John.

"Have you got the warrant?"

"Yes, we have it. To safely execute it, Interpol will send operatives to the ship on the supply delivery boat. Once they neutralize the crew, the HMCG will board and do the search."

"I want to be on that boat, John."

"No way. If you're recognized, it could throw everything off. You can be on the Coastguard ship when we come alongside the *Princess*."

"Okay."

"Meet me at the Coastguard HQ at zero-six-hundred. They already positioned one of their vessels out of sight in a nearby cove. We will be on it."

The cabin door swung open, and a harsh light streamed in from the hall, startling Brynne awake. She felt groggy from too much sleep.

"Where are you, my little kitten? Are you ready to come out to play with your new master?"

Brynne tried to disguise her hatred as she looked through the bars at him. "Please, Mr. Ivanov, I need to use the bathroom and clean myself up. Will you allow me to do that?"

"What is wrong, Kiska? Are you dirty? Did Gage leave his disgusting cum in you?"

"No! Please, I have my period."

"I don't know if I believe you." He dropped into a chair and stared at her.

"I promise, I need the toilet. I can't hold it much longer. Please."

His glassy eyes worried her, but she needed him to open the cage.

"I will let you out, but you will owe me something in return. Do you understand?"

Oh god.

She didn't dare ask what that was. She watched as he kneeled and took a gold keychain from around his neck to open the lock.

He moved back and swung the door open, beckoning her to crawl out. "Come, my fiery little Tinkerbell. But remember, you must stay on your knees."

Brynne stopped herself from getting up and shook her head in disbelief. He really was sick. She felt more at risk without the locked door between them and prayed he wouldn't force himself on her. "Could you take these off, please?" She held her cuffed wrists up to him.

"Nyet. You are not yet a trustworthy pet. Maybe once you understand your position."

Brynne's shoulders slumped in defeat.

"Hurry up and use the bathroom. I will order some vodka." He opened the door a fraction and barked at the man outside. The last thing he needed was more alcohol. Then again, if he got loaded, could she escape to the deck? Her chances were slim to none, and she would die after twenty minutes in the frigid water.

"May I have my suitcase, please? I need my toiletries."

He pointed to the closet. Her case was open, and someone had hung her clothes up. Maybe the food was drugged? She didn't remember them coming into the room. How fucked up was that?

She crawled across the floor with the things she needed and quickly closed the bathroom door.

"Remember, no locked doors between us, unless I lock them."

"Okay," she called out.

He burst in, and she screeched in shock. "When you answer me, you say 'Yes, Master Dima.' Do you understand?"

"Yes, Master Dima," she whispered, her breath still stuck in her throat. He dominated the small space. Her back was against the shower door when he grabbed her by the shoulders. His face came closer, and she held her breath, the panic making her dizzy. When he pressed his lips to her forehead, it was everything she could do not to flinch away. His eyes glittered, but he seemed placated. "Don't be long, or I'll come looking for you."

When he shut the door, she sank to the toilet, shaking. As quickly as possible, Brynne did her business. Her period had come, and brought with it a throbbing headache. She brushed her teeth, wincing when it grazed her cut cheek. Her face was clean now, but nothing could help the dark smudges under her eyes or the bruises darkening her jaw.

He banged on the door, and she almost lost it. "One minute."

When she opened the door, he roughly grabbed her hair and yanked her down to the floor. "Have you forgotten the rules already?"

Tears clouded her vision as she tried to grasp his hands, but it was futile.

He stood back and studied her, his face a mask of annoyance. "Why are you wearing these ugly clothes? I want to see you in the dress."

"I wanted to save it for when we have dinner together."

"You think you are clever, don't you? You think I don't know you are trying to manipulate me?"

"No, Master Dima, I promise you I'm not. It's just that time of the month and don't feel well."

He stared down at her, his eyes narrowing. "If you are lying to me, Malishka, I will make you bleed from someplace other than your pizda."

She shook her head vehemently. "I swear I'm not lying."

"Crawl over to the bed."

She remained rooted to the spot, fear clogging her throat. He started toward her when a knock sounded.

The servant hovered at the door until Dimitri directed him to set the vodka and glasses down. As he was leaving the cabin, the ugly henchman walked in and whispered something that set Dimitri off.

He swore and started barking orders. The man nodded and bowed as he backed out of the room.

Dimitri poured a large glass of vodka. Brynne watched him take out his cell phone and punch the screen. He paced around the room, yelling in Russian. When he hung up, his complexion was scarlet, and he sneered at her. "Don't you realize I could have a sniper take Gage out any time? My people are watching him, just like they were watching you."

All the blood left her head. "You don't need to. I'm here."

"Yes, but it seems he doesn't want to let you go. My team has just informed me he is in Stornoway. He came alone, which was quite stupid. But you're going to convince him you are with me now. I don't need him calling the police and claiming I kidnapped you."

Brynne felt dizzy and sick. "Let me call him and tell him. I will do whatever you want. Just promise not to hurt him."

"I have sent three of my crew to get him so you can tell him to his face that you don't love him."

God help her, she put him in danger! He must have found her note. What was to stop them from killing him?

Dimitri's eyes had a feral gleam as he stared at her old sweatshirt and leggings. "I want you to change into that black dress and fix your face. You better look radiant when he gets here."

He removed the handcuffs and left the cabin. She heard him speaking harshly to the guard stationed outside.

With shaking hands, Brynne did her makeup, using plenty of concealer to hide the bruises. She hated putting the special dress on when it held such amazing memories, but the most important thing was convincing Gage to walk away. She would do whatever it took to protect him.

To calm her rattled nerves, she drank a glass of vodka and sank into a chair.

The drink was a bad idea. She felt like she was no longer in her body, and her pulse pounded in her ears.

The sound of the helicopter several floors above signaled their return. She held out faint hope that Gage had eluded them, but when Dimitri burst through the door, she saw triumph in his eyes. She jumped out of the chair and wobbled in the high-heeled shoes. He stood for a long time, his possessive gaze raking over her from head to toe. Brynne mentally steeled herself for what was to come, her stomach churning with fear.

Dimitri stalked toward her, swinging a chain from one hand. "That dress shows off your figure to perfection." His smile was malevolent as he attached the chain to the collar still locked around her neck. "If you want him to live, you will convince him you are my cherished pet."

The lump in her throat threatened to choke her. "Yes sir, Master Dima."

They went up to the main deck and, when the elevator door opened, Dimitri yanked her close. "You may walk behind me until we reach the lounge, then you'll go to your knees."

Fury replaced fear at his ill treatment. "Yes, sir," she seethed.

When they reached the sumptuously decorated salon, Dimitri tugged the leash, and she dropped to her knees. When he moved aside, she saw Gage. A sob escaped before she could stop it. His face was battered. One eye was almost swollen shut and his shirt was spattered with blood. His good eye landed on her, and she saw unfathomable pain reflected there. It was like a knife to her heart. He was flanked by two armed men, with his bloodied hands cuffed in front. Gage must have fought them valiantly because they, too, were beaten and bruised.

If I don't comply with Dimitri, they will kill him, she realized soberly. She would find some way out of this for herself—but right now she had to get Gage released first.

Dimitri stroked the top of her head like a dog. Brynne closed her eyes, so she didn't see what it did to Gage.

"What would you like to say to him, my pet?" Dimitri's overly sweet tone was like nails on a chalkboard.

She cleared her throat, which felt like she had swallowed sand. "I…I've decided to leave with Dimitri. He didn't force me. I want a new life with him."

Gage stared at her. A twitching muscle in his jaw was the only sign that he heard her.

"Go on." Dimitri pulled on the leash to make his point.

"I used you." Her head started pounding, and she felt nauseous. "I needed the money and the job, but I realize I want more. Dimitri can give that to me. So, you should go. You need to let me go."

He nodded, his face giving nothing away. She hoped he bought it.

Dimitri nodded at his two goons, and they dragged him to his feet. "This is where she wants to be. And if you try to stop us, she will suffer my wrath every day until you desist. My people can take out everyone you care about, one by one."

Gage stared at Dimitri and spoke, his voice low and gritty. "She has made her decision. You can have her." Brynne heard the words and went numb.

"I'm glad you can see reason. She will live in the lap of luxury, provided she behaves." He yanked the leash to make his point. "My pilot will return you to the island now."

Brynne watched helplessly as the two men dragged Gage forward. She saw he was limping as they made their way through the wide glass doors to the main deck.

A siren pierced the night, making her flinch hard against Dimitri's leg. A voice rang out on a loudspeaker. "Stop where you are.

This is Interpol. We have a warrant to search your vessel!"

Dimitri moved quickly, grabbing a gun from one of the men holding Gage. He dragged Brynne to her feet and backed away, shouting at the crewman. She saw two men scurry to the helipad and start unlocking the steel tie-downs that held the aircraft to the deck.

Gage seized the moment. He elbowed the other guard and wrapped his cuffed wrists around his neck until he finally dropped his firearm to clutch at the metal crushing his throat. Brynne heard Dimitri cock the gun and point it at the two men. She had to do something.

Hysteria fueled the rush of adrenaline. She threw her weight against him and clawed at his face as the gun went off. Blood burst from the guard's neck and he and Gage fell backward onto the deck. Her scream echoed in her own ears as she watched a growing pool of red beneath them.

She had failed. Her legs gave way, but Dimitri yanked her roughly back against him. One huge hand was at her throat, squeezing as he spat into her ear, "You did this. You killed him." She closed her eyes, all the fight draining out of her body.

He started toward the helicopter when two officers in riot gear appeared on the deck with their weapons drawn. Dimitri pulled her in front of him and pointed the gun at her head.

"Everybody back off, or I will kill her."

The Interpol agent spoke. "We have you surrounded, Ivanov. Give yourself up."

Everyone turned to the sound of a steel latch releasing and watched the crewman leap over the side. Dimitri laughed maniacally when he heard the splash. "He's fired."

The rotors began turning over their heads, sending her heartbeat into overdrive. He pressed the gun to her temple and continued dragging her with him.

They were backed up against the cockpit door. She knew he would have to lower the gun or loosen his grip to open the door latch. If she could get free, the officers would have a clear shot. When he shifted her body to cover him, she made her move.

33

Surrender

Gage came to, pain hammering in his temples. He could hardly breathe with the dead weight on top of him. The last thing he remembered were Brynne's eyes, huge in her ashen face, staring at him, lying to him. His left shoulder hurt like a motherfucker. Some of the blood on the deck belonged to him, but he had to find a way to reach the gun. If it was the last thing he did, he would stop Dimitri from getting on that helicopter with her.

One officer spoke. "We have taken down your crew, Ivanov. If you try to board the chopper, our sniper will take the pilot out."

"Will you take that chance when I can end her life with one bullet?"

They had their weapons trained on him but had no clear shot.

Gage was a few inches from the gun when he saw something raw and resigned in Brynne's eyes, right before she sank her teeth into Ivanov's arm.

Seconds ticked by in slow motion.

The pain faded into the background, and he felt like his blood was injected with nitrous. He shoved the dead man's body off and reached for the gun.

Dimitri screamed in pain, rage clouding his features. When he flung Brynne away from him and raised his gun, Gage took the shot. Dimitri fell to his knees but fired a shot before another bullet took him down.

Gage watched in horror as Brynne launched herself over the railing.

The officers moved forward to subdue Dimitri and get the pilot out of the helicopter. Gage dragged himself up unsteadily. He had to get to Brynne. Cold water shock could kill even the strongest swimmer in minutes.

"Gage! Stop!" John rushed up behind him, pulling him back from the railing. "The Coastguard will go after Brynne. You can't help her like this."

"You don't understand. She could drown in seconds."

"So could you—you've been shot."

"Just get these cuffs off me."

A floodlight was shining into the inky darkness and Gage was preparing to dive in when one of the two divers yelled at the other. "I've got her!" He watched helplessly as they pulled her limp body from the water.

"God help me John, I need to get to her."

A paramedic arrived and started asking him questions.

"I'm okay. It's just a flesh wound."

The man looked at him skeptically. "Are you sure—you've lost a lot of blood!"

"It's not all mine, for Christ's sake." He pointed to the man whose body had shielded him, then almost crushed him. "It's his."

John held up his hand. Someone was talking in his earpiece. "Yes. Agreed. Go. MacLeod is okay. She is your priority." He turned to Gage. "They're airlifting her to Raigmore Hospital in Inverness. They have a trauma unit. I told them to go."

"Good, good." Gage sank to the deck, overcome with exhaustion. His heart ached like someone had cut open his chest cavity and left him to bleed. She'd put herself at grave risk. For him. She had to come through this.

Four days later

If she was dead, why did her body hurt so much? Brynne felt like a rock lay on her chest. Breathing hurt like she swallowed shards of glass. Her eyes refused to open; there was no reason to try. The man she fell in love with was gone. He would never know how she felt or how he made her world better. He cracked the ice around her heart, and she would never be the same.

Why was she so cold? She didn't remember getting pulled from the water. Maybe she didn't. Did she care? No. She didn't care.

Something warmed her icy hand. It felt nice. The incessant beeping noises were annoying. She wished they would stop. Her delusions were getting more elaborate. She could smell his spicy citrus scent. Maybe this was Heaven, and he was there, too.

Don't be an idiot, Brynne. You are imagining things.

Now she was hearing his voice. The fall must have damaged her brain.

God, she missed his grumpy, sexy excuse for a smile.

"Doc, if she's breathing on her own, why hasn't she woken up?"

"Mr. MacCallum, her body is on the mend, but her mind could be protecting her from the trauma she experienced. Give her time. You need to go home and rest. You still have a concussion and a healing wound."

"No, I'm not leaving. I need to keep talking to her."

John and Jared returned from the cafeteria with a sandwich and a bag of crisps for him. They arrived together the day before. As a couple. He was happy for them because John finally came out to his family and friends.

John put a hand on his shoulder. "Gage, you look like hell. You need a shower and a proper meal. We will stay and call you if there is any change."

His body was crooked from sleeping in the recliner for a week. He rubbed his scruffy jaw and stared at Brynne's pale face. He'd almost lost her to the cold North Atlantic, and it still made his pulse race. If the Coastguard diver hadn't been right there, they might not have found her in time. The diver had just pulled the body of the crewman out of the water and saw exactly where she went in. When they pulled her out, he started praying to a god he barely believed in. And he had not stopped.

"I must be here when she wakes up. There is a lot to explain."

Twenty-four hours later

"Brynne. God damn it, I am out of patience. When I am done with you, you won't be able to sit down for a week. You can't give up, for heaven's sake. I need you."

She stirred. "You need me?" she croaked. "Ow, my throat hurts."

Gage made a sound of anguish from deep in his chest. "Oh, thank god. Bree, can you hear me? I'm here. You're safe. Don't you dare leave me again—my heart can't take it."

She struggled to smile, but that hurt, too. She tried to touch her parched lips, but her hand couldn't reach. "Am I tied to your bed again?"

He groaned. "Not yet, but as soon as you're better, that's where you will be."

Brynne opened her eyes, but the sunlight was like pins and needles in her eyes. "Too bright. Where am I?"

"You're in the hospital in Inverness. You've been here for a week."

Her eyes focused on him, and she started sobbing. The machines beeped faster in her ears. "I thought I had lost you." She couldn't catch her breath. "I thought you were dead, and it was my fault. I'm sorry, I was so stupid."

"Shhh, love, I am fine. The bullet grazed my shoulder and missed everything vital, thanks to your quick thinking. I just can't carry you to my bed for a while."

A doctor walked in with a nurse in tow. "You gave us quite a scare, young lady." The doctor cleared his throat. "No lifting or carrying until both of you are fully healed."

They checked her vitals, but she waved them off, impatient for answers. When they were gone, she tried to sit up and groaned in pain.

"Bree, please, you need to rest—no sudden movements. You

bruised your ribs when you hit the water."

"That explains why I can't breathe without it hurting like a mother. Whatever. Did they get Dimitri? Is he dead? I heard gunshots."

"I shot him in the leg and the sniper got him in the shoulder as you went over the side. What in the bloody hell were you thinking?"

"I...I didn't want to be his pet. I lied to you. Is he dead?"

"Sadly no. He's locked him up in a maximum-security hospital. His pilot gave himself up when he saw the rifle trained on him." He kissed her on the forehead. "You need to rest now."

"No. How long have I been out of it? We have to talk."

"We have all the time in the world. I'm not going anywhere."

She swallowed and winced. "I need to say some things. First, can I have some water?"

He grabbed the cup and fed the straw into her mouth. The cool water soothed her throat. She needed a minute to collect her scrambled thoughts. How would she explain what went through her mind on that yacht?

He squeezed the straw closed. "Not too much at once."

"Do you remember the last time you rationed my water?"

"I remember it vividly. You called me an ogre." He smiled, and her heart melted.

"You had me at a distinct disadvantage, strapped down to that spanking bench with my ass on display."

"You loved every minute of it."

She snorted. "Ow, don't make me laugh. This is serious."

"I'm sorry. Please continue."

She wanted to sit up but settled for clutching his hand in hers. "I was nervous that night, but I felt safe, too. Because you were there. When he locked me in that cage, I thought I would never see you again. And I realized something."

Gage's face paled, a muscle twitching in his jaw.

"Magnus Gage MacCallum MacLeod, I know you don't feel the same as me, but that's okay. I want to be with you—not because you're paying me, not for book research, but because of you."

He just stared at her as she babbled on.

"If you agree to keep me around, I'll be the most obedient submissive you've ever known. I'll even learn to cook."

"Brynne, sweetheart. I need to tell you something, too. Do you remember that day in my office when I interviewed you?"

She nodded, drinking in the sight of him. Disheveled hair, bloodshot eyes, and a week's worth of beard growth... He was the most handsome man in the world.

"That day, I knew I was in trouble. A week later, when you told me you wanted to take me to bed, I fell a little more under your spell." He pulled her hand to his mouth and kissed it. "I didn't want to believe in your innocence. I thought I could keep you at a distance and protect myself from any real feelings. Can you forgive me for being such a fool?"

Tears were streaming down her cheeks, and he gently wiped them away.

"Of course I forgive you. Please tell me your investigator found out who wrote the article?"

"Yes. He intercepted Margaret Smythe on her river cruise. Dimitri threatened her family if she didn't write and submit the story. He gave her the details of everyone at the club. Then he paid her enough money to disappear until the heat died down and bribed the sub-editor to get the story printed."

"But how did he know where I worked?"

"Two months before he came back to London, he ensured one of his bodyguards, a British citizen, got a job at the club. He was the security guard who left you alone the night Dimitri came into the bar. He planted several bugs around the club and got your name from the recordings."

"Oh my god."

"Brynne. I'm sorry. I hired the investigator to prove that I couldn't trust you. But before he found out the truth, I already knew it. I knew you would never hurt me."

She squeezed his hand. "It's okay. I understand why you didn't trust me. That awful, smelly woman lied to you."

"Smelly woman?"

"That bitch who was spewing insults the day I first met you. Her perfume always gave me a raging headache."

He laughed and groaned, holding his own ribs. "Red?"

"Yes, sir?"

"I want you with me. Not for a month. Not because of our agreement. But because I love you."

She choked back a sob. "You do?"

"I'm afraid so. But there is one condition."

"Anything."

"I don't want blind obedience, I want the fiery pixie who challenges me at every turn. The one who misbehaves and gives me countless reasons to take her over my knee."

Brynne hiccupped. "I think I can manage that."

He leaned close and kissed her.

Her fingers entwined in his hair and held. "Mags. In case you haven't figured it out. I love you, too. And you've made me the happiest brat on the planet."

Epilogue

Six months later

"Are you comfortable, sweetheart?"

"Pffft, do I look comfortable? How long will you keep me like this?"

"Until you learn your lesson."

"I've learned my lesson. Please untie me, or at least make me come." She jangled the chains on the cuffs to make her point.

"You lied to me."

"It was just a lunch, for god's sake. Declan is a friend. I didn't tell you because you don't like him. He's not a threat, but you're acting like I cheated on you."

He leaned back in his office chair and smiled. His eyes gleamed with something sinister, making her shiver. "I think you did it on purpose. You've been a brat this whole week."

"I'm bratty because you've been making me wear these awful plugs in my butt for days!"

"They're for your own good. I don't want it to hurt too much when I fuck your sweet ass. You should thank me for being so thoughtful."

"This one is too big. It hurts," she whined plaintively, hoping for sympathy.

"If it was so terrible, you wouldn't be dripping all over my ottoman."

"I hate you." She laid her head back down to hide her secret smile. All attempts to sway him today had failed. He was ruthless. When he made her lie face down on the large leather hassock in his office, she expected to receive a spanking for being a brat. Because she deserved it. And she wanted it. Instead of keeping to her writing schedule yesterday, she surfed porn and read a dark novel, tapping the keyboard randomly so he would think she was writing. Somehow, he figured it out. So, she woke today to Mr. Hyde, who demanded she bathe, douche, and present herself for adornment in a leather collar, matching cuffs, and a huge stainless-steel plug. Whenever he got that forbidding look in his eye, her heart raced with anxiety. Or was it anticipation? In the last six months, he had discovered and exploited all her arousal triggers, one by one.

Today, he unearthed another. First, he clipped her wrists together behind her back. That started her motor running. Then he attached her ankle cuffs together. Her engine purred in anticipation of his open hand landing on her backside. But when he drew her cuffed ankles up and chained them to her wrists, she redlined.

Gage interrupted her musings. "I have another surprise for you."

She looked at him warily. "I don't think I can take any more of those."

"Do you want to use your safe word and stop everything?"

"What? No!"

He smiled like she'd just handed him the keys to the kingdom, and she swallowed a groan.

"Please, can I have your cock now? I need it or I'm going to perish."

"I have something almost as good."

She looked up and saw something in his hand that resembled a gag, only it was different. Her brow creased as he kneeled in front of her.

"I know you've fantasized about having two men at once, and I've devised a way to grant you that wish."

"What is that?" Her eyes studied the familiar size and shape, and her body readied for a total meltdown.

"It's a gag made to mimic my cock."

"Wait, how? You had a cast made of your dick?" Her breathing ratcheted up.

"In a manner of speaking. Now you can have me in your mouth and in your ass at the same time. Wasn't that thoughtful of me?"

She gulped in shock. But her insides went liquid molten. "That's crazy. You're crazy."

"Don't worry, it won't go too deep, it's only three inches long. Think of it as your own personal pacifier. For when you can't have the real thing."

"Holy mother of..." She shook her head, at a loss for words. It was diabolical and deviant, and she hated its effect on her.

"You can try it while I have my massage this afternoon."

Brynne inhaled sharply, and he noticed.

"What's that look for?"

"Um, I canceled Gemma, because I wanted to give you a massage myself. As a special surprise."

Her body started fidgeting and pulling against the cuffs. She saw the granite edge of his jaw and licked her lips nervously.

"Is that so? Are you sure it isn't a way to get back at me for what I've put you through?"

She could feel her face heating. The "No" died on her lips. There was no place to hide from those all-knowing eyes. He was a hungry jungle cat preparing to devour his prey, but he was going to play with his food first. What was she thinking, sharing her darkest fantasies with him? Now he could use them against her.

Her pupils had dilated, and her irises were the color of molasses. She was caught in a trap of her own making, and he'd never found her more irresistible. It took almost losing her to make him realize his life would be devoid of light and color without her in it. His fears and suspicions almost won.

There was a more pressing matter right now. His cock was subverting all rational thought and demanding he take immediate action.

"Open wide, little brat."

She sealed her lips and shook her head. "Please, I want the real thing."

"Baby, you're going to get the real thing. Just not in the hole you want it."

Shock registered and her mouth softened into an "Oh." One hand grasped her jaw and the other pushed the gag in. The sound she made as he buckled it behind her head sent a surge of primordial lust coursing through his veins.

Her body shook in reaction, and she struggled against the cuffs as he turned her on her side. He admired her voluptuous breasts which had been hidden too long, but he had a singular objective.

"Are you wet, little brat?"

She yelled something at him, but her mouth was full of a silicone dick mounted on a wide leather panel, so he wasn't sure of anything. Her dilated pupils conveyed fury mixed with arousal.

His fingers brushed lightly over her nipples repeatedly, until they resembled dark pink berries, begging to be nibbled on. When he abandoned them, her moan morphed into a low, angry growl. He reached between her spread thighs with a whisper of a touch, and she started panting and biting down on the gag.

"Shhh, baby. Relax your breathing. In through your nose, out through your mouth."

"Tuth me, pwees, make me come pwees."

The sound of her begging penetrated his armor, and he let his fingers sink between her swollen folds. She was soaking wet; her juices had left a glistening trail on her pale thighs. Between ragged breaths, she moaned again.

While his fingers lazily painted her lips, he leaned down and asked her, "Do you want it hard or soft, Brynne?"

Her eyes widened. At his wicked smile, she closed her eyes and sighed. "Arrd."

"That's my dirty girl." He lifted his hand and brought it down with a stinging slap on her pussy. Once, twice, and on the third, she came with a piercing scream. Her body shuddered for several seconds as he unfastened her ankles from her wrists. He could not wait another minute and hoisted her over his shoulder like a caveman and headed upstairs.

The massage table was already draped and ready for the massage he wasn't getting. He sat her down and unbuckled the gag, leaving it hanging loosely around her neck.

"How do you feel?"

Her eyes were glassy. She smiled shyly. "Thirsty. And still ravenous for you."

"Don't move. I'll get us some water."

He returned with water and a bottle of massage oil tucked in his pocket.

She guzzled a third of the bottle and handed it to him. "I can give you that massage now."

He quenched his thirst and put it on a side table. "No, my sweet, I would rather give you one. You've had a trying day."

A little crease appeared between her brows. She looked like she wanted to bolt, and he knew she saw his darkness coming into the light.

Before she could act, he moved in for a kiss. He felt her pulse hammering beneath his fingers as he held her head still and softly touched his lips to hers. He was gentle with his mouth and tongue, teasing her and pulling back when she tried to deepen the kiss. "Did you enjoy distracting me from my work this afternoon?"

She whispered against his mouth, "Mmm, yes."

He unclipped her wrists and helped her lie on her stomach on the table.

"You get comfortable. I'm going to change." As he stripped out of his clothes, he watched her stretch and roll her shoulders. He trailed his hands over her back and slowly down her legs as he circled the table. She let out a relaxed sigh. "This is very sweet of you. My muscles are so tight."

"I can feel how tense you are. We'll work those kinks out." Careful not to jangle the short chain attached to the table, he pulled her leg to the outer edge and fastened a metal carabiner to the D-ring on her ankle cuff.

She lifted her torso and craned to look at him. "What are you doing?"

As he secured the other ankle, he replied, "Delivering your bondage massage fantasy, sweetheart."

She giggled and lay back down. "Oh my god, you're the man of my dreams."

Gage quickly fastened her wrists to the top corners of the table and kissed the top of her head. "I hope you feel the same, after I have my wicked way with you."

"Mmm, how could I not?" She closed her eyes and rested her head.

He uncapped the oil and squirted a copious amount on her back. No way could he drag this out. His original plan was to have her suck his cock while he worked on her back and shoulders, but that was out the window. His balls were blue even though she went down on him before breakfast. Putting the collar and cuffs on her did him in every time.

"It's time to take the plug out. Lift your hips so I can put the bolster under you."

She lifted and then begged sweetly, "Please go slow, it's so big."

"I will, but you have to relax and bear down." He kept a steady circular motion on her lower back with one hand and slowly twisted and pulled on the jeweled end of the toy.

As the widest part tugged on her inner muscles, she pleaded with him, "Oh god. Stop, wait, it's too much, Gage!" Her squirming aided his progress, and she swore as it popped out a second later.

It dropped onto the tile floor with a loud clang, and he climbed onto the table between her legs.

Her skin glistened from her shoulders to her toes. He lay on top of her and used his whole body to slide up and down, kneading her generous curves and coating himself in oil. Using his thighs, he pushed her knees as far apart as they would go.

"Gage, please fuck me. I can't wait any longer!"

He needed no further encouragement and slid his full length into her pussy in one stroke.

"Christ!" He gasped when she pushed back and squeezed him like he'd taught her, but it was too much. "Stop and don't move a muscle. I am on the razor's edge."

She obeyed and relaxed immediately. "Yes, sir."

The little grin on her face told him all he needed to know. "So now you choose to behave?" He pulled out slowly and thrust again. "It won't save you. Your ass is mine tonight."

She looked back with those puppy dog eyes. "Oh no, please… haven't you tortured it enough for one day?"

"You know I won't hurt you." His voice deepened to that dark Scottish brogue. "And you know what to do if you want me to stop."

She nodded and dropped her forehead to the sheet. "Yes, I know. Please take me, sir. I am yours."

He dribbled lubricant at the dimple on her lower back and watched it travel between her cheeks to gather at her vulnerable hole. His cock was throbbing when he pulled out. It was going to take every ounce of his self-control to go slowly. He lay down on her again and dragged his shaft through the oil, then positioned it at her rear entrance. Holding his breath, he pushed forward. Through gritted teeth, he told her to exhale and push back on him. She whimpered, but did as he asked until he slipped in.

"Fucking hell, don't move. Let me control the pace." She was so tight, even after five days of progressively bigger toys. He felt like a thoroughbred held at the starting gate, waiting for the gun to release him to a full gallop. With herculean effort, he calmed his mind and pressed forward, one inch at a time, until he was fully seated.

"How do you feel?"

"Impaled. Full. Good." She wiggled her hips, and he tightened his grip on the table. They were both so slippery, he was in danger of sliding off. "What are you waiting for, Mags?"

"There's the cheeky brat I know and love. Now, I'll show you who owns you, body and soul."

He pulled back, added more oil between them, and sank balls deep. Brynne lifted her hips and spread herself to take him deeper. A buzzing sensation started in the base of his cock, and he knew he couldn't hold on much longer.

"Sir, please, I want your other cock in my throat when I come."

With his next thrust, he reached for the gag and put it in her open mouth. He left it loose but held on to the strap behind her neck. His other hand slid beneath her, with his palm resting on her mound and his fingers sinking into her folds.

He struggled to string words together. "You come when I come. Not before."

She nodded and growled in response to his command.

All semblance of control disintegrated as he slammed in and out of her. She met every thrust with one of her own and ground herself against his hand. With one final push, he buried himself as deep as humanly possible as his orgasm detonated. "Now! Come for me now!"

His fingers plunged into her pussy and his other hand tugged on the strap, pulling the phallus deeper in her mouth. She shattered into a million pieces beneath him, her keening wail one of pure ecstasy.

He lay there for several minutes, trying to catch his breath. Their bodies both twitched with the aftershocks. He didn't want to move, but knew his weight was bearing down on her, and she needed aftercare.

"Baby doll. Are you okay?"

"Hmm. I think you took me to heaven, but they've sent me back and I've just crashed down to earth."

"Come, let's get into a hot shower and then I will feed you."

Brynne sat curled up in front of the fireplace, sipping a cup of tea with a shot of Drambuie. She could not wipe the silly grin off her face. After a decadent steam shower, where Gage tended to her like she was a porcelain doll, he carried her downstairs, dressed her in her purple flannel nighty, and deposited her on the couch, with orders not to move.

He was making a racket in the kitchen, but she stayed put and let him have his way. There was something very satisfying about letting him pamper her. It took a while, but she had finally stopped worrying about giving up control. In surrendering, she found renewed self-confidence, safety, sexual fulfillment, and best of all, love. She was still a brat and enjoyed testing his patience, and he loved finding new and delicious ways to punish her.

Because of his tyrannical rule over her writing and editing schedule, she finished her revised manuscript in record time. The sizzle factor went up by a thousand degrees when he became her personal BDSM consultant. The cherry on top of her sundae was the three-book deal that her agent, Linda, secured. She was already outlining her second book and couldn't wait to test some of her theories in the name of research.

Gage returned with a charcuterie tray loaded with her favorite goodies. He took her empty teacup and handed her a plate. His head tilted with a questioning glance. "What's that dreamy smile all about?"

Brynne looked at him and swallowed a lump in her throat. "Just counting all my blessings. My life hasn't been the same since I met you. And I still pinch myself to prove that it's real."

He leaned across and kissed her gently. "It's me who is blessed, Brynne. You started by pushing my buttons and somehow broke through my armor."

She laughed. "I just wish that armor was bulletproof. Seeing you get shot took years off my life."

"We're even. Watching you jump overboard almost killed me. Enough talking—you need to eat."

"Yes sir, Mr. Bossy Pants."

"I almost forgot. Logan dropped off this letter today for you. He said he found it when they moved some furniture."

She looked at the envelope from him and burst into tears. "It's from Josie! I thought it was lost forever. I was supposed to open it eight weeks after the first one."

She ripped the seal, unfolded the letter, and took a deep breath.

Dear Brynnie,

I must confess something, and it is my deepest hope that you are not upset by what I am about to tell you.

There is a certain handsome, charismatic man moving into the house at the top of the hill, and I may have orchestrated a meet-cute between the two of you. You have undoubtedly heard from him about buying the house. That's because I gave him the distinct impression that I would sell it to him, even though I had already given it to you. He can be rather intimidating, but kind too. So, don't give in too easily. Men like a challenge.

The conditions of your inheritance were meant to wake you up to certain possibilities, so you wouldn't end up like me. Stubborn and alone. I hereby retract those conditions effective September 30 of this year.

Life is short. My wish is that you seize every opportunity to spread your wings, Live life juicy, and have no regrets when your time eventually comes.

I love you, my dearest.

Josie
xoxo

Brynne grinned at the handsome and charismatic man next to her and handed the letter to him. "It seems we're part of an elaborate ruse. Josie had no idea that you and I met in London, but she choreographed our meeting in Skye, from the great beyond."

"That sneaky little devil!" Gage laughed. "I'm impressed. But how did she know I'm dominant?"

"Seriously? Do you not realize it oozes out of your pores? If I met you anywhere outside of the club, I still would have known in a heartbeat."

He chuckled. "I suppose there's some truth to that. But compared to Aaron, I'm a pussycat. And Cole is the least scary of the three of us."

"When was the last time you guys got together?"

"It's been too long. But Aaron and Cole have promised to come to New York for your American book launch. And I'm looking forward to taking you to Lucifer's Eden."

Her eyes widened. "That sounds wonderful and terrifying."

Pulling her into his lap, he said, "Your education is far from over, Red. I look forward to expanding your horizons, but I will never compromise your safety."

She leaned in to kiss him. "I trust you with my life, Mags. I learned to trust you with my heart. But the true test was to trust you with my ass."

He grinned, and her heart melted.

"Your trust is the ultimate gift, Brynne. With it, you restored my irredeemable soul."

THE END

Acknowledgments

Massive, HUGE, to-the-moon-and-back love and appreciation to this group of people who helped bring this book into the world. Below is a long list of very dear friends and amazing people who went on this wild journey with me.

To the early beta readers—Roseann, Robyn, and Linda, thank you for your encouragement and positive feedback. You knew my ego was hanging in the balance, and you were oh so gentle!

To my editor, Kristen Hamilton—you understood my voice and vision, and you tended my baby with the same care and love you would your own. Thank you for bringing the manuscript into its final fabulous form.

To Abram Hodgens for answering that first weird email…and considering being the man on the cover of a juicy romance novel. You jumped in with both feet and made it happen! Special thanks go to Sarah Mireya for spending hours to get the best shots, and Natalie Fuller for celebrity-level styling. You all brought your A game to the photo shoot in LA. Stunning!

To Kari March for bringing my vision to life. You got me. You delivered and chose the best photos, colors, backgrounds, and fonts. And you were patient when I questioned perfection. Thank you for making my dream come to life.

To Kelley and Christa at Sweet Honey Marketing—you took the pain and suffering out of social media for me and tapped into my brain to deliver exactly what was needed to get my name out into the world. I am constantly impressed.

To all those agents who rejected my query letters—thank you, too! I am a firm believer that when one door closes, another more pivotal one opens. The experience of bringing this book to fruition was life-changing. Although it was a shit ton of work, I discovered I really like being the boss. ;-)

About the Author

Luce Sutherland has been reading juicy erotic romance since before it was mainstream and cool... when you couldn't hide behind a Kindle, and you had to bring the illicit book to the register - and be judged by the cashier.

When those books became harder to find, she resorted to writing her own stories with delicious, dominant alpha heroes and the bold, sassy heroines they aim to tame.

Luce lives with her own alpha husband in the Sunshine State, even though she gets sunburned walking from the car to the grocery store. She is passionate about living each day to the fullest which includes nurturing authentic friendships, savoring Maui coffee, indulging in Scottish gin, and being a devoted advocate for the benefits of self-care.

Her motto is LIVE LIFE JUICY!

Please follow Luce at:

Website | www.lucesutherland.com
Goodreads | Luce Sutherland
Facebook | Luce Sutherland Writes
Instagram | lucesutherlandwrites
Pinterest | lucesutherland1
Newsletter | https://lucesutherland.com/blog/

Made in United States
Orlando, FL
07 June 2025

61930212R00245